Praise for Mike Blakely

"Blakely's writing is crisp, enticing, and
underscored with depth."

—*American Cowboy*

"An almighty narrative talent."

—*Booklist*

"Mike Blakely turns the horses loose in all our souls."

—W. Michael Gear and Kathleen O'Neal Gear,
New York Times bestselling authors

"A fine spinner of tales."

—Elmer Kelton,
eight-time Spur Award winner

"Blakely writes with a beauty that rivals
the Big Bend country."

—Terry C. Johnston,
author of the Plainsmen series

D0104742

THE **SNOWY RANGE GANG**

· AND ·

VENDETTA GOLD

MIKE BLAKELY

FORGE®

A TOM DOHERTY ASSOCIATES BOOK | NEW YORK

This is a work of fiction. All of the characters, organizations, and events portrayed in these novels are either products of the author's imagination or are used fictitiously.

THE SNOWY RANGE GANG AND VENDETTA GOLD

The Snowy Range Gang copyright © 1991, 1996 by Mike Blakely

Vendetta Gold copyright © 1990 by Mike Blakely

A Forge Book
Published by Tom Doherty Associates
175 Fifth Avenue
New York, NY 10010

www.tor-forge.com

Forge® is a registered trademark of Macmillan Publishing Group, LLC.

ISBN 978-0-7653-9166-7

Our books may be purchased in bulk for promotional, educational, or business use. Please contact your local bookseller or the Macmillan Corporate and Premium Sales Department at 1-800-221-7945, extension 5442, or by e-mail at MacmillanSpecialMarkets@macmillan.com.

First Edition: January 2017

Printed in the United States of America

0 9 8 7 6 5 4 3 2 1

CONTENTS

THE SNOWY
RANGE GANG

ONE

Nine parts pistol and one part scattergun. Claude Duval judged his Le Mat grapeshot revolver the showpiece of his collection. He sat on the porch and tinkered with it as rain washed the pine-studded hills of his ranch and cooled the Laramie Plains below.

His finger drew the trigger in, his thumb holding the hammer back, easing it down on the firing pin. The action sounded like a clicking symphony of machined parts to Claude's ears, accompanied by the patter of raindrops on the shakes. His nostrils flared and took in the clean aroma of rain come down from the thunderclouds, pierced by the bite of gun oil.

Reaching under the bench, he touched the whiskey bottle but passed it over for the oil can. In his younger years he might have been well lit by this hour on a lazy day like today. But, at thirty-six, Claude Duval was finally learning to temper his bad habits. His fingers took in the oil can and let the whiskey bottle lie.

He put the hummingbird spout of the can to the revolving cylinder of the Le Mat and clicked the bottom of the can once, applying a single drop with restrained precision. To spread the oil, he turned the cylinder—an odd oversize design that chambered nine .42-caliber pistol rounds. The Le Mat didn't pack the knockdown power of a Smith & Wesson Russian or a Colt Peacemaker, but it chambered nine rounds instead of six. Three extra shots could come in handy these days, Claude thought, with every gun-lugging rustler on the range thinking six-shooters.

And the Le Mat still had a wild card to play. Instead of a solid steel pin, its cylinder revolved around a short, smoothbore, twenty-gauge shotgun barrel loaded with a blast of double aught. It was twice-barreled, over and under, the pistol barrel on top, the shot barrel underneath. The weapon was like a six-shooter and a half, with a sawed-off shotgun thrown in for grins.

Claude knew why the grapeshot revolver had never caught on. It had a movable tang on the hammer that the shooter flipped one way to fire the pistol rounds and the other way to fire the shotgun barrel. Under rough use, the tang had a tendency to break off, and then the hammer wouldn't fire anything. Still, it was the kind of piece Claude liked—one with unusual features.

He owned a Cooper's ring-trigger pepperbox, a six-shooter with six barrels; a Sharps carbine with a coffee mill built into the stock; a Jarre pinfire harmonica gun with a sliding magazine that looked like a mouth harp . . . They weren't worth much, but he didn't collect them for their pecuniary value. He just liked guns. He kept them in mint condition, the finest pieces hidden under the floorboards of his new frame house.

The Le Mat grapeshot revolver was his favorite. He loved to feel it work in his hand, yet every time he did, he wanted to kick himself for not thinking of the idea on his own. A shotgun barrel in the middle of the cylinder. Genius.

Claude had dreamed for years of inventing some firearm that would carry his name into posterity, but the only idea he had ever come up with was a thing he called the Duval Derringer—a pocket pistol that could be made to shoot backward as well as forward.

The idea had come to him a few years ago down in Texas when a cow thief he had been tracking snuck up on him in camp, disarmed him, and shot him with his own Colt. He remembered thinking just before the slug hit him in the chest that if his pistol could have been rigged to shoot backward at the flip of a lever or something, the rustler would have shot himself right in the eye. As it happened, though, he was lung-shot with his own gun and left for dead. Luckily, a couple of cowboys hunting strays had heard the shot and came to investigate. They took him to Mobeetie, where an army doctor from Fort Elliott announced he would probably die overnight. When Claude came around, he found a pine box at his bedside. They were efficient at burials in Mobeetie, but Claude had disappointed them.

Of course, the Duval Derringer would never reach production. Too dangerous. Some innocent fool would flip the switch the wrong way and shoot himself, sure as the world. Claude would have to think of something better.

He put the oil can down and pulled his watch from his vest pocket. Three minutes past the half hour. Time for a swallow. He picked up the whiskey bottle, pulled the stopper, and smelled the aroma as he put the spout to his lips. He doled the liquor out as he would oil on a fine collectible. Too much lubrication could break down a good grip, ruin one's stock.

Claude was forever thinking guns, hoping an idea for a new weapon would strike him one day. A patent in his name would sure show the folks back home.

Every man in the Duval family of Texas—except Claude—claimed a title of some kind. His father was Judge Duval, his brothers Senator and Major Duval. The only word he had ever heard spoken before his name was "Sabinal." And that wasn't a title, just a nickname given to him by his old friend Dusty Sanderson. He and Dusty had once owned a small ranch on the Sabinal River, west of San Antonio. Pretty place. Part of the Lost Maples woods grew on the ranch and turned beautiful colors in the fall. But they had lost that place to creditors.

A few years after that, he lost Dusty, too, and his life took some turns he had never planned.

Claude may not have cared where he stood with the Duval family—Dusty had never cared—but he was thankful to have his clan's good looks. He measured over six feet with his boots on, filled out the shoulders of his riding jacket, and looked at the world through twinkling sky-blue eyes. Those eyes were sprouting a lot of crow's-feet these days, but he had squinted at a lot of horizons. His eagle's nose was a Duval trademark, and his jaw was perhaps the finest in the family.

He knew his kin disapproved of him and the life he had chosen, so he had cultivated his own appearance, as if to set himself apart from the other Duval men. They were fond of ostentatious whiskers, so Claude had made a ritual of shaving. His brothers cropped their hair short, so he grew his in waving locks that fell on his shoulders.

He didn't even pronounce the family name the way his kin did. With the judge and the senator and the major, it was *dyu-VALLE*. With Sabinal Claude, it was just plain old *DOO-val*.

"You know, Sabinal," Dusty had told him one hot day on the trail to Dodge, both of them riding drag in the wake of the herd, "you could have stayed home and sat in the shade of your family tree. But look at you now, ridin' out in the sunshine."

"Yeah," Claude had replied, "if only I could see it through all this damned alkali dust."

When they were fifteen, Claude and Dusty had quit school in Austin, left their homes, and hired on with a South Texas ranch. After the war, when the big trail drives began, they had both made top hands, driving beeves as far north as Montana. It was on a return trip from Montana that they had first stumbled upon these pine-studded hills between the Laramie Plains and the Medicine Bow Mountains.

"If I could make a ranch go," Dusty had said, "this is where I'd put it. A man could tolerate poverty in a pretty place like this."

That had been more than a dozen years ago. It had taken him that long to make up his mind to leave Texas. Too many Dyu-VALLES down there looking down their Roman noses at him. Texas had never been the same, anyway, after Dusty's murder.

Of course, the deciding factor had nothing to do with his partner's death or his family. He had simply gotten nervous about some back-shooter slipping up on him. He had crossed a lot of hard cases over the years in Texas.

Claude had never intended to go into the stock detective business. It had happened by accident. The first winter after Dusty died, a gang of rustlers stole a herd out from under his nose near a line camp he was in charge of on a Panhandle ranch. Claude had taken out after them without even going for help, figuring the outlaw Giff Dearborn was ramrodding the rustlers. Dearborn was part of the reason Dusty had been murdered, and Claude wanted his scalp.

He trailed the rustlers until he caught them drunk in camp in New Mexico. They had already lost most of the cattle to stampede. It wasn't Giff Dearborn's bunch, but Claude brought them back to Texas, anyway, spending two sleepless days in the saddle guarding them. Most of the stolen cattle drifted back to home range. The affair made him look real good and started a lot of talk.

The next time a bunch of cattle turned up missing, the boss came looking for Claude Duval. "Sabinal," he said, "rustlers damn near cleaned out that herd down on the South Branch. I want you to go after 'em."

"Hell, boss, call the Texas Rangers. I ain't no regulator."

"You're a Duval, aren't you?"

"Damned if I ain't. What's that got to do with anything?"

"We need your kind of Duval backbone. Some of the other outfits have agreed to throw in for your wages. A hundred dollars for every cow thief you can kill or put in jail."

He could no more pass up earnings like those than he could let his family name get the better of him. His brothers had been Confederate heroes, his father a decorated volunteer in the war with Mexico. Claude's would be a range war.

He had only killed a couple of rustlers over the years, and then only to save his own skin. But he had sent dozens to jail. Maybe that was his mistake. Men tended to get out of prison sooner or later and drift back to their old ranges. Things had gotten hot for Claude down in Texas. It was well that he had come north.

He was starting something new in Wyoming. No more chasing rustlers. He had bought the section Dusty had been particularly fond of, here in the foothills of the Medicine Bows. He planned to run a few cattle and train some horses through the summer, maybe do a little gunsmithing.

When fall came, he would guide hunters into the Medicine Bows. A lot of those rich easterners were looking for sport out West nowadays. This was the perfect place to give them their taste of it. Laramie was only twenty miles to the northeast. He could pick them up at the Union Pacific depot and bunk them here before starting into the mountains. The Medicine Bows teemed with game: elk, deer, bear, lion, even mountain sheep.

He had a lot to do before the best fall hunting began. He had barns and corrals to build, horses and pack mules to buy. He needed to get up into the mountains to scout for the best hunting. But today he was content to sit on the porch and tinker with his guns. He wasn't going to stand out in the rain and dig post holes.

Looking down the irons of the Le Mat, Claude swept the Laramie Plains until a moving figure caught his eye. A yellow slicker emerged from the mist about half a mile away, the rider coming at a lope up the road.

"Now, who the hell is that?" he said to himself. He rose, shoved the Le Mat under his belt, and went into the house to choose a couple of weapons. He picked a Model 76 Winchester and a double-barreled shotgun. It didn't hurt to be careful. He didn't know anybody around here yet.

When he stepped back out onto the porch, the rider was within rifle range and still coming in plain view. The man obviously wasn't looking for trouble. Probably a social call. Some friendly neighbor wanting to sip a little whiskey on a rainy day.

But as the yellow slicker neared, Claude began to see recognizable features. By the time the visitor pulled rein in front of the house, he knew who it was.

TWO

Y ou've strayed off your range, Bob." Bob Steck dropped from the saddle, stomped up the porch steps, and shook Claude's hand. He took his hat off to slap the rain from it, revealing his thinning crop of gray hair. "I saw your advertisement for hunters in the Laramie paper. I was hopin' it would be the same Claude Duval I knew in Texas. The world ain't got room for another." His darting eyes caught the whiskey bottle, and he smiled.

Claude had worked for Bob Steck a few times as a stock detective, recovering dozens of stolen cattle and breaking up a ring of cow thieves. Steck owned one of the biggest ranches on the Texas coast. He was about fifty-five years old, but wild as a young buck, and used to doing whatever he damn well pleased. He was rather small, but built solid. He stayed in better condition than most twenty-year-olds, though he didn't work at it. He seemed to build muscle just going about his business, and every move he made was a thing of sure grace.

"So you came to hunt, did you?" Claude asked, picking up the bottle.

Steck grinned. "Yes. I sure did."

"Last I heard you were in Europe."

The rancher threw his wet slicker aside and took the whiskey bottle from Claude. "I had some trouble with some neighbors. Shot one of them in town one night, and I figured I needed a vacation about then."

"Have things cooled off?"

Steck nodded. "I made restitution, and the fellow I shot dropped the charges against me. Hell, we even went partners in a new venture. Raisin' bremmer crossbreeds." He put the neck of the bottle in his mouth and turned it upside down.

"What kind of crossbreeds?"

"Bremmers." Steck picked up the double barrel as he sat on the bench.

"Brimmers?"

"No, bremmers."

"Spell it."

"B-R-A-H-M-A-S."

Claude squinted one eye. "That spells brahmas, don't it?"

"Well, 'bremmers' is easier on my conversation. Didn't you ever see that bremmer bull I had at the ranch?"

"I don't recall. What did he look like?"

"If you'd have seen him, you'd remember. Big gray bull

with floppin' ears, enough dewlap and sheath to carpet your parlor, and a big hump on his shoulder."

"You mean like a buffalo?"

"No, more like a camel. But not the kind the army imported before the war. More like those two-hump camels."

Claude's eyebrows rose. "These bremmers have got two humps?"

"No, just one, but it sort of flops over to one side like a hump on one of them two-hump camels."

"I never saw anything like that," Claude said, lifting his flat-brimmed hat to rake his long hair back. "Where'd you get 'em?"

"They come from India. I bought that first one I had from a fellow in South Carolina after the war. I got to studying that bull, and I liked what I saw. You know how a longhorn will sweat around the nose?"

"Yeah."

"Well, this bremmer would sweat all over. And he'd sweat poison to ticks. When he'd sweat, they'd just drop off of him like rain."

Claude adjusted the Le Mat under his belt. "I guess that's good."

"Good, hell! That's a revolution in Texas beef! Most people haven't figured it out yet, Sabinal, but ticks is what causes Texas fever. I'm sure of it. Now, if we can breed that poisonous sweat into some bremmer-longhorn crosses, we can wipe out Texas fever and open the market for Texas cattle again."

Claude smiled and sank to the bench. Steck always had some revolution in mind. "Where you gonna get your breed stock?"

"Already got 'em. Had 'em, anyway. When I was on the lam in Europe, I figured I might just as well make use of the trip and take a tramp steamer over to India to see if I might buy some bremmer bulls. That's the damnedest, dirtiest country in the world, Sabinal. Don't ever go there."

"Worse than Mexico?"

"Oh, hell, you'd think Laredo was paradise next to Bombay. But the thing is, they've got bremmers runnin' loose in the streets. Fool Hindus won't eat 'em. Say they're sacred. They tame those bremmers like pet dogs, always hand-feedin' 'em and huggin' on 'em and what-not, but they won't eat 'em. Wouldn't even sell me any if I said I was gonna breed beef cattle with 'em. I had to lie and tell 'em I wanted those sacred bremmers to spread their Hindu religion around Texas, although whatever the hell their religion's all about, I don't know, and don't want to know. If it's against eatin' beef, I'm against it."

Claude smiled. "How many of these bremmers did you get?"

"Fifty bulls and a dozen heifers. By the time I sailed 'em across the Atlantic, I had almost a thousand dollars invested in every head. Then the damned Department of Agriculture says I've got to quarantine 'em and have a bunch of tests run to make sure they ain't diseased. So I quarantined 'em on Matagorda Island, right off the coast from my ranch, and that's when all hell broke loose."

"They get sick?"

"No, they got rustled! I had one of my hired boys out there to watch 'em for a couple of weeks. Well, when I sailed over to the island with this government inspector who was gonna run disease tests on 'em, I found my hired man shot dead and all my bremmers gone."

Claude squirmed a little on the hard bench. "How did they get 'em off the island?"

"Stolt a ferry boat and floated 'em across the bay to my ranch. We found the ferry owner shot dead, too. Whoever stolt 'em loaded 'em on a northbound. That's what brought me here."

Claude's eyebrows drew together. He didn't like the turn this conversation had taken. "I thought you said you came here to hunt."

"I did. Hunt rustlers. I traced those stolen bremmers up the railroads all the way to Laramie. Wasn't hard. They tend to draw attention. The rustlers put 'em off at Laramie and herded 'em west. I was about to take out after 'em alone when I saw your name in the newspaper. Imagine that. The best regulator in Texas shows up right in my trail way the hell up in Wyoming just when I need him!"

Claude stood and yanked his shotgun away from the rancher. "I'm not for hire," he said sternly. "I came up here to get out of that business." He picked up the Winchester and returned both weapons to the gun rack inside the door.

"You haven't even let me make an offer," Steck said. "I'll pay a hundred a head for every bremmer recovered and two hundred a head for every rustler. You don't have to go it alone, either. I'll come with you."

"No, you won't, because I ain't goin'," Claude insisted. He pulled his watch from his pocket. It wasn't time for a swallow yet, but he snatched the bottle up, anyway. His past hadn't taken long in catching up.

"All right, two hundred for every bremmer and five hundred for every rustler. You stand to make thousands, Sabinal."

"I stand to get killed. You've already got two dead men on your hands. I don't want to be the next."

They sat and argued, sipped whiskey, and watched the rain until Claude convinced Bob Steck that he would never chase another rustler. He invited Steck to stay overnight, but the rancher insisted on getting back to Laramie to find a real stock detective. Grousing, the old Texan put his slicker back on, tightened his saddle cinch, and mounted. But just as he was getting ready to use his spurs, he reached into his saddle pocket.

"Say, Sabinal, you know a thing or two about guns. What can you tell me about this?" He pulled something from the saddle pouch. "Of course, now, don't let me put you out none . . ."

Claude caught the empty brass shell casing that Steck tossed to him under the porch roof. It was a big one, about the size of a man's finger. He recognized the caliber and the distinctive necked outline, felt a long-buried pang of hatred come back to life. "A .44-90. Made for the old Model 73 Sharps Creedmoor." His glare rose to pierce Steck's eyes. "Where'd you get this?"

"Matagorda Island. We figured it was the shell used to kill my man I had guardin' the bremmers."

"What made you figure that?"

"We found it in his hand. We figured the killer put it there. That dead ferry operator had one in his hand, too."

Claude's jaws seized up on him for a second, and his fist clenched tight around the brass shell. He felt the heat of Texas on his face again. He spit into the rain and forgot all about hunting deer and elk.

"Bob," he said, "you just hired yourself a regulator."

THREE

Claude pushed his empty plate away and sloshed a shot of whiskey into his coffee cup. "We don't do anything until we get an answer to that telegram," he said to Steck.

The rancher frowned and sighed. "Who is this fellow Wolverton, anyway?"

It was midnight, and they had arrived in Laramie wet and hungry. One good thing about working for Bob Steck,

Claude thought. The rancher didn't skimp on grub. The food at the Depot Cafe was the best in town.

"They used to call him Lone Wolf," Claude muttered. "He was a stock detective and a bounty hunter years ago, before I got into the business."

"You callin' him in to help?"

Anger glinted in Claude's eyes. "Hell, no. I didn't send the telegram *to* Wolverton. I sent it *about* him. He's supposed to be servin' a life sentence in the Texas state pen. But that Creedmoor cartridge you found in the hands of those dead men—that was his sign."

"Sign?"

Claude nodded, his eyes staring into his coffee cup. "When he was regulatin' for those big outfits years ago, Wolverton would take his rustlers out at long range with a 73 model Sharps Creedmoor. He'd Lone-Wolf 'em—that's what they called it. After he killed 'em he'd just leave 'em lay and put that cartridge in their hand as a warning to other rustlers. Sharps only made that caliber rifle for a few years and they're hard to come by. When you found a Sharps .44-90 shell in some poor dead bastard's hand, there was no mistakin' who'd done it. It was known as Wolverton's sign from West Texas to Montana."

"How come I never heard of this Lone Wolf?" Steck said.

"He never worked down your way before. Besides, he didn't go in much for publicity. Laid low most of the time."

"You think he stolt my bremmers?"

"I sent that telegram to the prison to find out whether or not he's still there. If he's out, I'd say he's the man you're after."

Steck poured his coffee from his cup to his saucer and blew across it to cool it. "You know him?"

"Never actually met the son of a bitch. Seen him, though."

"What's he look like?"

"Big man. Carries a lot of weight. Got about a quarter Indian blood. Pawnee, I believe."

Steck sensed Duval holding something back. The range detective had ridden all the way to Laramie in a brood, refusing to say much until now. "What landed him in prison?"

Claude looked at the wall over the rancher's head. "His style of regulatin'. Never asked any questions, just shot his men dead from four, five hundred yards out. He was a back-shooter. Took 'em square between the shoulders every time. That .44-90 shoots a four-hundred-fifty-grain bullet. It'll tear a man wide open. Down in the Panhandle, dozen years ago, he mistook a cowboy for a rustler he was after. Killed him and left that cartridge in his hand. They should have hung him, but he turned himself in and gave a guilty plea, so the judge went easy on him and sentenced him to life."

Steck grunted. "So now he's escaped and gone from regulatin' to rustlin'."

"Looks that way."

"He must have lost his touch in prison. Those two we found dead weren't shot too clean."

The detective's sky-blue eyes narrowed and settled on the rancher's face. "That don't sound like Lone Wolf. He was steady."

"Maybe it ain't him at all. Maybe it's some imitator."

"We'll know when we get that telegram."

The Western Union boy found Claude bearded with shaving soap the next morning in his hotel room. The regulator tipped the boy, read the telegram alone in his room. He stared at the wall for a while, the page in his hand. He took an eye-opening swig from his flask, finished shaving, then went next door to rouse Steck from bed.

"Looks like Wolverton's our man," Claude said.

Steck's silver hair was standing on end. He had taken quite a few drinks at the Chugwater Saloon last night. He held the telegram at arm's length and squinted at it.

"Oh, hell," Claude said, snatching the page from the rancher, "when are you gonna get yourself some readin' glasses?" He read the telegram aloud:

"Lone Wolf model prisoner. Started Sunday school. Read entire prison library. Captain debating team. Full pardon by governor six weeks ago."

"That's about the time I got back with the bremmers," Steck said.

Claude shook his head and hissed. "They're pardonin' murderers now, Bob. Time was they'd hang 'em."

The rancher rubbed his face. "I'll still hang 'em, by God." When his eyes finally focused, he was surprised to see Claude smiling, but with more deviltry than joy. "Did you cut yourself shavin'?"

"Huh?" Claude stroked his face and felt blood smear under his fingers. "I guess so. Hurry up and get dressed. Let's go get those bremmers back."

While Steck bought saddle horses, pack mules, and supplies, Claude visited the shop of his only friend in Laramie, a gunsmith he had swapped collectibles with. The brass bell on the door announced his arrival. "Mornin', Phil," he said, raking his long hair back and fixing it in place with his hat.

"Claude!" the fat little gunsmith said. "What brings you to town?"

Claude smiled and shrugged. "Gets lonesome out there in the hills."

Phil put his fat oil-stained hand in Claude's. "With all those guns to keep you company?"

The Texan let out a genuine chuckle. Phil just had a way about him. "To tell you the truth, I thought I'd take one of my old long-range rifles up in the mountains after some elk. You got any Sharps .44-90s?"

The little man's eyes grew round and sparkled. "You're the second man to ask in two weeks! What's all the interest in these Creedmoors around here all of a sudden? I didn't even know you had one."

"What would I do with the ammunition if I didn't have one? Have you got the shells or not?"

"I found two boxes way in the back, but I sold them to that other fellow."

Claude gritted his teeth and shook his head. "I had my heart set on shootin' the old Creedmoor. Who was this other fellow? Maybe I can get a few rounds from him."

"Stranger," Phil said, shrugging.

"What did he look like?"

"Rough-lookin' little character. Between you and me in height, I guess. Dirty clothes. Bad complexion. You know, pockmarks. Haven't seen him since. I don't think you'll find him around here."

"Where was he goin'?"

"He didn't say, and I didn't ask. Say, what's that under your belt?"

Claude proudly drew the Le Mat and handed it to the gunsmith. He had found it under his belt the day before when he mounted to leave his ranch with Bob Steck. Instead of leaving it in the house, he had decided to bring it with him. It would make a nice addition to the Marlin repeater and the matched pair of .44-caliber Smith & Wesson Russians he had packed for the trip.

"You didn't tell me you had a Le Mat!" Phil said. "Say, this is a nice piece! You're a real collector, Claude, if you've got one of these *and* a .44 Sharps Creedmoor."

When he left the gun shop, Claude put the grapeshot revolver in his saddlebag and mounted the big paint stallion he called Casino. The horse had caught his eye the day he arrived in Laramie. He had always admired paint horses but had never owned one because Dusty didn't like them. He remembered well the highest praise Dusty had ever given to a paint horse: "His hide might make a good rug." But Dusty had been dead eleven years now and Claude figured he could ride whatever kind of horseflesh he wanted.

A day hadn't gone by that he hadn't thought of his old partner. Things Dusty had said came to him at odd hours, day and night. He remembered the way Dusty rode, walked, laughed. The only thing he couldn't remember was what he looked like. Oh, he could describe him to anybody, to a T. But he couldn't picture him anymore. Hadn't actually seen Dusty Sanderson's face since the day of his murder. He had never mentioned it to anybody, but he felt awful guilty about it. He should have been able to conjure a picture of the man's face at will, but try as he did, it would not come.

He reined Casino up the street and rode to the rail yard stock pens to meet Steck. Yesterday's rain clouds had broken apart and now looked like clean white sheep grazing a blue field. He found Steck sitting on a stockyard fence rail, taking in the sun, talking to one of the hands.

"This is the feller, Sabinal," Steck said, jumping down from the fence.

The stock pen foreman nodded at Claude through the rails. "What can I do for you?"

"I hear you saw some strange cattle here a while back."

"I sure did."

"Mind tellin' me about 'em?"

"I already told him yesterday," the foreman said, pointing at Steck. "Not much to tell, anyway. They looked like a cross between a camel and a big gray mule. About fifty or sixty head, I don't remember the exact count. Three cowboys took 'em off in the middle of the night."

"What about the men? What did they look like?"

The foreman scratched his head. "Didn't get a good look at 'em. It was dark, and I was sort of starin' at those flop-eared cattle."

"Did you see a big feller? Part Indian? Carried a long rifle?"

"Like I say, them cattle sort of got my attention away from everything else." The foreman rolled the quid in his cheek and spit.

"How about a dirty little cowboy with a pockmarked face?"

"That sounds more like the fellers I saw, but like I say, I didn't see any faces up close."

"And they headed west?"

He pointed across the plains. "Seemed to be headin' toward Big Hollow. Those cattle sure trailed easy. Like a bunch of old pet horses."

They started west across the Laramie Plains, leading their pack train and spare horses. The mules carried grub to last a month and enough ammunition for an extended campaign. Bob Steck had no aversion to spending money for the right cause. He had made and lost half a dozen fortunes in his life.

"You reckon Lone Wolf has put a gang together?" the rancher asked as they trotted across the plains. The wet ground was already pushing up tiny spikes of bright green grass.

"Seems likely, don't it?" Claude said. The gloom from the previous day had lifted from him, and he felt glad to be riding.

"How long you had that horse?" Steck said, admiring Casino.

"Since I come up here."

"You like him?"

"So far. He's got good bottom for a big horse. Mustang blood."

Steck let out a hoot that died somewhere on the prairie. "That ain't no mustang! Mustangs are little!"

"In Texas maybe. But up here they've bred with draft horses the Indians used to run off of the farms in Nebraska. Casino was caught wild on Powder River when he was a colt."

"Somebody sold you a bill of goods, Sabinal. I know a mustang when I see one, and that horse would make two of 'em."

Claude realized, traveling in Steck's good company, that he missed some things about regulating. Riding, camping, reading the sign. Now he was back in it, and his spirits were lifting, but this case still had him worried.

No one other than Lone Wolf Wolverton could have brought Claude out of his retirement as a stock detective. Yet he had to wonder what he had gotten himself into. Some of the evidence pointed to Lone Wolf, but not all of it. He had the Creedmoor shells and the pardon from prison. But there was also the sloppy shooting Steck had told him of and the fact that no one in Laramie could say they had seen Wolverton—only this little fellow with the pock-marked face.

He tried to tell himself it didn't matter. One way or another, this business with the sacred brahma cattle was going to bring him face-to-face with the man called Lone Wolf. Lying on his belly with his Creedmoor in his hands, the old murderer had killed many a man. Claude had waited years to show him how to do it standing up.

FOUR

The evening shadows fell across Big Hollow, a huge wind-scoured gouge in the Laramie Plains. It ran nine miles east to west, widened to three, and plunged a hundred and fifty feet below the surface of the surrounding plains. It held a little water in its bottom, but it wasn't a rain-carved feature. It was what Claude called a blowout—a wind-hollowed pit—the largest he had ever seen.

He and Bob Steck called on a small ranch near the hollow, hoping for an invitation to stay the night. The rancher, a man old enough to be Bob Steck's daddy, seemed pleased to have their company.

"Put your horses in the barn and bring your bedrolls in the house," he said. "I'll cook some steaks and potatoes for you."

A wind was whipping over the treeless rim of the hollow, carrying regular spouts of fine sand into the air, but the house was comfortable in spite of the dust, and the old man knew hospitality, breaking out the best whiskey for his guests.

He introduced himself as Jimmy McWhorter and talked nonstop as he cooked supper for three on the rusty wood stove. "Glad you showed up. Had to butcher a heifer last week and ought to eat it before it spoils."

Halfway through the meal, he finally ran out of talk and started asking questions. "Where you boys from?" he asked.

"Texas," Steck answered.

"Goin' huntin'?"

"Huntin' rustlers," Steck replied. "Seen any?"

Claude could only grimace, caught as he was with his mouth full. From now on, he was going to have to make sure Bob didn't do the talking for them. The rancher had never learned when not to advertise.

"Not that I'd know of," McWhorter replied. "What did they look like?"

Claude swallowed a chunk of steak and started carving another bite. "We don't know for sure, but I can tell you what the cattle they stole looked like. Big, gray, hump-backed rascals with dewlaps and flop ears."

McWhorter pounded the table with his fist. "Bremmers?"

The Texans looked at each other. "Well, yes," Steck answered. "How'd you know?"

"Five strangers trailed by here with a herd of 'em. Better than sixty, I'd say, mostly bulls. One heifer was draggin', so they sold her to me cheap. Ten dollars."

"Ten dollars!" Steck shouted.

"Where is she now?" Claude asked. He forced an over-size piece of meat into his mouth.

McWhorter gestured with his fork. "You just bit into a hunk of her."

Steck coughed up a swallow of whiskey and jumped back so quick that his chair slapped against the floor. "You butchered her!" he wheezed.

Claude took to laughing so that he couldn't swallow.

"She took sick and died," McWhorter explained.

The tenderloin in Claude's mouth suddenly lost its flavor, and he swallowed a chunk that felt big as his fist. He grimaced as he pushed his plate away.

"That's a thousand-dollar heifer you butchered!" the rancher said.

Claude picked up Steck's chair. "Now, settle down, Bob, and take your seat. He didn't know that heifer was yours." He turned to McWhorter. "How did you know to call that heifer a bremmer?"

"That's what they called her—them fellers that sold her

to me. Said it was some foreign breed that would sweat poison to ticks."

Steck plopped down in his chair, fuming.

"Mr. McWhorter," Claude explained, "those fellers were outlaws. Rustled them bremmers from Bob down in Texas. It would help if you could tell us what they looked like."

McWhorter had a good memory for details. He described all five men, their horses and tack, their chaps, spurs, hats, and guns. There was a pair of redheaded twin brothers, he said, a black man with a cavalry cap, and a squaw wearing a white man's suit.

"The one that done most of the talkin'," he continued, "and I reckon was sort of their leader, was a ugly little cuss looked like his face'd gone through a sausage grinder. Wore shotgun leggin's, gray felt hat all caved in, spurs didn't match. Had a buffalo gun so long he had to cut the end off his saddle boot and I saw the muzzle stickin' out. Had a covered front sight like a railroad tunnel."

"You sure there wasn't a big fellow with 'em?" Claude asked, his eyes glistening with excitement. "Bigger than me, heavyset, part Indian."

The old man shook his head. "No. Just them five. Odd outfit."

When they heard the old man snoring that night, the Texans added up what they knew.

"Whoever rustled those cattle had heard you talk about 'em," Claude said. "Who else would call 'em bremmers and talk about sweatin' tick poison? I figure somebody heard you braggin' about 'em in some saloon down in Texas and decided to go out on Matagorda Island and maverick 'em."

"You still reckon it was Wolverton? McWhorter didn't see anybody that looked like him."

"Wolverton's smart. He could just be layin' low while those five outlaws take all the risk for him. It was three men in Laramie. Now it's four men and a squaw. Wolverton may have put a gang together while he was teachin' Sunday school in prison."

"Maybe Lone Wolf rustled the cattle from Matagorda Island," Steck suggested, "then sold 'em to the gang that brought 'em up here."

"Maybe. But that little gang leader's carryin' a Creedmoor, and I'm not givin' up yet on it bein' Lone Wolf's gun. I don't know if you believe in hunches, Bob, but I've got one like an itch tellin' me we're gonna meet up with Wolverton before the hand is dealt." He pulled his hat over his eyes.

Steck lay back on his blankets and chuckled. "Damn, that old man can snore. I've heard quieter sawmills."

"Bob," the stock detective said, "I want you to promise me somethin'. When we come up against Wolverton, he's mine."

"Oh, hell, Sabinal. I know what you'll do. You'll march him back to town and let some judge have him."

Claude's hat muffled his voice. "Not this time. Not Wolverton. I intend to press an empty shell into his hand."

They saddled up in front of McWhorter's place at dawn, a hot breakfast in their stomachs.

"They trailed them bremmers west on the north rim of the holler," the old man said. "Looked like they was headin' for the Lafferty Ranch. You'll find it ten miles from here."

They shook the old man's hand and rode toward the mountains along the rim of Big Hollow. An hour into the morning they left the hollow behind and soon saw the barns and bunkhouses of the Lafferty Ranch wavering on the plains in the distance.

A few minutes later, Steck stood in his stirrups at the head of the pack train and leaned over the horn. "Hey!" he shouted, squinting. "Those look like my bremmers!"

Claude trotted up beside him, saw a pasture coming into view over a low roll. Then he spotted the first of the strange-looking cattle. They had horns no bigger than pinecones, ears too big to hold up, and dewlaps hanging like velvet curtains in a whorehouse. He hadn't given Steck's talk about the camel humps much credit until now. They were so big they listed to one side. Each hump looked like a second head growing from the shoulder of each animal. Even the heifers had humps. Some were almost black around the hump and head, others nearly white all over.

"I et one of those for supper last night?" he said.

"I only count forty-five," Steck said. "The rustlers must have sold these and taken the rest somewhere else."

"Don't be too sure," Claude warned. "Better not let on to these folks what we're up to until we ask 'em a few questions. Let me do the talkin'."

They rode through the herd of docile brahmas and found three young cowboys, armed and mounted, waiting to receive them at the main house. As they rode near, an older man stepped out onto the porch. Claude figured him for about forty to forty-five. The working duds he wore showed little wear. His boots held a shine.

The regulator tipped his hat. "Howdy. I'm Claude Duval, your new neighbor down south."

The man nodded, straight-faced. "I'm Ike Lafferty. Been plannin' on payin' you a visit. The boys said they saw a new house down there. What do you run? Cattle or sheep?"

"Just a few cows and horses," Claude said. "I plan to earn most of my wages guidin' hunters in the mountains. This is my first client, Bob Steck."

"What are you huntin' this time of year?" Lafferty asked.

"Bob's after bear," Claude said. He looked over his shoulder. "Those are the damnedest-lookin' cattle back there I ever seen. Where'd you get 'em?"

"Bought 'em from a herd that came through here a while back. The trail boss said he got 'em from an importer in Texas. They're called bremmers. Supposed to be just the thing for the northern ranges."

"They're mine," Steck blurted.

Claude groaned and found the grip of his right-hand Smith & Wesson. "Damn, Bob," he said through his teeth as he eyed the three Lafferty Ranch cowboys and wondered how many others might be watching over their rifle sights from barns or bunkhouses.

"Hell, Sabinal, I don't bluff. Fact is, Mr. Lafferty, you've bought stolen property. Those bremmers are mine. Didn't you ask for a bill of sale?"

"They're not even branded," Lafferty said. "How are you gonna prove those cattle are yours?"

"It's the only blasted herd of bremmers this side of Bombay! I don't have to brand 'em! Besides, I've got bills of sale, shipping records, even a letter from the Department of Agriculture authorizing me to import the son of a bitches." He swung down from his mount, opened the flap of his saddlebag, and removed the papers. He stalked over to the porch and handed the documents up to Lafferty.

Lafferty shuffled the records, then slapped them against his leg. "Damn! I paid a hundred dollars a head for those bremmers."

"A hundred!" Steck roared. "They're worth ten times that!"

Lafferty paced in front of the house. "That fast-talkin' little bastard took me . . . Where's that dog?" he shouted. "I want somethin' to kick!" He charged a pile of stovewood stacked on the front porch, booted chunks among his three cowboys, scattering their broncs. Claude's pack mules bolted and pitched, slinging camp utensils.

Steck jumped onto the porch with Lafferty as the three

cowboys started pulling leather. Claude managed to steer Casino clear of the stampede and keep him under control. When he looked back at the porch, he saw Lafferty still fuming and Steck slapping his leg. Bob liked a good laugh as much as a good fight.

"Me and my boys will join you," Lafferty said when the stock had settled down. "Maybe we can get my money back before those rustlers spend it all. They still have sixteen head of your bremmers, too."

"I don't work that way," Claude replied. "A big posse will just give us away. Me and Bob will get your money back for you."

"Well, I'll go with you myself, then," Lafferty said. "Just me."

"I'd rather you left it to us," Claude said.

"Neighbor, I don't care what you'd rather. Those bastards took me. I mean to get 'em. I've lived in this country since it opened up, so don't tell me I can't go after 'em if I want to. Besides, I know the mountains better than you do."

"He's got a point," Steck said. "Wouldn't hurt to have just one other man along."

Claude knew he couldn't keep Lafferty from going, but he wasn't about to let this thing get any further beyond his control. He looked sternly at Lafferty down his eagle's nose. "If you're ridin' with me, you don't flinch without askin' me first."

"Sabinal's the best, Ike," Steck said, already on a first-name basis with the rancher. "We're better off with him leadin' us."

"Fair enough," Lafferty said. "You seem to know what you're doin'. Let's get that pack string back in shape, get somethin' to eat, and get started. I can show you just the way those rustlers went."

FIVE

The darkened plains sloped up to the mountains, the mountains melding with black clouds, boiling back overhead, engulfing the three men on horseback. To Claude, it felt as if they were riding into a gigantic cave.

Dusty would have taken it as a sign, saying they were riding into a cave of no return, or something like that. Dusty used to look for signs in everything—wind, clouds, animals. Claude had never put much stock in such things, but he liked looking for them, anyway. They reminded him of Dusty and the cowboying days before the stock detective business, before Dusty was murdered for looking too much like the outlaw Giff Dearborn from a distance.

As they rode deeper into the cave of no return, Ike Lafferty described the five outlaws exactly as McWhorter had. "I've heard rumors for years about a gang that summers up around the Snowy Range. Maybe it was them. They've never bothered anybody down here on the Laramie Plains, but rumor has it they rustle a lot of stock as far up as the Wind River country. I guess I should have suspected somethin' funny out of that bunch. That squaw and the colored man with the army cap should have warned me off."

Lafferty knew nothing of anyone matching Lone Wolf's description.

As they climbed the foothills, they began to weave among ponderosa pines, their pace slowing to a walk.

"We'll come to Galloway's Sheep Camp over the next hill," Lafferty said. "I'm not very friendly with Galloway, so watch yourself when we get there."

"Not friendly with your neighbor?" Claude said. "Why not?"

"He runs sheep. Runs too damn many of 'em, if you ask

me. Most sheep men are peculiar, but this Galloway is just a mean little cuss. I don't like him. He's Scotch from the old country and stays drunk most of the time. Keeps a little wife with him, and she's mean as him."

When he led the party to the top of the hill, Claude stopped to look over the sheep camp. Ashes shifted where a cabin had stood. The poles of empty corrals lay scattered like splinters. A fire smoldered in a gully near the camp. There were two horses staked to graze, a wagon sheltered under a sheet of canvas. Then he noticed two broken fence rails lashed together to form a cross, planted at the head of a fresh mound of dirt.

"Lordy," Lafferty said, stopping beside the stock detective. "Looks like them outlaws came through here, all right."

"Somebody survived to dig that grave," Claude answered. "How many people lived here?"

"Galloway, his wife, and a hired Indian boy. But the boy usually stayed up in the mountains herdin' sheep."

They eased their pack train down the trail, Claude watching for movement. He passed a broken-down corral fence and noticed signs of blood on the ground. Sheep blood, he surmised. A plain trail led to the smoldering gully. Someone had dragged dead sheep there to burn. The stench of scorched wool was still in the air.

When he got to the grave, he stopped, looking for a name on the cross, finding none. The other riders and the pack train shuffled noisily up behind him. But above the hooves, the squeaking of saddle leather, and the rattle of the packs, he heard the lever of a repeating rifle go through its strokes.

He reached for his side arm as he twisted in the saddle, but the voice stopped him short of drawing the weapon. A smooth, sweet voice, etched with the lilt of Old Scotland. He found its source in a woman who stepped from the gully behind the horsemen, covering them with her rifle, the smoke rising behind her.

"So now you've landed back, have you?" she said, glaring at Ike Lafferty with hard green eyes. She looked small with the big Winchester against her hip, but she seemed sure and agile. Her pretty face was streaked with dirt and sweat. Her grimy green print dress hugged her waist. She wore no hat or bonnet, and tousled brown hair fell over and around her shoulders.

"Now, Correen," Lafferty said, "you don't think I had anything to do with this."

"Who but yourself?" She circled the men to get the best angle on all three, moving like a dancer. "I'm sure I might have thanked you for murderin' my husband, savin' me the trouble, but you never should have killed my dogs and sheep and taken my horses, nor burned my house."

"You've got it wrong, Correen," Lafferty said. "We're on the trail of the gang that did this. Steck here has trailed them all the way from Texas."

"That's right, miss," Steck said.

Claude turned Casino for a better look at the woman. "And just how did you come through this alive?" he asked, his suspicion showing in his face.

The barrel of Correen's Winchester swept quickly around to him, her eyes following. "You're in a more likely way to do the explainin' to me, sir," she said.

Her nerve made Claude smile, and he removed his hand from his pistol butt. He chuckled and raised his hands a little, his reins draped over his left palm. "All right, I see your point. I'll explain . . ."

He told her about the rustled herd of bremmers, the murders in Texas, and the trail to Lafferty Ranch. Thunder rumbled in the mountains and a light rain began to fall.

When she had heard the story, Correen finally lowered

her rifle and allowed the men to get their slickers out. "Have you got a tent?" she asked.

Claude nodded.

"Pitch it up over here." She eased the hammer down on the rifle and started toward her wagon.

"You still haven't said how you managed to escape gettin' killed with your husband," Claude said.

She shook her hair over her shoulders. "I wasn't here when it happened." Her eyes narrowed and knifed toward the wooden cross. "My late husband—may God curse his soul—fell from his horse drunk a couple of weeks ago and broke his leg. He couldn't travel, so I took the wagon to town for my messages."

"Your what?"

"My supplies and groceries, you know. Have you never heard the mother tongue?"

"Not the way you speak it. What happened when you came back with your . . . your messages?"

"I found my farm in ashes and my husband dead. I just this mornin' got the last of the sheep dragged together and burned."

Claude reached into his vest pocket. "What do you know about this?" He tossed the Sharps Creedmoor cartridge to Correen.

She snatched the shell from the air, glanced at it briefly. "I've one that matches it. Found in my husband's hand."

"Mrs. Galloway," Bob Steck said, "looks like you and me were visited by the same outlaws."

She tossed the cartridge back to Claude and turned her hardened eyes on Steck. "Don't call me by that devil's name," she said as a large raindrop hit her brow. "You may address me as Correen. I'll take no offense to the familiarity."

When the rain slacked off after dark, Steck and Lafferty left the tent to look after their animals. Claude went out after them, stopping to observe a strange little tent beside the woman's wagon. It looked as though she had taken the bows off her wagon, jammed them in the ground, and covered them with canvas. Through the flapping tent door, he saw her bed inside: straw covered with an old quilt.

He found Correen under the canvas roof that shielded her wagon, washing the supper dishes in a caldron of hot water. "Can I chunk up the fire for you?" he asked, ducking in under the canvas. "Carry some wood or somethin'?"

She glanced at the two revolvers he wore. "Thank you, no. I've gone without a man's help many years now, Mr. Duval."

He had never heard his name spoken with such timbre, but he knew better than to fall for pretty faces and pleasant voices. "Now, don't exaggerate. You're not that old."

"I was taken very young from Scotland. My husband brought me here when I was only fifteen, and I had little to say about it."

His hat was pressing against the canvas, so he took it off, raking his long hair back between his fingers. "Your folks let you marry that young?" He saw Correen pulling at her own tangled trusses, soiled from days of dragging dead sheep. He heard rainwater trickling into a pot under the edge of the canvas and knew she was thinking of making herself presentable.

"I'm sure they did," she said. "We were poor traveler folk. My father a tinsmith, my mother a basket maker. We never lived in a house. Just wandered about, hawkin' tinware and baskets. My darlin' old mother wanted somethin' better for her children, so she urged me to marry this man, this widower, a sheepherder comin' to America, and the wickedest man ever I knew."

Claude sniffed. He had heard a lot of hard-luck stories. "Now, your mama wouldn't let you marry him if he was that bad."

"Aye, but he was canny, Mr. Duval. He was darlin' enough at first, until we landed in this country. Then he'd take a dram or two and get to behavin' rather droll. The first time he got drunk, I'm sure he knocked me scatterin', but I repaid him with a shovel when he went to sleep that night. From that hour it was a constant battle between us, but anyway, he's dead now, and I would just as soon not talk about him."

"All right," Claude said, looking over his shoulder. "Let's talk about Ike Lafferty. What made you think he was the one who ransacked your place?"

She turned to him and put her wet hands over the curves of her hips. "I cannot talk about him without talkin' about my husband again. Is it your purpose to torture me with his memory?"

He glanced into the dark. "I know my timing's bad, Correen, but I need to know. Lafferty is a stranger to me. I don't know if I can trust him or not."

"Nor do I," she said, turning back to her dishes. "He argued with my husband every time he came around here, and they threatened each other with every manner of unpleasantry. That's why I suspected him at first, but I don't think he had anything to do with it now."

"I didn't hear you apologize to him."

"Nor will you."

He fought back a smile. "Have you ever heard of an outfit called the Snowy Range Gang?"

"Only rumors."

"Ever seen any outlaws around here?"

She tilted her head and smirked at him. "Not unless I'm lookin' at one right now." Her eyes darted to the twin revolvers.

He grinned, pulled his watch from his pocket, and turned it to catch the lantern light.

"Are you takin' medicine?" she asked. "You've pulled

that watch from your vest a dozen times since you landed here."

"Waitin' for my next dose of whiskey," he said. "One swallow on the half hour keeps a man healthy and sober."

"I admire your temperance." She clanged some tin plates together and shoved them into a box in the wagon. "I would admire more your abstinence."

Claude grunted and put his hat on. "I would appreciate it if you didn't tell Lafferty I was askin' about him."

"I have no plans to speak to him," she said.

He nodded and touched his brim. "Good night."

"Till the morn."

He walked to his tent and uncorked his whiskey flask. He tried to concentrate on the case at hand, Lone Wolf Wolverton, Ike Lafferty, the Snowy Range Gang. But instead he caught himself wondering if Correen would stay on in this country now that her husband had been murdered and her sheep herd wiped out. He wouldn't mind looking in on her every now and then.

"There you go again," he heard Dusty say. He felt him there, a faceless presence. "When are you gonna learn, boy? That girl could hog-tie you with a spiderweb right now if she wanted to."

SIX

Correen woke the men before dawn for breakfast. Her hair was washed, combed, and tied back in a twisted, shining bundle. Claude gathered that she had done some shopping for herself in Laramie. She wore a new riding skirt, a white blouse tied at the throat with a black ribbon, and a new pair of leather riding boots buttoned up to her calves.

The stars were still in the sky when she served the bacon and biscuits, the clouds having drifted away. Yesterday's dark cavern of no return had vanished.

After breakfast, Claude stropped his razor and whipped some shaving soap in a bowl of rainwater. He watched Correen as he took his whiskers off. She was getting ready to go somewhere. Not too far away, he hoped. She happened to walk by and glance at him as he was rinsing his face. The other men were striking tents, packing mules.

"Your sideburns are lopsided," she said, shaking her head.

He felt them with his fingertips. "Feel straight to me."

She took the razor from him, flipped the blade from the handle, and compared the two sides of his face. "You shouldn't be shavin' if you don't have a lookin' glass."

He felt her small hand grab his jaw and wrench his head to one side. The blade made two swipes at the left sideburn. She twisted his neck the other way, and he heard the razor scrape the right side of his face in short, hard strokes.

"There now," she said, swizzling the blade in the bowl of water. "That squared it up. Now I won't have to look at crooked sideburns all day." She slapped the folded razor in his hand.

As she walked away, Claude rubbed the tender skin she had scraped. "What do you mean all day?" he said. "We're fixin' to ride up after those outlaws."

She whirled and pierced him with a glare. "And I'll be ridin' with you."

Claude threw the razor into the bowl of water. "Like hell you will. That's a wild outfit we're going after up there."

Bob Steck came to the regulator's side.

"I've got a hired boy and a flock of sheep in those mountains," she said. "I'll not stay below until I know they're alive and well. I've got to look after what's mine."

"I'll look after it for you," Claude said.

"No, thank you, Mr. Duval. I don't need your help."

"And the last thing I need is a woman to look after."

Steck slapped him on the shoulder. "Wyoming gives 'em the vote and they think they can wear britches!" He laughed loudly.

Correen marched to her wagon and drew her Winchester from a leather scabbard. "Have you still got that empty cartridge?" she asked.

Claude patted his vest pocket. "Yeah," he said, puzzled.

She cocked the rifle. "Throw it just as high as you please above your head, Mr. Duval." She put the stock against her cheek.

Taking the big casing from his pocket, Claude smirked at Steck and sent the shell arching against the pale blue sky. Correen swept her barrel in pursuit and squeezed off a shot that twisted her with its recoil. The brass shell angled up and away, whirling, singing through the air. Steck hollered with joy and bounded across the ground to retrieve the target.

"I can look after myself," Correen said. She ejected the smoking shell, chambered a live one, savagely wrenching the lever of the Winchester. She let the hammer down, plucked a fresh cartridge from a box in the wagon, and refilled the magazine before replacing the rifle in its scabbard.

"Who taught you to shoot like that?" Claude asked.

"My father had an old musket, and I, bein' the oldest, learned to hunt rabbits and deer with it. Only it was poachin' in the old country, and you had to be canny."

Steck strode back with the empty shell, torn open by Correen's shot. "Look at that, Sabinal!" he said joyfully. "I've never seen the likes of it!"

"She still can't go with us."

"Then I'll go alone," she said.

"Aw, let her come along," Steck said. "She's proved she can shoot, and we could use a cook."

"Forget it. Too dangerous. She's not comin'."

Claude had his knee braced against a mule, taking the slack out of a diamond hitch, when he heard Correen ride out. He watched her trot away on her black pony, her spare horse carrying a small pack, expertly secured. When she got to the rise above her homestead, she turned west, toward the mountains.

Steck laughed. "She don't take you serious, Sabinal!"

Ike Lafferty sighed and rolled his eyes.

Claude saddled Casino and chased her half a mile before he caught up. "I told you it was too dangerous for you!" he shouted, standing Casino broadside in front of her on the trail.

She simply reined her mount onto rockier ground and went around the regulator, ignoring him.

He stood there after she passed, cussing her persistence. At last, he loped up the trail and overtook her again.

"All right," he said, "if you're determined to come along, you might as well ride with us where I can keep an eye on you." He wasn't totally against her going, though he suspected she would be more trouble than she was worth.

"No, thank you, Mr. Duval," she said, almost smiling at him. "I'd rather go on alone." She urged her mare up the trail.

"Dang it, Correen. Wait for the rest of us, I said!"

She pulled her reins and turned in the saddle. "Ask me," she said, her voice almost purring.

"What?"

"Ask me nicely."

Claude groaned. "Will you *please* wait on the rest of us?" He was thankful that Steck and Lafferty weren't listening, but knew Dusty was, and heard the echo of his partner's laughter.

"Well," she said, letting her eyelids sag as she felt her bundle of hair for loose strands, "I'm sure I might wait if you'd hurry along." She reined her mare under a pine and hopped down from the saddle.

"You have no idea what kind of a mess you're gettin' into," he said.

She glanced at him over her shoulder as she loosened the saddle girth. "And you, Mr. Duval, have no idea what kind of messes I have overcome long before I met you."

Correen grilled the men for information as the pack train moved slowly into the forests of fir, pine, and spruce that covered the high country.

"Sacred cattle in the sacred mountains," she remarked.

Steck was riding beside her, enjoying her conversation. "What do you mean by that?" he asked.

"Little Crow, my shepherd boy, has told me his people's lore of these mountains. He's from the Ute tribe. His people once came to these mountains to get wood for makin' bows, and to make 'medicine' as he calls it: magic." Her green eyes flared at mention of the word. "That's how these became known as the Medicine Bow Mountains. They are sacred to the Ute people, and now you have come for your sacred cattle here."

"How'd you come by a Ute boy?" Claude asked, looking back at her, resting his hand on the cantle as he rode. "I thought they were all on reservations."

"They were going to send Little Crow to school and make him learn English. His father thought bad of it and urged him to run away. I found him a year ago in the mountains, fed him, and put him to work with the sheep."

"How do you get along with him if he don't speak English?" Steck said.

"I know a few words of Ute, and he a few of English. And he has taught me some of the hand signs. We communicate well enough."

They rounded a bend in the trail, Claude pausing to admire a small mountain brook running along the edge of a meadow. Beavers had dammed it, forming a small lake. "We'll stop here to have lunch and let the horses graze," he said.

"I'll bet it's full of trout," Correen said, smiling at him as if she had come for a holiday picnic.

As the other men went for firewood, Claude walked around the pond to scout for signs of deer, elk, and rustlers. He looked across the water and saw the reflections of the horses in the still water. He liked what he saw here. Dusty sure knew how to pick a ranch site. Mountains, plains, foothills, and Correen all within a day's ride.

He caught Correen looking at him across the pond and turned his eyes to the ground again. He was trying not to think of her as available. One of the bad habits he had learned to temper over the years concerned women. "A pretty girl can knock you over with an eyelash," Dusty had once told him. In the past, various members of the gender had stolen Claude's heart, money, pride, or combinations of the three. He had trained himself to watch for deceptions. He hadn't found any in Correen yet, but wasn't about to let himself get taken in by her looks or her lilting talk.

And, after all, the woman's husband had just died. Even if she did hate the man, she wasn't going to be in a hurry to replace him. But could she ever be interested in a black sheep like Claude Duval? He would have to proceed carefully with her. He knew his weaknesses. He was still feeling her firm grip on his clean-shaven jaw.

He risked another glance at her, caught her removing

something from a long tube on her packhorse. Putting sticks together now, end-to-end. Stringing them with . . . Thread? What the . . . ? A damned fishing pole? Yes, a crank reel fixed to the handle.

He stormed back around the pond, but by the time he jumped the brook below the beaver dam, she had her line played out, flicking it gracefully out over the water and back over her shoulder. He stopped to watch her for a moment, fascinated. Never had he seen such fishing, flogging the surface of the water like a stage driver flicking the rump of a horse.

"Woman, what in the name of the devil do you think you're doin'?" he growled.

"Angling, Mr. Duval. I've brought along my new pole I ordered from—"

"Do you think this is a damned pleasure trip?" he said, interrupting her. "Do you think we've got time to . . ." His eyes got stuck on the end of the line that kept whipping over her shoulder. "What are you usin' for bait?"

"A wee bucktail fly," she said, letting the end of the line light finally, her alert eyes staying with it.

"A fly?"

"I'm sure I never said it wasn't. Now, stand back if you will, sir, or you'll frighten our lunch away."

"Correen, if you catch a fish with a fly, I'll . . ."

The surface of the pond erupted in a spout of water and a glint of scales. The angler snapped her rod back, bending it, and began taking line up on her reel. "You'll what, Mr. Duval? Have it for lunch?"

Claude stared in stupefaction as she played the trout to the shore and into her waiting hand. He looked over her shoulder as she removed the hook, a tiny bend of steel with bits of feather and hair tied to it. "Well, I'll be damned," he said. "That's not a bad fish."

"Past the common," she replied, handing the catch to him. "You might as well start guttin'."

As they ate their fresh fried trout, Claude laid down the rules for the rest of the expedition. "No shootin', except in self-defense. I don't want any hollerin', whistlin', or loud talkin'. Don't do anything that might spook the horses. Correen, keep the cook fires small, and douse 'em as soon as possible after dark. We don't know how close they are, so we'll start takin' turns at guard duty tonight. That means you, too, Correen."

She tried to respond, but he had purposefully caught her with her mouth full.

"Remember, if Wolverton's up here with 'em, he can blow a hole in any one of us from four hundred yards. Maybe farther. That means we have to watch a circle a half mile across all the time. You see where you're sittin' right now, Bob?"

"Huh?" Steck said, looking at the ground under him.

"You're liable to get Lone-Wolfed right there. Wolverton has a clean shot at your back from that ridge yonder, right at three hundred yards. He likes to take 'em in the back."

The Texan craned his neck, looked wild-eyed at the ridge behind him, picked up his plate, and found a safer place against a tree.

"Ike," the regulator said, "have you got any idea where this gang might be holed up?"

The rancher had finished eating and was whittling a soft piece of pine. "Not really. There's hundreds of hidin' places in these mountains."

"How do you aim to find 'em, Sabinal, with no tracks to follow?" Steck asked.

"First thing we need to worry about is findin' Correen's Indian boy. After we find him, we'll scout the ridges and look for campfire smoke. Correen, where you reckon that boy is?"

"He'll be near the Snowy Range this time of year. He's expectin' me to bring his supplies in a few days. He'll be easy enough to find."

"Just pray that Wolverton's gang doesn't find him before we do." He slung a fish spine from his plate, pulled his watch from his pocket, and smiled. "You gentlemen care for an after-dinner drink?"

Late in the afternoon, Claude led his party over a ridge and got his first look at the Snowy Range through a gap in the trees. The row of rocky peaks jutted above the timberline, bathed in sunlight, streaked with year-round snow. He felt compelled to ride over and see them, but knew they were farther away than they looked through the thin alpine air.

"We'll camp down in this draw," he said. "Looks like we'll make the Snowy Range by tomorrow afternoon." He let the pack train file by him and stayed on the ridge to admire the barren pinnacles. As he tried to take it all in, the breeze and the sweet Scottish lilt chilled him so that he almost shivered.

"Beautiful, isn't it?" Correen said.

Claude grunted, allowing himself a glimpse of her face. "Reminds me of the Highlands of home."

"It looks like this over there?"

"A bit tamer, I'm sure."

He gripped his saddle horn. "A tamer country's a good place for a woman on her own."

"I have no desire to go back now, Mr. Duval. I have come to love it here and will love it all the more now that my husband is dead. I only need to get my horses back and punish those who slaughtered my sheep."

"Without gettin' killed," Claude added. She's going to stay, he thought. That's good, but this ain't the time to think about it. Wolverton's out there somewhere. Hell, for all you know, she begged Lone Wolf to kill her husband. She may be in it with him. You've been fooled by pretty faces before, boy. Watch yourself.

"You haven't told us everything, have you?" she said.

He tried to look dumbfounded. "Huh?"

"You're following their trail, and you haven't told Mr. Steck and Mr. Lafferty."

"What trail?" Claude said. "The rain's washed all the tracks away."

"And beaten down the heaps of horse and cattle dung, but they're still underfoot of us."

Claude couldn't prevent his eyebrows from raising. "Anybody's stock could have left that sign. Lafferty runs cattle up here."

"Aye, but this sign runs a straight path. They were movin' slow, lettin' the sacred cattle graze. The grass they cropped is still plain to see. And don't think I didn't spot their campfire ashes at the pond."

Claude smiled in spite of himself. "Where'd you learn to read sign like that?"

"Trailin' my flocks, huntin' food. Little Crow teaches me something new every time I see him."

"Well, don't let on to Bob and Ike that we're on the trail of those outlaws."

"Why not?"

"Because Bob flies off the handle, and I don't know what Lafferty is liable to do. I don't want them gettin' nervous till the last minute."

She nodded. "There's still something you're not telling us, Mr. Duval. I'd say you're more than a hired detective to this shootin' party. You've got something personal at stake."

Claude scoffed and looked away. "What gave you that kind of idea?"

"There's sign to read on the ground, Mr. Duval, then there's that in a man's eyes. I see blood in yours."

Her keen stare stayed with him even after she rode down to the campsite. He pulled his watch from his pocket. Still twelve minutes shy of the hour. "Damn," he said.

SEVEN

Claude picked up his Marlin repeater as he left camp. "Bob, you'll relieve me at nine o'clock. Correen, put the fire out as soon as you get through with it." He looked at Lafferty, who was leaning against a tree, whittling. "You better turn in early, Ike. You'll stand morning guard."

He walked to a slope overlooking the camp and sat down against a tree trunk, relieved to be beyond the eyes of his campmates. The pistol grip of the Marlin felt good in his palm. He could sort things out up here.

Bob Steck? Not afraid to fight. The trouble was holding him back until the fight started.

Ike Lafferty? Quiet. Calm. But he's got a temper. Showed that back at his ranch. Correen doesn't like him, and she's a good judge. Agreeable enough so far, but watch him.

And what about Correen? Can't control her. Does what she pleases. Good hand around camp, but she's trouble. A woman is always trouble.

He looked at the stars over the Snowy Range and remembered the nights he and Dusty rode night-herd together on the trail. One would circle the herd to the right, the other to the left, and Dusty always had something funny to say every time they crossed paths. Claude was young then, felt old now.

He sat against his tree for an hour, until a peal of Bob Steck's laughter caught his attention. He shook his head in

disgust when he saw the campfire burning brightly. He figured he'd better go back and lay down the law.

"Correen!" he said, stepping from the shadows. "I told
you to put that fire out! And you, Bob, I can hear you laughin'
half a mile from camp! This ain't no damn pleasure trip!"

He propped his Marlin against a saddle and began
kicking dirt on the fire. Dust and smoke filled the air as the
light dwindled. But before the last tongues of fire could die,
Claude sensed something near. Looking up, he glimpsed
an image across the smoking wood that jolted him with a
pang of terror.

A form emerged from the shadows, swaggering through
the smoke and dust. He saw the dull glint of a weapon and
the glare of the eyes under the dark brim. The face came
clear, a sunken version of an old nightmare. It rode a lank
human frame that skulked silently in among the campers
and towered over them.

Claude tried to get his revolver out of the holster but
found the rifle barrel of the intruder covering him.

"Don't do it," the voice said. It was so low that it almost
croaked, and it rattled an old chord of hatred in the pit of
Claude's heart. "I don't mean to harm anybody." His black
hair was cropped short, barely sticking out under his hat.

Bob Steck sprang to his feet and stepped in front of Correen. "What the hell do you mean, wadin' into our camp
gun-first?"

The eyes, sparkling in their narrow slots, darted to every member of the party, then lingered on Claude. "Take it
easy. I don't want any trouble. I'm lookin' for a gentleman
named Bob Steck, of Texas. I have a letter for him." He
pulled an envelope from his coat pocket.

"I'm Steck."

The big man continued to guard Claude as he handed
the envelope to Steck. He squinted again at the regulator.
"You look familiar."

"You've got a good memory," Claude said. "You only laid eyes on me once before. You've taken off a lot of weight since I saw you last."

"Hard labor," the visitor said.

"You two know each other?" Steck asked, tearing open the envelope.

"This is the man we came up here after," Claude said. "This is Lone Wolf Wolverton."

Ike Lafferty dropped the piece of wood he had been whittling and got to his feet.

"I'm not the man you're after," Wolverton said. "That letter will prove it."

Steck was trying to make out the writing. "I can't see a damn thing. Correen, what does it say?"

She took the letter from Steck and knelt by the fire to catch the light. Claude's temper flared when he saw Wolverton's eyes look her up and down.

"Dear Bob . . ." Her accent attracted another glance from the rifleman. "A gentleman known as Lone Wolf Wolverton has taken up residence near me and engaged in agriculture. I have seen him every day on his farm since he located here and know he could have had no part in the recent crimes occurring on your ranch. The Texas Rangers have investigated him and found him faultless. I know Mr. Wolverton as a good neighbor and churchgoer. Kindest regards, Bill Johnson."

"Bill Johnson!" Steck said, taking the letter back from Correen. "That's an old friend of mine, Sabinal. His word's good."

"You could have forced anybody to write that," Claude said to Wolverton. "Anyway, why would you travel across half the country to deliver it?"

"I'm after those outlaws, like the rest of you."

"Why?"

"They're tryin' to make it look like I'm with 'em."

"Why would they do that?"

"Maybe to put the blame on me. Maybe to scare posses off their trail. Either way, I can't allow it."

Claude sneered at the big man, his anger building. "I say you *are* with 'em. Your empty cartridges keep turnin' up in the hands of dead men."

"I don't even own a Creedmoor now. I give you my word."

"Your word doesn't mean shit to me, Wolverton."

The big man frowned and glowered at Claude. "Where do I know you from?"

He met Wolverton's stare, turned it back. "I'm Dusty Sanderson's partner."

Wolverton's eyes widened, and his jaw dropped.

"Who the hell is Dusty Sanderson?" Steck blurted.

"Tell him," Claude said to Wolverton. "I want to hear *you* explain it."

Wolverton's stare dropped to the ground. "He was the man I went to prison for killin'. I mistook him for a rustler I was after name of Giff Dearborn."

"Mistake, hell. You murdered him," Claude said.

"I gave a guilty plea. I owned up to what I did and paid for it."

"You haven't paid squat. You're still breathin' and Dusty's still dead. I was the one who found him, Wolverton. Shot in the back. A hole through him big as my fist. That cartridge shell in his hand. His face burned off where your bullet knocked him into the fire, and you just left him there."

The glistening eyes looked up at Claude again. "Now I remember you. The courtroom, the day the judge sentenced me."

"I should have killed you then," Claude said. "I had the gun in my pocket."

"Things are different now. I've changed."

Claude chuckled. "Yeah, I see you have. You've gone from regulatin' to rustlin'."

"Why would I barge into your camp if that was true? I came here to clear myself with Mr. Steck and to help him catch those rustlers."

"He's talkin' sense, Sabinal. He could have already shot you."

Wolverton's eyes caught another flash of surprise. "Sabinal? Are you Claude Duval?"

"I am."

"I've met a dozen men you sent to prison. By golly, I never knew Dusty was partners with Sabinal Claude."

Claude quivered with rage. "You dare speak his name like you knew him! Goddamn you, Wolverton! First chance I get, you're a dead man!"

Wolverton sighed and set his jaw. "I don't think so," he said.

"Try me."

"Oh, I know you'd do it. But not tonight. Not here. A gunshot might bring those outlaws down on your camp. You've got to think of your friends. Especially the woman. I know your reputation, Duval. You're a fair man. You'll wait." As he stared into Claude's pale eyes, he raised the barrel of his rifle to the sky and eased the hammer down to the safety position. Then he lowered the rifle butt to the ground and put his hand on the muzzle.

Claude snatched a big Russian from his right-hand holster.

"No!" Correen cried.

"Don't do it, Sabinal," Steck warned. "Wolverton's right. We don't want to stampede them outlaws."

Claude felt his hand trembling, hoped it didn't show. He had sworn long ago that if he ever got this chance, nothing would stop him. But he hadn't counted on circumstances like these. He fought the urge to jerk the trigger, and lowered his revolver. "Get the hell out of my sight, Wolverton."

"Wait," Lafferty said, stepping forward. "I don't trust him out there with that rifle. I'd rather he stay in camp where we can watch him. He says he's after the same rustlers we're after. Let's give him a chance to prove it."

Claude thought for a few seconds, then nodded. "You may have somethin' there, Ike." He put his revolver in the holster and picked up his Marlin. "All right, Wolverton, bring your gear in. But, like you said, I'm a fair man, so I'll give you advance warnin'. As soon as we take care of this Snowy Range Gang, you'd better make yourself scarce if you want a chance to live." He stalked back into the dark to take his guard.

EIGHT

She came up behind him, silently, while he was shaving. "Do you know why they tremble so?" she asked. Claude flinched, felt the blade nick him, turned to upbraid her for sneaking in on him. But she was looking at the fluttering leaves of the quaking aspens, her eyes reflecting their tremulous energy, and he couldn't speak harshly to her. "Huh?"

"Little Crow says the leaves tremble at the passing of the wind god. The trees must show their fear, or the wind god will tear their limbs asunder." She broke off a small branch with about a dozen leaves on it.

Claude smiled, his face half covered with shaving soap. "You believe in that sort of thing?"

"I might if I didn't study things so." She plucked a single leaf and held it in front of his face. "The stem is flat, with a quarter twist. You would tremble, too, if you had to stand like that in the wind." She swept her aspen branch gracefully over her head, its leaves fluttering through the cool morning air.

"You just took the wind out of a thousand years of Indian legend."

She shrugged and tossed the branch carelessly aside. "I believe what I see, Mr. Duval."

Claude took another swipe at his chin with the razor. "What were you talkin' to Lone Wolf about this mornin'?" He had seen the gaunt man towering over her as she cooked, and it had bothered him.

"Just talkin'. He's a nice man to talk to."

"Correen, I know you don't like me tellin' you what to do, but I advise you to keep your distance from that man. He'd shoot you in the back if somebody'd pay him to do it, and never give it a second thought."

"Strange," she answered. "That's not at all the sort of thing he said about you this mornin'."

"What?"

She lifted his chin with her finger and studied his neck. "He said you were a fine man. Tough but fair. Brave, honest, and bound by the law." She took the towel from Claude's shoulder and dabbed at his throat. "You cut yourself," she said, showing him the blood.

"You believe what he says?" Claude took the towel from her and held it against his cut.

"I don't believe either one of you any more than I believe the leaves tremble before the wind god. I believe what I see." She tossed her brown hair as she turned, and went to pack her gear.

Claude finished shaving, wondering how Wolverton had managed to make him look bad by saying good things about him. He put his shaving kit in his saddlebag with the Le Mat revolver and reached for the gun belt holding the twin Russians.

As he buckled the belt around his hips, he caught Wolverton staring at him. "What're you lookin' at?" he said.

"Your hardware. What do you carry all that weight for?"

"The likes of you."

Ike Lafferty led a packhorse between them. "I'm no gunman," he said, patting his Peacemaker, "but I thought Colt built the best weapon. What do you see in those Smiths?"

"Solid weapon," Claude said, drawing the right-hand one. "Good balance." He put his thumb under the rear sight and lifted the latch, breaking the revolver open. The action kicked all six rounds out at once into his waiting palm. "Reloads faster than that gate-loader you're wearin'."

Lafferty nodded thoughtfully.

"If you can't hit what you're shootin' at with twelve rounds," Wolverton said, "reloading won't do you much good."

Claude snapped the empty revolver shut and pointed it at Wolverton, cocking it, looking down the sights at the bridge of the big man's nose. "I've never shot more than one at a time into a man. Never had to. I might use a dozen or more on you, though. Just for fun." He pulled the trigger and let the hammer fall on an empty cylinder.

Wolverton sighed. "You'd give that idea up if you'd been where I've been."

"I don't care where you've been. Just where you're goin'. Straight to hell, and it's my job to send you there."

Wolverton frowned and turned away, shaking his head.

After replacing the six live rounds, Claude looked up and saw Correen staring at him, arms crossed like a schoolmarm about to scold a rowdy pupil. He felt ridiculous. He had never used such reckless talk in his life, and now she had to be on hand to hear it. But his beef with Wolverton went back long before he ever laid eyes on Correen. He wasn't going to let Lone Wolf get away alive to please a woman he hardly knew. He had to think of Dusty.

When they took to the trail, Correen rode up past the pack mules, pacing Claude once she reached the head of the string.

"I wanted to kill Mr. Galloway sure as you've got it in for Mr. Wolverton," she said. "I swore I'd do it the next time he raised his hand to me. I was lucky. Someone else came along and did the killin' for me, else I'd burn in hell for murder."

"Hell?" Claude said, raking his long hair back. "I thought you only believed in things you've seen."

"I'm sure I've seen my share," she said. And they rode on together in silence.

NINE

The three riders came over the Medicine Bow Divide, past the scrubby wind-twisted evergreens, over the tundralike graze. The peaks of the Snowy Range loomed five miles to their left. Only Strikes the Dog looked at the rock pinnacles jutting skyward above the trees like the jagged edges of a broken pot left out in the snow. Behind her, the black man and the gang leader were too busy talking to take notice.

"One: Lone Wolf Wolverton gets pardoned out of prison. Two: This fellow Steck comes back from India with all them bremmer cattle. Three: Wild Roy Wiloughby puts 'em together and makes history for cattle rustlin'."

It was Wild Roy himself talking—short, ugly, face like an old plow pitted with rust. To Strikes the Dog his face resembled the cratered surface of the moon, and she thought of him as Moon Face, though she never called him that out loud. Never spoke to him at all, in fact.

The only one in the gang she spoke to was the black one, the one the others called Squaw Man. He was her man—to sleep with, to cook for. He protected her from the others: Moon Face and the two red-haired brothers—the evil twins, like two humans sharing a single soul.

She hated all these white men. She cursed them for coming back to her mountains. When she was a girl, the white men had poisoned her brother's mind with firewater. Poisoned him to the point that he sold her to the soldiers at the fort to get more money for more firewater. Now they simply called her Squaw, but she knew she was Strikes the Dog, and the name was medicine to her wounds.

"How do you know about them cattle sweatin' poison and all?" Squaw Man said, tilting his cavalry cap on his head. He was bearded with dense curls, always sleepy-eyed except in a fight. He was still trying to get all the details about the bremmers out of Wild Roy. They hadn't had much time to talk since Laramie.

"I heard Steck braggin' on 'em in a saloon down in Texas. Damn fool all but told me how to steal 'em. Just had one man guardin' 'em, quarantined on Matagorda Island." He patted the stock of the long rifle in his saddle boot. "Figured I'd better get a old Sharps Creedmoor like Lone Wolf used to use if I was gonna make it look like him. Couldn't find one, though, so you know what I did?"

"No."

"I tracked down Lone Wolf's old rifle. Yeah, found out a judge up in the Panhandle had kept it after Lone Wolf's trial, so I broke into the judge's house and stolt it. Anyway, once I had the Creedmoor, I shot a fellow owned a little steamboat. Put that shell in his hand like Wolverton always done. Took the boat to Matagorda Island, killed the cowboy guardin' the bremmers, and herded 'em onto the steamboat. Sailed up into Lavaca Bay, let the cattle rest a day till dark, then herded 'em twenty miles overnight to the depot at Telferner."

"Reckon they're missin' them cattle yet?"

"Don't give a damn if they are. They'll be lookin' for

Wolverton down there. Time they figure out he didn't do it, it'll be too late to trail me."

"How do you know this Wolverton ain't comin' after you?"

Wiloughby laughed. "Preacher Wolverton? He'll stay put in Texas. Prison took all the killin' out of him. Used to read the Gospel to us Sundays."

"You listen to any of it?"

"Hell, yes. Sunday school got you out of chores."

They rode silently into a line of trees, passing the white trunks of aspens, mottled with black scars.

Squaw Man was worried. Without Roy Wiloughby, life had been hard but enjoyable for the past year and a half. It had been just him and the squaw, living off the land in the Medicine Bows.

He had come to the mountains three years ago, on the run for killing a smart-mouthed sutler at Fort Casper. The squaw was a Fort Casper whore he had brought with him. Up near the Snowy Range, he had stumbled onto Wiloughby and the Sickle twins, Clay and Frank, driving a herd of stolen beeves. He and his squaw had helped the outlaws move the cattle, earning an uneasy trust.

"What do we call you?" Wild Roy had said, the day he took the former buffalo soldier into the Snowy Range Gang.

"I ain't tellin' my name."

"Shit, I ain't gonna shoot you for bounty."

"I said I ain't tellin'."

"Damn, you're a spooky squaw man."

It had seemed like a good thing a couple of years ago, raiding the ranches to the north, selling the cattle in Colorado. Then Wild Roy and the Sickle twins had gone to Texas for a tear, landed in prison for a year for stealing a saddle. Squaw Man had found that he and his woman could get along all right in the mountains on their own—hunting, trapping, living in a tepee, avoiding civilization.

He went to Laramie once or twice a year for supplies, and there he had found a letter, sent care of the outfitter the Snowy Range Gang had always done business with. It was from Roy Wiloughby: "Out of prison in Texas. Wait for me early September, Big Hollow."

Now the gang was back together, and Squaw Man wasn't so sure he liked it. Imported cattle rustled from a rich Texas rancher, using the sign of a bloody ex-regulator. Could be trouble, but he would go along with it. He always went along with Wild Roy for some reason. He didn't know why. He didn't really like the son of a bitch.

"How'd you get them bremmers on the train with nobody seein' 'em?" Squaw Man asked.

"I knew the foreman at Telferner. Paid him to keep quiet. Clay and Frank helped me put 'em on in the middle of the night, and we was on our way north."

Squaw Man shook his head. "Somebody seen them cattle between here and Texas. Had to."

"I hope they did. I hope they know I took 'em. I never heard tell of nobody rustlin' no cattle like that. I hope they put my name in the paper."

Squaw Man frowned. "That fellow Steck gonna come lookin'?"

"That old bastard? Hell, no. He might hire some detectives, but they'll go after Wolverton first. Time they figure out he didn't do it, we'll have them bremmers scattered all over the territory. Then we'll split up for the winter, spend all our money, get back together next spring."

Squaw Man grunted. Wild Roy thought he was some outlaw. Damn fool was going to get them all lynched one day.

Strikes the Dog's Indian pony crunched tracks in a patch of snow that hadn't seen sunlight all summer. She couldn't hear the forest very well over the clopping hooves of the trotting horses and the squeaking saddle leather. But she could see and smell. She knew they were getting close.

Suddenly, she jerked her horse to a stop as the men came up beside her. She made a few fluid signs, mostly with her right hand.

"She smells 'em," Squaw Man said. "Maybe two miles upwind."

"The hell," Wiloughby said. "Sheep stink, but that squaw can't smell 'em two miles."

"She says remind you not to kill the boy."

"Why don't she tell me herself? She talks to you. What the hell does she want with that boy, anyway?"

"I keep him," Strikes the Dog said, answering Wiloughby, but looking at Squaw Man. "He work."

"The boy's Ute," Squaw Man explained. "The Cheyenne used to catch Ute boys and adopt 'em. Make 'em slaves first, then turn 'em into braves."

Wiloughby looked at the woman. "He causes me trouble one time, I'll kill him." He knew she understood, though she ignored him. "Hell, maybe he'll make a rustler. At least he can carry water, chop wood."

Strikes the Dog slacked her reins and kicked her pony, leading the men into the wind, across a meadow, then winding through the trees, ducking branches. They went quietly, at a walk. After a mile, the bleating of sheep reached them through the forest.

"Goddamn stinkin' woollies," the gang leader said. "Listen at 'em."

Roy Wiloughby hated sheep. They took range from cattle, and he couldn't stand to think of rustling sheep someday, the cattle all pressed out of the country. He hated the way they smelled, though he wasn't fond of the scent of cattle, either. He hated their cowardly little voices, their stupidity, their bug eyes.

The only thing he liked about sheep was killing them. Sheep and sheep people, he had found, were usually easy targets. The animals would bunch together when threatened, where they could be easily shot, or clubbed if he didn't want to waste ammunition. And shepherds often worked alone, far from the law.

Coming over a timbered ridge, they saw glimpses of wool below, through the trees, sunlit in a meadow. The bleating voices came clearer.

"Look like a bunch of goddamn maggots," Wiloughby said.

"How you wanna do it?" Squaw Man asked quietly.

"Give your squaw a few minutes to sneak close to the boy. Then . . ." He stroked his thinly bearded jaw, trying to look thoughtful. "There a bluff close to here?"

Squaw Man pointed. "About half a mile that way. Seventy-, eighty-foot drop."

"We'll rimrock 'em, by God. Always wanted to try that. But first I'll limber up ol' Creed. Gotta keep the eye in." He squinted his left eye, rolling the right one. Grinning, he pulled the Creedmoor from the saddle boot, stroked the stock. "You still a bettin' man?"

The black man shrugged. "What's the bet?"

"A hundred dollars says ol' Creed will shoot through three sheep with one shot."

"I reckon she might," Squaw Man said, "you line 'em up just right, hit 'em through the guts."

"How 'bout four?"

"You got a bet." He shook the little white man's hand.

Strikes the Dog rode north to get around the meadow and find the Ute boy she wanted to capture. Wiloughby and Squaw Man went south, got below the meadow, and dismounted in the timber. They snuck toward the clearing until they could see the hundred grazing sheep, their woolly backs undulating like a giant living rug.

They heard the sheepdog bark, then a pistol shot and a yelp. The woman burst into the meadow at a gallop and they saw the Indian boy running for cover, the squaw pouncing on him from the saddle. Sheep scattered in a moment of panic, then bunched in the middle of the clearing. The Creedmoor roared, hazing the air with black powder smoke. The flock surged as one, some sheep jumping over others, a hundred bleats filling the air like the hollering of spoiled children.

"Four down!" Wiloughby shouted, laughing. "Pay up!"

"Let's go see," Squaw Man said, his sleepy eyes turning away from the meadow as he walked for his horse.

They loped into the meadow, found two wounded sheep lying on their sides, gut-shot, heaving, eyes rolling. A third stood on wobbly legs, head hanging, blood dripping from its belly. A fourth butted against the flock, seeking protection, a busted leg dragging.

Squaw Man scattered the flock, reaching low to grab the fourth sheep by the ear. He lifted it and could hear its terrified voice calling his name: "Squaw Maaaaan! Squaw Maaaaan!" He dropped the poor beast, unnerved. He had been living like an Indian too long. The animals were talking to him.

"You owe me a hundred," Wiloughby said.

"That fourth one's not shot through," Squaw Man replied.

"I said ol' Creed would hit four with one shot."

"You said you'd shoot *through* four. You pay *me*."

"Bullshit, boy. I'll take a hundred out of your cut when we sell the rest of them bremmers."

Squaw Man was riled, his eyes showing it, wide with anger. He rode toward Wiloughby, his hand on his pistol butt. "Won't do you no good dead."

Wild Roy laughed. "You gonna kill me over a hundred dollars?"

"Call me boy again, I'll kill you for that."

"Oh, goddamn," the little white man said, rolling his eyes. "Bet's off. You didn't make yourself clear. Shoot all the way through four sheep, hell. Which way is that bluff?"

Squaw Man tilted his head, keeping his eyes on Wiloughby.

The little man pressed the flock toward the bluff. "Come on, let's rimrock these little pill-shitters."

They passed Strikes the Dog, kneeling on the squirming Ute boy's back, tying his hands behind him with a rawhide thong. Squaw Man shook his head at the strangeness of the sight. A squaw and a longhaired boy, both in white men's clothing, thrashing the ground in their struggle.

They reached the bluff after a short stampede and pressed the surging body of sheep toward the rim. The leaders reached the drop-off, balked, then tried to back up or turn around. But Wiloughby drew his pistol and fired into the air, hollering and whistling at the sheep. The animals in back pressed frantically against the leaders, forcing them over the brink.

Squaw Man heard the blatting voices fade as they fell. Then the bodies of the animals began to thud against the rocks below. He worked with Wiloughby, pushing the sheep toward the rim. They followed the leaders almost willingly now, leaping into thin air, somersaulting as they plummeted. He heard Wiloughby laughing with joy, impact jolting dying blats from the sheep. He wished Wild Roy had stayed in Texas. The dying sheep were calling his name again: "Squaw Maaaan! Squaw Maaaan!"

TEN

Little Crow stumbled along at a trot behind the Cheyenne woman's horse, his hands bound behind him, the rawhide noose tightening around his neck whenever he tried to slow down. He knew he was alone in this. The squaw had pounced on him from one of Correen's horses. He figured Correen and her mean drunk of a husband for dead. He expected no rescue.

He had seen sign of Squaw Man and Strikes the Dog in the mountains before, spotted them once from a distance. But they had always let him alone. It seemed the little ugly white man had caused them to kill his sheep and take him captive. He was scared but hoped his face didn't show it. He wanted this Cheyenne woman to know he was a brave Ute.

He was trying to act more exhausted than he really was. If they thought he had nothing left to run with, they would ease their guard on him, and he could try to escape. But they had already dragged him past the Snowy Range, across the divide to the western slopes. Sharp rocks had bruised his feet through his moccasins. He had fallen three times on the trail, and the ground had scraped a shoulder and a cheek raw. The squaw could have dragged him and choked him to death, but she didn't want to kill him. Not yet, anyway.

The trail finally led over the rim of a bluff and Little Crow got a glimpse of the gang's camp in a park below. He saw the tepee the black man and Strikes the Dog lived in and the log walls of the cabin the gang had begun to build. Between the unfinished cabin and the tepee, he saw something hanging from a slanting timber, but it disappeared behind treetops before he could make it out.

He staggered down the steep trail behind the squaw's horse until she came to a stream. Strikes the Dog stopped him in the rushing water and turned in the saddle to look at him.

Little Crow was thirsty, so he lowered himself to one knee to put his mouth against the surface of the stream, shin-deep where he had stopped. He was ready for what happened next. The noose tightened around his neck and the cold water engulfed him. Floundering to his feet, he heard the little ugly white man laughing, then the squaw's horse jerked him toward the bank. But he had sucked in a mouthful of water, and that would help.

There was nothing but the cool breeze to dry him, the sun having sunk behind the treetops. But there was plenty of daylight left and Little Crow knew he would dry before the frigid night came on. He was trying to see his advantages, though they numbered few.

When Strikes the Dog led him into the camp, the boy collapsed as if he couldn't take another step. She untied the leash from her saddle horn and dropped it. He thought for a moment of running but knew it would get him nowhere. He would rest, wait for night, use the darkness to his advantage.

He lay on his side, gasping, taking in his surroundings. The slanting timber between the tepee and the cabin stood nearby—a sweep used to suspend camp meat above the reach of bears and wolves. It consisted of a long pine timber, propped up at an angle on an old tree stump. The stump was four feet high and almost as thick, with a saddle chopped into the top of it to cradle the meat pole. The butt of the pole rested on the ground and had two logs bound to it with rope and rawhide to give it counterweight. Little Crow saw a beef carcass swaying on the tip of the pole but doubted he would get any of it.

The black man rode by him, dismounted, and began stripping the saddle from his horse. The gang leader trotted toward the log walls. Beyond the unfinished cabin, the boy saw the two redheaded brothers coming on their horses, and beyond them, a herd of humped bulls, ghost-colored with sagging ears, staring at him as if they felt sorry for him.

Something hit him in the back, and he looked up to see Strikes the Dog glaring down at him. She had come over just to kick him. He didn't move. She kicked him again and padded silently away on her moccasins.

When he looked toward the white men again, he saw the ugly one coming with an axe and an iron stake, coming right at him, grinning. The boy fought his fear and lay still.

"Squaw Man," Roy Wiloughby said. "You ever heard tell of a Indian runnin' ten, twenty miles and such? This one here looks plumb give out runnin' just six or seven."

Little Crow winced as Wiloughby jabbed the iron stake into the ground in front of his face. With the blunt end of the axe, the gang leader drove the stake pin deep into the ground, the Indian boy hoping the axe wouldn't glance and cave in his skull.

"What are you doin'?" Squaw Man asked.

"Stakin' the little bastard down." He threw the axe aside and pulled Little Crow's face against the stake pin with the rawhide loop.

"That's Squaw's boy. She'll train him."

Wiloughby jerked a hard rawhide knot around the stake pin and raised up, his hands propped defiantly on his hips. "I'll stake down whatever I damn well want in my camp."

Squaw Man's frown deepened, but he said nothing. He led his horse toward the pole corral.

Little Crow felt the squaw's toe jab him in the back again and heard Wiloughby's hoarse laughter.

The redheaded twins trotted up and dismounted in unison. They frightened the boy more than the squaw or the ugly gang leader. They didn't menace him, but their every move seemed coordinated, and he knew they had some evil medicine about them that made them look and act so much alike. When they looked at him, their eyes hit him at once.

He heard Strikes the Dog's moccasins turn in the sand behind him and knew she was walking back toward the tepee. With her back turned to them, the eyes of the evil twins rose together and searched her from the ankles up, and back down again. Then they looked at each other and communicated something without speaking. All this Little Crow saw through his squint of false anguish.

He was shivering now, lying on his side on the ground, the tether around his neck tied so short to the stake pin that he couldn't sit up. He had dried from his fall in the creek, but it was still cold. His arms were cramped behind his back, the rawhide cutting his wrists. But he had a plan.

Wiloughby had tied the knot tight around the stake pin, but he hadn't doubled it. Little Crow would wait for dark, then he would begin loosening the knot with his teeth. It might take an hour or more to untie. The axe was still lying where Wiloughby had tossed it aside. He would pick it up on his way out of camp and use it to cut his wrists free. After that he didn't know what he would do, except run.

Strikes the Dog suddenly stepped over him from behind and glared down at him, as if she might have felt him plotting. She had a knife in her hand and Little Crow feared for a second that she might torture him with it, but she walked instead toward the sweep where the beef carcass hung.

She grabbed a rope dangling from the high end of the sweep and cried, "Squaw Man! Squaw Man!" When the black man looked from the corral, she pointed at the beef hanging above her.

"Frank!" Squaw Man shouted. "You and Clay come help me get some meat down for the squaw."

The Sickle twins threw their tools down at the cabin where they had been notching and laying up logs with Wiloughby. They marched in stride, like soldiers.

It took Squaw Man, Strikes the Dog, and both Sickle twins to lower the meat pole. The gang had made the counterweight heavy enough to keep two or three elk carcasses in the air and still prevent big bears from pulling down on the pole and stealing the camp meat. As they pulled on the rope, the beef descended, the long timber pivoting in its cradle on the stump, the weighted butt lifting unwillingly from the ground.

Little Crow noticed the Sickle twins pressing against the woman harder than the task demanded. He was young and didn't understand completely, but had a vague instinct for what they were doing, and it made him uncomfortable. He didn't want anyone getting the squaw mad, for she would probably take it out on him.

With the beef carcass within reach, Strikes the Dog stood on the rope while the men held it, and carved a section of hindquarter.

"Tell her to cut us some, too," Frank Sickle said.

"No cook," the woman replied. "Only Squaw Man."

"What the hell does she mean by that?"

"She'll cut a chunk off for you, but you got to cook it yourself," the black man replied.

"Don't we always do our own cookin'?" Clay said.

Little Crow watched the woman carve the meat and hand the chunks to the men. Then, without so much as a glance at each other, the Sickle twins released the rope together and jumped clear. The boom swept upward like a catapult, jerking the rope out from under Strikes the Dog's feet, flipping her to the ground. It hummed through Squaw Man's hands until they clenched tighter, and he rose like a lamb in the talons of an eagle. The counterweight hit the ground, the beef carcass hit the bottom of the timber it hung from, and Squaw Man looked fearfully at the ground as the rope slacked above him. He came down, snapping the rope tight with his weight, and swung six feet above the ground.

The twins laughed, their guffaws sounding like each other's echoes. They slapped their knees alike and stomped rhythm like clog dancers. Strikes the Dog picked up her knife and lunged at them, but Squaw Man dropped in front of her.

"Cook the meat, woman," he said, shoving her toward the tepee. "The boys was just havin' some fun." He looked at the rope burns on his palms.

The squaw's face writhed with anger as she picked up the meat she had dropped and knocked the dirt from it. She stepped over Little Crow on her way back to the tepee, pausing only to kick him once between the shoulders.

As he watched the twins carry their meat toward the cabin, Little Crow heard the squaw rattle a metal bucket behind him at the tepee. His ears trailed the rattling sound to the creek, and he knew she was fetching water to cook with. But the bucket didn't rattle full, and the boy could no longer track the squaw with his ears as she came back. Then the cold wave hit him, and he flinched so hard that his noose choked him.

Strikes the Dog was standing over him with the empty bucket. She rattled it in his face, pointed her finger at him, then at the creek, and shook the bucket at him again. He lay shivering in the mud as she walked back to the creek. Now he knew what she wanted with him. He would be her slave. Carry her wood and water, do whatever else she demanded.

Darkness came and the cook fires flared. Little Crow crawled closer to the iron stake pin, shivering uncontrollably, and began working on the rawhide knot with his teeth.

ELEVEN

He saw the smoke first, then the light of the fires, three miles distant. Claude Duval was sitting on the Medicine Bow Divide, the Snowy Range to his right, a cloud bank far to the west—maybe as far as Utah—glowing like an ocean of floating coals over the setting sun.

Correen's ears had been the first to catch the muffled rumble of gunfire that afternoon, rolling like echoes of distant thunder across the mountain peaks. They had known instantly that Little Crow was in trouble: maybe hiding, maybe captured, maybe killed.

They had spurred their horses to a fast trot and arrived a couple of hours later to find the four dead sheep in the meadow, the dead sheepdog, the great heap of carcasses at the base of the bluff. Claude had ordered the others to stay in camp—Correen against her will—and had taken to the trail after the sheep haters. He had found the boy's moccasin tracks in a few soft places, wincing where Little Crow had left blood on the sharp rocks.

Now it was too dark to read the sign, but it didn't matter. He had spotted their smoke. He climbed to the high seat on Casino's back, the campfires of the Snowy Range Gang in his view. He didn't know what he was going to do when he got there, but he had to have a closer look.

It was pitch-dark when he reached the bluff overlooking the camp. He was on foot, having left Casino a few hundred yards behind. In the firelight he saw the tepee, the unfinished cabin, the meat pole hung with beef. Big gray ghosts were moving beyond camp: the sacred bremmer bulls. Something lay on the ground near the meat pole. Claude thought he saw it move, but he couldn't be sure. A big dog curled up?

He crept silently down the bluff trail, the sound of running water covering his approach. He stopped before crossing the creek, not anxious to get his boots soaked. As he was looking for stepping-stones, or a foot log to cross on, he heard a woman shout from the camp.

"Squaw Man! Squaw Man!"

Boots scuffled on the ground for several seconds, and something thrashed the bushes along the stream above him.

"Wiloughby! The squaw's boy got loose!"

"Goddammit! Come on, boys, let's go find him."

"Tracks go to the creek!"

Claude drew a pistol when he saw the black man approaching with a burning stob, reading the ground. More men appeared up the creek, formless movements in the darkness. One slogged through the water, followed by another. The black man with the torch came closer and Claude thought he would be surrounded, discovered. He shrank into a clump of scrub oak. Three of the outlaws were on his side of the creek now, two still on the side of the camp.

"There he goes!" a new voice shouted—a squeak compared to the black man's baritone.

The brush up the creek popped as if a stampede were coming. Claude saw the boy running, carrying something behind his back: an axe. The black man with the burning stob splashed across the creek to cut the boy's path, crossing right above Claude's hiding place. The boy dropped the axe, but a short man pounced on him from behind. Another man jumped on the pile, orange hair illuminated by the torch.

"Got him!" Wiloughby said.

Claude aimed, but held his fire. The three men were wearing side arms. He would be lucky to get all three in the dark, luckier still to miss the boy. And there were others upstream. He could hear them rustling in the bushes. He wouldn't fire unless they intended to kill Little Crow. He wasn't about to go back to camp and tell Correen he had watched the boy die.

The three men dragged the boy back across the creek, bending his arms up behind him. Claude knew it hurt, but the boy didn't whimper.

"Squaw!" the black man yelled when he had crossed. "We got him!"

Claude heard the ruckus in the bushes upstream again—not the kind of noise an Indian woman would make coming back to camp. Puzzled, he rose from his clump of oak and snuck toward the noise, his Smith & Wesson leading the way.

He couldn't make it out at first: the writhing mass of humanity on the ground. Then he saw a faint glint of red hair, a hand over the squaw's mouth. She was pinned to the ground, but fighting, the man clawing at her clothes. Claude saw her knee hit the redhead in the groin, almost flipping him. The woman squirmed out from under him, stumbled into the creek.

"Shit," the man groaned, humped with pain as he crawled into the darkness upstream.

Claude watched the woman flounder out at the other side of the creek. She ran toward the three men and the captive boy at the meat pole.

Wiloughby was putting a noose around Little Crow's neck. The second redheaded twin, standing there, looked at the approaching squaw, then into the darkness along the creek, a pained expression on his face. He turned quickly toward the cabin, leaving Squaw Man and Wiloughby with the captive.

Were they going to hang him? Claude braced the revolver in both hands for a long shot into camp. No, they were just tying the boy to the sweep. He would have to stand there all night, or his weight would tighten the noose and choke him. Wiloughby picked up a stick from the woodpile and cut the air with it a couple of times.

Now what? Let them beat the boy? He couldn't get them all from this distance with a pistol. The twins were out of sight. He could take Wiloughby out first, but then the black man, if he thought quick enough, would make Little Crow a hostage—put a gun against his head. Still, he didn't want to see them beat that boy.

Wiloughby was rearing back to hit Little Crow when the Indian woman stumbled up to Squaw Man, grabbing his vest. She made signs with her hands so fast that she seemed to be swatting at mosquitoes, finally pointing back toward the place where the redheaded outlaw had jumped her.

Wiloughby lowered his stick. "What the hell's wrong with her now?"

"Frank! Clay!" Squaw Man bellowed. "Come here!"

Claude saw the twins coming from the cabin together.

"What the hell's goin' on?" Wiloughby demanded.

Little Crow stood shivering, his wet clothes plastered against his skin, the rope tying him close to the timber above his head.

"Which one of you did it?" Squaw Man said as the twins joined the others.

"Did what?" one of them said. They were both wet below the knees from crossing the stream. They wore identical suits, no hats. Each looked as though he had been in a fight.

Squaw Man turned to the woman. "Which one did it?"

She looked at one, then the other, then back at the first. She chose the one to the right and pointed.

"I didn't do nothin' to her," he said.

She pointed at the other, certain now. "Him," she said, jabbing the air in his direction with her finger. "Him, him!"

"I didn't do nothin'," the other twin said.

"All right, both of you!" The black man's rich voice came clearly to Claude across the creek. He walked about half-way to the tepee, then turned around to face the twins, drawing a long knife from a belt scabbard, beckoning the redheads with the blade.

The twins looked at each other, reached for their knives in tandem, and began flanking the black man.

"Wait just a goddamn minute!" Wiloughby shouted, stalking in between the duelers with his stick. "If I have to sew somebody up, I want daylight. You boys can fight in the mornin'. And, Squaw Man, I don't aim to see my gang killed off now that I just got it back together. If you kill one of 'em, I'll kill you!"

The twins came out of their fighting stances. "What if we git him?" one of them said.

"Oh, hell, you boys don't stand a chance in hell of cuttin' Squaw Man. I don't care if you do read each other's minds, the two of you together ain't half the brawler he is."

"We'll see at dawn," Squaw Man said.

Wiloughby shook his stick at the twins. "You two git back to the cabin. Squaw Man, you git in the lodge. And you . . ." He pointed the stick at the Indian woman. "If that boy gits loose again, I'll bust his skull in."

Claude saw the gang leader wield the stick of firewood viciously overhead, felt his finger tighten on the trigger. But the stick broke across the heavy timber of the meat sweep, above Little Crow's head. The boy flinched, but wasn't touched by the stick.

"You camp right here tonight," the gang leader ordered, "and make sure he don't get loose again."

The woman got a blanket from the tepee and threw it down beside the boy. She sat there a few seconds, and Claude thought it was all over. But then the woman jumped up and walked to the fire. She pulled out a chunk with a glowing end and came at the boy like a cat stalking game. Little Crow shuddered. Claude felt his muscles tense with dread again, until Squaw Man jumped out of the tepee, took the hot coal away from the woman, and sat her back down on her blanket as he would a child.

Claude watched until the woman rolled herself in the blanket and lay down. It would be a long, cold night for the boy, standing there in the dark. But rescue would come with dawn.

TWELVE

Claude found Bob Steck snoring on guard duty, curled up in his blanket with his Winchester. He put his lips next to Steck's ear. "If I'm an outlaw, you're dead," he said.

The old rancher snorted, flinched, and banged himself in the forehead with his rifle barrel. "Hell, Sabinal," he said, his senses restored, "let them others stand guard and I'll make the charge. Did you see the rest of my bremmers?"

"I saw 'em."

"Correen's Indian boy?"

"Yeah. Come on back to camp with me. I don't want to have to tell it but once."

"What about guard duty?"

"No more guard duty tonight. I want everybody to get some rest. You're a worthless guard, anyway, Bob."

When he heard the voices from camp, Claude held Steck back. "Let's have a listen at what they're sayin' about us before we go in." Claude was still in a mood to reconnoiter. He had always enjoyed sneaking around in the night, whether to line a roost of wild turkeys up against a full moon or to judge his enemy's defenses. And sometimes it made sense to spy on one's own camp.

They snuck close enough to make out the conversation and see the three campers huddled near a small fire. Ike Lafferty was whittling so close to the flames that his shavings flared as they fell. Correen's small hands were wrapped around a tin cup, her hair loose to help keep her neck warm. Claude didn't like her expression. She was smiling at Wolverton as the big man spoke:

"... so the Pharaoh's men came after 'em, just a-whippin' their horses like stagecoach drivers, except they drove chariots back then. They had six hundred of 'em! Now, Moses' folks were backed up against the Red Sea and somebody said, 'We'd been better off slaves, and now here you've brought us out in the wilderness where Pharaoh can slaughter us.'

"But God used to talk to Moses, just as sure as I'm talkin' to you, and God told him to hold up his walkin' stick and stretch his hand over the sea, and the waters would part. And Moses tried it, and by golly, it worked, and all his folks walked down on the bottom of the sea, and it was dry ground, just like what we're sittin' on. And on either side of 'em, the water rose up like a wall, and they could see fish swimmin' around in there!

"So the only thing that kept the Pharaoh's chariots and the whole Egyptian cavalry from harassin' Moses' rear was a big ol' whirlwind, or a twister, dark on Pharaoh's side, but bright as fire on Moses' side, so his folks could see their way across the bottom of the Red Sea, because I forgot to tell you that all this happened in the middle of the night.

"Anyway, in the mornin', when Moses had his people across, I guess this pillar of cloud and fire blew away, because Pharaoh took his whole army down onto the bed of the Red Sea after Moses. Now, there was six hundred chariots, and I don't know if they were one-horse or two-horse chariots, but there was a lot of livestock and soldiers down in there.

"Well, all of a sudden, the wheels fell off of all the chariots, and that spooked Pharaoh's men so bad that they called a retreat. About that time, over in Moses' camp, God told Moses to put his hand out over the water again, and when he did, the whole Red Sea slammed back together and you should have heard the hollerin' and screamin' of dyin' men and horses. And in a couple of days all that stock and all those dead soldiers washed up on Moses' side of the sea, and you talk about stink . . ."

Bob Steck burst into laughter. Wolverton and Correen reached for their rifles, but Ike Lafferty merely ceased his whittling and looked into the darkness.

"It's just us," Claude said. "We're comin' in."

Steck was still chuckling when he strode into camp. "Lone Wolf, I'd like to have you tell me the whole Bible that way. I've never heard it explained in the language I savvy."

"I don't understand the half of it myself," Wolverton admitted. "It was told by better men than me."

"Any man's better than you," Claude said, muscling his way in between Wolverton and Correen.

Lafferty went back to whittling.

"Did you find Little Crow?" Correen asked.

"I did," Claude answered, soothing her worries with his eyes. "He's alive and well, but tied up and guarded. Looks like the squaw wants him for a slave. I couldn't risk goin' in after him alone, but we'll get him back in the mornin'."

"What's your plan?" Lafferty asked.

Claude squatted by the fire, and the others sat down to hear him. "There's five of 'em. They've got Bob's cattle, so they're the same ones we're all after, no doubt. The leader's name is Wiloughby. He looks like a mean one. The colored feller's called Squaw Man, and he claims the squaw. Then there's the redheaded brothers. Twins. You can't tell 'em apart lookin' at 'em. Their names are Clay and Frank."

"The Sickle twins," Wolverton said. "And Wild Roy Wiloughby. I figured it was them."

Every eye shifted to Wolverton and stared.

"You figured what?" Claude growled.

"They used to come to my Sunday school behind the walls. I confessed all my sins before God and the men in prison. Thought I might get them to do the same, get all them sins off their chests and repent. Wiloughby and the Sickle brothers heard it all: the Creedmoor, the killin', the sign I used to use. I figured it was them that stole Bob's cattle when I heard about the redheaded twins and the leader's pockmarked face."

"You let me go in there without tellin' me who I was up against?" Claude said, glaring at the big man.

"Tried to tell you three times today. You wouldn't listen to me."

"You should've tried harder, damn you."

"I would have if I thought it was that important. Wouldn't have made much difference, though, so I didn't bother."

"You didn't bother? Why, you sorry—"

"Gentlemen!" Correen said. "Can't you put your dashit differences aside until we've rescued Little Crow?"

Claude fumed, but held his tongue. Wolverton looked into the fire like a scolded child. Lafferty seemed to be ignoring them.

"She's right," Steck said. "You two hard cases are gonna have to call a truce if you're gonna be any good to each other or the boy. How do you suggest we go about it, Sabinal?"

Claude heaved, rubbed his face, collected himself. "There's a bluff overlookin' their camp. It's within rifle range."

Steck's eyes shifted as he visualized the elevation. "We'd have to wait for all five of 'em to come out in the open at once."

"There's gonna be a knife fight at dawn."

"What?" Lafferty said, looking up from his whittling stick.

"Those redheaded twins got to foolin' with the colored man's squaw, and he wants to fight 'em both at dawn."

Steck slapped Claude on the back, almost knocking him into the fire. "I told y'all Sabinal was the best. Hell, we'll line up on that bluff like a firin' squad and perforate every one of the bastards!"

"The squaw is mine," Correen said, brandishing her brass-bellied Winchester. "She'll answer to me for takin' the lad."

Claude thought it odd to see such a hard set to the pretty green eyes.

Lafferty nodded. "As long as we stay together on the bluff, I'm with you. Divide our forces, and we're beat."

The camp was silent for a moment, except for the crackling of the small fire.

"You goin' along with all this, Duval?" Wolverton asked, his voice like a bull's moan.

"Why not?"

"Firin' down on people you don't even know?"

"I know they've got Bob's bremmers and Correen's Indian boy."

"I heard you took your men alive."

"I take rustlers alive if I can. These are kidnappers. They've got the boy tied by the neck to a pole, like a dog. Any one of us misses our shot, and they'll put a gun to that boy's head, and then they've got a hostage. No need to risk it. Shoot 'em all dead—that's the only thing we can do. Hell, they've left dead bodies from here to Texas. I'd say they've got it comin'."

Wolverton stood up, lifting his saddle as he rose.

"Where you goin'?" Claude asked.

"Back to Texas."

The other four exchanged looks.

"You came all the way up here to turn back now?" Steck said.

"I don't aim to repeat any old mistakes. I came here to take 'em alive, and if y'all mean to slaughter 'em from ambush, I don't want any part of it."

Correen stood. "We'll be one rifle shy."

"That's not my problem."

She walked toward Wolverton. "Stay and think about it the night," she pleaded. "You may see it our way in the morn."

"No, ma'am. I don't even want to be close enough to hear the gunshots."

"You've lost your nerve," Claude said.

"Think whatever you want. I've learned my lesson. You ought to know better, too, Duval, if Dusty Sanderson was really your friend."

Claude sprang to his feet, jumped across the fire, and lunged at Wolverton. But Lafferty dropped his knife and came between them, moving quicker than Claude ever suspected he might. The rancher caught him by the collar of his jacket and held him back.

"Let him go, Sabinal," he said. "We're better off without him. I wouldn't trust him to hit his man, anyway."

Claude put his hand on Lafferty's forearm and nodded at him. When the rancher turned him loose, he pointed his trigger finger at Wolverton. "I'll catch up to you someday," he said.

Lone Wolf glanced at the men, touched his hat brim for Correen's sake, and disappeared in the dark with his saddle and guns. A minute later, they heard his horse's hooves fade down the trail.

"Better off without him," Claude said. "One less man to watch. I can pick off the two twins, and we'll still rescue the boy. Now, let's rest a few hours."

Bob Steck rolled himself in a blanket. Correen stalked away to her tent. Ike Lafferty picked up his knife and commenced whittling. Claude lay down and watched Lafferty under the brim of the hat he put over his eyes. He was beginning to think of Ike as his surest hand.

THIRTEEN

They couldn't see the glow of the rising sun across the mountains, wouldn't feel its warmth for a couple of hours. Dawn came on slowly west of the Snowy Range.

They had left their horses in the trees and crept to the bluff overlooking the outlaw camp. Bob Steck was on the right with his back against a boulder and his rifle on his knee. Correen lay prone in an attitude that Claude found rather distracting. He was next to her, slightly behind her, his rifle propped on the thick branch of a dead pine. To his left, Ike Lafferty stood behind a boulder, ready to hit his mark.

As morning's light came on, Claude made out the shape of the squaw, wrapped in a blanket, still sitting up and guarding the captive boy. Little Crow was shivering, his legs wobbling uncontrollably under him. Every minute or so they would fail him, and the rope would tighten around his neck, then he would have to get his legs under him again.

Correen looked over her shoulder, up at Claude, her eyes holding back tears of anger.

"Wait," Claude whispered.

The features of the camp stood clear in the gray morning light when Squaw Man came out of the tepee wearing his knife in a belt scabbard. "Frank!" he yelled, his echo repeating the challenge three times before it faded. "Clay!" The mountain seemed to tremble at the break of morning calm.

Strikes the Dog didn't even turn to look at her man. She stared at the cabin, waiting for the brothers to appear.

"Oh, hell, Squaw Man," one of them said from the log walls. "We don't want to fight anymore."

"Come out or I'll come in," the black man shouted.

Claude heard Wiloughby's laughter and saw the ugly little cuss come out from the cabin walls. The regulator looked back at Ike Lafferty. Lafferty nodded. Claude looked to his right. Correen and Steck were ready, their thumbs on their rifle hammers. As soon as the knife fight began, they would do it.

He was glad Wolverton had gone. All that damn preaching—and the way Correen listened so contentedly to it—had unsettled him something fierce. He would help Correen rescue her boy while Lone Wolf ran back to Texas.

Strikes the Dog glared at the twins as they passed her, then turned her back to Little Crow to watch Squaw Man fight the Sickle brothers.

The black man drew his long blade, cut circles with it in the cold air. It would be a tough fight. Squaw Man had seen them act on each other's thoughts before. Still, he was more than a match for them. He would teach them once and for all about fooling with his property.

Claude rubbed the stubble on his chin. He hadn't taken the time to shave before leaving camp, and the growth bothered him. He began easing his Marlin to his shoulder as the squaw got up to get a closer view of the fight. Correen already had her rifle in position, and Bob was settling his on his knees. Then Claude heard Ike's hammer catch over his left shoulder. Lordy, didn't the man know how to cock a rifle silently? He shot a glare toward Lafferty and found the rancher's muzzle staring him in the face.

"Put your hands up, Sabinal," Lafferty said. "You, too, Steck. Both of you get away from your guns. And, Correen, I'll shoot you sure as any man if you try anything. Take your hands off that rifle."

"Ike, what in the hell . . ." Claude whispered, glowering.

"Wiloughby!" the rancher shouted, climbing onto the boulder he had been hiding behind. "Get up here with your guns, you dumb son of a bitch!"

FOURTEEN

Claude stared up at the muzzle, his heart pounding, his stomach feeling suddenly as cold and heavy as the boulder Lafferty stood on. Of all the stupid things he had ever done . . . He had come to trust Ike Lafferty, a total stranger, after just three nights in camp. Some bit of philosophy Dusty had once uttered came to him: "You can't trust a man till you've got drunk with him."

"Get away from your guns," Lafferty ordered. "Leave 'em there. Move!" He waved his three prisoners away from the rifles left lying on the ground. "Take the gun belt off slow, Duval."

Claude let the twin Russians drop at his ankles and thought about the Le Mat revolver. Still in his saddlebag. Lafferty didn't know about it. Right now he was hoping Correen didn't try anything. She was madder than hell. Probably at herself for the most part. He heard the outlaws scrambling up the bluff on foot.

"Now you, Steck," Lafferty said. "Drop that Colt, and step away from it."

Claude gave Steck a look to calm him. He knew Bob was willing to draw Lafferty's fire, die a hero. But if he did, Claude wouldn't be able to get to Lafferty on top of the boulder quick enough to save himself or Correen. They would have to wait for a better chance, though he didn't see one coming just yet. The Le Mat grapeshot revolver was his only hope.

Steck kicked his Colt away as the outlaws reached the top of the bluff, clouding the air with breath. They stared with open mouths at the three strangers.

"By God!" Wiloughby said, recognizing the old Texan. "You're Bob Steck! How'd you trail me? Who talked?"

Steck stood with his hands clenched, grinding his teeth.

"Frank and Clay, go get our horses," Lafferty ordered, jumping down from the boulder. "In the trees yonder. Squaw Man, you and the squaw cover 'em. Wiloughby, over here."

When Wiloughby got close enough, Lafferty lunged suddenly, bringing his rifle butt around to hit the gang leader in the jaw. The little ruffian managed to block some of the impact with his forearm, but the blow still knocked him down. Lafferty kicked him in the stomach as he got up, then hit him across the back with the rifle barrel.

"Shit, Ike!" Wiloughby squealed. "What's the damn deal?"

"I thought you said you got out of Texas clean!"

"I did, dammit! Somebody must've talked!"

"I thought you said you pinned the cattle rustlin' on Wolverton."

"I damn sure did! I used his sign."

"You didn't do squat, Roy."

The outlaw's eyes shifted to Correen. "Whose little sister is this?"

"She's the widow of that sheepherder I told you to stay clear of until we got rid of the bremmers!" He kicked Wiloughby in the knee, starting him hopping.

"Son of a bitch told me his wife left him!" Roy said, rubbing the joint.

"You expect a man you're about to kill to tell you the truth?"

"Hell, I thought he was too drunk to lie." Wiloughby grinned as he looked Correen over again. "But if I'da knowed she was comin' back, I'da waited."

"You touch her and I'll kill you," Claude said.

Wiloughby smirked. "Who's this longhaired son of a bitch?"

"Name's Sabinal Claude Duval," Lafferty said.

"No bullshit? Away up here in Wyoming? I met a lot of boys you sent to prison, Duval." He frowned at the long locks covering Claude's collar. "This'll make a hell of a scalp for my bridle," he said, reaching.

Claude jerked a fist up into Wiloughby's stomach, snapped a second punch up under his jaw. From the corner of his eye, he saw the squaw moving toward him, but let her take a clean swipe at him with the barrel of the Marlin she had picked up. She caught him on the back of the head, just under the hat brim where no felt would pad the blow. Claude collapsed and braced himself for Wiloughby's boot. He felt the toe jab the tight muscles of his stomach, let the kick flip him, and grunted as if Wild Roy had knocked all the wind out of him.

Correen was over him for a second, then the squaw forced her away.

"Son of a bitch," Wiloughby said, spitting blood down on the regulator.

Claude heard the horses approaching, rolled to all fours, and hung his head as if barely conscious.

"Let's take 'em down to camp," Lafferty said. "Squaw Man, get Duval on his horse."

"We're not gonna kill the girl, are we?" one of the twins asked. "I mean, not yet, anyhow."

"Hell, no," Wiloughby said, grinning. "Not till we get some service out of her."

"If you lay one finger on me, I'll tear you to pieces," Correen said through clenched teeth, her eyes darting frantically.

"Mercy, but don't she talk pretty!" Wiloughby said.

"I said get 'em down to camp!" Lafferty shouted. "We don't have time for you to fool with the woman. We've got to catch Wolverton before he gets off the mountain."

Wild Roy's eyes bulged. "Wolverton? Lone Wolf?"

"Yes, you damn fool," Lafferty was saying. "You had

him figured wrong, too. Came all the way from Texas to get you, but didn't like our plans of slaughterin' you all from this bluff. Now you and Frank and Clay are gonna have to go kill him."

Claude stumbled around Casino's hind end as Squaw Man pushed him toward the stirrup. He put his hand on his saddlebag and shot a hidden glance at Steck.

"How come *we* gotta kill him?" one of the Sickle twins asked.

"You brought him here," Lafferty said.

Bob Steck suddenly jumped. He leaped right off the brink of the bluff, into the branches of a lodgepole pine. Claude heard the limbs popping as the rancher fell through them, heard Lafferty shouting orders, felt Squaw Man's rifle muzzle at the back of his head. His right hand, hidden from the black gunman by his body, was unbuckling one of the two leather straps that held down the flap of his saddlebag.

Wiloughby scrambled to the brink of the bluff and shot down at Steck, working his revolver like a pump handle.

Lafferty locked an arm around Correen's neck and put his revolver to her head. "Steck!" he yelled, forcing the woman to the brink. "I've got Correen. You come back, or I'll kill her right now!"

Claude, still acting dazed, shook his head and rubbed the bloody spot under his hat. But his hidden fingers continued unbuckling the saddlebag strap.

"Steck, you hear me?" Lafferty shouted.

"Probably killed hisself jumpin' off," one of the twins said.

"I believe I killed him," Roy said, craning to see over the bluff.

Then the Texan's shaky voice came from below. "Ike?"

"Yeah, Bob."

Like two friends having a conversation.

"Don't hurt her. I ain't goin' nowhere. I think I busted my damn knee."

"See there?" Wiloughby said. "Shot him in the leg."

"Shut up, Roy, and help Squaw Man get Duval on his horse."

Claude hoped no one would notice the strap he had unbuckled as Squaw Man put his foot in the stirrup for him and lifted him into the saddle. He would have to wait to unbuckle the other strap and reach in for the Le Mat.

He held the horn with both hands, swayed side-to-side in the saddle as one of the Sickle twins led him down the trail to camp. The party stopped to lift Steck onto his horse, Steck favoring his right knee, groaning with pain.

Little Crow watched them helplessly as they crossed the creek and went to the pole corral at the edge of the trees. He had recognized Correen on the bluff and felt ashamed that he could do nothing to help her. Now he felt sick with dread for her, because she had come to rescue him. It was his fault. Though the sight of her alive charged his weary legs with energy, he thought about letting his knees buckle, letting his weight tighten the noose around his neck. Watching them abuse her would be a shame he could not bear.

But when Correen got off the horse, she smiled at him and glanced at the longhaired man. Little Crow and Correen could read each other's thoughts almost as well as the evil redheaded twins. Correen's eyes told him there was a chance.

Claude leaned against the saddlebag after climbing down at the corrals. He put his hat over his right hand and ran his left hand back through his hair, feeling the blood. Under his hat, his fingers groped desperately at the second buckle. Squaw Man's rifle muzzle was against his ribs. Bob Steck was drawing the attention of the outlaws with his busted knee, wailing pitifully as one of the redheads tried to pull him down from the saddle.

"March 'em out there with the boy," Lafferty said.

"Even the girl?" Wiloughby whined.

Steck hopped on his good leg, checked Claude's progress at the saddlebag with a glance.

"Do as I say, or I'll line you up with 'em," Lafferty ordered.

Claude's hand reached into the saddlebag, touched cold Le Mat steel, but then Squaw Man was shoving him away. A loose buckle jingled, but the black man thought nothing of it. Squaw Man marched the regulator into the open, toward the sweep where the boy stood. Steck was limping along behind, guarded by the twins. Strikes the Dog made Correen follow.

"Let's shoot these two," Wiloughby was suggesting, "and take a quick turn or two with the woman before we ride after Wolverton."

Ike shook his head in disgust. "You are no gentleman, Roy. That's what makes you such a damn fool. Don't you understand there's no time for you to defile this girl?"

The Le Mat was getting farther away, hope shrinking.

"I'll make time, dammit." The ugly little rake-hell trotted to the head of the file, drew his Colt, pushed Squaw Man aside. He kicked Claude in the back of the knees, bringing him down. He turned the regulator to face the others, grabbed a handful of long, bloody hair. "Let's get it over with."

The Colt came around toward Claude's face. It was time. He didn't see himself getting out of this alive, but he was not going to go easy on his knees. He would shoot a glance at Correen and Bob, then come alive all over Wild Roy Wiloughby. That had been something, the way Steck had jumped off of that bluff. A good thought to die with. Maybe he could make it to the Le Mat. Probably not.

His eyes flashed at Bob, then Wiloughby's chest exploded. Wild Roy went down as if a rope had jerked him.

Claude felt the blood spatter him. The mountain peaks tossed a gunshot among them. A wisp of smoke trailed away from the bluff on a new morning breeze.

Wild Roy Wiloughby had been Lone-Wolfed.

FIFTEEN

t's Wolverton!" Ike Lafferty cried, trying a blind shot at the bluff as he dodged, feeling Lone Wolf's rifle sights on him. The Snowy Range Gang bolted for the trees beside the corral, leaving their prisoners with a few stray shots.

Steck's busted knee suddenly worked well enough to carry him in three great bounds past Claude, to Wiloughby's revolver. The ugly little gang leader was staring at the sky, his body heaving grotesquely.

"Let's go git 'em, Sabinal!" Steck charged the outlaws' rear with a rebel yell punctuated by three shots, chasing them all the way to the cover along the creek. Claude and Correen came to his side at the corrals.

"Give me a knife," Correen said, looking back at Little Crow, the boy vulnerable to gunshots under the slanting meat pole. "Quickly!"

A bullet hit a corral pole, Ike trying to regroup the outlaws.

Claude ducked under Casino's belly, got the Le Mat and his shaving kit out of the saddlebag. "How many shots you got left?" he asked Steck as he flipped the razor from the groove in its handle.

"Three," Steck said.

Correen was reaching for the razor. He tossed her the Le Mat instead.

"Keep 'em busy." He sprinted for the sweep where the boy was tied, gunshots following him from the trees. He cut the rope above Little Crow's head with a swipe of the razor, pulled the boy behind the bulky counterweight for cover.

Carefully, Claude cut the rawhide binding the boy's wrists. Bullets splintered the long arm of the sweep. He glanced to his right, saw Wiloughby's body, dead. To the left, the sacred bremmer cattle standing in a line, watching the fight with curiosity.

"Ready?" he said, though he wasn't sure the boy understood. He tilted his head toward the corrals and stepped from cover, the boy behind him. He felt a bullet sting the flesh of his inner thigh just before he reached the horses. Bob Steck and Correen were mounting. Correen tossed the Le Mat back to Claude, her hand free to catch the boy's arm and pull him up. Little Crow lit behind her as Claude vaulted into his saddle.

Steck's pistol clicked. He shoved it into his pants and spurred his mount. Claude overtook him, leading the way to the creek. Reaching the water, he plunged in, crossing without drawing fire. At the far side, he turned Casino to guard the others as they crossed, wondering how many rounds the Le Mat had left. He heard the hooves of Wolverton's mount coming down the bluff trail.

Steck was in the middle of the stream, and Correen prepared to plunge in, when Claude saw the squaw racing downstream on the other side of the creek, his Marlin rifle in her hands. "Correen!" he shouted, trying to find a shot at the squaw between the trunks of the oaks and the young lodgepole pines.

A rifle blast from upstream knocked Steck's horse down in the water, pinning the Texan's leg to the streambed. Claude rode by him, spurring Casino back across the creek

toward Correen. The rancher's head was above water, the
horse shielding him from the gang's bullets. A little cold
water wouldn't hurt him.

The squaw raised the Marlin as Correen spotted her and
reined toward her, ducking behind the horse's neck for
cover. The rifle erupted and Correen's horse collapsed,
pitching her and Little Crow into the brush. Claude saw
them scramble through the underbrush in different directions. Strikes the Dog charged again as he reached the
creek bank. A gunshot cracked and a bullet cut his hat brim.
He glimpsed red hair upstream.

The squaw spotted Correen crawling away and stopped to
fire, when Little Crow sprang from nowhere, knocking the
Cheyenne woman down. As she hit the ground, she fired
a round that tore through the boy's ribs, spinning him.
Correen screamed.

Claude rode between the two women as the muffled clatter of hooves came from behind—Wolverton charging up
the creek, attacking the gang.

Looking down the sights of the Le Mat, Claude found
the squaw on her knees, swinging the rifle his way, raising
the stock to her cheek. He fired, the .42-caliber load cracking like a whip after the roar of the big-bore weapons. The
butt of the Marlin splintered in Strikes the Dog's face,
knocking her back as she fired. Claude pulled the trigger
again and heard the click of the firing pin on a dead shell.

Strikes the Dog sprang to her feet, pumped the lever
of the Marlin, raised the shattered stock to her cheek,
found the longhaired white man between the tree trunks.

Claude was fumbling with the lever on the hammer of
the Le Mat. He flipped it to fire the scattergun barrel, raised
the weapon, pulled the trigger as he saw the muzzle of his
own Marlin coming around on him.

Buckshot knocked the Indian woman down. Wounded,
she tried to rise, but Correen was on top of her, wrenching

the Marlin away, using the last three rifle rounds on her. She dropped the weapon on the dead squaw and rushed back to Little Crow.

Claude heard stray shots upstream, the Snowy Range Gang stampeding away. He rode Casino through the brush to look down on Correen and Little Crow. The boy was alive, smiling up at her, shot bad.

"Oh, laddie," she was saying. "Oh, no . . ."

The regulator reined Casino back to the creek and found Bob craning his neck to keep his head above the rapids. "Through with your bath?" he asked, taking his rope down from the horn strings.

"And ready for a toddy," Steck said, his voice shuddering.

Claude dropped his loop over the saddle horn of Steck's dead horse, took a dally on his own horn, and urged Casino upstream. The big paint searched for footing on the slippery streambed, put his head down, and rolled the carcass from Steck's leg. The rancher got up and staggered in the stream, trying to make his numbed limbs obey.

Claude shook his loop from the dead horse's saddle, grabbed the collar of the rancher's vest, and led him to the creek bank, noticing a limp. "You bust your knee for real this time?"

Steck shook his head. "Just strained it some."

Claude pulled his whiskey flask from his coat pocket, took a swig, and handed it to Steck. He looked upstream to see Wolverton marching one of the redheaded twins back to the camp, both of them on foot. "Where's your horse?"

"Lafferty shot it out from under me. They ran the spare horses off. Left Sickle, here, behind."

Steck shook the whiskey down his throat with a shiver. "Why didn't you kill him?"

"Didn't have to. He was out of shells." He threw Claude's

gun belt up to him, the two Smith & Wesson Russians in it. "He was wearin' your guns."

Steck handed the whiskey flask back to Claude, drew the Colt revolver from the front of his pants, and started punching the spent brass casings from it. "Let me borrow some loads," he said to Wolverton.

The big man took six rounds from his belt and gave them to Steck. Claude broke open one of his Smiths and began reloading with .44s. The captured Sickle brother looked on uneasily.

"Sabinal, let me borrow your horse," Steck said when he had his pistol loaded.

"Where are you goin'?"

"After them rustlers."

"Alone?"

"Just to make sure they ain't doublin' back on us. Come on, get down. A ride will warm me up."

Claude stepped down with his guns and his rope. "All right, but don't go attackin' 'em by yourself. We'd better keep all our shooters healthy if we want to get down from this mountain."

Steck climbed stiffly into the saddle. "Don't do nothin' to that redheaded peckerwood till I get back. I don't want to miss it." He spurred Casino and left at a gallop.

Claude dropped his loop around the outlaw's neck, tightened it, and led him toward the meat pole in the middle of the camp.

Wolverton followed. "What did he mean about us not doin' anything to Sickle?"

"This ain't no time for us to be guardin' prisoners," Claude answered. "Lafferty doesn't mean to let us get off this mountain alive."

Wolverton's eyes shifted nervously. "I won't take part in anything that doesn't sit right with the law or with the Lord."

Claude smirked at the big man. "Don't preach to me, Wolverton. I know what you've taken part in before." He reached the sweep and tossed the end of his rope over it where Little Crow had been tied before.

"How bad is the kid shot?" Lone Wolf asked.

"Bad. Jumped up and took Correen's bullet. Looks plumb proud of himself, dyin' over there." He tied the rope to the timber, taking as much slack out as he could without strangling the outlaw. "I want to know one thing, Wolverton. Why'd you leave last night? How'd you know not to trust Ike?"

"Ike had me fooled," Lone Wolf admitted. "It was you I didn't trust."

"Me?" Claude said, jerking a knot into the rope, looping the loose end around the redhead's wrists.

Lone Wolf nodded. "It was too convenient, you livin' up here so close to Wiloughby's hideout, leadin' us right to his camp. I figured you were in it with him. I was wrong, of course, and I apologize."

The redheaded outlaw suddenly burst into laughter. "Apologize! My brother's thinkin' about how he's gonna kill you both right now. Damned if he'll apologize."

"Not with his head blowed off," Claude said. He grinned at the worried look on Wolverton's face.

They walked back to the trees to stand over the dying boy. Correen's one hand held Little Crow's while her other stroked the black hair back from his face. He was still smiling, his face pale. Claude saw Wolverton taking off his coat, and quickly unbuttoned his own. They covered the boy with their garments, hoping he would die warm. Claude's coat sleeve fell in a pool of blood when he draped it over the boy, but he let it lie.

They left Correen with Little Crow and stood speechlessly at the creek for a few minutes, listening, watching the bluffs around them through the treetops. Claude heard a horse galloping and saw Steck returning to the camp. Correen was covering Little Crow's face with Wolverton's coat. They met Steck at the body of the dead boy.

"They hit the high places," Steck said. "I saw 'em go over a ridge, about two miles east." He looked down and saw Little Crow's blood oozing out from under the two coats that covered him. "Sorry about the boy, Correen. I wish I could have taken that bullet for him."

Correen's eyes were wet, alive with anger. She looked each of them in the face, then glared across the open ground, past Wiloughby's body, at the red-haired Sickle twin tied to the sweep.

"What are we gonna do with that Sickle boy?" Lone Wolf said.

"You know fine what we're gonna do," Correen said, her mouth drawn up like an angry child's.

"What?"

Steck adjusted the Colt revolver under his belt. "Hang him from that meat pole, by God."

SIXTEEN

Clay Sickle saw Steck stalking toward him, favoring a leg. The woman and the longhaired gunman followed. Lone Wolf came along in the rear, uncertainly. But from the looks on the first three faces, the outlaw knew his minutes numbered few.

Steck drew a folding knife from his pocket and cut Claude's rope, leaving a short piece tied around the outlaw's wrists. He untied the long portion of the rope from the timber angling overhead. Keeping the noose tight around Sickle's neck, he led the outlaw to the rope that dangled under the beef carcass at the end of the sweep. He pulled down on the meat rope, but the pole didn't give.

Sickle sniffed.

Correen took hold of the rope, adding her slight heft to the effort. The pole merely bent. Claude's hands grasped the rope above Correen's, and the three drew their feet up under them, hanging from the meat rope. The counter-weight rose an inch from the ground, then settled in its rut again.

"Lend a hand, Lone Wolf," Steck said.

The big man shook his head.

"You wanted part of this manhunt," Claude said. "Now do your share."

"It's justice," Correen added. "He deserves it."

"That's not for us to decide. I refuse to lynch anybody."

Sickle laughed.

"Hell, we don't have to lynch the son of a bitch," Steck said, drawing the Colt from his waist. "I'd just as soon blow his damn head off." He cocked the weapon and put the muzzle against Sickle's greasy red locks.

"Wait!" the outlaw said. "I'll . . . I'll help you. I'll help you pull the meat pole down."

Claude squinted. "Why the hell would you help us hang you?"

Sickle shrugged, searched for words, glanced at the Colt in Steck's hand. "A minute from now just seems like a better time to die."

Steck exchanged looks with Correen and Claude. He put the Colt back into the front of his pants and turned Sickle around to untie his hands. "All right, friend, you've got one last chance to do somethin' good for the world—execute yourself. But try somethin' tricky and I'll gut-shoot you and hang you, anyway." He put the short piece of rope between his teeth.

Sickle rubbed his wrists, paused, stepped up to the meat rope. He saw the eyes of his three executioners guarding him, put his hands with theirs on the rope, pulled with them. The high end of the sweep began to descend. They hauled down on the rope until the beef carcass touched the dirt beside them, and the pole was within reach overhead.

"Stand on the rope," Steck ordered.

Sickle put his boots on the rope and slowly released his grip. The others kept their hold.

"Hands behind your back," Steck said. He held the meat rope with one hand, took the short rope from his mouth with the other hand, and looped it around Sickle's wrist. "Hold this end so I can pull it tight." He pressed a length of rope into the redhead's palm.

The outlaw helped his hangman tie his hands back.

"What's your name?" Steck asked, jerking the knot tight around the doomed man's wrists.

"Frank Sickle." Frank was across the divide somewhere. It was Clay standing next to the beef carcass with the rope around his neck. But Frank was wanted in Nebraska for killing a stagecoach driver and Clay figured his hanging might as well do his brother some good. Frank would know to switch names after today. Hell, he knew already. "He's gonna feel it," Clay said, speaking low.

"Huh?" Claude grunted, catching a strange quiver from the outlaw's shoulder, pressed against his own.

"My brother's gonna feel it when y'all kill me."

Steck scoffed. "Maybe you'll feel it in hell when we kill him." He tied the end of the lynch rope to the meat pole, doubling the knot, pulling it tight. "I'm leavin' you plenty of slack so it'll jerk you up hard. You won't choke slow."

Sickle swallowed, then smirked at Steck. "I'll be obliged to you as long as I live." He chuckled, amused at himself.

"We gonna let go now?" Claude said, anxious to get it over with.

"No," Steck answered, pulling out his pocket-knife again. "I'll cut it." He held the bone handle in his mouth, unfolded a blade with his free hand. "That way nothin' will tangle." He put the blade against the meat rope holding the pole down.

"Don't do it," Wolverton said, his voice a low croak.

Steck looked at the big man over his shoulder. "Hell, Lone Wolf, he's takin' it better than you, and he's the one gettin' hung." His blade sawed through one strand of the lariat; another twisted away.

"Remember, Sickle," Wolverton said, "God forgives."

The third strand stretched and tore. The three executioners fell back as the meat pole whipped upward, cutting the air with a sigh, moaning on its fulcrum, carrying the beef carcass with it. Clay Sickle suddenly took an urge to run, thinking maybe the lynch rope wouldn't jerk him quite so hard if he got out from under the pole. He had taken three steps when his slack played out—a short whir of the tightening noose, a thump of tension, a groan of stretching fibers.

Sickle's legs kicked once, froglike, as his boots left the dirt. The body rose like a rocket, tracing a curve in the air as the rope swung it back to center.

The counterweight hit hard and bounced, the high end of the long timber springing like the tip of a cane pole, the beef carcass hitting its underside. The lynch rope slacked, the body arching high through the air, as if shot from a cannon. It reached a zenith, then fell like a goose killed on the wing, limp, plunging headfirst toward the ground.

The rope was going to tighten and whip the dead man around like a calf hitting the end of a lariat. Claude doubted a human neck could take it, and he turned away. He found himself looking into Wolverton's damning stare as he heard the lynch rope snap taut and creak against the meat pole.

His eyes escaped Lone Wolf's glare and found Correen

staring toward the corpse, her face suddenly pale, her mouth open. Then the body swung between them, its neck bent like an elbow, the dead man's eyes looking through Claude, like Wolverton's, damning him.

"Son of a bitch!" Steck cried. "I didn't think it would hang him that hard. It's a wonder his damn head didn't come off!"

As they watched the body swing, an echo reached the valley: maybe the caw of a crow or the morning bark of a stray coyote. Or maybe, Claude thought, the yell of a red-headed outlaw feeling the lynch rope tighten around his brother's neck.

SEVENTEEN

A men," Wolverton said, putting his hat back on his head. He got down on his knees and pushed the first handful of dirt in on Little Crow's body, wrapped in a blanket in a shallow grave.

Claude put his hand on Correen's shoulder for a moment, then began pushing dirt in with his boot.

"What do we do next, Sabinal?" Steck said.

Claude thought about Ike Lafferty, Squaw Man, the other Sickle twin. "We'll ransack this camp for anything we can use. Lafferty will do the same to our camp over the divide. We've got one horse. Can't chase 'em down and attack. Can't even run."

"They'll come back after us," Steck said.

Claude nodded. "Probably not today. We've got one more gun than they do, and we've got 'em scared. They know we're short on ridin' stock and can't get out of the mountains anytime soon, so they'll probably go back to Ike's ranch and get some more boys."

"Yes," Correen said, throwing handfuls of dirt onto the blanket. "Lafferty will come back after us with twice as many men."

"We'll get ready for 'em," Claude said, nodding to convince himself. "The bastards will think they've never seen a fight before."

"That's what I like to hear!" Steck brandished a fist.

Lone Wolf looked up from the graveside. "Now we're the Snowy Range Gang, and they're the posse. 'Whatsoever a man soweth, that shall he also reap.'"

Claude groaned. "Bob, go up on the bluff and stand guard," he ordered.

Steck didn't care much for guard duty, but grave digging appealed to him even less. He picked up his rifle and limped away from the fresh grave. By the time he was in place on the bluff, Claude had put the last stone on the mound. He left Correen and Wolverton and went to find his Marlin rifle.

The weapon was still lying across the body of Strikes the Dog, where Correen had dropped it. The bullet from the Le Mat had splintered the stock, the hardwood cracked from grip to butt as if by an axe. Only a few grains held it together.

Claude went back to the tepee and found a square of rawhide. He cut a spiral from it, making a narrow strip about six feet long. He put the rawhide strip under a rock in the creek to soak, also rinsing Little Crow's blood from the sleeve of his coat.

When he came back to camp, he saw Wolverton dragging Roy Wiloughby's body to the meat pole. The big man cut the Sickle brother down, then dragged both dead men to a shallow grave he had dug.

Claude shook his head. He would have left the outlaws to the buzzards. At least Lone Wolf had the decency not to bury them near Little Crow. They were across the camp from the Indian boy, Little Crow on higher ground.

Claude found Correen working at the tepee, making herself useful, putting the contents of the lodge into two piles. One was made up of usable things: blankets, food, guns. The other pile was for things of no value: skins, holey buffalo robes, trinkets.

Claude picked up Squaw Man's .45-70 Winchester. "Find any ammunition for this thing?" he asked, looking up at the bluff to make sure Bob Steck was still on guard, and not off engaging the enemy.

"Maybe fifty rounds," she answered. Much of the pleasant lilt had left her voice this morning.

Claude grunted, saw Wolverton coming. "There'll probably be more in the cabin."

"Why was he smiling so?" she said quietly, looking at a piece of tanned deerskin, as if unaware that the thought had escaped. "Didn't he know he was dying?"

Claude rubbed his chin and wondered where he had dropped his razor. "Proud of himself. He wanted to do right by you because you came to rescue him. Gave him a chance to die a hero. He did all right."

Correen saw through Claude and what he was trying to do: ease her guilt. She gave him a forced smile for trying.

Wolverton strode up to the pile of goods Correen had tossed aside from the tepee. "Mind if I have this?" he said, picking up an old buffalo robe.

"What on earth would you want with it?"

"I'm gonna wrap the Indian woman in it."

Correen looked at Claude, then back at Wolverton. "Whatever for?" she said.

"Bury her."

She threw an old saddle blanket into a pile and scowled at Wolverton. "Leave her to the wolves!"

Wolverton picked up the robe. " 'Rejoice not over thy greatest enemy being dead, but remember that we die all.' "

"Do not quote the Good Book to me, Mr. Wolverton. I

rejoice in nothing this morning!" She threw the bearskin flap aside from the entrance hole and stepped into the tepee.

Claude caught a part of the anger she left behind. "How the hell can you leave a good man to burn in his own fire, then bury a bunch of dirty outlaws?"

Wolverton winced. He had been wondering when Duval would remind him of Dusty Sanderson again. "Too late to take back the things I've done. All I can do is change."

Claude faked a laugh, then stepped closer to Wolverton, glaring. "I hope you don't think I'm gonna let you go back to Texas alive just because you saved my life this mornin'." He stalked away toward the creek.

The strip of rawhide he had put in the creek was soft now. He pulled it between his fingers to wring some of the water from it, then began wrapping it carefully around the split stock of his Marlin. He tucked the end under the last three coils, fiddled with it until it was snug.

The sun was shining down on the outlaw camp now, so Claude carried his rawhide-wound Marlin out into the light. He propped it against the counterweight of the meat sweep at such an angle as to catch the hottest rays of the sun.

As his eyes swept upward to check on Steck's position, he caught an unexpected movement about halfway up a tree. It was Wolverton, putting the squaw to rest the Cheyenne way, on a platform of poles built into a tree. He shook his head in bewilderment.

Correen stopped at the meat pole on her way to search the unfinished cabin. "I don't know what to think of him," she said, watching Wolverton hoist the shrouded body into the tree. He's either a better Christian than I or a dashit fool."

"I don't believe he's either one of those."

"Why don't you use one of the Winchesters?" she asked, observing his rawhide-wrapped rifle stock in the sunshine.

"I've grown partial to that Marlin."

"Why? Certainly it shoots no better than a good Winchester."

"Winchester's a good gun, but when you have to shoot fast, it goes to slingin' those spent shells over your head, up under your hat brim. That side-eject puts the Marlin one up in my judgment."

She shook her head. "You with your twin pistols and your fast-shootin' repeaters. You're a short-trigger man, Mr. Duval."

"Come on. Let's have a look in that cabin."

Stepping through the doorway sawed into the new log wall, Claude found wads of blankets and clothes, stacks of dirty pots and pans, coils of ropes and piles of tools. A rifle leaning against the rear wall caught his eye, its long barrel sticking through a hole cut in the end of a leather saddle scabbard.

"Look here," Claude said, stepping across the cabin to the weapon. "I'll wager the caliber of that piece is .44-90." As he pulled the rifle from the scabbard, a checkered pistol grip appeared. Then a long-range tang sight, folded down. Then the single-shot falling-block action, about three feet of octagonal barrel, and a hooded front sight. Claude had never before held such a piece. He had seen only one, in the courtroom during Wolverton's hearing.

"Sharps Model 73 Creedmoor," he muttered. "The same kind of gun Wolverton used to kill with."

"I've seen a Creedmoor rifle before," Correen said. "I'm sure it was a Remington, and not a Sharps."

Claude shouldered the weapon, its barrel longer than a goose gun's. "Remington's made some. So has Ballard, and Wesson, and some others. Sharps still makes one, too, but they use .45 caliber now. The old 73 model was the only Sharps Creedmoor to chamber a .44."

Correen held her hand out for the weapon, tested its

balance when Claude handed it to her. "Mr. Creedmoor had a lot of partners," she said, putting the slender stock to her cheek.

Claude chuckled. "Creedmoor's not a fellow's name. It's the name of a shootin' range at Long Island, New York. They have long-range matches there." He took the rifle back from her. "Creedmoor's just another name for a long-range gun." He showed her the hooded sight on the barrel tip. "The front sight's got a level in it, and you can adjust it for windage." He flipped the rear tang sight up. "And you can adjust this one to a thousandth of an inch for distance."

"How far will it shoot?"

"They use 'em up to a thousand yards in match shootin'. Now, you take an expert like Wolverton. If he lays down on his stomach and judges wind and distance right, he might kill a man a thousand yards away. He got Wiloughby this mornin' at about two hundred yards with a regular Winchester. Four or five hundred yards is a sure thing for him with a good Creedmoor rifle."

Her cold eyes studied him. "You sound as if you admire him for it."

"I admire marksmanship. Like you shootin' that brass casing out of the air. But I cannot abide a murderer."

A shadow filled the doorway, and Lone Wolf stepped in, quickly sensing the eyes on him. He stopped, saw the rifle in Duval's hands.

"I found you somethin' to work with," Claude said, pitching the Creedmoor across the cabin.

The big man had to catch the gun, his left hand grasping the forestock, his right the checkered grip. He turned the weapon a couple of times, letting the sun glint from its facets. He let it lie upside down in his open palms. One side of his mouth smiled, but only for a second, then his eyes bulged as if entranced by the evil stare of a rattlesnake he held in his hands.

"Remember how to use it?" the regulator asked. He saw Wolverton flinch and found the Creedmoor flying back at him.

Lone Wolf stumbled back out of the cabin, wiping his palms on his shirt. He tripped over the threshold and fell backward into the sunlight. He rolled and ran, like a scared child.

Claude stepped to the doorway with the rifle in his hands, Correen coming up beside him. They watched the big man stumble forward into the brush along the creek.

"My God," Correen said. "What got into him?"

Claude stood silent for a second, watching the place where Wolverton had disappeared. He held the Creedmoor before him one-handed like a flagstaff. "The devil, I reckon."

EIGHTEEN

Frank Sickle sat on his horse, his head cocked at an unnatural angle, watching Ike Lafferty and Squaw Man as they pulled up Correen's bow tent and threw it into the fire.

"Get off your horse, Frank, and lend a hand," Lafferty said.

"I'm Clay."

Lafferty squinted. Usually, neither brother complained when called by the other's name. No one could tell them apart, anyway. "I thought that was Frank's horse."

"They hung Frank," Sickle said.

"I wouldn't doubt it." Lafferty added a pack saddle to the blaze. "Old Steck's been itchin' to kill somebody."

"What about my woman?" Squaw Man asked, as if Sickle could conjure a vision of her.

"I hope they hung her, too," the redhead said.

Squaw Man's mouth pulled tight across his teeth. He reached for his reins and bounded into the saddle.

"Hey, where you goin'?" Lafferty demanded.

"Goin' back to see about the squaw."

"Don't be a damned fool. They're not in the frame of mind to take prisoners. Like Frank says, they probably hung 'em if they didn't shoot 'em."

"I'm Clay," Sickle repeated. He scratched at his neck, starting at the throat, working all the way around to the back. His skin was red from clawing. It had started itching right after he had caught the crick in his neck. He had been riding at the time, crossing the divide, and the pain had struck him like a knife between his neck joints. He had coughed, and wheezed, and almost fallen out of the saddle.

Squaw Man held a tight rein. "What are we gonna do?"

"Use our heads. They've got one more gun than we do now, and believe me, that sheep woman can shoot as good as any of us. On top of that, they've got the Creedmoor. Wolverton can kill a man at five hundred yards with that thing, so we don't want to just go chargin' in after 'em."

"We ain't lettin' 'em go," Squaw Man insisted.

"They aren't goin' anywhere," Lafferty replied. "They've only got one horse left. Frank shot Steck's horse down in the creek. The squaw shot that horse out from under Correen and the boy. When we turned to run, I fired over my shoulder and killed Wolverton's horse, and we drove all the spare mounts off with us. Duval is the only one left with a mount."

"So what?" Sickle said.

"They can't all four ride one horse. The worst they could do is send somebody out for help. That's why you two are gonna go back and watch 'em from a distance. If one of 'em rides that big paint horse out of camp, you hunt 'im down. I'll go back to the ranch, round up some of the boys, and be back in a couple of days. Then we'll finish 'em off."

"Then what?" Squaw Man said. "What about the bremmer cattle? The gang?"

"You'll scatter the bremmers. Trade 'em to the west. If anybody comes up from Texas lookin' for Steck, I'll tell 'em the Snowy Range Gang killed him and got away with all his cattle. Then you'll build up another gang, Squaw Man, and come next spring, it'll be business as usual. Hell, it's a blessing to get shed of Wild Roy. He'd of got us all caught sooner or later."

Sickle was rubbing his neck. He felt a chill. Looking to the east, he saw clouds building. He found breathing difficult—pressure on his chest. "Let's go," he said, buttoning his coat up to the collar. "I don't feel worth shit."

NINETEEN

Damn, I hate this," Steck said. He was helping Claude and Correen raise the lodge poles near the base of the Snowy Range.

"It'll keep your rear end out of the weather," Claude said, glancing at the darkening sky.

"I don't mean the tepee. I mean sittin' up here waitin' to get shot at."

They had made a travois of the lodge poles, using Casino to haul everything of value five miles up from the outlaw camp. Now the Snowy Range loomed above them, a colossal wall of rock jutting above the timber, marked with streaks of snow. Several high mountain lakes nestled between the Snowy Range and the trees, huge pools of ink today, drawing darkness from the storm clouds that had gathered overhead. Claude had chosen to camp beside a body that Steck had named Lake Correen—Loch Correen, as her mouth spoke it.

"The fishin' rod was for Little Crow," she had said, looking out over the clear pool. "If only he had lived to use it."

Wolverton was somewhere in the timber. He hadn't spoken to anyone since running from the Creedmoor. He had come back to camp, his eyes as red as if he had been on a three-day drunk, but he hadn't spoken a word.

"We don't have a choice," Claude said. "We have to fort up and wait. Might as well count our advantages and quit whinin' about our sorry luck."

"What advantages?" Steck said, using a big rock to pound an iron pin into the ground near the center of the lodge. A rawhide strap running from the pin to the crossed tops of the lodge poles would hold the tepee firmly to the ground in case the wind got up.

"Well, we can pick our own ground," Claude said.

"That's true. I want to die over there," Steck said, pointing. "How 'bout you, Correen?"

Correen's dark laughter felt good, but didn't last long.

"We've got the Creedmoor. Wolverton can hold them off at five hundred yards or better with that."

"No." The voice croaked from the tree line. Wolverton followed it to the campsite and began unfolding the old hides that would cover the lodge poles. "I won't use that Sharps or any other gun against any man, except to defend myself or one of you." His eyes were clear now, bright and sure.

"That's what I'm talkin' about," Claude said. "Shoot 'em before they can get in range of us."

Wolverton shook his head. "I won't fire unless they fire at us first."

"The hell you won't!" Claude shouted, his voice hitting the rocks and bouncing back. "If they figure out you're not gonna hold 'em back, they'll move in range and rush us."

Wolverton shook his head. "I can't. The Good Lord's testin' me."

Claude's mouth dropped open, and he stared at the old killer.

"There goes another advantage." Steck groaned, but he was actually enjoying this. The worse it got, the more he liked it. "That Creedmoor might as well be just another gun with any of us lookin' through the sights." He helped Correen and Wolverton spread the hides around the framework of lodge poles. It blocked the cold wind and mist, made him eager to get a fire going.

Claude stood and stared at Lone Wolf in disbelief while the others worked. He put his hands on his hips, noticed his breath trailing away on the cold wind. It was summer down in Texas, green grass sprouting from Dusty's grave on the plains. But up here it was freezing cold. Raindrops began to thump against his hat brim.

Steck built a fire in the tepee, and Correen began cooking. Claude carried in the guns. Wolverton brought in everything else. They sat in a circle in the captured hide tent, staring at the spaces between one another. Wolverton's eyes avoided looking at the Creedmoor, standing tall where it leaned against a lodge pole.

Claude went out, filled a small pot with lake water, put it over some coals, and found his shaving kit. He sat down again to think and wait for the water to heat up.

"There's ranches down in North Park," Wolverton said, breaking the silence. "Correen could ride the horse down and bring back help."

"You'd all be dead by the time I got back," she said quickly.

"*If* you got back," Claude added. "Ike may have left Squaw Man and that other Sickle boy behind to watch us. One rider's too easy to ambush." He smirked. "Anyway, if anybody was to try it, it would be you, Wolverton. Correen's too valuable to us. She's willin' to fight."

They stared at the lodge poles again, the tension between them like a snowbank.

"Correen, how many rounds did we find for the Creed-moor?" Claude said after a minute.

"No more than twenty, if that many."

Claude spread the contents of his shaving kit on a rag in front of him. "Wolverton, you're gonna teach me how to shoot that damn long-range Sharps. We've got a couple of days to practice before Ike comes back with his boys."

The big man shook his head. "You'd use all your rounds and still not be worth a darn."

"Then we'll reload the damn cartridges! Take some powder from some other shells!"

"We don't have primers or bullet molds," Correen said, glancing up from the fire.

"Anyway, what's the difference in my shootin' 'em or teachin' you to?" Wolverton said. "I won't have part of it either way."

They fell silent again, listening to the bacon sizzle, smelling the aroma. Claude got up once to put his finger in the water, then sat back down.

"All right, how's this?" he said, turning to Wolverton. "We'll find an open place where we can see five hundred yards or so. When Ike and his boys find us, I'll ride out on Casino and draw their fire. If they shoot at me, you'll have to shoot back, right?"

"Better to let me draw their fire," Correen said, turning the bacon in a skillet. "I'm smaller and lighter. I can ride faster and Will make a smaller target."

"Now, wait just a doggone minute," Steck said. "I ain't no braggart, Correen, but I can outride you. And you're a better rifle shot than me, so we'd be better off lettin' me draw their fire while you and Sabinal and Lone Wolf cover me."

"Stupid plan," Wolverton said. "They'll shoot our only horse out from under you, then we'll be in a worse fix."

"Don't talk to me about stupid!" Claude shouted. "You're the one too damn stupid to shoot for your own life! The only chance we've got is to whittle their forces down with that Creedmoor before they get inside of normal rifle range!"

Wolverton's dark face frowned, but he said nothing.

Claude dipped his shaving brush in the hot water and began viciously whipping up soap. "Where's the best place to fort up, Correen?"

She pulled her dark hair back and bent over the fire again, crouching, balancing on her toes with the agility of a bird. "If we're lookin' for open ground to fight on, I would say to go to the south, along the divide where the wind gnarls the trees so." She paused, stirred the beans. "I wish Little Crow was here. He knew every canyon. He grazed sheep on the western slope, shot deer to the south, hunted mustangs north of the Snowy Range. He could tell us where to bide an army."

Claude's shaving brush pulled slowly away from his face, leaving a smear of white soap. He looked at Correen, found her stirring beans. He looked at Steck, found him pouting across the tepee. Then he looked at Wolverton and found the big man looking back, eyes ablaze with new energy.

"Mustangs?" Claude said.

Correen looked up from the fire. "Yes, a small band of them north of here."

"Why didn't you say so before?" He rinsed his brush in the hot water, yanked the rag out from under his shaving tools, and wiped the soap from his face.

"Why would I mention it?"

"Horses, Correen! With mounts we can take the fight to Lafferty!"

She gawked. "But these are wild horses."

"I've rode green stock before."

"It's not possible," Correen argued. "These horses have never worn a saddle."

"I broke horses with the Indians when I was a boy," Wolverton said. "I can train 'em good enough to ride in three days. Maybe even two."

"How you gonna catch 'em?" Steck said. "Might be able to rope one or two if Sabinal's big paint can get close enough."

Correen pulled a skillet from the fire. "Little Crow said he built a trap across the mouth of a canyon. A high fence of poles and brush. I brought him some salt and an auger so he could make a salt lick to attract them."

"How long ago was this?" Claude asked.

"Weeks. He said he would give them time to get used to the pen, then sneak back and catch them in it, close the opening with some poles he had cut and left there."

Claude wrung his hands together, put his razor back in the shaving kit. "Where is this trap?"

"North of the Snowy Range and east of Rock Creek. That's all I know."

"That's enough." He stood up and put his coat on.

"Where are you going?"

"Saddle up Casino. I'll eat some supper, wait for dark, then slip out of camp. Head north. With some luck maybe I can find the boy's mustang trap in the mornin' and catch us some horses."

As he left the tepee, he rubbed the coarse stubble on his chin, almost glad now that he hadn't found time to shave. A little whisker would keep his face warm tonight in the freezing rain.

TWENTY

The boy had built a damn fine trap. Claude looked down on it from the bluff, his stomach growling against the rimrock, the warm morning sun drying his backside. It seemed he was getting to know Little Crow better now, and was liking him.

He quietly raked some gravel out from under his belly and settled in again, like a rattler taking sun on the rocks. He was more comfortable than he had been all night.

After leaving the tepee, he had ridden east around the Snowy Range, then loped north for an hour in the sleet, until it became too dark to see. He had dismounted, rolled himself in a blanket, a tarpaulin folded below and over him. No fire. Little sleep.

It had snowed briefly before the clouds broke, about midnight, letting the moonlight through. He had mounted again and continued north, riding at a walk, listening to the wolves howl and the panthers scream, knowing the mustangs heard them, too. He found Rock Creek, made another camp, caught an hour of sleep before sunrise.

He was riding Casino in the creek when he found the crossing. The mustangs had used the ford often, their unshod hooves stomping down the brink of the creek bank. Their trail seemed to lead toward a narrow canyon to the east.

He rode wide around the downwind side, peered into the canyon from the rim above. Now, from the bluff, where the sun thawed him out, Claude studied the barricade built across a narrow place in the canyon floor. Little Crow had strapped stout poles to pine saplings with rawhide. He had laced the pole fence with brush and evergreen boughs, copper-colored now, making the barricade appear solid up to seven feet high. He had left an opening in the middle, through which the mustang trail led. Claude could see the cut poles lying ready to close the gap, a pile of pine boughs and brush nearby.

The sun was making him drowsy, but he fought off sleep. Mustangs might come and go before he knew it. He hoped they'd want to gnaw at Little Crow's salt lick today. Tomorrow might be too late. He put his palm on the rocks, rested his chin on the back of his hand, waited.

The others would be well on their way by now, carrying guns, saddles, and provisions on their backs. He hoped they wouldn't get here too soon and spook the mustangs. Not likely, though. A long walk. He'd have to go back and find them. First, catch the mustangs. Then find the others . . . Yes, find them . . . Find Correen . . . Correen . . .

A clatter woke him, and he felt a chill. The rim-rock was in the shade now, the sun behind a tree. Must have been asleep an hour, he thought. What about the mustangs? What was that sound?

His eyes focused on horses below, moving like deer among islands of brush. His heart pounded against the rock. A dream? He saw the stallion lunge, nipping at a mare's flank, chasing her back into the band, hooves rattling like an alarm clock. They were real. The steel-gray stallion, four mares, and a foal.

They approached the barricade cautiously, nostrils flaring, ears pivoting, necks craning. Only the foal took time to gambol, rearing back from a windblown blade of grass, kicking his heels. The lead mare stepped inside the barricade and stood, head high, for almost a minute. Then she lowered her nose and stalked toward a log on the ground.

Claude hadn't noticed before, but the log had been bored with holes and gnawed into a rough hourglass shape. The holes, once filled with salt, were now empty. The lead mare sniffed the log, moved farther up the canyon. The stallion herded his other harem members into the trap as the lead mare nuzzled another log, also with holes bored in it.

Little Crow had set his baits perfectly. Now the lead mare was checking the third salt lick, also empty. She continued searching for a fresh lick, taking the herd all the way around a bend in the canyon.

The stallion, bringing up the rear, stopped and turned to look once at the hole in the barricade. He waited long enough to let the lead mare get to the head of the canyon. If anything was wrong, she would scream and come galloping out. But she did not. The old boy tasted salt. He waited a few more moments, then walked up the canyon, around the bend.

Carefully, Claude slid back from the rim of the canyon and pushed himself to his knees. He was stiff from sleeping on the rocks but determined to control his every movement. One clattering rock or breaking branch would warn the wild horses, and his slim hopes of obtaining mounts would vanish.

He used several minutes getting into the next canyon, where he had left Casino, all the while imagining the mustangs trotting out of the trap and escaping across the valley. He finally mounted, made Casino walk. He didn't want hooves warning the mustangs. It wasn't easy, for he wanted to get there before the wild horses left, but he remained calm and walked.

Rounding the bend to Little Crow's canyon, Claude saw no sign of the wild horses. Either they were still up in the head of the canyon or they had left. He rode quietly toward the narrow place where the boy had built the barricade. A hundred yards from the gate, he saw the lead mare appear around the bend. She flinched as if stung by a hornet, whistled, and lunged back toward the head of the canyon.

Claude put spurs to Casino, and a thunder of hooves

shook the canyon. He had a good idea what would happen. The mustangs would charge to the head of the canyon, see that they were trapped, and stampede back toward the opening in the barricade. He would have to get it closed before they returned, otherwise he might not be able to turn them.

As he hit the ground beside the gap, he could hear the stallion screaming at his mares. He grabbed a pole that Little Crow had left, and slid it into its notches, starting with the top rail. By the time he had the second pole in his hands, the percussion of hooves had burst around the bend in the canyon, and the horses were galloping his way.

He tried not to look up as he put the second rail in place, but he caught a glimpse of the huge gray stallion charging, neck bowed, ears back, legs sprawled. He got the rail in its notches and looked again. The mares and the foal had dropped back, but the stallion was challenging. Claude took off his hat and waved it, whistled, hollered, and jumped up on the lower rail so he would stand taller.

Casino began grunting and pulling against the bridle reins as the gray beast came on. He felt an old twinge of wild savagery but restrained himself, too long under the saddle.

The gray finally planted his hooves just a few leaps short of the gate. He stood whistling breath from his nostrils, glaring with defiance, too proud to turn tail. He reared and slung his head as he backed away. Finally, he wheeled, kicked toward Claude, and darted after his mares, pawing them, biting, driving them up the canyon.

Claude wrapped Casino's reins around a branch, hoping the big paint wouldn't pull loose to fight the gray. He put two more rails in place. If he hadn't known better, he might have thought there was an avalanche coming down from the head of the canyon.

The gray stallion stopped even closer this time as Claude

stood in front of Casino, waved his hat, and hollered. He didn't want to give away his location to Squaw Man or the Sickle twin by shooting, but he was ready to reach for a Smith & Wesson if the gray decided to do more than bluff. He couldn't afford to get Casino hurt in a fight. But the big gray turned tail again and angled across the canyon floor, looking for a trail out of the trap.

Claude began lacing brush into the new section of fence. He spaced the dried pine boughs out at first, then started filling in the gaps between them as the wild herd thundered down the canyon a third time.

The regulator leaped into the saddle, felt Casino trembling under him. He stood in the stirrups and waved his hat high, shouting at the stallion across the barricade. The big gray was fuming now, grunting, slinging his head in rage. He stopped just short of the fence, reared and pawed at Casino through the brush. His hooves came down on the rails as a screaming roar rattled from his lungs in a cloud of vapor.

Claude was holding a tight rein on Casino, but the big paint was feeling his mustang blood.

The gray dropped behind the brush barricade for a second, then reappeared, wall-eyed, ears low, lips curling back from his teeth. He pawed blindly, parting brush, and came across the top rail, his belly bowing the stout pine pole.

"Oh, dammit!" Claude yelled, wrapping a hand around his right-hand revolver.

The gray wielded his head like a battle axe and climbed the fence rails with his hind hooves. He stumbled as he cleared the barricade, landing on his knees, using his face to break his fall.

Claude spurred Casino between the wild stud and the hole he had started in the fence. The gray came up off his knees and bit Casino on the shoulder. The paint roared with rage and sprang forward, bumping the gray, then felt the bit in his mouth and gave ground, guarding the opening in the fence.

The gray reared and pawed, hopping toward the horse and rider on his hind legs. Claude drew his pistol. Casino wanted to rear and face the attack but remembered his training and stayed on all fours, letting the gray come down on him.

Claude was swinging the barrel of his .44 up when the huge mass of gray landed in his lap and bounced, the stud thrashing head and hooves everywhere. The hot gray horse was on his hand, his revolver, his reins. He had no control over Casino now, astounded that the paint hadn't collapsed under the weight.

He reached for his left-hand pistol as Casino whirled right, dropping his head. The gray flinched, screamed, and Claude knew his mount must have sunk teeth into a thigh. The wild stud slipped down over Casino's neck, throwing hooves like a prize fighter as he retreated. One chopped the back of the rider's hand against the saddle horn.

The gray stumbled back and gathered himself for another lunge when Claude jerked his trigger. The four mares and the foal shied away across the barricade and thundered up the canyon. The gray darted aside, lowered his neck, and ran, abandoning his harem in the trap, his instinct for survival overcoming his love of combat. His huge gray rump shrank away toward the creek. Then he was gone, his screeching roar sounding across the valley, drowning out the echo of his hooves.

Claude stumbled down from the saddle, holstered both revolvers, and had a look at Casino. The paint's muzzle was red, but that was the gray's blood. A couple of bites on the shoulders, a cut or two on the neck. Nothing too deep. He stepped in front of the stallion and saw Casino's ears angle back.

He popped the paint across the muzzle and held his head

down with the reins. "Don't you cock your ears at me!" he said, not interested in getting bitten. He stared the stallion down until Casino shook his head, pitched his ears forward, and heaved.

Claude grinned. "I know you could have whipped him, but I can't have you all cut up." He reached out to pat the paint's broad neck and saw something flapping on the back of his right hand. A hunk of skin, peeled back by the gray's sharp hooves. He stared, as if at someone else's wound.

"Oh, shit," he muttered, remembering the blow from the hoof on the saddle horn. He had felt a little pain, but expected only a scratch. Now it hurt like hell, of course. And no time to fool with it. The mares were coming back.

He pressed the skin down on the back of his hand, avoided looking at it, and started repairing the damage the big gray stallion had done to the barricade.

TWENTY-ONE

Correen saw plainly where the tracks were leading, but she kept quiet and let Wolverton go ahead of her to read the sign.

The big man paced, searched the ground, then stopped. "I figured he might ride into the creek sooner or later," he said, lowering his saddle to the gravel. "Doesn't want the mustangs to smell him on the ground."

Correen dropped her saddle. Across it, she put a Winchester and the Creedmoor, which Wolverton had refused to take up. "Shall we camp here until he comes back for us? We don't want to stumble onto Little Crow's trap and frighten the wild horses away." Her joints were aching from the hike, her arm and shoulder muscles burning from carrying the load.

Steck dropped his tack beside Correen's. "Ain't no easy way to carry a saddle if you ain't a horse." He had woken this morning to find his right knee swollen tight inside his pants leg where his horse had fallen on it the day before. He had walked in the rear all this morning, so the others wouldn't see him limping. "I ain't marched so damn much since the war. Hated it then, too."

Correen began gathering wood for a cook fire. Claude would be hungry when he came back.

"I'm gonna have a look around," Wolverton said. He stood over Correen's saddle for a moment, staring down on the weapons. She saw his eyes on the old Sharps, the fear still in them. He reached toward the gun but grabbed a Winchester instead, and left.

Steck rolled himself in a blanket and put his hat over his face.

Correen stacked her kindling, took in a deep breath of cool mountain air. This was a pleasant place, the sun shining down through the leaves of small oaks, Rock Creek rushing nearby. If only they had rescued Little Crow. How different she might feel now. And yet he was here in a way, helping them catch the wild horses.

Steck was already asleep, breathing deep.

Correen knew she should have been tired, too, but instead she was anxious. The outlaws were running loose while Little Crow lay in his grave. They had all taken part in murdering the boy. She wanted them all dead. The black man, the other redhead, and especially Ike Lafferty. If her late husband had taught her one thing, it was how to hate a man.

But these were good men in her company, if strange. Bob Steck: gentlemanly yet violent. Wolverton: struggling with bloodshed and righteousness. Boyish in a way, seeking a mother's affection.

And Claude, the strangest of all. Running from something?

Restless? Haunted. Could he truly so love a friend that he would grieve still for this dead man, this Dusty Sanderson? Still seeking vengeance after eleven years? He wasn't as tough as he let on. She had seen his face, horrified, when the Sickle twin swung between them, and she had felt the same way.

Maybe they were more alike than she cared to admit. Maybe, eleven years from now, she would still be plotting Ike Lafferty's death.

What would happen when this was over? After she took her revenge on Lafferty, would she stand and watch Claude take his on Lone Wolf? Even if she understood Claude's hatred, she didn't want to see Wolverton die. Something about the old murderer charmed her. Something rare and sincere.

She shook her head—she might not live to worry about it. It wasn't her business, anyway. These men—these big strong fools—would do what they wanted in the end.

She kept the fire burning small but hot until she heard Wolverton slogging across the shallow creek. The big man put the Winchester down beside the Creedmoor and began pulling his boots off. "I don't see anybody on our trail," he said. He got one boot free and put it near the fire to dry. While pulling the second one off, the Creedmoor caught his eye again, and he stared at it as a drunk would a bottle of whiskey.

"It's not a snake, you know," Correen said. "It won't bite."

"Like hell it won't," he said as his boot came free. Then he looked at her, embarrassed. "Pardon my language, but it bites, all right."

"So will any other weapon. What's different about that one?" She watched as he unwrapped a square of wet cloth from each foot. Two different fabrics in different prints. He wrung them out and draped them over his boot tops. "It makes me smell blood again," he said, stretching his feet toward the fire. "It tempts me."

"To kill?"

He nodded, looked at the long rifle again. He reached for it, put his hand around the breech. "Like nobody knows." He lifted the gun, snapped it to his shoulder. His eyes grew wet looking down the barrel, until he squinted them shut. He put the Creedmoor across his lap. "I'd sooner hold the devil's pitchfork, but I guess I'd better get used to it in case we need it."

Correen added a branch to the fire. "How did it start, Mr. Wolverton? The killin'?"

The big man shrugged. "When I was a kid in Indian Territory, I got the idea I wanted to kill somebody one day. I don't know why. The Indian in me, maybe. Maybe the white man. Maybe the devil. I figured there wasn't any harm in it, as long as I picked somebody who deserved to die."

The water was steaming out of one boot, so he moved it a little farther from the fire.

"You went lookin' for someone to kill?"

"You might say so. A lot of outlaws in the territory then. Bounties on 'em. I went to Fort Smith, Arkansas, collected some Wanted posters, and went huntin'. I was seventeen when I killed my first outlaw. Tracked him to his camp. Waited for him to finish cookin' his biscuits and beans. Shot him in the back, then ate his supper."

"Just as you shot Dusty Sanderson?"

Wolverton sighed. "That was a couple of dozen corpses later, but it all led to that. The devil's work, and I enjoyed every second of it, and every drop of blood I spilt, till I shot the wrong man."

Correen shook her head as if annoyed at the big man. "How could you have made such a mistake?"

"Killin' had gotten casual with me," he said, his face staring blankly. "I got careless about it. Some ranchers had hired me to kill a rustler name of Giff Dearborn. I came across a fellow who looked like Giff from afar, but didn't even bother to get close enough to make sure. I just shot him in the back, and like Duval says, left him lay in his own fire, puttin' that cartridge shell in his hand. Later, when I found out I'd killed the wrong man, I finally saw myself for what I was."

They sat in silence beside the fire. Wolverton turned the rags draped over his boots until they had dried all over. Correen pitied him for some reason and yet admired him. She tried to hate him like Claude did, but couldn't.

Bob Steck began to snore.

"I didn't know Dusty, but he was my own personal savior," Lone Wolf finally said. "Just like Jesus, he died for my sins, so I could know what it really means to live. God bless his soul, and save mine. I'm a sinner, Correen. I'd go to hell if it wasn't for Jesus Christ and Dusty Sanderson."

She watched him wrap the rags back around his feet, working with nimble familiarity as a woman might tie up her hair. He tucked the loose corners in under his arches and caught her curious eyes. "California socks," he said, smiling. "The only kind I've ever worn."

She smiled as she rose. She fetched another branch for the fire, pausing to put her hand on Wolverton's shoulder. She didn't know why. She felt he needed it.

Hoofbeats came from downstream and Wolverton lifted the Creedmoor before he could recognize Claude on Casino. Correen pulled away from the big man, stroked back a strand of hair blowing across her face.

"You got friendly with that gun quick," the regulator said, pivoting on the stirrup. He had a piece of his shirttail wrapped around his right hand.

The new voice in camp woke Steck.

"Sorry," Lone Wolf said, lowering the long barrel. "Didn't know it was you."

"That's all right," Claude said, kicking Lone Wolf's boots aside so he could stand at the fire. "I know you wouldn't shoot a man who was lookin' you in the eye. That's not your style."

Correen's eyes scolded him for antagonizing the big man. "What's wrong with your hand?" she asked.

"Nothin'."

Steck sat up on the ground. "Then what the hell did you bandage it for?"

"I boogered it up a little, that's all. Anything to eat in this camp?"

"I'll make you somethin' after I doctor that hand," Correen said, taking him by the wrist. "Mr. Wolverton, will you fetch a pot of water to boil, please?"

"God A'mighty," Claude groaned. "You'd think I was sick as a thousand head of sheep."

Steck came to look at the hand as Correen unwrapped the dirty bandage. "Boogered it up a little, huh?" the Texan said. "I'd hate to see the booger."

Claude grimaced for several minutes as Correen cleaned the wound, pulling the loosened skin back and forth to examine it, getting every speck of dirt out. She boiled the bandages, dressed the wound in pork fat, and wrapped it again.

"Now I'll cook you a fine tightener," she said when she was done.

"Hell, I've lost my appetite."

"You'll get it back when you smell food. Try not to use that hand for several days. Keep your fingers straight, or you'll pull the wound open again."

"I'm afraid I can't do that, Correen," Claude said, trying to make a fist with his right hand.

"Why not?"

"Because we've got some horses to break."

TWENTY-TWO

ke Lafferty turned his horse into the corral and walked toward his front porch. The Laramie Plains felt stifling hot compared to the mountains where he had risen before dawn. He was tired of this, but it wasn't half over yet. He would be back in the saddle before noon.

"Emmett!" he shouted as he approached the house. "Emmett, where the hell are you?"

The foreman opened the front door and stepped out, a cup of coffee in his hand. "Howdy, boss," he said nervously. "You back?"

"Emmett, why in the hell are you sittin' around here this time of day, drinkin' coffee?" He stomped up onto the porch and glared at his top hand.

The foreman pointed his thumb over his shoulder and grinned sheepishly. "Sleepin' off a drunk," he said. "How did it go up there?"

"It didn't go worth a damn. They killed Wiloughby, the squaw, and one of the Sickle boys."

Emmett's jaw dropped. "Which one?"

"What damn difference does it make?"

"Frank owes me fifty dollars. Unless it was Clay, sayin' he was Frank. They'll do that sometimes, you know."

"Shut up, Emmett. Did a fellow named Wolverton ride through here after I left?"

"Yes, sir. Lone Wolf."

"Then why the hell didn't you and some of the boys ride up with him to help me?"

"You said when you left you could handle 'em better alone."

"That was before Wolverton joined 'em. You know who he is?"

"Yes, sir."

"Then why didn't you ride up with him and give me a hand?"

"Well, I didn't know exactly who he was at the time. He just said he was lookin' for Bob Steck to give him a message from Texas."

Lafferty put his hands on his hips. "But you know who he is now?"

"Yes, sir."

"How did you happen to find out who he was after he left?" the rancher asked, glowering, his head jutting forward on his neck.

"I told him," a voice said from the house. A stranger stepped onto the porch, a cup of coffee in one hand, a sweat-stained felt hat in the other. He stood about five-ten, spare, a balding scalp leaving an island of hair perched over his forehead. He seemed proud of it, having gathered it and combed it into a curl. His eyes seemed bottomless, like two cups of black coffee, sprouting red veins this morning. He wore a sheepskin vest, a revolver belted high on his hip, brown corduroys worn slick at the knees.

"Who are you?" Lafferty asked.

The stranger pressed his hat on the back of his head, leaving the lone curl in view. He shifted his coffee cup to his left hand. "Giff Dearborn," he said, thrusting his right hand toward the rancher. "It's my fault Emmett got drunk last night. I brought the whiskey."

Lafferty shook the man's hand, turning the name over several times in his head. "What brings you around here?"

"Lone Wolf."

"What do you want with him?"

Dearborn slurped his coffee. "A clean shot." He grinned.

Lafferty took his hat off and scratched his head, squinting at the stranger. Suddenly, the name engaged a cog in his memory. "You're the rustler Lone Wolf thought he killed when he shot Dusty Sanderson."

"That's right," Dearborn said. "Nothin' makes me madder than somebody shootin' me dead. Even if I don't turn out to be me."

Emmett laughed, sloshed his coffee, and rubbed at a deep piercing pain over his right eye.

Lafferty smirked. "Lone Wolf's got three others with him up there. All sure shots, even though one's a woman. I wouldn't go after 'em alone if I was you."

Dearborn shuffled his boots, looked far out across the Laramie Plains. "I couldn't help overhearin' what you were sayin' just before I stepped out. Sounds like your Snowy Range Gang has just about been wiped out."

"Snowy Range Gang?" Lafferty said.

"Emmett told me all about it last night," Dearborn explained. "His tongue gets looser the more he drinks."

Lafferty shot an angry glance at his foreman.

"Tell you what," Dearborn suggested. "You help me get Wolverton, and I'll help you with the other three. Then we'll put a new Snowy Range Gang together and take to tradin' stock."

Lafferty frowned, but inside his spirits lifted. He had not been looking forward to facing Wolverton, Duval, Steck, and the woman with just a handful of cowboys. Giff Dearborn looked like a godsend standing on his front porch, if God could send a devil. This Dearborn was no idiot blowhard like Wild Roy Wiloughby, but a serious customer with experience.

"You still carry a runnin' iron?" Lafferty said.

Dearborn licked his fingers and twisted the curl on his crown as if it were a mustache. "I haven't carried one in a few years, but I haven't forgot how to improve a brand with one, either. I could practice on those humpbacked bulls you've got out there."

"What kind of business have you been in lately?"

"Gravel."

"Huh?"

"Minin' it from boulders."

Emmett laughed. "He pulled the same one on me last night! Said he's been a *guest* of the state of Colorado."

"I had a damn fine position there," Dearborn said. "The state give me three square meals a day, though the squares was awful small, a suit of striped clothes, a blanket, a hammer, and even some jewelry to wear. But I decided to take my leave when I heard about Wolverton's pardon in Texas."

"He escaped," Emmett said, patting the outlaw on the shoulder. "Knocked a guard's head in with a sledgehammer, stole his horse, and rode hell for leather!"

"I just missed Wolverton in Texas," Dearborn added. "Trailed him up here."

Lafferty could not hold his grin back any longer. "Mr. Dearborn—Giff—I'm in need of a man like you. You help me clean Wolverton and his bunch out of my mountains, and I believe we can go partners in this territory."

"Well, then," Dearborn said, taking his hat off, "if you don't mind me invitin' you into your own house, why don't you tell me what we're up against over a cup of coffee." He kicked the door open, bowed, and gestured toward the doorway with his brim.

TWENTY-THREE

The afternoon sun shone into the canyon bright and warm where frost had sparkled this morning. Claude breathed a sigh of relief when he saw the barricade still intact, the mustangs milling nervously inside. The thought of the gray stallion coming back to rescue his mares had dogged him the whole time he was gone.

The wild horses stampeded around the bend to the head of the canyon when he began taking the section out of the barricade. After leading Casino in, he replaced the rails and brush, untied a lariat from his saddle string, and swung a loop in it. He rode up the left side of the canyon, the noose ready at his right leg.

When the lead mare saw him come around the bend, she tried to climb the canyon walls, her eyes rolling with fear. The other horses panicked, scattering. Claude let the mare with the foal run by, then spurred Casino to cut off the second mare, a sleek bay with a white face. He whirled his loop twice, threw it as the mare balked, saw it hit her neck and flip around her head.

The bay hit the end of the short lariat, tied fast to the saddle horn. Hemp stretched and leather squeaked, but everything held. Casino had the advantage in size and strength, turning his rump to the roped mare, pulling her toward the mouth of the canyon.

The other two horses stampeded down from the head of the canyon, and the lead mare hit the rope stretched between Casino and his catch. For a moment, Claude thought he would see a bad tangle, then the lead mare jumped, the rope catching her hooves and throwing her. She grunted as she hit, squealed, and jumped to her feet again, uninjured.

Claude tried to keep a tight rope on the bay, but she was dodging, trying to shake the loop around her throat. The twists of hemp whirred against pine saplings, the mare stupidly wrapping herself around every slender tree trunk that came between her and the big paint. Claude wondered how Little Crow had intended to handle this part, roping his wild horse afoot.

As he worked the mustang toward the mouth of the

canyon, tediously unwrapping her from trees, he saw the lead mare prancing along the barricade, gathering herself repeatedly for a jump she never took. He decided to avoid looking at her, afraid he would see her lead the other mares in escape. As Casino pulled the darting bay near the barricade, the other mustangs charged again toward the head of the canyon.

The bay would not go near the one tree Claude wanted her to wrap around—a sapling standing a few yards away from the pole fence. After several minutes of maneuvering, he finally forced his catch to wind herself around the trunk, with only a few feet of slack. She shook needles from the sapling, jerking against the rope.

Casino leaned against the lariat, keeping it tight, as Claude climbed down. He took an old rope from the cantle strings, tied a bowline in one end. He worked his way around to the side of the roped bay, tossed the bowline under her neck. Then he tossed the other end of the rope over her withers. Staying clear of her hooves, he moved around to her other side and gathered both ends of the rope he had tossed over and under her neck. He ran one end through the bowline on the other end and quickly drew the new noose tight.

This second rope Claude wrapped around one of the trees supporting Little Crow's barricade. He wrapped it low, three feet from the ground, taking just one turn around the tree before tying the rope off at a third tree.

The mare was roped twice now, tied to two different trees. Claude got back on Casino, spurred him forward a few steps, and untied the lariat from the saddle horn. It was his best rope, and he wanted to use it to catch the other horses. He let the mare pull away from the first tree, then got down and went to his second rope. Every time the bay took a step toward the fence, Claude took another foot of slack out of the rope. In a few minutes, he had her tied close to the fence. The fence would keep her from wrapping herself around a tree and strangling herself. The rope was wrapped low so that even if she fell, she wouldn't choke.

The mare seemed ready to die of fright when Claude reached through the fence to take his good lariat from her head. He spoke to her in a low voice, trying to calm her, but she rammed the fence several times before he could catch the loop and pull it over her ears.

He coiled his lariat and mounted Casino again. He hoped to have two more mares caught and tied by the time Correen and the others arrived on foot. The thought of her keeping company with Lone Wolf all this time bothered him. He had seen her hand on the big man's shoulder when he came back to camp. But it was probably better this way. He was doing something useful, carrying the fight against Ike Lafferty and his cutthroats. Lone Wolf wouldn't even agree to shoot at the bastards unless they shot first.

He had never thought of settling down with a woman before, but now it felt as if the idea had always been with him. He was going to bust up this Ike Lafferty bunch, get Steck's cattle back, and take up with Correen. He was thinking way ahead, and that wasn't good, but he couldn't help himself.

He was trotting back up the canyon when he felt Dusty Sanderson riding beside him—only a momentary lapse, but it felt as certain as if they had never been broken apart.

He had forgotten something: kill Wolverton.

TWENTY-FOUR

Claude was fighting the lead mare when the three hikers arrived at the mustang trap. He had decided not to rope the mare with the foal, thinking the little one might get in the way. The lead mare, older and more set in her ways, would prove ornery, but could be broken.

Wolverton crawled through the brush and roped the big mare a second time, using his lariat to draw the horse up to the fence. A third mare, a rather poor-looking claybank, was already tied some distance away.

"All right, you're such an expert," Claude said. "Show us how the Indians break 'em." He loosened the end of the rope from his saddle horn and dropped it.

"Looks like you know about as much as I do," Wolverton replied. "You started out like I would've." He looked over the lead mare for a minute or two, then walked to the other two horses, judging them. "I'll work the big one," he finally said. "Bob, you take that little claybank. Sabinal, you get the bay."

"I've told you not to call me that," Claude said, staking Casino to graze.

Steck plowed through the barricade, spooking the mares. "How come you give me the scrawny one?"

"For goodness' sake," Correen said, her voice knifing through the brush. "Stop bickerin' among yourselves and break the horses!" She began setting up a camp in the mouth of the canyon.

"She's right," Wolverton said. "Now, the first thing you do is get a second rope on your mare around the base of her neck. The safe way to do it is to tie a bowline in the end of a rope, throw it under her neck, and—"

"I know how to do it!" Claude snapped.

"I don't!" Steck said.

Wolverton helped the rancher get the second rope on the claybank. The little horse fought when the end of the rope flew over her withers, but she could go nowhere.

"Stay away from her feet, Bob," Wolverton said. "Especially those front ones. She'll put one over your shoulder before you know it and stomp you down." He watched Steck bend over to pick up the end of the rope, noticing that the old Texan's right knee wouldn't bend. That leg he had been favoring all day must be hurting bad.

Wolverton went back to the lead mare and picked up the rope lying on the ground beside her. Keeping the rope tight, he swung around behind the horse, letting the rope slap against her left shoulder, flank, and hip. The mare shied every time the rope touched her, pulling hard against the fence.

"They think that rope's gonna hurt 'em," he explained. "Just let 'em fight it for a while. They'll get used to it."

When the mare had settled down some, the big man let the rope sag along her back left leg and rub against her cannon and ankle. She kicked at it until she had stepped over it, then Wolverton drew it up tight between her thighs. The mare came near tearing the tree she was tied to out by the roots.

"You call this breakin' 'em?" Steck said. "Looks more like you're tryin' to loco 'em to me."

"She's just a little skittish," Wolverton said. "It's like somebody tyin' you up hand and foot and droppin' a chicken snake in your shirt. Drive you crazy for a few minutes, then you'd get used to it and could carry a snake in your shirt like a money belt if you wanted to."

Claude followed Wolverton's example with his white-face bay, laughing at the mustang's wild contortions with the rope between her legs.

"Now, keep the rope up high between her legs," Wolverton directed, "and swing back around to her neck." He showed them how, keeping the rope pulled tight around the back of the mare's left thigh. "Stick the end of your rope through the noose around her neck. Watch those hooves!" He pulled the rope end through and drew it tight, making a loop around the mare's back left leg.

"Now watch," he said. "Let the loop drop down to her fetlock, but keep it tight. When she steps or kicks, draw it tighter, pullin' her leg up off the ground." He hauled in the rope as he explained, cinching the mare's leg up several inches from her belly. "Pull hard," he said, gritting his teeth as he fought the rope, "because she'll try to kick and get a rope burn around the back of her ankle if you let the rope slip." He tied it off to the noose around her neck and turned to watch the other two men.

"Now, Bob," he said, "you don't have to watch out for those hooves anymore. She can't rear up to paw on just one back leg. Can't kick, either."

"The worst she can do now is fall on you, Bob," Claude added.

"I'll bet she can still bite, too."

"When you get a foot tied up," Wolverton said, "you two come on over here and we'll all three work 'em over real good one at a time. Grab a saddle and a blanket."

Claude brought the saddle and Steck limped over with the blanket.

"All right, Bob, I want you to start rubbin' the blanket all over her. Start on her neck and go easy, then get a little rougher. Then throw it on and off of her all over. Don't hurt her with it because I want her to learn that it won't hurt her, but work up to slappin' it against her until she's used to it."

Steck started rubbing the blanket on the shivering mare's neck.

"Duval, just pick that saddle up every now and then and drop it," Wolverton suggested. "Then flap it around a little."

"What are *you* gonna do?" Claude said. "Watch?"

"No, I'm gonna run a rope around her legs so she'll get used to that and won't panic if she ever gets tangled. Now, let's work her over real good."

For several minutes they rubbed the mare with the blanket, shook saddle and straps at her, ran ropes around her legs.

"Usually, you'd do all this to her one thing at a time," Wolverton said, "but we're hard up for time. She's no outlaw, anyway. She'll be all right." He backed off and threw his rope at her head, over her neck, over her back.

"You let that leg down and she's liable to turn outlaw," Steck said. He walked around her rump, rubbing the blanket on her, lifting it and letting it fall.

"Naw, she's fine," Wolverton replied. "I've seen 'em so bad you'd have to draw both legs up like that and throw 'em on the ground to work 'em. This old hoss ain't no trouble. Duval, press that saddle against her now, shake it around. Rub that cinch under her belly."

"I'm workin' up to that," Claude said.

In half an hour the big mare was covered with sweat, but she had stopped pulling against the rope tying her to the fence and was breathing easier.

"Bob, put the blanket on," Lone Wolf said. "Duval, you throw the saddle on and off a few times."

"Do it yourself," Claude said, dropping the saddle at Wolverton's feet. "I'm gonna get a bridle."

He walked down the fence to the place where he and Steck had pushed all the riding tack through the brush in the barricade. He picked up a bridle and looked for Correen through the gap in the brush. She had stretched a rope between two trees and thrown a tarp over it to make a tent, in case the weather turned wet again. He searched until he found her, climbing the northern canyon wall, a Winchester in her hand.

Claude grunted his approval and couldn't help grinning a little. That woman beat any he had ever seen, standing guard so the men could play with horses.

Wolverton had thrown the saddle on and off several times and was cinching it down when Claude got back with the bridle. Before climbing on, the big man put some weight on the saddle seat with his hands, then his elbows, finally pulling his feet off the ground. The mare pranced a little but couldn't move much with just three legs under her.

The big man stepped into the stirrup then and mounted as if the mare had been ridden a thousand times. She craned her neck and humped her back but was too tired to make trouble. Wolverton got down after just a few seconds, then got back on again. He stayed longer, shifted his weight. He climbed up and down a dozen times before he was through.

"Let's put that bridle on her," he said. "Then we'll let her foot down so she can rest, and go work with the others."

Claude eased the headstall over the mare's ears, slipped the bit between her teeth. She didn't like the feel of the metal in her mouth but could do nothing about it.

Claude removed the bridle reins so the mare wouldn't step on them and break them off, and Wolverton lowered her hind foot to the ground.

"She'll make a good mount," the big man said as they started toward the little claybank.

"If she'll rein," Steck said. "I don't know that a mustang will learn to rein in two days."

"That'll be a problem, but we'll train 'em as best we can," Wolverton said. He looked through the brush at the camp. "Where's Correen?"

"On the canyon rim, standing guard," Claude said. He stopped and looked toward the point of rocks above.

"I don't see her," Steck said, shading his eyes.

"You sure she's up there?" Wolverton added.

"I saw her headin' that way with a rifle."

They saw Correen rise from the rocks, wave at them, and disappear again. All three men waved back.

"That's a heck of a gal," Wolverton said, an admiring grin on his face.

Claude lowered his arm and glowered at the big man, his upper lip curling.

"Oh, hell," Steck groaned, catching the look on Claude's face. "All we need now is for you two short-trigger men to go sweet over the same damn woman."

TWENTY-FIVE

Sickle couldn't remember ailing a day in his life, ruling out hangovers. But now he had hot spells that made him sweat, chills that made him shiver. He felt stiff all over. He was tired of riding, looking. He wanted to roll up in a blanket and sleep. "I don't think he come this way," he said. "We've cut every trail headin' west, and there ain't a track one."

"Where else would he go?" Squaw Man said, leaning on his saddle horn. Early this morning, he had snuck near enough to the tepee under the Snowy Range to count heads. He had seen the woman at the fire, Wolverton and Steck drinking coffee. But Duval had slipped away in the night on the big paint stallion, and all trails were covered with melting slush. He had assumed that Duval was riding west to find help in North Park.

"Maybe we should split up," Sickle suggested. "I'll keep lookin' for his trail this way, and you go back to their camp, see if he came back. Hell, he may have just gone out for a scout." He pulled his coat tight around his neck, the chills coming on again, shivering him in his own sweat.

"Don't know where else he'd go," Squaw Man said. "Ain't nothin' to the south or north. He wouldn't go east, chance runnin' onto Ike."

"That's what I say!" Sickle growled. "Either I'll find his trail headin' west or you'll find him back at their camp."

Squaw Man shifted in the saddle, rubbed his chin. "All right, you look over here the rest of the day. If you find his tracks, go after him. If you don't, come back tomorrow and meet me where we camped last night."

Sickle nodded.

Squaw Man reined east and started back toward the Snowy Range. When he had gone, Sickle got down, unsaddled and hobbled his horse, rolled himself in a blanket, and went to sleep.

It was late in the afternoon when Squaw Man saw the tip of the meat pole through the treetops. He approached carefully but expected to find no living souls around the deserted camp of the old Snowy Range Gang. He heard hooves and turned to see the bremmer cattle grazing around two fresh graves.

As he sat in the saddle, wondering which grave held his squaw, he spotted the scaffold in the tree by the creek. Strange that they should bury her the Cheyenne way. Then he remembered hearing that Wolverton had some Indian blood. He must have done it out of some tribal superstition.

Trotting to the scaffold, he rode under it, took hold of a limb, and pulled himself up. His pocketknife cut the rawhide thongs around the old buffalo robe. He unwrapped the hide, found Strikes the Dog's eyes open, her mouth gaping. He tried to close them, but the corpse was rigid. He counted three bullet holes in her chest and many more places where buckshot had hit her. At least they hadn't hanged her.

An hour later, he reached the base of the Snowy Range, left his horse in a thicket of scrub oak, and began sneaking toward the tepee beside the lake. When it came into view over a ridge, he sat down to watch. It seemed abandoned, but he had to make sure.

He moved closer, thinking it might be a trap to lure him

into the open. He could imagine Wolverton waiting in the rocks across the lake, the long Sharps Creedmoor in his hands. It wouldn't be a difficult shot for an expert. Maybe four hundred yards. The bullet could go damn near through four sheep.

He stopped a couple of hundred yards away and studied the camp. Everything but the tepee was gone. Of course, they could have put everything inside to fool him. Maybe they were waiting inside themselves. He wanted badly to hike down there and see, but the thought of ambush held him back.

For several minutes he planned his approach. He would dodge from this tree to that, remaining shielded from shots fired across the lake. When he had every step memorized, he skulked closer, holding his rifle ready before him.

The last ten paces were the most dangerous. Nothing to shield him as he ran to the entrance hole of the lodge. But the flap was open, and he could see inside. He sprinted across the open ground and leaped in.

A few blankets. An iron pot. Some unused firewood. Cool ashes. They had taken everything they could carry on their backs. Had Duval stranded them? No, not the sort. He remembered the regulator risking his life to cut the Indian boy loose yesterday.

He sat down to think. Yesterday he had watched from a distance as they hauled their saddles up from the outlaw camp below. Now the saddles were gone. Why would they carry their saddles on their backs unless they expected to get some horses somewhere?

The vision of the steel-gray stallion galloped across the hide wall of the lodge. Squaw Man remembered finding the trap the Ute boy had built in the canyon to the north. Strikes the Dog had planned to use it to catch the wild horses after making the boy her slave. Were they going to try to ride wild horses out of the mountains?

Squaw Man stepped out of the tepee, looking for tracks, oblivious to the thought of ambush now. He found footprints along the lake at the base of the Snowy Range. Long strides in a straight line. They knew where they were going and wanted to get there quick. The tracks pressed deep in the mud, even the woman's, though she couldn't have weighed over a hundred pounds by herself. They were carrying heavy loads. Steck was limping. Maybe he really had injured his leg jumping from the bluff yesterday morning. Something had dragged beside him here. A cinch buckle?

Yes, he had them figured now. Duval had ridden around the Snowy Range in the night, then headed north to find the mustang trap. The others had followed this morning on foot. They were desperate for horses.

He turned back for his mount. He would find them tomorrow, see how they had fared with the mustang trap, then ride to warn Lafferty. He wouldn't let them get away. He wanted them alive. He wanted to know which one had killed his woman.

Sickle woke in the middle of the night, suffocating. He sat up, gasping for breath as if someone had knocked his wind out in his sleep. But he was alone. He had dreamed of nothing but blackness. A chill shivered him. Then he felt the call. Neither name nor voice, but a cool grip, a tortured plea.

He found his horse nearby, put the bridle on, took the hobbles off. He saddled up and rode.

At dawn he reached the abandoned outlaw camp, his head throbbing with pain, his skin burning as if scalded. Somehow, he knew where to look, finding two mounds, rock-covered, marked with sorry crosses. He fell on one and raked the dirt and rocks back until his hands were bleeding. Day broke as he felt a handful of cloth and hauled up with all his strength, unearthing the body. The light of day struck his face as he unwrapped the death shroud.

It was like finding his own corpse, robbing his own grave. The crick in his neck knifed him with new pain, and his limbs stiffened. He looked up and saw the humpbacked cattle in a line, staring at him, their short black horns jutting. He was tired, cold in his own sweat, weak. He lay down beside the body of his brother and went to sleep.

TWENTY-SIX

Claude rode the bay mare back to the fence Little Crow had built, pulling wide on the reins to turn the green-broke mount. "Hell, she didn't hardly buck at all," he said, his boots hitting the ground. The mustang wore streaks of lather from the thirty-minute ride.

Wolverton was sitting on Casino, ready to chase down the bay had she thrown Duval. "I figured the lead mare for the worst outlaw," he said.

"That explains the fact of her landin' you on your ass," Steck said, chuckling. He was throwing his saddle on and off of the scrawny claybank. "I think this one's ready now. She don't even flinch anymore when this old kack lands on her."

"Then get on," Claude suggested.

Steck cinched the saddle down, mounted and dismounted several times. "Yeah, she's ready. Poor thing's already plumb wore out."

He untied the rope around her back left foot, letting her get four hooves under her. Claude removed the rope from the mare's head and held her by the ears as Steck climbed once more into the saddle.

"Let her buck!" the old rancher said.

Claude released the mare's head and backed away, but she merely stood there, spraddle-legged, confused.

"Touch her with the spurs," Wolverton said. "Not hard."

When she felt the steel against her ribs, the pony flinched and took a few awkward steps. Steck poked her again, and she began to walk. "Look at that!" Steck shouted over his shoulder. "By God, a three-year-old could ride this hoss!"

Wolverton followed on Casino. "See if she'll stop."

The Texan pulled back on the reins. "Whoa," he said, and the mare stopped, twisting her head against the bit in her mouth. "This ain't no mustang," he said. "That silver stud must have stolt this mare from a farm somewhere."

Claude picked up a rock. "If you want her to buck, Bob, I can oblige you."

Steck started the mare walking again. "I didn't say that." He rode the claybank slowly, a hundred yards up the canyon. "I can feel her humpin' her back all up. What do you reckon that means?"

Wolverton was following on Casino. "Hard to say. See if she'll rein."

Steck pulled the right rein wide and the claybank followed the bit in her mouth. "I'm tellin' you she's been rode before," he said.

"Her back still humped up?"

"No, she quit that. This is some kid's saddle horse, Lone Wolf." He put the spurs to her ribs, and the claybank leaped forward, trotting toward the barricade.

"Looks like you got shortchanged," Claude shouted as the horse and rider came toward him. "Want to ride mine next time?"

"Hell, no," Steck said, nonchalantly drawing his reins. "I generally hire boys to buck out my horses. This little nag suits me just—"

The claybank jerked her head down between her front

legs, kicked her hind legs, twisted, sent Steck flying, then went to hopping around the canyon on all fours.

Claude brought his knee up, slapped it, and laughed as Wolverton chased down the claybank on Casino. The regulator helped the stiff-legged rancher to his feet. "What happened to your saddle horse, Bob?"

"She jumped astraddle of her head and like to broke in two, damn her. Bring her back over here, Lone Wolf, and let me settle the score!"

Wolverton led the claybank back to Steck, and Claude grabbed her by the ears to keep her still. The rancher mounted again, swinging his stiff right leg over the cantle.

"All right, Sabinal, let her go."

The claybank ducked her head again, but this time Steck was ready. He leaned back in the saddle and fought her head with the reins. She whirled, bowing her neck to the left, kicking her hind legs to the right. With his right leg in pain, the Texan had trouble hooking his knees under the swells of the saddle, and he lost his right stirrup. The mare seemed to sense it and jumped to the left, dumping the rider.

Claude helped Steck up from the ground again. "That bum leg's foulin' you up, Bob. Let me buck her out for you."

"Like hell. Bring her back, Lone Wolf!"

Wolverton led the claybank back to Steck, smiling. "Before you get on again, I want to show you a trick," he said, getting down from Casino. He fetched a piece of old rope from the fence and tied one end of it to the ring on the left side of the claybank's bridle bit. "Now, you run this rope up the bridle and through the headstall," he said, threading the rope as he explained. "Then you take the rope back to the saddle horn, wrap it around once, and go back to the other side of the bridle."

He threaded the rope down the right side of the bridle, as he had come up the left side. Then he tied the end to the right-hand ring in the bit and cut the excess rope off. "We'll use this piece to make sure that loop doesn't slip off the saddle horn." He tied the leftover length of rope just in front of the horn, securely linking the bridle and saddle together.

"The bit will keep her from duckin' her head too low," Wolverton explained. "Somebody's grandmother could ride her now."

Steck smirked at the strange bridle rig but put his foot in the stirrup to try again. "I ain't nobody's grandmother, but I'll try, anyway."

Claude gave the claybank her head, and she attempted a buck but pulled up short and stood testing the new restraint. Steck spurred her, and she kicked a little but couldn't put much into it with her head trussed up.

"That knee's botherin' him worse than he lets on, ain't it?" Wolverton said as Steck rode away on the mustang.

"He wouldn't complain if it was busted clean off," Claude replied. He heard the big man chuckle and started to smile himself but remembered whom he was talking to.

TWENTY-SEVEN

Claude sucked bacon grease from the fingers of his left hand as Correen inspected his right. At least this time she had waited until after he ate before she went to poking at his wound.

"Your fingers are a bit puffy, Mr. Duval." She unbuttoned his sleeve and rolled it up. Turning his wrist up, she found the beginnings of a red streak reaching toward his elbow. "It's infected." She pursed her lips and began removing the bandage.

"I'll get some more water to boil," Wolverton said, leaving camp with a small pot.

When he returned from the creek, the big man had the pot in one hand, a bundle of greenery in the other. "Try this," he said to Correen. "Mash the leaves and stems up together and make a poultice."

"What is it?" Correen asked, taking the plants from Wolverton.

"Wild lettuce."

Claude smirked. "What makes you think that'll help?"

"Horse bit me one time in New Mexico," Lone Wolf said, rubbing his shoulder as if the injury still hurt. "Got infected. Some old medicine woman wrapped it up in some of that wild lettuce. Cleared it up overnight."

Claude rolled his eyes. "Hell, throw some lizard tails and snake tongues in with it." He winced as Correen poked a tender spot on his wound. It was an ugly mess today, red and swollen.

"It couldn't make anything worse," she said, "and might help."

"I wouldn't pass judgment on those old Mexican herb women, Sabinal," Steck said. "One time I was down south of San Antonio buyin' stock to take up the trail, and I got a big ol' boil on my . . ." He rubbed his rear end and glanced toward Correen. "Well, I couldn't ride, it hurt so bad. But this old herb woman down there sold me a mess made of mashed-up pokeberries and red oak bark. By golly, it drew that boil to a head overnight, and I went on about my business."

"I know a thing or two about home remedies myself," Claude argued. "One time up in North Texas, one of the boys got snake-bit. One feller said to put coal oil on it, and another said gunpowder, so they doubled up and put both, and I mean a bunch of it, too. That night the boys built a fire out of some old cedarwood, and you know how that stuff pops when it burns. Well, a spark jumped out of the fire and blew the boy's whole leg off."

"Oh, my Lord," Correen said.

"Kill him?" Steck asked.

"Didn't have to. He was already dead from the snakebite."

Steck broke into laughter.

"Sounds like a tall tale to me," Wolverton said. "Did you see this happen?"

"No, but I talked to some boys that did. It was up on the Four Sixes." He drew his watch just far enough from his vest pocket for a glance.

Correen put the water on to boil and began crushing the wild lettuce.

"You know how the Four Sixes got its name?" Steck asked.

"Poker game," Claude answered, pulling his whiskey flask out with his free hand.

"Now, that is puredee bull . . ."

As they argued, Claude unstoppered his flask and turned it upside down over his mouth. "Correen, didn't you find some whiskey in that outlaw camp?"

"Aye." She dipped a bandage from the boiling water with a knife blade.

"What did you do with it?"

"Didn't I pour it out?" she said, smiling smugly at the regulator.

"Damn," Steck said. "I didn't know a Scot could make a temperance fanatic."

"Maybe that's why they ran her out of the old country," Claude suggested. "Ouch!" he said, taking a jab in the back of his hand.

"Sorry," Correen said, smiling as she arranged the crushed herbs on the wound. "Mr. Wolverton, when will the horses be ready? We wouldn't want to get discovered and pinned down in this canyon."

"They're ready now," Lone Wolf said.

She looked up at him in amazement. "You're not serious."

"Yes, ma'am, I am. You saw us ride 'em this mornin', didn't you? Claude didn't even get thrown. We'd better finish 'em out on the trail if they're gonna be any use to us against Ike and his boys."

"Does that mean you're ready to fight?" Claude asked.

"Like I said before, I'll fight to protect myself or my friends."

"Don't count me as one of 'em," Claude said. He looked into Correen's eyes as she finished tying the bandage around his hand. She was disappointed in him, but what did she expect?

Steck started laughing, slapping his good knee, his guffaws echoing across the narrow canyon.

"What's so damn funny?" Claude demanded.

"I just got a picture of myself ridin' that green claybank through an outlaw gang, tryin' to draw enemy fire so we can get Lone Wolf, here, to fight. I'll eat horse dung if this ain't the damnedest fix I ever got myself into!"

TWENTY-EIGHT

Claude squatted to study the elk sign on the ground, finally feeling relaxed after the long ride on the newly broken horse. His Marlin rested across his thighs, and a long shank of hair dangled from his hat as he pushed his fingers into one of the tracks. Two young bulls, trotting for cover, last night or this morning.

This was what he had come to Wyoming for. To hunt game, not outlaws. Life sure took its little twists.

"I need practice," the voice said behind him.

Claude looked back toward camp to find the long barrel

of the Creedmoor propped on the big man's shoulder. He shook his head. "It'll give our position away."

"I know, but I haven't shot long-range in years. I need to brush up in case I have to use this thing. The mustangs are likely gun-shy, too. We'd better get 'em used to shootin'."

Steck limped up beside Wolverton. "He's got two good points, Sabinal." He was dying to see Lone Wolf use the old Sharps.

Claude scratched his itchy beard and looked at Correen, as if to ask her opinion, but she simply looked away from him and went back to her camp chores. "All right," he said. "Take a few shots before it gets dark." He took it as a good sign. Maybe Wolverton was feeling the urge to fight now.

Their camp was eight miles up Rock Creek from Little Crow's mustang trap. They had left the canyon after dinner, riding their green mounts up a crooked trail, training them to rein at every bend. Now the Snowy Range was again in view, bathed in the reds and pinks of a falling sun.

The mustangs had been tied to a stout rope stretched between two trees and were also hobbled to further discourage escape. The men had found it necessary to tie a foot up when hobbling the lead mare, but now she stood resigned with the others, worn out from the day's work.

"I'll get a couple of hundred yards away from the horses for the first shot," Lone Wolf said, "then I'll move closer. The three of you had better stay with 'em to calm 'em down after I shoot."

"What are you gonna shoot at?" Claude asked.

Wolverton's eyes swept the valley to the north. "That dead pine on that little bluff." He pointed a steady finger on the end of a gangling arm. "That'll be about three hundred yards for the first shot, then four hundred, then five hundred. I'll be satisfied if I can hit it in the middle at five hundred."

"I'd be satisfied if I could just see it good," Steck said, squinting. "I hope some of Ike's boys are watchin' and see you hit it. That'll put the fear in 'em."

"And let 'em know we've got mounts now, too," Claude said. "I had planned that for a surprise."

Wolverton marched two hundred yards downstream and lay down on his stomach. Claude could see him adjusting the rear sight for range and throwing sand in the air to judge windage. The marksman settled in behind the graceful stock and lay like a fallen statue for several long seconds.

The long barrel spouted black smoke. The pine on the bluff splintered chest-high. The blast hit like nearby thunder, electrifying the horseflesh tied at the hitching rope.

"Easy," Claude said to his bay mustang, stroking the shivering horse on the neck. Steck scratched his claybank, and Correen handled the lead mare. Casino, picketed nearby, merely looked up, grass sticking out of his mouth.

Wolverton strolled closer to camp and lay down again. He made his adjustments for the longer shot, aimed, and slammed another bullet into the dead tree.

He opened the breech to let the long rifle cool as he walked into camp for the third try. He stood and looked at the target for a moment, his face intense. He made a minute adjustment on the long-range sight. Reaching into his pocket, he removed a cartridge and slid it into the breech. He sank to his knees as if ready to pray. Then he lowered himself to his belly and put the rifle against his shoulder.

The blast made the mustangs pull against their ropes, but they fought less now than when the first shot came from down the valley. Chunks sprayed from the dead tree, over a quarter mile away.

Steck gave his claybank a good pat on the neck. "By golly, Lone Wolf, you'll do if we can get you to shoot!"

Claude grunted. "Five hundred yards ain't nothin'. Billy

Dixon knocked an Indian off a horse from a mile away at the Battle of Adobe Walls."

"Not quite a mile," Wolverton said, leaning the Creedmoor across a saddle seat. He turned his back, walked away from the gun, and sat on the ground, seemingly exhausted. "About seven-eighths of a mile."

"How do you know?" Claude asked. "Were you there?"

"No. But I went back there with Dixon the year after the battle. He showed me where he was when he shot, and where the Indian fell. I measured it with a wagon wheel. It was short of a mile."

"Back during the war," Steck said, "a Union sharpshooter wounded one of our generals from a mile away. Got him when he stepped out of his tent."

"Captain John Metcalf," Lone Wolf said. "Now, that was a shot of true skill."

"I heard about that," Claude replied. "That Yank had a bunch of soldiers build him a platform to shoot off of, had him a surveyor's transit to find the range, even had a telescope on his rifle. Billy Dixon's shot was better. He didn't have any of that crap. He just drew on experience and Kentucky windage and let her rip."

"But it wasn't skill," Wolverton said. "Dixon himself told me it was nothin' but a scratch shot. It ended the battle, though. I didn't think about it back then, but I believe now that the Good Lord had a hand in that shot. He dwells upon battlegrounds as well as in churches."

Claude scoffed as he came to stand over the big man. "He don't dwell in hell where you're goin'."

Correen jabbed the regulator with an armful of wood she was carrying into camp.

"My savior goes with me wherever I wander, no matter the danger."

Claude rolled his eyes, walked across camp, and collapsed on a saddle blanket.

"I don't know, Lone Wolf," Steck said. "I fought with Terry's Texas Rangers in the war, and I saw some scraps a fellow like that wouldn't get within earshot of."

"A fellow like what?" Wolverton said.

"You know, always prayin' and kneelin' down. A man on his knees wouldn't last long in some of the tight places I've seen."

"You talkin' about Jesus?"

Steck nodded.

Wolverton chuckled and shook his head. "You don't understand who Jesus Christ was. He could get riled and ornery as you, Bob, when he wanted to."

"Like when?" Steck said.

"Like in Jerusalem that time the Good Book tells about. Jesus walked in there one day—he was sort of a circuit preacher then—and he found a lot of people tradin' and swappin' money around the church."

Lone Wolf's eyes caught a spark from the air, and he pulled himself up to a squatting position. "Now, the likes of this church—the Temple, they called it—was somethin' we don't see much of out here in the territories. It was about eight or nine hundred years old, made of stone, cedar, and cypress. Had gold angels in it and bronze columns on the front porch. And all around it was a wall that closed in, I'd say, five or six acres." He spread his arms, indicating the valley floor around him, and his eyes looked as though they could conjure the Temple there.

"If you've ever seen the Palace of the Governors in Santa Fe, or any of them old missions down in San Antone, well, maybe it looked kind of like that. Anyway, Jesus walks in there one day, and here's all these horse traders makin' deals. Now, over here was a herd of sheep," he said, pointing at nothing up the valley. "And over yonder, a big bunch of oxen—maybe fifty yokes of 'em. Another fellow was sellin' doves up against a wall over there. There was manure all over the place, and a lot of folks went barefoot back then."

Correen laughed at Wolverton as the big man stood and shook a foot.

"All this riled Jesus, goin' on in the shadow of the church like that, because these were some rough characters, and the brands on some of the stock was still scabbed over. But the thing that really twisted his tail was the money changers. They had all different kinds of money back then—like we've got dollars and pesos down on the border—and these money changers would swap the different kinds for a cut. And they were generally considered a no-'count bunch of thieves."

Taking immense strides across the campground, Wolverton snatched up a coiled length of rope and unwound it. "Now, Jesus was good with his hands, so he got him some rope and built a whip right quick. He was a carpenter most of his life, so he had a good grip and a strong arm. He galloped into the Temple with his whip—riled like all get-out—and stampeded a herd of sheep."

Lone Wolf whistled the rope around his head and popped it at Claude's heels, causing the mustangs to lunge against the hitching line. "You never heard the likes of blattin' sheep as when he got 'em runnin'. Then he got into a mess of oxen and scattered 'em, and they started the jackasses goin', and busted open the doves' cages, and you'd have thought ball lightning was bouncin' on their rumps the way all them critters lit out of there.

"But Jesus still hadn't got it out of his craw, so he waded in with the money changers and knocked over all their jars of different kinds of money. Then he went to throwin' tables around. Kicked a stool out from under the ol' boy hawkin' the doves. And like I say, these were rough characters, but they got out of the Temple, all right, and the folks who needed to get in there to go to church came in."

Wolverton laughed as he coiled the rope. He shook his head. "Lordy, what a sight . . ."

Claude hated thinking it, but he wanted to hear the big man go on. Then he looked at Correen, saw her lively eyes smiling at Lone Wolf, and got mad.

"Didn't they have law back then?" Steck asked. "Didn't they get after him?"

The smile dropped from Lone Wolf's face. "Oh, they got after him, all right. Yes, Bob, in the end they sure got after him. Nailed him to that cross."

Claude hissed. "That's almost as bad as shootin' a feller in the back and lettin' him burn in his own fire."

TWENTY-NINE

Dusty used to call it a rustler's moon. Bright enough to steal cattle by; too dark to shoot by. Claude watched it slide down the ragged silhouette of the Snowy Range, remembering, listening to the sounds of the night.

He never understood men who dozed off standing night guard. Too much going on. Owls sailing between the trees on silent wings. Wolves howling. Deer stamping alarms to each other. Birds calling. Here the wind rustled pine needles and the creek pulled its waters noisily down the valley. He trusted his ears in this light.

The three mustangs were still, sleeping on their feet, he supposed. How did they do that? Casino's white rump and withers glowed faintly in the meadow nearby. Bob Steck's snore rattled from his bedroll.

Then it came: a single thud somewhere up the slope, in the timber. Casino heard, too. The sparse moonlight caught his mane as his head rose high. Man and horse listened.

Claude hooked his thumb over the hammer of the Marlin. Casino tossed his head.

Nothing happened, so they relaxed, Claude settling back against a lodgepole pine, Casino cocking his hip as his head drooped again.

What followed came through the air first, like a wheezing scream, then through the very bedrock of the mountain: a drumroll of hooves. Branches snapped as the wild gray stallion came down for his mares, grunting anger with every stride. He burst into the open, a wayward shadow.

Casino lurched to cut the gray off but hit the end of his picket rope. The mustang charged across the clearing and screamed in the ears of his mares. In the night they looked like a single fantastic beast, the claybank's head and neck rising above the withers of the bay, the gray pawing at the ropes. The line they were tied to shook the two trees like a twister would whip a weed, and their shrill voices split the night air.

"Hey!" Claude shouted, running for the string of mounts. "Get the hell out of here!" He growled and hissed, spooking the tethered mares worse than the gray stud. They broke one end of their rope away from a tree and fought each other for freedom. The lead mare reared, got her leg over the claybank's back. Claude saw a wreck coming, then he heard Casino's charge.

The big paint had pulled his picket pin out of the ground and was coming with his head low like a stalking cat. The gray wheeled away from the mares to meet him. They rushed together like a couple of locomotives, dodging each other's teeth, slamming their shoulders together.

The bay mare was on the ground now and trying to get up under the claybank, tangling her rope around the feet of the others.

Both stallions reared and traded blows with sharp

hooves, the paint's white patches bobbing like fragments of glowing fury. Claude froze, awed by their screams, a tingle pricking the back of his neck.

"Stop them!" Correen said, her warm hand touching his.

Claude put the Marlin to his cheek. "I can't see the sights!" he cried. He felt Steck and Wolverton step up beside him.

The stallions reared and pawed again, the gray tangling his feet in Casino's halter rope, jerking the paint forward, off balance. The wild one came down on the paint's neck, biting him on the withers. Casino's scream grew to a roar.

"Frighten him away!" Correen said.

"Not now. They're tangled!"

Casino whirled out from under the gray, spinning in a blur of white streaks. The halter rope tightened around the gray's front hooves and jerked him down, then the paint's heels stomped the broad gray flank and the wild stallion rolled.

Claude sensed a skirmish at his side and turned to see Correen drawing Bob Steck's knife from his belt scabbard. She ran toward the melee in the clearing, past the tangle of tethered mares, into the storm of flying hooves.

"Correen!" Claude yelled, running after her.

As the gray rolled to his feet, Casino kicked again, catching the wild stallion on the shoulder. The rope tightened between them for an instant, then the gray charged, jabbing the paint behind the ears with his sharp front hooves, hobbled though they were by the tangled rope. Casino ducked, snapped his teeth at gray flesh.

Correen rushed between them as they braced for another clash. She grabbed Casino's halter and sawed at the rope. Both horses reared, and the woman rose from the ground between them. Claude raised the rifle, but the gray circled behind Casino. Their hooves cut the air all around Correen.

A frayed rope end flew as the horses parted. Correen let the knife fall and clung to Casino's halter, swinging like a rag doll in the hand of a galloping child. The gray shadow bucked and screamed, snapping at the rope tangled around his forelegs.

Claude caught the paint first, adding his weight to Correen's on the halter. When the stallion quit pulling, Claude cocked his Marlin and turned on the gray. The wild horse had kicked his feet free of the tangled rope and was bolting for the timber. Claude swung the barrel around on him as he faded behind branches and tree trunks. He let three slugs fly but heard the gray continue up the slope. There was silence, then a defiant scream, and the hoofbeats faded.

Steck and Wolverton calmed the mares, the three horses on their feet now, but still tangled, pulling nervously against one another.

"You all right?" Claude said, his hand taking the halter beside Correen's.

"Aye," she said. "I think so."

"What kind of damned fool thing was that to do?"

She saw his eyes glaring in the moonlight and tossed her hair back. "Someone had to do something. I could see you weren't going to."

"You have no idea what I was gonna do!" he shouted. "You could have got your pretty little head kicked clean off of your shoulders!"

"But I didn't, did I?"

"By the damnedest luck I've ever seen!"

"I'm not afraid of horses, Mr. Duval, and I'm not afraid of you."

Claude felt warm blood under his palm as he touched Casino's withers. "Look here. Those hooves could have laid your hide back just like this." He soothed the heaving stallion as he checked for more wounds.

"My hide is tougher than you think," she argued. "And my head on tighter than—"

Claude grabbed her by the arm and shushed her. "You hear that?"

They stood for a couple of seconds, then heard the crazed roar of the gray again, somewhere up the mountain.

"What the hell is he doin' now?" Claude asked.

Two shots cracked, not a mile away, and echoed across the valley. A third rang out, giving Claude a bearing.

"Somebody's up there," he said. "One of Ike's boys. Get my bridle, Correen!"

THIRTY

Squaw Man looked over his rifle barrel at the huge gray hulk of horseflesh on the ground. "Damn," he said. It had taken three bullets to bring the beast down, still twitching now with the last quivers of life. He would have killed the stallion with one shot if he could have seen his sights. But three. He knew they would be coming after him now.

After all, hadn't he located them before dark by the three shots from the Creedmoor? In fact, he had peeked over the ridge in time to see Lone Wolf fire the last volley, splintering a dead tree five hundred yards away. He had seen the mustang mares tied at the hitching rope. He had retreated a mile or so and made a dry camp, no fire. He would ride in the morning to warn Lafferty that the enemy had horses.

But this gray stallion had ruined everything. The old boy had turned killer, crazed by the loss of his harem. He had come to kill Squaw Man's gelding, frightening the mount so badly that he had pulled his pin from the ground to run for the timber.

The sound of hooves thumped in the dark forest, the picket rope whirring against a tree trunk. "Come on, boy," Squaw Man said, stepping away from the dead stallion. He whistled and clucked his tongue. He heard the hooves circle his clearing, the gelding unsure. He bent and pulled grass, that the horse might hear him and come to eat a handful.

Now a tree shook in the darkness and the gelding grumbled in confusion.

"Whoa, boy," Squaw Man said. The picket rope was tangled: a stroke of luck. He had to saddle up and run. They would be here any minute. Maybe not all of them, but certainly one. Probably the one called Duval, on his big paint stallion. The others wouldn't want to ride the green mounts in the dark if they could help it.

He spotted the movement in the trees and ran forward. "Easy, boy," he said, his voice lending comfort to the horse. He cut the picket rope and led the mount back to camp at a trot. Hoofbeats were coming already as he grabbed his bridle. Should he stay and fight? No, too dark to see his target in this moonlight. Too close to the enemy camp. Run now, fight in the morning.

He threw the blanket on with one hand, the saddle with the other, fumbled with the cinch as the hoofbeats approached. Duval had good ears. Coming on a beeline. This was going to be close. He jammed his Winchester in the saddle scabbard, buckled his gun belt around his waist, left his bedroll on the ground, and mounted. He jabbed the gelding with his spurs and headed south at a dead run.

Casino planted his hooves and shied when he smelled the stallion, almost wrenching Claude from the saddle. The regulator saw the gray hulk on the ground and drew a revolver. Above the creaking of his own saddle leather, and Casino's heaving for air, he heard the retreating hooves.

Searching the black horizon, he glimpsed the rider against the stars, going over a ridge. He slid his pistol back into its holster and spurred the paint.

At a gallop, the trail was barely visible in the moonlight. He gave Casino his head, leaning low over the mane to avoid tree branches. He topped the ridge the rider had crossed before him, straining to see ahead. Down the grade, the trail opened up into a big park, and at the far side he saw a hint of motion. Nothing more than a shadow flitting into blackness. Still a quarter mile ahead. He knew Casino had the scent now and braced himself for a long run.

He rode until the chase had taken him almost due east of the Snowy Range. Another mile south, and he would fall into the shadow of the pinnacles where not even the rustler's moon would light his way. He ducked his head to keep some limbs from whipping his face and cut his own path down a timbered slope.

He was beginning to think Casino had lost the trail when he caught another glimpse of the rider, struggling to get up a steep grade strewn with deadfalls. He reined in for a look at the terrain. Something compelled him to look west, toward the Snowy Range, into the moonlight, and there he saw the unexplainable.

The sacred Indian bulls stood in a line on the ridge, staring down at him, and the moon revealed a clear path snaking up to them. It would take him out of his way but would prove easier to negotiate than the one the outlaw had chosen.

Claude turned the paint west, spurred him to a gallop. He pulled his hat low over his brow to keep the feeble moon rays from shining directly into his eyes. Reaching high ground, the regulator looked around for the bulls, but they had vanished.

He turned south again and saw the rider pass over the divide ahead of him. Much closer now. Maybe two hundred yards. He had made up a lot of ground, and Casino was probably less winded than the outlaw's horse, who had fought the steeper slope and the fallen trees in his path.

As he leaned back into the chase, he glanced behind him for the bremmers. They had been standing there bigger than life. But, now . . . Gone.

Squaw Man unlimbered his quirt when he saw the big paint almost within shooting range behind him. He would stick to the downhill runs now. He wasn't really sure where he was, looking over his shoulder like this, letting his mount choose the path. Did he know this meadow? That bluff? Hard to say in the dark. And it was getting darker, too. Riding into the shadow of the Snowy Range.

He wasn't lost, of course. The high rocky pinnacles were sure landmarks. But exactly what lay around the next bend or over the next rise—he could not say.

He glanced back again. Damn! Duval making an all-out effort now, wanting to end this thing before they ran into the darkest corner of the range. He looked up at the peaks, haloed by moonlight.

"Stop!" the voice said from behind. "I'll shoot, dammit!"

Shoot at what? The noise? The night? The report came and Squaw Man lay low in the saddle. Damn, he *was* shooting! He looked back, saw a muzzle blast as the next round came. He drew his pistol and fired back, aiming by instinct at the powder flare.

What a ride! He looked ahead, grinning at darkness. His eyes opened wide but he could see nothing. He trusted his mount. The old gelding was still a little spooked—rattled by the gray stallion—but he knew this range well enough. Squaw Man had to trust him to smell the way.

He fired back at another muzzle blast, then heard a bullet sing against a boulder at his side. Duval homing in on him. This wasn't working. Maybe he should stop and fight. Yes, hand-to-hand. See how the Texan fared at close quarters in the dark. The next piece of good ground he found, he would stop.

Keep riding south. Get the moon in view again. Choose your ground. Too dark here. Darker than a cat could see in. The pony running downhill. The stars like jewels in the sunlight.

Duval fired again, but Squaw Man ignored him. Don't give the Texan a target to shoot at. He couldn't see his horse's ears, but this place felt familiar. He looked up at the Snowy Range. Yes, he recognized the silhouette from this angle. What was this place? He rode blind but felt the terrain around him.

The horse grunted, then Squaw Man smelled it, too. Death. Stinking, rotting death. He remembered Wild Roy with the Creedmoor: four dead sheep. The Indian boy, the bleating voices.

Rocks clattered under his pony's hooves, and the stench welled up around him, sticking like lard in his throat. The odor stung his eyes, useless though they were.

Like a shot he found his place on the mountain, visualized every roll and swell. He jerked back on the reins, but too late. The hooves were silent under him, the great odor engulfing him. He remembered rimrocking the sheep with Wild Roy. He remembered their frightened, bulging eyes and felt his own mocking them. He remembered the way they kicked as they fell, and he flailed his feet free of the stirrups. He remembered their voices and heard them again. "Squaw Maaaan!" Louder now, as he fell to join them. He screamed in terror as the wind roared up at him. It was dark, but he saw them all clearly: looking up at him, their tongues lolling out, voices calling his name.

"Squaw Maaaan! Squaw Maaaan!"

THIRTY-ONE

U h-oh," Steck said, looking expectantly down at the claybank between his legs.

"What's wrong?" Wolverton asked.

"She's got her back all humped up again. I'd say we've got about thirty seconds before she turns herself inside out."

Wolverton flanked the claybank on the left, riding the big lead mare. Correen moved to the right on Claude's bay mustang.

They had worried all night about the far-off gunshots they heard after Claude rode out in the dark. When the regulator failed to return by daybreak, Correen had insisted on riding, though she would have to mount a green-broke horse. They had found Squaw Man's camp and were following the trail of the chase at a trot, a mile into it now, expecting the claybank to start bucking any second.

The mare suddenly stretched her neck and kicked her hind legs straight back. The rig running from the saddle horn, through the head-stall, and to the bit kept her from getting her head down low enough to really buck, but she compensated by rearing and whirling. Steck held his seat until the mare threatened to fall over backward on him, then he bailed out and lost his reins.

Correen hazed the runaway claybank toward Wolverton as the big man angled in and leaned from the saddle to grab a dangling rein. The mustangs lunged against each other for a few seconds, but Lone Wolf talked horse to them, settling them down with a few low grunts.

Steck got up and dusted himself off. "She's had her pitch for the day. She'll ride all right now." He took the rein from Wolverton and climbed back on, grimacing as he swung his stiff right leg over the saddle.

"Correen," Wolverton said, "you handle a wild horse right well."

"You call that pet horse wild?" Steck said. "Let her get astraddle of this outlaw and see who handles what . . ."

Claude stopped as he came over the rise and watched the three riders in the clearing. Steck was gesturing, pointing onc finger in the air as he spoke. Wolverton was next to Correen, patting her on the back. It riled Claude, and he took it out on Casino, jabbing the big paint with his spurs.

Every time he came back to camp, he found Lone Wolf trying to sweet-talk Correen, now going so far as to reach out and touch her. While he was off chasing outlaws, Lone Wolf was courting, refusing to fight until fired upon. It made him sick.

"Hey, here's Sabinal!" Steck said, seeing the regulator approach.

"Thank God you're all right," Correen said. "We heard shootin'."

Claude got down and motioned for her to take his mount.

"What happened?" Bob asked.

"It was the one they called Squaw Man. We had a runnin' fight and he got to ridin' so hard in the dark that he rimrocked himself. Rode right off the bluff where all those dead sheep were. Killed him deader than hell."

"That's one less outlaw to worry about," Steck said.

"And eight more to take his place," Claude replied. "I spotted Ike's bunch this mornin'. About a mile away when I saw 'em, and ridin' this way. They probably heard the shootin' last night, too. They'll be on my trail by now."

"Eight riders?" Lone Wolf said. "They'll have good horses, and us with these mustangs. Maybe we'd better make a run for Laramie."

Claude had been waiting for this. "And guard our hind ends all the way there? Hell, no. You've got to feel some grit, Wolverton. Right now they don't know we're mounted, so it's the best time to attack. See if we can't even the odds some."

Wolverton shook his head. "I think we should go back to Laramie and get some kind of legal authority before we start killin' any more men."

"I've got legal authority," Steck said. "I'm a reserve deputy sheriff back home."

Claude mounted the bay mare and sighed as if in disgust. "Dammit, Wolverton, they've killed Little Crow and shot at every one of us. They've killed our horses and stolen Bob's cattle. What more do you want?"

"He's right," Correen said. "We've got to attack now while we have the one advantage."

Wolverton's head was still shaking. "If we get more men, we can surround 'em and make 'em surrender. I'll fight when I have to, but till then I'll go out of my way to keep from killin' another man."

"Then you can hold the horses while this old cripple and this little hundred-pound woman does your fightin' for you," Claude said.

"Here now!" Steck said. "No need to get all that familiar, Sabinal. I'm still bankrollin' this outfit."

"No offense, Bob, but that leg of yours don't look good."

"Callin' me cripple don't rile me, but don't you go callin' me old!"

"And don't you go callin' me a coward," Wolverton warned.

Correen moved between the two men. "No one spoke that word."

"No, but he's talkin' all around it," Wolverton said, "and I'm tired of it."

"Hell, I'll say it. I think you're a coward. By God, a man who won't fight when he ought to is a coward."

Wolverton got down from the lead mare and handed his

reins to Correen. "Years ago I'd have killed you for sayin' that. Now I'll satisfy myself with just beatin' the tar out of you. Get down."

"Don't mind if I do," Claude said. He gave his reins to Steck as he hit the ground and let his gun belt drop.

"Stop it!" Correen ordered.

But Claude was already in motion, running toward the big man. Wolverton came ahead, too, and they rushed together like two fighting bulls, even to the point that they butted heads, knocking each other's hats off. Each grabbed with one hand and punched with the other. Claude lost his footing and fell, but pulled Wolverton down with him, and they rolled like schoolboys in the dirt.

"Get up!" Correen shouted. "Stop that!"

Wolverton tried to pin Claude, but the regulator swung a knee into the big man's ribs and they rolled far enough apart to get back on their feet.

Correen got down from Casino and handed Steck the reins of the lead mare, the old rancher absorbed in the fight, hardly noticing her.

The brawlers panted and circled for a few seconds, until Claude rushed Lone Wolf again. They traded a few solid punches, the toes of their boots inches apart, until Correen came between them with a pine stick. "Stop it!" she said, hitting Claude over the left shoulder. The regulator staggered back as the stick broke over Wolverton's forehead.

"Whoa," Steck said, holding the two skittish mounts.

Correen cleared the air between the two men with what was left of her stick. "Stop behavin' so stupid! We've got eight killers almost upon us, and all you can think of is fightin' each other!"

Claude took his mustang from Steck, stepped up on the stirrup. She was right, of course, but he had taunted Wolverton with purpose. For one thing, it had felt good to release some of his old anger. For another, he thought maybe he had gotten Wolverton into a fighting mood.

The big man rubbed his head, spit blood, took the reins of the lead mare from Steck.

The rancher chuckled. "You're gonna have to let 'em get it out of their craw sooner or later, Correen. I don't care if you break a whole forest of sticks over their head, them boys are gonna fight. Probably make best friends once they get it over with."

Claude reined south. "My best friend's dead."

THIRTY-TWO

Giff Dearborn lay on his back, balancing his foot on a spur rowel, a roll of blankets under his head. The smell of frying bacon drifted under his nose as he drummed his fingers against the canteen on his chest.

"Let me go over it one more time," he said. "You got this character, Claude Duval, in charge. Good tracker, good with a gun."

"Right," Lafferty said, a curl of wood dropping from his whittling stick. "If he's good enough to run Squaw Man off the mountain, he's damn good."

"Then there's Wolverton. Got the Creedmoor now, but he's turned preacher and won't fight unless he has to."

"That's the way it looks. He could have picked us off anytime at Wild Roy's hideout, but he waited till the last possible second. Didn't he, Clay?"

Sickle nodded his drooping head. He sat against a big deadfall, a blanket over his shoulders, his face pale as snow.

"And Duval don't get along with Wolverton," Dearborn

continued. "That could work in our favor." He adjusted his hat around the curl on his crown. "Then there's the feisty old bastard from Texas, and the crack-shot woman."

"Crack shot is right," Lafferty said. "And she don't panic under fire."

"And one horse among 'em." Dearborn inhaled the aroma of biscuits, rolling his eyes to one side to see how far along the cook was with lunch. He swept his eyes around the circle of gunmen. They weren't professionals, but they had all done a little shooting. His hunch was that not all of them would be riding out of these mountains. "This ought to be easy enough," he said.

The coffeepot rang suddenly like a bell as two holes appeared in it, one circled by curled points of torn metal. It swung violently over the fire, issuing two streams that hissed on hot coals, going up in steam. The gunmen flinched, the rifle blast still ringing in their ears.

"Don't move!" a voice said from the timber. "Give up, Ike, or we'll shoot in there among you."

Dearborn shot a look at Lafferty, drew his Colt, rolled to the big deadfall for cover, and fired toward the voice in the timber. Lafferty rolled in beside him.

The cook reached for a rifle but fell with a bullet hole in his chest. Three points of fire opened up, all on the north side of camp. Sickle fell over on his side, caressing a rifle but feeling too weak to use it.

Two cowboys fell, one screaming in pain. Others scattered, looking for cover, firing blindly.

Dearborn stuck his head up, fired four quick rounds, glimpsed a woman retreating up the slope and over the rise. "Get the horses!" he shouted, jumping to his feet. "Run 'em down!"

Ike Lafferty rose calmly beside him and took off his hat. He put his finger through a hole in the side of the crown.

"That one parted my hair," he said, walking with Dearborn to the horses.

"Yeah, crosswise," Dearborn replied. "Wonder what they've got planned. They shouldn't be harassin' us like that."

Lafferty glanced back at the two dying men on the ground. "Maybe they're just tryin' to draw us out where Wolverton can get a bead on us. I haven't heard that Creedmoor fire yet."

Dearborn pulled himself up by the saddle horn as he grabbed his reins. "He can't shoot us all with a single-shot rifle."

"Dammit," Lafferty said, looking back over the camp before riding out. "They got my cook. Now the grub's gonna burn."

They put spurs to their mounts and rode for the rise where Dearborn had seen the woman disappear. The cowboys in front of them stopped at the ridge, staring down at the terrain below.

"Emmett, what are you waitin' for?" Lafferty asked as he rode up beside his foreman. He expected to see the three attackers on foot down below, but found nothing.

"Where the hell did they go?" Dearborn said.

Along a trail on the next ridge, they glimpsed two riders passing a gap in the trees, neither riding the big paint they had expected.

"Son of a bitch," Lafferty said. "They got horses somewhere."

"Now what are we gonna do?" Emmett said.

Dearborn lifted his hat, briefly twisting the scalp lock on his crown. "You all stay behind 'em, but don't press 'em too hard," he replied. "Give me a chance to get around in front of 'em."

"What are you gonna do?" Lafferty asked.

"Hell, I don't know. I ain't there yet." He spurred his mount down from the rise and left the other riders behind, his stirrups slapping against the flanks of his mount as he plunged down the grassy slope.

"I guess we hit four of 'em hard enough to keep 'em out of the saddle," Claude said, watching the gang lope toward him. "Could have got five if you'd have done more than hold the horses."

Wolverton ignored the taunt, his eyes sweeping the parks and ridges for more riders. "Did you give 'em a chance to surrender?"

"I'm sure we did," Correen said. "But we didn't expect they would."

"Maybe they will now, the odds bein' even."

"They don't look like they're surrenderin' to me," Steck said. "Looks like they're comin' for a fight."

"Wonder why they're comin' so slow," Wolverton said. "You sure you got four? They may have split up."

"They ain't splittin' up, they're just comin' to kill us," Claude said. "You remember that big park west of here?"

Lone Wolf nodded.

"You and Creedmoor go get ready on the west side of it. We'll see if we can draw 'em out in the open after us, and you can pick Lafferty off."

Wolverton sat silent in the saddle.

"Well, git!" Claude ordered.

The big man frowned and turned his worried eyes to Correen. Only when she nodded would he touch his spurs to the lead mare. Claude ground his teeth and felt a vast distance between Correen and himself. Not the kind of thing he wanted to worry about now. When this business was over, maybe he could show her how much of a gentleman he could be when he wasn't hunting outlaws. Then again, maybe it would be too late.

* * *

Dearborn leaped from the saddle and loosened the cinch as the pony stood heaving. He let his reins drop and scrambled up the slope. Approaching the rise, he threw his hat down, dropped to his stomach, and slithered ahead. He could hear his mount puffing behind him as he peeked over the ridge.

A single rider caught his eye. A big man on a big bay horse, far off, riding hard across a wide park. Had to be Wolverton. A flash of white drew his attention to the east. He made out the paint stallion, the woman perched on top like a child. She was riding just behind two men head-reining their horses. They must have come across some green-broke stock somewhere. Searching farther east, he saw Ike and his boys loping over a rise, stopping to look at the sign on the ground.

Looking back to the west, he saw Wolverton dismount at the far edge of the park, a long rifle in his hand—a mere toothpick from this distance. Was the old assassin going to fight? Looked that way. Lying down on his stomach now, preparing to shoot.

Dearborn scooted back from the ridge, grabbed his hat, and ran back down to his mount. In a few seconds he had tightened the girth and was on his way, still not sure what he was going to do. All he really wanted was Wolverton's scalp. This idea of running Ike's rustling gang wasn't altogether unattractive, but it wasn't what he had come here for.

He circled, keeping high ground between himself and the other riders. He had to get closer if he was going to make something happen. He would figure out what to do when the time came. That was the way he liked it, anyway.

A hard push got him to the big park somewhere between Wolverton and the other three vigilantes. He stayed back in the timber, not anxious to let Lone Wolf find him in the sights of the Creedmoor. He found a heavily timbered draw at the lower end of the park and stayed in its cover, watching and listening for opportunities.

He had been sneaking through the brush long enough to let his pony catch some wind when he heard the approach of the horses. Through the oak leaves he saw Duval, the gray-haired rancher, and the woman on the big paint. Duval searched the park and pointed toward Wolverton at the far side. They looked over their shoulders for pursuers, then angled toward the head of Dearborn's wooded draw.

Dearborn guessed what they were doing. Luring Lafferty and his men into the open where Wolverton could pick them off with the Creedmoor. Yet, they were playing it safe, staying close to cover, skirting the edge of the park. In fact, it looked as though they would come right by the heavy timber of the draw Dearborn was hiding in.

He drew his revolver and moved his pony step by step, closer to the sunlit openness of the park. As long as they were moving, they probably wouldn't see him coming through the shadows. It was time to make something happen.

He caught it like a spark. The woman was the key. The bargaining chip. He could get whatever he wanted out of this expedition through her. She was riding in the rear still, two or three lengths behind the men, the big paint she rode prancing like a wild stallion herding his harem. Dearborn could hear their saddles squeak.

"Come on," Duval growled, trying to wrench his mustang's head away from the timber. The claybank Steck rode proved no more cooperative, and the riders found little opportunity to watch for enemies.

Dearborn remained motionless, let them pass the draw. Then he came out silently, at a walk, trailing Correen. Once in the open, he spurred his horse hard and rode for the woman.

Casino sensed the attack first, craning his neck to see behind. Correen gasped as she reached for the Winchester in her saddle scabbard. "Claude!" she shouted.

Dearborn let loose a Comanche yell as he closed the gap between himself and the woman. The green-broke horses lunged against every effort to turn them. The woman had the Winchester out, but Dearborn was there, springing from his saddle, landing right behind Correen on the big prancing paint. He wrenched the Winchester away and dropped it. He put his hand around her tiny fist, mastering the reins. The muzzle of his pistol felt cold under her chin.

Claude was on the ground, drawing a pistol, holding a rein. But it was too late. The stranger had Correen, had Casino, had control.

"I love ridin' double with a pretty woman!" Dearborn shouted. "Turn loose of that pistol, and she'll be all right."

"Turn loose of her, or you won't!" Claude warned.

"Can't do that! Once you get aholt of a wildcat, you'd better keep a firm grip!" His maniacal laughter ripped across the park like a donkey's bray.

Steck had his claybank turned around and was heading back toward Dearborn. "You'd better not harm her!" the old rancher shouted.

Dearborn rode Casino in front of his mount, herding the riderless pony toward timber. "She'll be all right. Y'all just stay put here and I'll be back directly—let you know what it'll cost you to get her back."

Claude thought about chancing a shot as Dearborn rode broadside into cover. Correen's eyes told him to do it, but he couldn't with the pistol barrel at her throat.

As she disappeared, he felt a pang in his chest. Little things she had said to him over the past few days came unexplainably to mind:

"Your sideburns are lopsided . . . Sacred cattle in the sacred mountains . . . Thank God you're all right."

And even his own name in her lovely Old World voice. Yes, just now. She had called him by his Christian name. Before she could think, she had called it out: "Claude!" And he had done nothing.

THIRTY-THREE

Duval!"

The voice knifed through the trees, a shrill cry reaching Claude's ears.

"I know you're out there! Let's talk!"

He got up and showed himself to the man who had taken Correen.

He had followed the kidnapper to Ike's camp, ordering Steck and Wolverton to stay back unless they heard gunfire. He had watched the camp for an hour as Ike's men planned their strategy and guarded Correen. Now the shadows were long, the cold night coming on. But at least something was happening.

The stranger left the tents behind and approached him, weaving his way among the trembling aspens, armed with a single revolver in his gun belt. He was smiling. As he walked up to Claude he stuck out his hand, as if he wanted to shake. "Howdy," he said.

Claude looked disdainfully at the callus-armored grip. "What do you want?"

"You don't remember me, do you?" He spoke low, his voice falling short of the camp.

"Should I?"

"We stood in the same courtroom eleven years ago. I'm Giff Dearborn."

The regulator's eyes shifted. He remembered now: the outlaw showing up at Lone Wolf's sentencing. Someone next to him had elbowed him and said, "That's Giff Dearborn. That's the feller Lone Wolf thought he was killin' when he shot that poor cowboy."

He looked the man over from spurs to hat.

"You remember now?"

Claude remembered plenty. Would any of this be happening if Wolverton had killed the right man eleven years ago? He hated this: dealing with Dearborn for Correen's life. Dearborn was no better than Wolverton, maybe lower. "You had gall showin' up in a court of law," he said.

Dearborn laughed as if having the time of his life. "Hell, wasn't no gall about it. The law didn't have a damn thing on me. Why do you think them ranchers wanted me Lone-Wolfed?"

The regulator scratched his beard. "What are you doin' up here in this country?"

"Same as you. Came to kill Lone Wolf. It's riled me for years, thinkin' he'd back-shoot me."

"If that's all you wanted, why'd you throw in with Lafferty? Why'd you take the girl?"

Dearborn set his sweatband back behind the tuft on his head and twisted the curl. "Seemed like a good idea at the time. Thought I'd take over the Snowy Range Gang, but now I've changed my mind. Gettin' too dangerous." He flashed a smile. "I'm willin' to give the girl back."

"What about Lafferty?"

"I don't give a damn for Lafferty. All I want is Lone Wolf. You and Steck and the girl can go your own way as far as I'm concerned."

Claude shifted his weight to his other foot, tucked his thumbs under his gun belt. "What do you have in mind?"

Dearborn grinned. "Simple. I'll swap you the girl for a clean shot at Lone Wolf."

Claude stared, no expression on his face. "There's not a damn simple thing about it. What about Ike and his boys with all those complications strapped around their hips?"

Dearborn nodded. "I've been thinkin' about that." He crossed his arms over his chest. "How's this: Let's tell Ike you killed Lone Wolf."

"What the hell for?"

"Ike knows you want Lone Wolf dead, and he hasn't seen the big bastard since you all had that scrape at the outlaw camp. If Ike thinks it's just you and Steck, he'll get over-confident. He'll think it's us five outlaws against you two regulators."

"The truth is, it's you five outlaws against us three regulators. And you have Correen. I still don't like the odds."

"Goddamn, Duval, you're missin' the mark. I'm comin' over to your side. Loyalty never was one of my stronger points, anyway." He jabbed a trigger finger at the Texan, leered with a ridiculous face. "It'll be me, you, Steck, and Wolverton against Ike and his three boys. Four against four. But we'll have the surprise on 'em. Anyway, that one red-headed feller's got the grippe so bad he won't be no good for nothin'."

"And nobody will be shootin' at you, because everybody thinks you're on their side."

Dearborn smirked at the sky. "By God, I hadn't thought of that!"

Claude was mulling the deal over from every angle. "So you want to beat Ike out of the girl, then you want to turn on Wolverton and kill him?"

"Don't you?"

Claude didn't like it. He didn't like a man who changed sides in the middle of a fight. He didn't like selling some-body out—not even Wolverton. The only thing he did like was the glimmer of hope this conniving Giff Dearborn had brought. Hope that he would see Correen alive again. He forced his cracked lips into a smile. "I like it," he said.

Dearborn scraped some ground bare with his boot and squatted on his heels. He urged Claude to hunker down beside him and began drawing a rough map in the dirt. "Here's how Ike wants to do it. There's a bare pass in the divide south of here . . ."

"Well?" Steck said when Claude came back to their hideout in the timber. "What do they want?"

Claude pulled his knife from his pocket and unfolded a blade he had filed square at the end. He picked up his Marlin rifle and began removing a screw holding the rawhide-wrapped stock to the gun. "We may have a chance. One of Ike's boys says he wants to turn on Ike and help us get Correen back."

"Bullshit," Steck said. "You believe that?"

"I think he means it. Says he doesn't want any part of killin' a woman."

"Sounds like bait to me," Steck said.

"You know Correen," Claude said. "She could charm a snake into bitin' itself. She's already got this outlaw halter broke and leadin'."

Steck put his hand on his chin and raised an eyebrow. "Well, now, that does sound like Correen. What's he gonna do? Sneak her over to us tonight?"

"I suggested that. Too risky for him. He wants us to take all the chances while he guards his hind end."

"What do we do?" Wolverton asked.

Claude glowered at the big man in the dying light. "Are you ready to shoot now?"

"Yes."

"You'd better hope it's not too late." He threw the stock

of the Marlin aside and started unscrewing the barrel band to remove the forestock. "Now, to make this work, Bob, your leg's got to be busted. And, Wolverton, you've got to be dead . . ."

THIRTY-FOUR

They found the place in the moonlight—a treeless, saddle-shaped pass in the Medicine Bow Divide. By the time they crawled into position on the high northern rim, the moon had sunk beyond the Park Range, draining the mountains of light. They hid between clumps of wind-twisted evergreens, staring silently down at the pass, barely visible in the starlight.

"I see why Ike picked this place," Claude said, his words trailing away on a cold breeze. "Must be a mile across with no cover. That makes for a long ambush, even for you and the Creedmoor."

"I thought Ike was supposed to think I'm dead."

"He's supposed to, but that doesn't mean he does."

Wolverton grunted and they looked down at the wind-swept saddle in silence.

"Ike will come up the east slope with Correen and all his boys," Claude finally said, pointing. "Me and Bob will come up from the west. My guess is they'll try to talk us out of our guns first. When we refuse, Ike will probably have some signal planned for his boys to start shootin'. He'll have Correen shieldin' him, so his boys will be takin' all the chances. He won't know about you up here, though. With any luck, you'll get to take your shot first."

"How's your hand?" Lone Wolf asked. "That sore's not gonna slow you down, is it?"

Claude flexed the bandaged hand. The swelling was

down, the pain hardly noticeable. He had to admit, the wild lettuce seemed to have helped. "You worry about your own shots. How far away you reckon the bottom of that saddle is?"

"Hard to tell in the dark. I'd say close to seven hundred yards."

Claude shook his head and sighed. "You ever shot that far?"

"I've shot targets at a thousand yards."

"How long was the farthest shot you ever took at a man?"

"A little over six hundred," the big man muttered.

Claude whistled under his breath. "Hit him?"

"Killed him."

"Who was it?"

Lone Wolf stared blankly down at the saddle, the Creedmoor lying in his open palms. His silence gripped Claude like a stranglehold as a quarter mile of wind whipped between them.

Everything kept coming back to Dusty. He couldn't forget if he wanted to. And he *didn't* want to. In fact, he was scared senseless that someday he'd forget. What kind of man would that make him, if he failed to keep that promise he had spoken to his dead partner the day he found Dusty facedown in his own campfire?

He wished he had never gotten to know Wolverton. It would have been easy killing him as a stranger. He still didn't like the man but had found qualities there he had never expected.

He thought about Giff Dearborn's deal. "You should have stayed in Texas, Lone Wolf. You know what I have to do if I make it past tomorrow alive."

"I know what you think you have to do. I even understand it. Used to think along those lines myself. I just hope you change your mind when the time comes."

Claude scoffed into the wind. "I can't wait to haul off

and kick your carcass and see that you don't even flinch. Dreamed of it for years. Maybe you think you've paid for killin' my partner, but I just see one way you can pay. I don't care that you made a mistake, either. There's some things you just can't let go as accidents."

"It wasn't an accident."

"What?" Claude growled.

"It was God's will. If it hadn't been for Dusty, I'd still be murderin' now."

Claude's muscles writhed, his hands gathering fists full of gravel. "What the hell do you know about God's will, you back-shootin' son of a bitch?"

Lone Wolf took his hat off and looked at the stars around him. Here, on this high, barren ridge, he felt as if among them—one shining soul in a flock. The Milky Way coursed lazily down upon him, bathing him. He rolled onto his back, pillowed his head on his old hat, watched his breath-cloud catch the starlight.

"I believe a star burns for every soul who ever lived," he said. "I believe a life is like a light. Maybe you think you kill it when you snuff it out, but it don't die. It just keeps goin' into space, shootin' quicker than a sound, or a glance, or a bullet. Farther than you can see. Farther than you ever thought things went. Look at 'em up there. Millions of 'em."

Claude looked around in spite of himself, felt the cold night on the back of his neck as his long hair fell away from his skin. A shooting star raked far across the sky, leaving a trail in a quick flash.

"Now, you see that?" Wolverton said. "There went somebody's lifetime spent wasted. That was me before I knew Dusty."

"You *didn't* know Dusty."

"No, not the way you did."

"What the hell does that mean?"

Lone Wolf let the Creedmoor lie across his chest, and

put his hands in his coat pockets. "The day after I shot your partner, one of the ranchers who'd hired me asked me why I hadn't killed Giff Dearborn yet. Said he'd seen him in town. I figured out what I'd done then, so I tore out for New Mexico.

"That night I stared up at the sky. Couldn't sleep. And I saw a new star come out right in front of my open eyes, takin' up a patch of dark sky that never saw light before.

"I never looked at Dusty Sanderson's face. Never heard his voice. That night I didn't even know his name. Didn't know yet who I'd killed. But I knew that was his light, and I knew what I had to do. I started livin' that night."

Claude searched the sky. He felt depth he had never noticed before, distance he had never fathomed, loneliness he knew too well.

"I know Dusty," Wolverton said, "and he won't let me forget. He crosses over every night, straight and steady. He shines true. That's his star way up yonder."

Claude felt the cold air in his windpipe, the solid mountain pressing up under him. The sky all but swallowed him in a spray of light. "What star?" he groaned, as if to ridicule. But he wanted to know that light. It was just like Dusty to come back as such.

The long arm swept slowly upward, a gnarled finger jutting. "There . . ."

THIRTY-FIVE

Like a smile, the great curve of the saddle appeared against the dawn sky. When the light suited Ike Lafferty, he arrived at the bottom of the curve, his arm wrapped around Correen, holding her as a shield in front of him, his pistol under her ear. Four men appeared beside him.

"Here we go," Claude said. They stepped out of the trees and started up the slope to the divide, Claude on foot, Steck riding the bay mare. "When we get close, stay over to the left," he said. "I don't want to be lookin' right into the sun."

"Our left or their left?" Steck asked.

"Our left, dammit. What do I care about their left?"

Steck chuckled. "Take it easy, Sabinal. I was just needlin' you some to take the edge off."

Claude shot a glance up at him. "Whatever you do, don't look up at Wolverton's position. They'll catch you lookin' and know he's up there."

"Hell, I didn't want to look till you said that."

"Well, don't."

They walked the rest of the way in silence, squinting into the eastern sky. Lafferty stood at the left, pressing Correen against him with more familiarity than Claude could enjoy. Emmett, the ranch foreman, stood next to Lafferty. Then there was the redheaded Sickle twin, looking pale and poorly, shivering visibly. Next, a cowboy called Joe, if Claude remembered the name correctly. And finally, Giff Dearborn at the far right.

A breeze tossed his hair back from his collar when he reached the divide, and Claude wondered what the windage adjustment would be on the Creedmoor for this distance, this wind speed. The Laramie Plains stretched away into a haze far below. He looked each man in the eye as Steck reined in the bay mare. Then he looked at Correen, her big green eyes alert and misty.

"Mornin', Sabinal; Bob," Ike said smugly.

Steck grimaced as he swung a splinted right leg over the saddle and lowered himself from the seat, holding a rein. He took a couple of hops away from the horse, stretched his right leg out in front of him, and sat awkwardly on the cold ground. The leg had two pine boughs lashed to it with rawhide. He rubbed his knee tenderly as he looked up at the outlaws, resisting a glance at Lone Wolf's position on the high ridge to the left.

"That leg botherin' you where you fell off the bluff?" Ike said.

"I didn't fall, I jumped," Steck replied. "And it wasn't the jump that busted it, it was you bastards shootin' my horse dead in the creek." He lifted the splinted leg from the ground as he rubbed it.

"What do you hold it up like that for?" Emmett said.

"Because it don't hurt so much when I do, stupid." He pointed his boot heel at a gap between two of the men and massaged his knee.

"Let's get down to business," Claude said. "Let the girl go and give her ten minutes' head start on the horse, then the rest of us will decide how to finish this thing off."

Lafferty glanced down the line of men at Dearborn. "Is that what you told him we were gonna do, Giff?"

"Wasn't that the plan?" Giff said, smiling and shrugging.

"I'm afraid there's been a little mix-up, Sabinal. I ain't about to turn loose of this woman until you and Steck lay your guns down."

Steck lowered his splinted leg gingerly to the ground and lay back on his elbows.

Claude shook his head. "The odds are against me bad enough as it is, Ike. You've got five men against two."

"Five against three, for all I know. Wolverton could be out there with that old Sharps."

"He's dead."

Correen suddenly kicked a spray of rocks at Claude, causing every man but Sickle to flinch. "You fool!" she said, her voice a savage growl. "Did you have to tell them you'd killed him?"

Claude quickly caught her drift. "Oh, shut up, Correen. It don't do no good to bluff like he's out there if he ain't."

Ike chuckled. "It hasn't been a real pleasant couple of days in camp for you all, has it?"

Steck elevated his leg and rubbed his knee again.

"We had an agreement," Claude said. "Let the woman go, like we decided."

Lafferty shook his head. "I'm still not convinced about Wolverton. If he's dead, where's the Creedmoor?"

"Busted," Bob said, lowering his splints. "Sabinal used it to cave in Lone Wolf's skull, and just kept beatin' his brains out till he'd busted that skinny little stock off that rifle and boogered the block all up. Then he just threw it out in the woods somewhere."

Lafferty studied Steck's face, then looked at Claude. "If you wanted to kill him, why didn't you just shoot him?"

"I didn't want to advertise where we were. You had that black man huntin' us."

Ike grunted. "You believe 'em, Giff?"

Dearborn crossed his arms over his chest and cocked his head to one side. "I believe if I was them, I'd be lyin' my ass off about now. But I ain't seen no sign of Wolverton, and we are way out here away from cover."

"You want proof he's dead?" Claude asked. "I got it in my saddlebag." He stepped toward the horse.

"Careful," Lafferty warned. "Last time you reached into that saddlebag you pulled out a pistol."

"No, you be careful," Claude said, raking the men with his eyes. "Any of your boys touches a gun butt and all hell's gonna break loose." He unbuckled the saddlebag flap with one hand, watching the men. He reached inside and slowly withdrew a patch of black hair.

"What's that supposed to be?" Lafferty said.

"It's what's left of Lone Wolf's scalp," Bob replied.

"Oh, son of a bitch," Emmett groaned, his lip curling.

"Let me see it," Ike ordered.

Claude took a few steps toward Lafferty, then stopped, and tossed the scalp toward the outlaw boss, landing it at Correen's feet.

"Darlin'," Ike said, keeping his eyes riveted to Duval, "bend over and pick that up, will you?"

The right side of Correen's mouth smiled at Claude, where only he could see, and she bent slowly to pick up the tuft of hair, her own trusses falling around it as she reached. For an instant, the barrel of Ike's revolver angled away from her head.

Claude saw the wind tear a stream of black smoke away from the ridge to his left, high and far away, out of focus. Time slowed, like molasses through an hourglass. To his right, he sensed Bob's splinted leg rising and knew the old rancher had seen the muzzle blast of the Creedmoor, too.

Sickle started to say something.

The regulator concentrated on what he had to do. When the big slug from the Sharps hit Lafferty, he would draw a Russian to gun down the man next to Ike—the ranch foreman called Emmett. Bob would take the Sickle boy. Giff Dearborn would turn on the man at his side—the cowboy called Joe.

Sickle's words had arrived slow as a bayou: "They scalped that squaw."

The slug popped against Ike Lafferty's shoulder, whipping his head back as his chest spewed blood. He fell on top of Correen as Claude reached toward his holster and the green mare broke to run down the mountain.

Steck pointed his boot heel at Sickle and reached into a slit in his pants leg. He pulled the trigger of the Marlin rifle, stripped of butt and forestock, lashed to his leg under the fabric of his trousers. The bullet tore through boot leather at his ankle and hit Sickle high in the stomach, folding him back like a cellar door slamming shut on a freight hole.

Claude had Emmett covered before the foreman could get his grip around his pistol, but something was wrong. Dearborn was standing, waiting. Cowboy Joe was drawing a side arm. Steck was trying to get his Colt out of his holster.

Claude saw the fear in Emmett's eyes when he fired, spinning the foreman. He thumbed the hammer as he turned.

Cowboy Joe shot down at Bob Steck, and now, too late, Giff Dearborn drew a weapon and fired at the man beside him, as Claude did the same, catching the cowboy in a cross fire that doubled him over and rolled him down the mountain slope.

Dearborn looked back at Duval to find the big Smith & Wesson staring him in the face. He waited for the sounds of the runaway horse and the echoing gunshots to die.

"He was fast with that pistol," Dearborn said. "Faster than I thought." He let his Colt slip into its holster and pitched his hat back on his head, feeling for the curl of his scalp lock.

"He wasn't fast," Claude said, stalking toward the outlaw. "You were slow. You waited, you son of a bitch." He brought the barrel of his .44 down on the twisted curl atop Dearborn's head. The outlaw collapsed.

Turning, he saw Correen crawling out from under Ike's limp body. He followed her eyes to Bob Steck, saw the old Texan holding back a current of blood streaming from his vest. He knelt to one side of Steck as Correen came to the other.

"Hang on, Bob. We'll get you out of here and take a look at that wound."

Steck shook his head. "Don't waste your strength. I'm hit too bad."

Correeen put her thigh under Steck's head like a pillow.

He smiled up at her, then looked at Claude. "Send them bremmers back to Texas, Sabinal, but keep a couple of bulls for yourself. I left instructions to get you paid, in case I didn't come back." He grinned. "And it don't look like I'm goin' back."

Claude caught a glimpse of motion and glanced up to find Wolverton running down into the saddle, still a few hundred yards away.

Steck lifted his head to look at his wound. "Lone Wolf made a hell of a shot on Ike, didn't he? I didn't want to say it, Sabinal, and crush what little morale we had, but I didn't think he could make that shot." He let his head sink back to Correeen's thigh as she stroked his white hair back over his head. "What are you gonna do about Lone Wolf? You gonna let him go back to Texas?"

Claude looked over his shoulder to check on Dearborn. "I don't know."

Correeen looked across the dying man and stared in astonishment at the regulator.

"Well, anyway," Steck said, heaving now, his eyelids sinking, "it ain't my worry. You'll do what's right. Your folks down in Texas ought to be proud of you." His eyes closed, and his bloody hand slid to the ground. "Have Lone Wolf say a few words over me." He smiled. "Thank God I ain't dyin' in no rockin' chair."

Claude stared down at Steck until he realized the life had left him. He could hear Wolverton's footsteps now, rattling rocks as the big man trotted toward the bloody ground of the fight.

Correeen slipped her leg out from under Steck's head. She ran to meet Wolverton over the body of Ike Lafferty. Claude felt the morning chill when he saw her embrace the big man, pressing her face against his chest as she wrapped her arms around him. He had never felt such a helpless jealous rage.

He turned away and looked down the slope to the west, where the mustang had disappeared. He squinted, blinked. There they were again. Standing in a line, staring at him, their humps listing. Sacred cattle in the sacred mountains.

THIRTY-SIX

The broad flat neck of the claybank felt warm where the strong sunlight struck her. Claude patted her as he led her to the mound of dirt Correen and Lone Wolf were smoothing.

They had chosen an open park with a good view west to bury Bob Steck. Wolverton had fashioned a cross of pine boughs and set it deep at the head of the grave.

"Ol' Bob can see the Great Divide from here," Claude said, his voice expressionless. He slipped Steck's Winchester into its scabbard.

Correen looked up from the grave and saw the claybank wearing Steck's saddle, rope, bedroll. "Mr. Duval, what on earth . . ."

Wolverton silenced her with a touch on the shoulder.

Claude turned the mare to the west, looking out over the slope of the park. "I cut almost all the way through the cinch. She'll bust it in a few days and shake the saddle off. If she's lucky, she'll never wear one again."

The wild mare rolled her eyes nervously as Claude worked his hand toward her head. "Well, ol' girl, you're carryin' everything he'll need. A good rifle and a stout rope." He put his hand on the headstall, and the mare flinched, jumping aside. "Whoa, now, it ain't so bad. If you were a Indian horse, we'd shoot you and leave you lay on the grave."

He worked his hand under the bridle and pulled it off. The mare jerked her head back, then stood confused, unsure of her freedom.

"Go on!" Claude shouted. "Git!" He lashed the clay-bank's rump with the reins of Steck's bridle. The mare bolted, ran halfway across the park, then started pitching. "Run, you knothead!" the regulator shouted. He dropped the bridle and pulled both Russians from his holsters, firing them alternately in the air until the mustang had run for the timber, her head and tail high, mane streaming over the empty saddle.

"Now, that's a cowboy funeral," Claude said, the echoes of gunfire sounding like thunder from his throat. "Would have suited Bob." He picked up the bridle and left it hanging on the pine cross as he hiked uphill for the horses.

Correen and Lone Wolf looked uncertainly at each other, wondering what Claude had in mind next. They followed him up the mountainside.

Giff Dearborn was sitting against a tree, his hands tied in front of him, his neck leashed to the trunk. A streak of dried blood—cracked like parched soil—ran from his scalp lock, between his eyes, down one side of his nose. It jumped his mouth and disappeared under his chin. He had a fierce headache, and his stomach was fighting pangs of nausea.

"Hey, Duval," he said as the three regulators began shaping up their midday camp. "What about our deal?"

"I don't hold to deals with horse thieves," he said, stroking Casino. "Anyway, you didn't keep your end."

"What deal?" Correen asked.

Claude glanced at her, but he was still reeling with envy over the way she had embraced Wolverton, and he couldn't look her in the eye. "Ol' Giff here sold out on Ike. He was

supposed to help us get you back in exchange for me givin'
him a shot at Wolverton. But when it came time to shoot it
out with Ike's bunch, he waited to see who would win the
fight. He knew nobody would be shootin' at him. He
waited, and got Bob killed."

Correen tried to get in front of Claude, but he turned
away. "You weren't really going to let this man shoot Mr.
Wolverton?"

"If anybody's gonna shoot Mr. Wolverton, it's gonna be
me."

"Hell, I don't care who shoots him, long as I get to see
it!" Dearborn said.

"Shut up," Claude warned.

"Duval!" Lone Wolf's voice said, barking across the
camp. He was pulling the long barrel of the Creedmoor
from his saddle boot. "I'm tired of all this talk. If you're
gonna kill me, you're gonna do it before we leave this camp."

"Don't tempt me," Claude said.

"That's exactly what I intend to do." He pitched the rifle
at the regulator. "You can use this and add it to your collection."

Claude caught the gun, tossed it back. "You're the one
knows how to shoot it."

Wolverton frowned at the Creedmoor, threw it back at
Claude, putting his muscle behind it this time. "I don't want
it," he growled.

Claude enjoyed seeing the big man flustered, felt an urge
to taunt him. "Why not? It fired true enough for you this
mornin'. What's wrong with it?"

"The serial number."

"Huh?" Claude rolled the Creedmoor onto its back and
looked at the number stamped on the belly. "What's wrong
with it? Not low enough for you?"

"That's not just any Sharps Creedmoor. That's my old
gun. That's the gun I killed Dusty with."

"Oh, I'd shoot the son of a bitch now for sure," Dearborn said.

Correen stepped in front of Wolverton, as if to shield him, though he looked twice as tall as she. "You're not going to do any more killin', Mr. Duval."

Wolverton moved her aside with a long arm. "Get out of the way, Correen. I have to get this over with."

Claude swung the Creedmoor around on Wolverton. "You want it over with? I can oblige you." The gun in his hands made him think of the moment he had visualized in a thousand nightmares: the long rifle kicking, Dusty falling, Wolverton pressing the cartridge into his dead partner's hand, the smell of burning flesh in the air.

"I tried to explain it to you last night," Lone Wolf said, standing tall, legs apart, the Snowy Range over his shoulder. "Dusty means somethin' good to me. To you he's just a reason to kill. You call Dusty your partner, but since I killed him, he's been closer to me than he has been to you. Dusty's *my* partner now. He don't ride with you anymore."

Claude vaguely heard his own jaw teeth grinding. The mountains darkened, and he saw only Wolverton, standing in a half-light. He thumbed back the hammer of the Creedmoor. "You want to die, don't you?"

"No," the big man said. "I want to live. But I don't mean walkin' this earth with a dead soul rottin' inside me. If I'm gonna live, I have to get this behind me for good. I've got to have your forgiveness, Sabinal. Otherwise, I might as well be dead."

Claude raised the rifle to his shoulder and stared at the big man through the hooded front sight. "How 'bout if I send my forgiveness right down this long barrel?" His finger wrapped around the trigger.

"It doesn't help," Correen said, her voice calm, like an angel's. "It doesn't make you feel one wee bit better."

"Hell, kill him!" Dearborn said, kicking his boots in the

dirt. "The goddamn son of a bitch shot your partner! Shot him in the back and left him lay in the fire!"

"Don't do it," Correen said.

"Kill him, goddammit! Kill him, kill him, kill him!"

The half-light faded around Wolverton, and Claude remembered the horror of rolling Dusty from the fire—flesh burned to the bone; cooked, blackened, blistered; the gaping death smile of Dusty's skull. His finger felt the spring behind the trigger.

Then he blinked, and during the instant of darkness, he began to see it. First the left eyebrow, peaked like a mountaintop. Then the eyes, green like Correen's. Dirty blond hair hat-flattened to Dusty's white brow. A crooked nose, broken that time in Abilene. The high cheeks, sun-browned. The jaw, sharp like a plowshare. And the right corner of Dusty's mouth, curving in perpetual smile . . .

Where you been? he thought, as if his partner had come in late from hunting strays.

"Don't do it, Claude. It ain't worth it. It was supposed to happen this way. Go home, Sabinal. Go on home."

The white mountain sun and the cold fresh air burst upon him, and he heard Giff Dearborn's hellish voice growling:

"Kill him, goddammit! Kill the son of a bitch now!"

Claude swung the long barrel around like a boom, stopping the muzzle between Dearborn's eyes. "If I do any more killin' today, I'm gonna start with you."

Dearborn quaked like an aspen before the wind god, his mouth stuck open.

Claude wheeled, aimed into the sun, and pulled the trigger. The hammer fell on an empty chamber, and only clicked. He looked at Wolverton, and the big man smiled—a friendly smile, almost an apology.

It was a fine acquisition. A collector's item. A showpiece, like the Le Mat grapeshot revolver. The Sharps long-range Creedmoor rifle, Model 73. It would be rare someday.

Claude flipped it in midair, caught the barrel behind the hooded sight. He swung like a lumberjack, cracking the hardwood stock off on the tree trunk above Dearborn's head. Overhanded, splitting stovewood. One-handed, like an ape with a stick, spooking the horses. Like a mad farmer with a hoe, a section worker driving spikes.

The trigger guard rang, glinting sunlight as it flipped away. The breech shot a spark from a boulder. The forestock cracked like a walnut. The long steel barrel sailed away, end over end, above Bob Steck's grave, landing in the middle of the park.

Claude panted for a while, then turned to Lone Wolf. "You're not worth it. Probably just end up back in prison, anyway." He drew his knife, cut Dearborn's leash, and pulled the outlaw to his feet.

"Maybe I will," Wolverton said. "For plowin' too deep, or singin' too loud in church."

Claude led Dearborn to one of the captured mounts. "Get on," he said, virtually lifting the outlaw into the saddle. He mounted Casino and started his prisoner up the slope.

"Where are you goin'?" Correen demanded.

"Takin' this outlaw to Laramie. I'm sure he's wanted somewhere for somethin'."

"Don't you want some help guardin' him?" Wolverton said.

"Hell, no."

"What about the bremmers?" Lone Wolf shouted after the riders in the timber.

"I'll come back for 'em. Don't worry, I'll see that you both get your share of the reward money."

"Aren't you going to say goodbye?" Correen pleaded, her fine voice romping through the forest like frisking squirrels. But she heard only hoofbeats in reply.

THIRTY-SEVEN

laude's boot plowed through the cold ashes until it thumped against a chunk of something solid. Stooping, he picked up a discolored rifle barrel, studied the breech. It looked like the remnants of his old Henry repeater. The fire had destroyed his entire collection, hidden under the floor planks of his frame house. The only piece he had left that was worth anything was the Le Mat grapeshot revolver.

Ike's boys had come calling while he had been away hunting the Snowy Range Gang. They had torched his new house, his shed, his corral. He would be hard-pressed to rebuild before winter.

He tossed the ruined rifle aside as a gust enveloped him in a swirl of dust and ashes.

It didn't really matter. Nothing seemed to matter anymore. He looked back at Casino, standing sleepy-eyed beside a small ponderosa pine, a bremmer bull to either side of him. The big paint looked gaunt from his ordeal in the Medicine Bows, but now he would have time to rest and put some fat on before winter.

Claude had a good deal of money coming: rewards from Bob Steck's family and the state of Colorado. He had the two bremmer bulls to start a breeding program with. He still had his section of pine-studded hills and a share of the Laramie Plains to graze. A bigger share, now that Ike Lafferty's outfit was wiped out.

But it all seemed worthless. He trudged out of the ashes, then stopped. He didn't even know where to stand, what to do, how to start. He joined the horse and the two sacred bulls under the little pine. Casino's reins made a circle on the ground where they dangled from his bridle. Good horse.

Never stepped on a rein. He wished he had a dozen like him. Needed them, too, now that the Lafferty boys had run off all his other mounts.

As he sat down under the tree, he pulled his whiskey flask from a pocket, not bothering to check his watch. He took a big swallow and leaned back, letting the tree trunk push his hat over his eyes. For the past couple of weeks, since leaving her without a goodbye in the mountains, he had thought of almost nothing but Correen.

"You've got it bad this time, boy," Dusty was saying to him. He could conjure his partner's face now. Clearly, as if they had parted only yesterday. Dusty would be eleven years older, wouldn't he? Wouldn't there be a few more lines on the face? It didn't matter. Flesh aged, not the soul.

It wasn't Dusty he wanted to see, anyway, but Correen. He wondered where she was. Rebuilding her place in the foothills? If so, Lone Wolf was there with her. Or maybe she had gone with him back to Texas. He would have to find out when the rewards came, to send them their shares. He was hoping they had gone back to Texas. Didn't want to see them together. He wanted to see Correen, of course, but he didn't care to look at Lone Wolf again as long as he lived.

Now that it was all over, he was having nightmares about Wolverton. In the worst one, he and Lone Wolf were friends, standing the rigid corpse of the squaw up against a tree, giving it a haircut to resemble Lone Wolf's, then scalping it. It had really happened, of course, but in the dream they enjoyed it—laughing like ghouls as they worked. Then the corpse would come to life and start screaming, and Claude would wake in a cold sweat, his heart beating so hard that it hurt.

So he hadn't slept nights much lately, and now the sun was warming him, making him drowsy. He heard her voice: "Aren't you going to say goodbye?" But then he saw her embracing Wolverton. She had touched him a few times, too, to straighten his sideburns or bandage his injured hand. But there hadn't been any hugging between them.

Better to doze. Forget about her for a while. He scratched his beard, three weeks old now and still itching. It was going to have to come off.

The squeak and rattle of a rolling wagon woke him, and he jumped up from the ground, knocking his hat aside, dropping his whiskey flask, feeling for his pistols. Casino bolted, startled. The big paint stepped on a rein, broke it off.

Damn, nothing was certain anymore, he thought, trying to make his eyes focus on the road. He found the wagon, two mules, a cargo of odds and ends—and Correen with the reins in her hands, perched lightly on the seat like mist in the air, her hair tied back and bouncing on the wind behind her pretty face.

He rubbed his eyes and took a few steps toward her. Should he wave? What did she want?

He pulled himself together, picked up his hat, raked back his long hair, and fixed the felt crown over it. He waited until she stopped the team, then approached her, his heart gushing blood in his chest.

"What brings you here?" he said carefully.

She set the brake, wrapped the reins around the handle. She looked at him and shrugged. "I came for my reward." She sprang down from the wagon, landing flat-footed beside the front wheel.

"It ain't come yet."

"Perhaps I'll wait for it." She looked around at the ashes, wondering what his place had looked like before the Lafferty boys raided. "A wee bonnie croft you have here, Mr. Duval," she said, laying the lilt on thick.

Claude's eyes shifted, and his tongue felt his front teeth. "Where's Lone Wolf?"

She started walking slowly toward him, like a lioness stalking something. "He went back to Texas, of course."

He studied the stuff in the wagon, knowing she was reading his eyes. What was this, anyway? "You goin' after him?"

She stopped in her tracks. "Why would I?" She looked at him suspiciously.

Claude guarded himself, circled away from her, toward the wagon team. He had to remind himself of what he had seen up there. She had made him feel like a helpless fool. Not again . . . "He ran out on you, did he?"

She put her small hands on the curve of her hips. "Whatever do you mean?"

He nodded knowingly, circling the sun to his back, judging the cargo in the wagon. "So now you come crawlin' to your second choice?" He saw the astonishment in her face turn to anger and knew he had picked a bad fight.

"You bloody fool," she growled. "Surely you don't think . . . "

Did he think? He groped desperately for ammunition. "I had my eye on you two up there. Every time I'd come back to camp, there you'd be." He pointed his finger at her as if something had just occurred to him. "And I saw the way you hugged on him that last mornin'."

She gasped. "He had just saved my life!"

"I had a little to do with it, too, but you didn't hug me that way."

She took two menacing steps toward him. "It would have meant something entirely different with you, and it wasn't the time nor the place to start skylarkin' up there."

"And what about you standin' in my way to protect him," he went on, only now interpreting what she had last said.

"Didn't I do so for your sake, not his? If you had

murdered him, you would have lived the rest of your life as he must, and you would be of no use to me whatsoever."

Claude glared for a moment, then stomped his foot like a five-year-old. "You didn't have to go huggin' him!"

She laughed, flailing her arms. "I don't believe it. You're jealous of him. You are actually jealous of a single hug."

"Jealous?" He scoffed. "I am not!"

"You are! Do you think I ever felt the least bit attracted to him?" He turned away from her, but she circled and got in front of him. "That big, awkward ox of a man? His eyes squint like old bullet wounds in his head. Not like those poor, tortured, blind eyes of yours." She grabbed his arm and pressed her small fingers against his palm. "His hands are petrified, compared to these. These are warm and strong. He's an old killer, Mr. Duval. I could never condone the things he's done." She glared a warning at him. "I'm not that forgivin'."

Claude moved his mouth in an attempt to speak, but nothing came out. He wrapped his hand around hers, closing it gently.

Her eyes softened, and she shook her head in wonder. "You poor jealous fool. Can't you see what you've done? You did more than save my life. You rescued me." She leaned into him, put an arm around the back of his neck, and lifted herself toward his lips.

Claude felt himself weakening in her powerful embrace, drew back only an inch as her face neared his. "I thought you said you came here for your reward." He felt her hand slip from his and touch the small of his back, her fingers curling in against him like the claws of a playful cat.

"Perhaps I came to deliver one as well."

Claude slipped his arms around her and pressed his lips down on hers. For two weeks—delivering Giff Dearborn, herding the bremmers down from the mountains—he had sulked and thought of this. He had lain on his back alone at night to watch Dusty's star pass over him. Maybe Lone Wolf was right. Maybe there were no accidents. Maybe the humpbacked cattle really were sacred, the mountains possessed of real medicine. Maybe even the Creedmoor had been wrought by God's hand.

She pushed away from him, her cheeks reddened where his beard had scratched her. She ran her fingers roughly through his whiskers.

"Mr. Duval," she said, shaking her head, "you're badly needin' a shave."

VENDETTA
GOLD

To Rebecca

ACKNOWLEDGMENTS

For helping me understand the land laws of Texas and the ways of the frontier surveyors, I wish to thank the General Land Office of Texas and the Texas Surveyors Association. A special thanks to Ralph Harris, R.P.S., Austin, Texas, for sharing his collection of antique surveying instruments.

ONE

I had just one ambition the day the old Mexican died. One ideal controlled my every action. A single goal for life went before all my daily needs and immediate desires. I had vowed to dedicate the rest of my days on earth to the complete and unceasing avoidance of criminal activity and nothing I could imagine would ever have the power to sway me from that mission.

It may not sound like much of an aspiration or one that would prove particularly difficult to achieve, but to me it was a cause so crucial and absorbing that I felt precariously near to failure at every turn. Dreams of hard labor haunted my nights, and memories of close confinement filled my waking thoughts. I had just finished a stretch of three years and it was my sole aim to make it the only sentence Roy Huckaby would ever serve. Of course, all that began to change the day I met the old Mexican.

When I first saw him, I must have mistaken him for a wooden Indian. He was standing board-stiff in front of a cigar store on Dolorosa Street, across from the Old Southern Hotel. But when I looked his way again, several minutes later, I caught him shuffling along in front of the Buckhorn Saloon and I knew he was human.

He wore the dress of an old-fashioned vaquero except for the faded red bandanna tied on his head in place of a sombrero. Years had cracked his face like parched soil and I couldn't locate a single tooth amid the white stubble of his beard. He wore a frayed vest under a jacket resplendent with patches. The ends of his bowed pant legs disappeared down the tops of boots that had once stood straight as stove pipes but now slouched like the features of his weathered face. The rowels of his spurs had lost almost as many teeth as his mouth. He used a walking stick to maintain his balance and his only means of getting around was to totter a few feet, then rest.

One of San Antonio's municipal water carts was sprinkling the street to keep the dust down. By the time it had circled Main Plaza, the old Mexican had only taken about a dozen steps. A German merchant left his store at the corner of Quinta and Main and walked all the way across the plaza to the Buckhorn Saloon in the time it took the old Mexican to negotiate the width of three or four planks on the boardwalk. A horseman rode by and the old man raised his hand to wave, but too late, and the rider didn't notice. He paused with his hand in the air and watched the horseman ride out of sight.

He continued to inch along until his squint found my horse under the shade of an oak in the gardens of Main Plaza. He stopped and stared for a full minute. Then I caught a glimmer of desperation in his eyes and knew he wanted something of me, so I crossed the street, tipped my hat, and stepped up on the boardwalk. "Good afternoon, sir," I said. "Can I be of some help to you?"

Conversation didn't come easily between us because he spoke no English and I spoke no Spanish. But I soon figured out from his gestures that he wanted to ride my horse somewhere. Given my recent inclination toward acts of philanthropy, I had no objection to letting him borrow a ride.

The old man didn't look spry enough to climb a stirrup so I led my horse to the edge of the boardwalk and helped him get one leg over the saddle. I did most of the work and he simply leaned in the appropriate direction. He indicated that he would have no further use for his walking stick, in fact he scorned the thing once he was in the saddle, so I left it leaning against the wall of the Buckhorn Saloon.

"Which way?" I asked, giving him the choice of turning up or down the street. He began to point so I would know where to lead him, and we turned onto Flores Street and walked slowly south.

It didn't take me long to learn my first two words of Spanish. "*Derecho*" meant right and "*izquierda*" meant left. I was very familiar with those commands by the time we reached the vaquero's destination, which was the beautiful old Mission Conception, three miles south of Main Plaza.

"*Izquierda, izquierda!*" he ordered, and I made the last left turn through the gate of a split-rail fence surrounding the mission.

I helped the vaquero down from the saddle, and he sat on a rock under a tree to rest. With his eyes and a motion of his hand, he asked me to stay with him. So I sat and listened to him mutter in his foreign tongue. He seemed to have a great many things to tell me. He pointed and gestured incomprehensibly as he spoke. I got the idea he was thanking me for the use of my mare so I merely nodded at him as if I understood. "Okay, old-timer," I said. "Whatever you say. Yes, yes, I understand."

Then the old man grinned, patted me on the shoulder, and reached into his jacket. He pulled out a rolled piece of tanned sheepskin tied with a leather thong. He handed it to me. When I took it, he wrapped his rough old hands around mine and shook them weakly. He tried to get up then but didn't succeed until I helped him.

The moment we both got on our feet, I heard the whistling of mourning doves on the wing. Six of them flew between the twin stone belfries of the old Spanish mission and landed in the tree limbs above us. I knew there were six because I had gotten into the habit of counting birds in prison when they flew overhead or landed on the walls, as if they represented some sort of index to freedom from which I was excluded.

The old man noticed the doves, too, and pointed at them as they found their perches among the branches over our heads. He raised his hands to them and spoke as if to a woman he had once loved. A toothless grin covered his face as he turned to me and made his old arms move slowly like wings and then swept his knotty fingers over his head to indicate the great blue expanses of sky over Texas.

Finally he clutched the cloth of his vest and hobbled toward the mission. There was an altar in front of the ancient building with a statue and a cross and some wilted flowers, and the vaquero shuffled over to it and sank to his knees to pray.

I untied the thong around the sheepskin and unrolled it. There was something written or drawn on it in ink. I didn't have time to figure it out because the doves jumped their perches and took to the sky again. They numbered seven when I counted. I glanced toward the statue and found the old man slumped over in front of it, dead.

I remember letting a shameful thought cross my mind: Now you've wasted your time, Roy. What kind of character witness will a dead Mexican make? I rolled the sheepskin up and put it in my pocket.

In the chapel I found a Mexican boy carrying candles into a baptismal chamber. "Hey, boy. There's an old man out here who just died," I said.

"Where?" he asked.

"Out in front by that statue."

"Which one? The image of the Virgin?"

"I don't know whose image it is. How many statues have you got at this church, anyway?"

The boy put his candles down. "Show me," he said.

I took him out to the altar and he explained that it was indeed the likeness of the Virgin Mary from whose feet the old Mexican's spirit had flown. He didn't seem to regard the corpse as any form of novelty.

"He asked if he could ride my horse here," I said. "Who is he?"

He shrugged and said, "Who knows? The old ones sometime come here to die."

The boy let me know I had nothing more to do there, so I mounted my horse and eased back toward Main Plaza. Halfway there I remembered the sheepskin the old man had given me and I took it out of my pocket for another look. It would take me some time to make sense of the thing, but, once translated, the gift of the dying vaquero would both haunt and enthrall me. It would cause me anguish and rapture. It would rob me of control over my own destiny and change my life forever.

TWO

Something more than chance drew me to San Antonio the day the old Mexican died. The Alamo City was part of a plan I had formulated to keep me forever beyond the grasp of felony. The plan had come to me in Huntsville, the day the underkeeper opened the gate of the Texas state penitentiary to let me out. "We'll see you back here soon enough, convict," he said.

"You'll meet the devil before you lay your eyes on Royal Strickland Huckaby again," I replied. Then I walked into the rain and started stomping red mud puddles down the road, as carefree as a boy out of school. When the clouds broke I found a sunny spot at the edge of a pine wood on the east side of a hill, just outside of town. I sat there all morning and strung together the pieces of my plan for a long, free, honest existence.

The last thing I wanted to do was return to my home in Matagorda County, on the Texas Gulf Coast. A few of my sister's letters had gotten through to me, telling me that the feud had died out there after I left for prison. But I couldn't rely on her word even though I knew she would never intentionally mislead me. I was afraid the feud had simply lain dormant for the past three years and might erupt anew as soon as I stepped off the train at the depot. I intended to spend the rest of my days in a place that offered the least potential for violent conflict and Matagorda County was not it. Neither my folks nor my three sisters would understand that, of course, so I decided not to tell them or any other past acquaintance where I would go.

It occurred to me on the hill outside of Huntsville, as the sun dried the cheap freedom suit the state had provided for me, that *people* had caused all my troubles. People as individuals and people as a society. Well-meaning people, ill-intentioned people, people I knew well and some I had never even seen. They had caused all my misfortunes. It made sense to me, then, that I should look for a place where few people lived and go there to start staying out of trouble.

The frontier had the fewest people, but moving to the frontier to shun trouble made no more sense than joining a leper colony to avoid smallpox. I decided I would drift just shy of the frontier, to the edge of the settlements, and find work in a quiet town or on a lonely ranch where I could mind my own business and avoid people. The one product of humanity I most fervently wished to elude was that anomaly of civilization variously known as a vendetta or a blood feud or "a trouble" and my plan would not allow me to come within one hundred miles of such an abomination.

That plan I put into effect at Huntsville. I had made my

preparations for the day of my release well in advance and had asked my banker back home to establish an account for me in Huntsville. I drew on it to buy a horse and a saddle. I could have ridden the rails, but trains moved fast and my plan dictated that I take things slow and keep my eyes open for any form of turmoil I might have to sidestep. So I mounted my horse—a five-year-old seal brown mare I named Liberty—and set out for the Alamo City.

San Antonio was not the most likely place in Texas to stay out of trouble, but I reasoned that if I hung around the hotels and stockyards—and avoided the saloons and brothels—I could probably find work and stay clear of vice. I wasn't particular about the type of employment I found, and I was willing to work for little pay as long as I could work alone and mind my own business. It seemed odd that a college-educated man of a wealthy plantation family should consider a career of servility, but circumstances had conducted me to that end and there was nothing I could do about it.

I started out toward San Antonio at such a crawl that even my mare found the pace lacking. I thought I would feel safer if I traveled slow, but the sluggishness only gave me time to contemplate the various species of mischief that could undermine my intricately formed plans. I started to wonder if simply avoiding calamity would suffice. It might prove beneficial, I thought, to actively work against trouble—to begin a practice of doing *good*. That way, if I earned a reputation as one who habitually did his neighbor a kind turn, it could fare in my favor in a court of law. I would have no trouble producing witnesses who could testify to my fine character.

I had no intention of going on trial for anything, but neither had I had that intention in Matagorda County, three years before. I had learned there that a man could find himself at odds with the law simply by going about his business as usual. If I had worked harder at establishing character witnesses in Matagorda County, I might have gotten off with a lighter sentence or been acquitted altogether. My new formula for avoiding incarceration took those kinds of things into account.

So, by the time I reached San Antonio, I had already carried out a half-dozen feats of good will. I had helped an old man fix a stake-and-rider fence southwest of Bryan. I had caught a boy's saddle horse for him near Caldwell. Just outside of Giddings, I had helped a farmer and his sons get their hay under the barn ahead of a thunderstorm. I had done my part in extinguishing a small kitchen fire in Bastrop. And in San Marcos I had accomplished two acts of benevolence at once by escorting the town cow from the premises of a boarding house whose matron was beating the animal soundly with a broom handle to get rid of it. I had become a virtual samaritan.

The afternoon I tied my horse in the shade on Main Plaza, I was still lumbering through life with one eye trained for eminent disaster and the other for potential deeds of generosity. From my vantage on the plaza, I could watch the door of the Old Southern Hotel and look for cattlemen I might hit up for work.

That was when I met the old Mexican and agreed to let him ride my horse to Mission Conception. Now he was dead and I was wandering back toward my shade tree on the plaza, trying to analyze the peculiar design on the sheepskin he had given me.

I turned it over, around, and sideways several times before I settled on a way to study it. It was essentially a line drawn between two points. One point was labeled "*el tesoro*" and the other "*la piedra del cero*." If it had said *derecho* or *izquierda* I would have had some understanding of it, but as it was, I didn't have a clue. I swatted at a horsefly that lit on my neck and continued to ogle the gift of the dead vaquero.

There were a few ideas that I could comprehend because they were in numerals and Spanish speakers write numerals the same way English speakers do. A bracket-like manifestation seemed to suggest that the distance between *el tesoro* and *la piedra del cero* was "189 *cadenas,* 7 *varas.*" But of what length a *cadena* was, or a *vara,* I could only imagine. I finally began to grasp the gist of the diagram when I saw "N 49 W" scrawled beside the line that ran between the two points. I recognized "N 49 W" as a compass bearing. The old Mexican had given me a map.

THREE

I remembered the way the old Mexican had gestured and talked at length before giving me the gift. He had probably been telling me what the map would lead to and I hadn't understood a syllable.

I returned to my place under the shade tree from which I had first seen the old man and continued to study the map. *El tesoro. La piedra del cero.* Those were the two key phrases. Two points, a line running between them. North and 49 degrees west.

North was zero degrees. I remembered that much from a cartography lecture I had attended at Southwestern University. I also recalled that there were 90 degrees between north and west. That would cause 49 degrees to bear almost exactly northwest. *El tesoro* stood somewhere to the northwest of *la piedra del cero* and I didn't have the faintest idea what either of them represented.

I almost flagged a passing citizen to ask for a translation, but I remembered my plan and rolled the sheepskin back up. Until I knew what I had, I would not flaunt it in the faces of strangers. Prudence was my hallmark. I leaned back against the plaza oak to contemplate my strategy.

I rolled and unrolled the map twenty times in the next hour until I arrived at a plan to translate it. I would do it one word at a time, using a different translator for each word. I would not mention or show the map to anyone or call the least bit of unnecessary attention to myself. I would go about it casually and carefully. If possible, I would have some knowledge of each translator before I asked for assistance and that was where the Buckhorn Saloon fell into my plan.

I knew the proprietor of the Buckhorn, but was sure he wouldn't remember me. I hadn't seen Albert Friedrich in years and didn't think he had ever known me by name. He was a sober and agreeable man—just the candidate to translate a word for me. Of course, I would have to enter the Buckhorn to talk to him, and I had vowed to stay out of saloons. But one minor violation of my master plan for a crime-free life would matter little in the long run, I decided. Besides, I was burning with curiosity to decipher the old Mexican's map.

"Good afternoon, sir," Friedrich said as I stepped up to his polished cherry-wood bar. He ran a topnotch saloon. "What can I get for you?"

"Beer," I said. Sweet cigar smoke filled the air, glasses clinked together and laughing voices reminded me of the many hours I had spent in saloons before prison. I forced those halcyon memories from my mind, though, because I knew now that beneath the pleasant facade of any saloon rushed an undercurrent of pure wickedness. Some of the same men I had once toasted were now dead.

Friedrich slid a mug to me across the bar. "Say, don't I know you?"

"Nope," I said.

"You look like Champ Huckaby's boy, grown up. Yes, I didn't recognize you in those rags. Have you been ill? You look thin." He turned to a group of businessmen at a nearby table. "Hey, boys, look who's here. I want you to meet . . . "

"How much for this beer?" I said, interrupting him in a severe tone of voice. I had heard of Friedrich's great memory, but never dreamed he would remember me from a single visit to his saloon several years before.

Friedrich instantly caught on to my situation. "Never mind, boys. My mistake," he said to the men at the table. Then he spoke softly to me. "Sorry, Royal. I forgot about the trouble down your way. I thought that was over."

"I'm not Royal. You have me mixed up with somebody else. How much for the beer?"

"On the house with my apologies. I could have sworn you were one of the Huckaby clan." He winked and went to sit with the men at the nearby table.

Friedrich's saloon wasn't called the Buckhorn for the heck of it. He owned a collection of antlers that has never been matched anywhere. Antlers protruded from all the walls and parts of the ceiling, in some places as dense as a bed of nails. A hundred glass-eyed deer heads stared at one another across the billiard and card tables. The most tremendous specimens hung between the marbled columns of the back bar and a few pairs were mounted as they had died, with their antlers locked together in combat. Even the chandeliers were made of deer horns.

Friedrich loved to hunt deer and he loved just as much to talk about deer hunting. He probably remembered me from my only previous visit to his saloon because I had told him a story about a big buck I had killed. As I sipped my beer, I heard him talking about one of his hunts to the gents at the table and he got up to show them the buck he had killed on that hunt. The antlers were tacked to the ceiling

with about a hundred other pairs. He used a billiard stick
to single it out. "It was this one right here. When that old
buck came over the hill, he never knew what hit him . . . "
The Buckhorn Saloon virtually bristled inside.

As I turned my beer mug up, five cowboys burst in,
dressed in new boots, hats, or handkerchiefs, and already
somewhat drunk even though it was an hour till dark. They
had just returned from a drive, I figured, and were bent on
trading their wages for fancy clothes and whiskey. They all
wore pistols and surged about as one blustering body of
havoc, making me nervous. "Look what we brung you from
the Sabinal," one of the cowboys said, holding up a huge
pair of deer antlers bearing fourteen points. "Old Ben
Saddler kilt this buck last winter and throwed the horns up
in a tree. We borrowed 'em when we left the ranch. Figured
you might trade us a few drinks for 'em."

"I should say I'll trade!" Friedrich said. "That rack will
earn a drink for each of you."

"Make it drinks for the house, and we'll swap," another
cowboy said.

The men at the table approved and Friedrich began drawing the beer and pouring the whiskey.

"Say," I ventured when he brought my new mug, "do you
speak any Spanish?" The cowboys were laughing it up
along the bar next to me and covering my conversation with
Friedrich adequately.

"Enough to get business done," Friedrich said.

"Well, I don't speak any. But there was a Mexican talking to me today and, of course, I couldn't understand anything he said, but there was one word he used a lot. I was
wondering if you could translate it for me."

"It was probably profane," Friedrich said, "so don't get
offended at me when I tell it to you. Sometimes they'll
smile at you like they mean the greatest compliment and

all the while they are cursing every member of your family. What was the word he used so much?"

"The word, as I recall it, was *tesoro*."

Friedrich stood bolt upright and began to laugh. He shot his eyes toward the cowboys lining the bar next to me. "Hey, boys, this young fellow needs a Mexican word translated. Does anybody know what *tesoro* means?"

The punchers thought for an instant and then began spouting jeers. One of them cuffed me about the neck. "By God, he must have gone and bought him a treasure map!"

The men at the table turned their faces to the antlered ceiling and laughed in unison. "Give him one on us, Albert," one of them said, "he won't have any money left if he's bought a treasure map!"

There was more laughter at my expense and I could not even attempt to deny purchasing the map. Friedrich brought me another beer. "How much did you pay for it? Fifty dollars is the going rate."

"I didn't pay that much."

"No, he got swindled at a bargain!" the cowboy next to me said. "Give him a drink on us. He's a good sport to take such a ribbin'!"

Friedrich continued to set up drinks for everybody. "Don't feel bad," he said to me. "Some of these boys have probably invested in buried Spanish treasure, too. Who took you?"

I shrugged. "An old man."

"The old men sell the most maps," a cowboy said. "I guess they're supposed to be old enough to remember where the damned Spaniards buried the stuff."

They went on about old Mexicans selling bogus treasure maps, but my thoughts drifted as I drank my beers quicker—the mugs were backing up. I remembered what Friedrich had said about Mexicans smiling and cussing one's family members at the same time. Was that what the old Mexican had pulled over on me? Had that feeble old man chosen me as the victim of his final hoax? A last jab at the almighty gringo? After I had let him ride my horse?

I couldn't believe it. He had spoken to me as he had to the doves he dreamed of flying with. I thought I knew enough about deceit that I could have detected it in his eyes at Mission Conception. And I had not paid a red cent for that map. The old man had *given* it to me. That should have accounted for something. Yes, his gift to me was given in sincerity—a map labeled with lost treasure. *El tesoro.*

The beer shone golden through the mug in my hand and glistened through the facets of the glass like polished pieces of eight. Maybe there really was a treasure. But even if there was, I knew nothing about it except that it lay buried 49 degrees northwest of a thing labeled *la piedra del cero.* And just what in the hell was *la piedra del cero?*

"Well, which one was it?" a cowboy asked, nudging me on the shoulder.

"Which one was what?"

"Haven't you been listenin'? Was it parchment or sheepskin?"

"Sheepskin," I muttered.

"That's five you owe me, Dick! Pay up!" The cowboys made good on their bets.

"India ink or blood?" they asked next.

"Blood?" I responded, astounded at the thought.

"It must be India ink, then!" Dick said. "Now *you* owe *me* five," and the money changed hands again. "Where is it? Let's have a look at it."

"No, I better not," I said. "I've drunk my last beer so I better get going."

Friedrich had a full stein in my face before I could reach my hat on a nearby antler tine. I had forgotten how easily beer could flow down one's gullet. "Here's another, friend," the barkeeper said. "Now, let's see that map. Maybe one of these boys will recognize it."

I shrugged and pulled the sheepskin from my pocket and unrolled it on the bar. We bunched our heads together to study it and I could smell three or four different species of liquor riding the rough voices of the cowhands. The gentlemen from the table came over to look, too. They all told some fine jokes on me, but even I was laughing by then. The beer and the visions of treasure had improved my disposition.

"Here's the treasure," one said, pointing at *el tesoro*. "Have you a pickax and shovel, Albert?"

"It lies forty-nine degrees northwest of this, whatever that means," I said, pointing to *la piedra del cero*.

"Let me see," said a businessman from the table. "I speak some of the lingo. I have Mexicans on my payroll."

"I aim to have one on my bedroll, tonight," one particularly randy cowboy said. The rest of them howled like wolves.

"I don't know what it means," the employer of Mexicans said, "but here's the distance between the two points. One hundred eighty-nine *cadenas,* seven *varas*. What in the hell is a *cadena?*"

"What in the hell is a *vara?*"

"A vara is about two or three feet or so," a cowboy said.

"How the hell would you know?"

"My uncle's a surveyor. He's always talkin' about varas and leagues and labors and things like that."

"But what's this part mean?" I asked anxiously, pointing my finger again at *la piedra del cero*.

"I think he's still aimin' to dig!"

A great laugh went up among the deer antlers.

"No, it's not that," I explained. "But I'm going to frame this and put it in my parlor. It will make a better story if I know what all the words mean."

The men around the treasure map became studious. Finally one of the cowboys spoke up. "This here means rock," he said, indicating *piedra*. "I know because me and a Mexican kid I grew up with used to chuck 'em at each other all day and that's what he called 'em—*piedras*."

"The rock of the something-or-other," a businessman said. "Who knows what *cero* means?" He pronounced the word, "care-oh."

"It ain't 'care-oh,' it's 'chair-oh,'" one cowboy insisted. "Or maybe 'share-oh.' Damn these Mexican words!"

The cowboy with the hopes of having a *señorita* on his bedroll spoke up then. "What's your name, gold-digger?"

"Charlie Fischer," I said, quickly assuming the name of a former prison mate.

"Well, Charlie, I know a girl across town that can help us change these last two words to American—this share-oh and this here *cadena*. Stick with ol' Matt Cottle and we'll go see her later."

Stepping into the Buckhorn had been a severe enough transgression against my designs for avoiding trouble but visiting a whorehouse was unthinkable. "No, I have no business there," I said.

"Of course you haven't," Matt said. "You've done all your business with an old mapmaker." The boys howled, especially the one named Dick who seemed to be getting drunk faster than the others. "But we'll loan you a buck a head and you can pay us back when you get your treasure. Ain't that right, boys?"

"Why the hell not!" joyous Dick yelled.

Things looked grim for me. I had five drunken cowboys buying me beer and staking me to a night at the whorehouse. They would not let me refuse their charity. I finally had to give in and decided I could just give my five to a girl and then get the hell out of San Antonio and go treasure hunting and return to the formula I had conceived in Huntsville—the one I was currently straying so far from.

When we left the Buckhorn Saloon after dark, all of us were still passably sober except for Dick. He tried to pick a fight with a stagecoach guard carrying a shotgun, and we had to drag him away kicking.

We mounted our horses and rode toward the whorehouse across town. On the way, there was some discussion about shooting out the gas streetlights, but Matt told his friends to wait until after he had bedded his señorita in case they all had to make a gallop for the ranch.

I was still sober enough to feel uneasy about the prospects ahead. I considered turning my horse to make a break from my corrupting acquaintances, but my mind was still on the treasure map and the two words yet uninterpreted.

And also, though I was uneasy, I was having certain carnal visions about the house of ill repute at which we would soon arrive. I had visited such an establishment on one or two occasions in Matagorda County—a lonely, sequestered two-story mansion where buxom belles played classical music and curtsied to the wealthy ranchers and plantation owners who frequented the place. I was curious to find out how the San Antonio brothel and its personnel would compare.

It disappointed me to find that the cowboys' whorehouse was nothing more than a shotgun shanty. We hitched our horses outside and the boys chipped in their dollars for my benefit before we went in.

The madam was a fat, painted woman who had tried to improve the looks of her establishment on the inside with a bunch of cheap curtains and tapestries. She played an ill-tuned piano with a half-dozen dead keys while a couple of scurrilous jacks danced with the working girls. "Welcome, boys," the madam said when we entered. Dick started dancing by himself and his friends stomped and clapped for him until he whirled himself to the floor.

The girls, about eight or nine of them, were of every nationality, race, and tribe I could imagine in my present condition of inebriation. One yellow-haired girl didn't look a day over sixteen. Overall, the place represented the vilest example of iniquity I had ever stood in outside of the state penitentiary.

"Where's the Mexican girl you know?" I asked Matt.

"She must be busy. Wait a few minutes. She'll show."

Matt and I sat on a dusty sofa and waited. The few minutes turned into half an hour. The rest of the cowboys danced with various whores, "to get a feel for 'em," Dick said. He finally disappeared down a hallway with the young, yellow-haired girl. My head was pounding by that time and I realized I had drunk near two gallons of beer on an empty stomach. I longed to be sober and sleeping alone under the stars.

But the sheepskin map rolled in my pocket made me stay. The old Mexican had *given* it to me. That virtually guaranteed its authenticity. He would have *sold* it to me for a hoax. Wasn't a chance at buried treasure worth the risk of five more minutes in a whorehouse? Then an awful thought occurred to me. The old swindler knew damn good and well that he was about to keel over at Mission Conception. What use would he have for my money where he was going? By *giving* me the map, he had perpetrated the perfect fraud—one I would scarcely suspect in a hundred years.

The lady of the house quit punishing the piano and approached Matt and me. She leaned over and swung her huge breasts in front of our faces. "Are you boys shy?" she asked.

"No, just particular," Matt said. "I'm waiting for Juana. There she is now!"

Juana had emerged from the hallway, a slip of a *señorita*. She came running at Matt when she saw him and, flinging herself at him, wrapped her legs about his waist and bit his ear playfully.

"Ouch, damn it!" he said, and slapped her on the rear end. He began carrying her back toward the hallway and I followed.

"Now, wait a minute," the huge madam said. "You get your own girl. We don't double up here."

I should have made a break for the door, but I had come that far and there were only two more words to translate on the map. Yes, it was probably a worthless piece of sheepskin, but I had done the old Mexican a kindness and therefore there was just the slightest chance that he had given me an authentic map out of gratitude.

"You," I said, pointing at the nearest prostitute, "come on." I felt more depraved than I had in my entire life. I caught up to Matt before he got Juana locked away behind her door. She was prattling nonstop in Spanish.

"Slow down," Matt said. "No savvy." He started to close the door.

"Hey, what about the map?" I asked. The girl I had chosen was a half-dressed half-Indian and she was going through my pockets for money and I was squirming like a wounded centipede, trying to retain some particle of dignity. I won't admit everything I was thinking then, but I had been locked away from women for three years and there was a conflict going on within me between proper moral conduct and acute lust. I was thinking that I had already fallen far enough from grace as it was and would have to give the girl the money anyway . . .

"Can't you wait till later?" Matt said.

"No."

"Well, damn it, come on in here and let's let her have a look at it." Matt laboriously used his limited Spanish to let

Juana know what we were about. She looked suspicious at
first, but finally allowed us all to enter her cubicle and the
half-Indian whore kicked the door shut behind us. I unrolled the map and Matt showed it to Juana. He stuttered
through some more Spanish and pointed at the words we
wanted translated. When Juana stopped laughing, about my
having purchased the map, I suppose, she began trying to
explain. First she addressed the reference to 189 *cadenas.*

Her words came too quick and Matt had to get her to
slow down. She wore a silver chain around her neck and
she kept showing it to Matt as she explained.

"I think she's sayin' a *cadena* is like this necklace she's
got, but men wear it in jail."

That made perfect sense to me. "Chains," I said. "One
hundred and eighty-nine chains. The distance is measured
in chains and varas."

"Yeah, but how long of a chain?" Matt asked.

"It's not as if it matters. This is just going to hang in my
parlor."

"Oh, yeah. Let me see if I can get her to change this other
word to American—this 'share-oh.'"

"*Sí, cero,*" Juana said. "*Como, como, como . . .*" She
couldn't find a word Matt could comprehend.

With me the struggle was with morality, not language,
for the half-Indian whore had found things in my pockets
I had forgotten I kept there.

"*Como, como, como . . . Nada!*"

"*Nada?*" Matt said.

"*Nada,*" Juana repeated.

"She says it don't mean nothin'," Matt told me.

"How could it mean nothing? Are you sure?"

Matt asked her again if the word had no meaning.

"No, no, no," she shrieked. "*Es como nada. Cero es
como nada.*"

"I don't know what the hell she means, Charlie. Let's forget about it. These girls work on time."

Juana punched Matt in the stomach. She did not like being misunderstood. The half-Indian girl was trying to strip me, much to my moral degradation and lascivious gratification. I tried to fasten the buttons as quickly as she undid them, but I was quickly losing ground.

"Mira," Juana said, holding five fingers in front of Matt's face. *"Cinco,"* she said. She turned her thumb in against her palm and said, *"Cuatro."* Her fingers went down one by one as she said, *"Tres, dos, uno."* Then she brandished her closed fist in Matt's face and said, *"Cero!"*

"Oh, I git it," Matt said, handing the map to me. "She don't mean that it don't mean nothin'. She means that it means absolutely nothin'. *Cero* is zero."

Of course! Only one letter differed between the two. Zero! *La piedra del cero* was the rock of the zero. That was where my treasure hunt would begin thanks to the generosity of the kind old Mexican. But what and where in the hell was the rock of the zero?

I might have had something of a tussle with temptation at that juncture. With the map translated, the only matter left unresolved was that of the half-Indian prostitute. But a sudden shotgun blast relieved me of my moral responsibilities to resist her advances.

Juana jumped onto her bed, bounced off holding the mattress, and landed in the corner with it on top of her. The half-Indian whore jerked her hands out of my pockets so fast that the rough fabric of my trousers chafed me in a sensitive area. She joined Juana behind the mattress. Matt pulled his pistol out and cocked it.

Another blast went off somewhere in the shack and I could hear the courtesans screaming and doors slamming and one big, loud, angry voice railing above it all. If Juana's room had had a window, I would have leapt through it at that point, but there was no such avenue of escape available. The ruckus outside of the room continued as Matt and I backed speechlessly away from the door, he with his revolver cocked and aimed in that direction, I holding my pants up so they wouldn't fall below my knees—the half-Indian whore had undone most of the buttons. The thundering voice roared again in the hallway and filled me with dread—and disdain for the old Mexican for getting me into this fix.

Suddenly the door burst open and we beheld a huge, grizzled frontiersman in the doorway with a double-barreled shotgun. Matt dropped his pistol and it went off. The frontiersman sent a blast of buckshot through the ceiling in retaliation.

"Who's under that beddin'?" he demanded.

"Just whores," Matt said.

"Let me see 'em!" His voice rivaled the bellow of a crazed bull.

Juana and the half-breed peeked over the top of the mattress and then ducked under again. The frontiersman cursed and moved down the hall. I eased cautiously to the door, holding my trousers up with one hand, hoping to make my break up the hall and out into the street to my mare, Liberty.

Just then drunken Dick fell into the corridor in front of the frontiersman, pulling up his pants and holding onto his pistol. "What the hell is going on out here?" he asked, swaying as he stood. From the same room, now, came the yellow-haired minx, clutching Dick's shirt in front of her naked body. She took one look at the big man with the shotgun, said, "Papa!" and ducked her head of yellow hair back into her room. Other heads ducked into other rooms and only Dick was left standing in front of the double-barrel.

"Why, you whorin' little son of a bitch!" the old settler bellowed. He thumbed back the hammer of his live barrel and leveled it on Dick. I was Dick's only hope for salvation and as such I foolishly disregarded my own safety and used both fists to strike the enraged father on the back of the head, causing him to blow a huge chunk of wall away as he fell.

Dick must have sobered up instantly, because he made a marvelously agile leap over the old pioneer and shot past me at a sprint. Matt ran out behind him and so did several other customers. "Run, Charlie!" Matt yelled to me. That was the last I ever heard from Matt Cottle, however, because my trousers had dropped down around my ankles, hindering my escape. A shotgun barrel tapped me on the skull about then, and I fell into a compulsory form of slumber.

I awoke in the San Antonio City Jail, arrested for causing a drunken row in a whorehouse. I found out the old settler had escaped with his yellow-haired daughter, leaving only me to pay for the damages. Thus, less than one day after my arrival in the city where my permanent avoidance of trouble was to have begun, I found myself jailed, wounded, ashamed, and utterly miserable.

FOUR

The judge let me wire my banker in Matagorda County for the money I needed to pay for my fine and the damages. I included strict instructions that no one in the vicinity should know of my whereabouts. I had to drop my alias and go back to being Royal Strickland Huckaby, which was neither an honor nor a pleasure. Until I could produce the cash, I had to remain in jail. The authorities were rather upset with me and I was furious at the old Mexican. And at myself for having believed in him.

One jailer, however, listened to my story that I was but little responsible for the disastrous outcome of the previous night, and he checked the bank for me at intervals to see if the transfer of funds had been accomplished. This man was a short bundle of muscles whose head consisted of a thick skull and an anvil jaw, the hinges of which he seemed to keep working by greasing their joints regularly with profanities.

"Hey, Huckaby," he said when the beans and bread came that evening. "The goddamn bank ain't got your money yet. Tomorrow you'll get out for sure, though. Anyway, we'll keep your ass out of trouble tonight." He slid the tin plate through a slot in the grating. "Here, I got you a newspaper to pass the time with."

One of the other prisoners scowled at me from his cell. "I guess if I had me some money in the bank I could buy me a guard, too."

"Shut up, you thievin' bastard," shouted the guard, and spit on the prisoner's food before sliding it through the cell grate.

The newspaper distracted me with satirical commentary and accounts of all the local disasters and social engagements. I remembered the specifics of only two articles, however. One was a cryptic report of the rechartering of the Colorado River Navigation Company that was, according to the newspaper, engaged in clearing the raft at the mouth of the Colorado River to open that stream to steamer traffic. I knew that to be pure bunkum.

The Huckabys owned ranch land along the lower Colorado and I had seen the raft many times over the years and had seen several attempts to clear it fail. The Colorado River Navigation Company was an impotent, graft-ridden governmental entity that, each time it was reactivated, ran out of money before a fraction of the raft could be blasted or carved away.

As a boy I had once walked across the raft and shot a great many water moccasins in the crossing. It was a permanent fixture on the river. Every year, floods tore trees from the banks hundreds of miles along the Colorado and pulled them downstream to add to the driftwood raft. In time, they became waterlogged, sank, and were driven into the riverbed by other sinking debris with the force of a pile driver. The river current seeped through the raft but steamers could not enter from the Gulf of Mexico. Only a couple of land-locked boats serviced the river above the raft.

About once every ten years, some legislator who had never laid eyes on the tangled mass of timber would undertake to remove it with public funds, and the Colorado River Navigation Company would quit the grave, usually fed by taxes levied on steamers and other merchant boats. It would slow the growth of the raft for a while, until some bureaucrat had sufficiently lined his pockets, then it would fold for lack of funds and hibernate for another decade or so while the great raft remained forever intact.

That brief newspaper article predicting the ultimate navigability of the river made me chuckle a little, sarcastically, despite my aching head and dejected frame of mind. The idea seemed even more peculiar now that railroads served almost every town along the Colorado as high up as Austin. Why did the river need steamer traffic? Besides, I had seen the Colorado shrink to a trickle during drought years. I decided not to fret anymore over it. I had my own concerns to look after and, so far, I had done a sorry job of looking after them.

On the same page with the report of the Navigation Company, however, I found an article that *did* require every particle of my concern. Reading it made my cell darken.

SPECTACULAR MURDER
Four Dead in Burnet County War

The Burnet *Messenger* reports a stunning double murder in the area of southern Burnet County on the 14th inst., the two victims, brothers, being members of the Standard family currently embroiled in a trouble with a neighboring family by the name of Flatt.

The Standard brothers were shot in the back from ambush near their ranch on the south bank of the Colorado River below the Marble Falls, their bodies filled with bullets. These murders bring to four the number of victims killed in the Flatt-Standard feud. Two Flatt brothers died in a battle two months ago.

The *Messenger* credits a land dispute as the source of the conflict, the two families both claiming the same parcel of land along Double Horn Creek where it empties into the Colorado River.

The *Messenger* reports the neighborhood of southern Burnet and northern Blanco counties in a state of extreme agitation. Texas Rangers have been summoned to help locate the boundary between the two clans and end the hostilities.

I could not say where Burnet County was in relation to my jail cell, but I knew I would have to find out before I left the city. I did not intend to get anywhere within fifty miles of any feud between families or any other opposing factions.

I suffered from fitful nightmares of ambush and violence that night. The next morning the guard at the San Antonio City Jail secured my fine from the bank and opened my cell door.

"Your old nag is in the livery around the block," he said. "You'll have to pay the bill there, too."

"Where is Burnet County from here?" I asked.

"Burnet County? Shit, I don't know. What town is in Burnet County?"

"Burnet, naturally."

"Well, how the hell was I to know? Houston ain't in Houston County. Austin ain't in Austin County."

"Just tell me where the town of Burnet is from here."

"Ninety miles due north, past the Marble Falls on the Colorado. Is that where you're heading?"

"Nope. That's the place I intend to avoid."

"Oh, yes, I understand. So, if anyone was to ask where Roy Huckaby was headed after raking hell in San Antonio, I should tell them anywhere but Burnet County."

"Tell them what you like. I simply mean to say that I intend to avoid the place."

"Yes, sir, Mr. Huckaby. I understand. You are going anywhere, but you damn sure as hell are not going to Burnet County. That I will remember."

"I don't care if you remember it or not," I said.

The guard shrugged his burly shoulders and brought my personal belongings to me, the most conspicuous item among them being the rolled sheepskin stained with India ink.

"What son of a bitch sold you that worthless piece of horse shit?" he asked, snorting out a laugh or two. "Money just sort of has a way of flowing with you, don't it?"

I had no objection to the guard keeping a small stipend for serving as my liaison with the local bank, but for the amount he took from my cash reserves he should have been locked up in his own jail. I had no intention of starting another altercation in San Antonio, however, because I had found them to be accompanied by the most serious of consequences. I let the jailer keep the money and bid farewell to San Antonio, its jail, its whorehouses, its saloons, and its devious, old citizens bearing gifts of bogus treasure maps.

FIVE

Things change northwest of San Antonio. Limestone rears suddenly through the topsoil. Running springs carve it into craggy ranges. Stunted trees spread a general cloak over the hills, but where their roots probe the spring beds they gain ample, even heroic, proportions.

I stopped among these first outriders of the Texas hills and asked myself what I would do now and how I would prevent myself from straying again from my plan to lead a life free of criminal activity. As I had done in Huntsville, I found a hillside to recline against.

Where would I go now? It seemed easier at the time to decide where I would not go. Not Burnet County, where the Flatt-Standard trouble was leading to murder and ambuscade. Not Matagorda County, where my own vendetta was lying dormant, waiting to flare at my return. Not San Antonio. Not the frontier. I unhooked my canteen from my saddle horn and took a swallow. Liberty was staked and grazing nearby.

I wanted to go to the most peaceful town in Texas. Where was it? After some deliberation, I decided Fredericksburg would be my destination. The Germans who had settled there loved peace and had even managed to get along with the Comanches before that tribe was run into the Indian Territory. I thought I could probably find work on one of the farms or ranches in the area. I was desperate for a job now, willing to work for room and board. San Antonio had proven true the adage about idle hands.

I got up and moved my mare to another part of the hill. She had eaten all the grass in her circle around the picket pin. Then I moved my own place of repose farther into the shadows. The sun had crept dangerously close.

To get to Fredericksburg, I resolved to use the same mode of travel that had delivered me from Huntsville to San Antonio without incident. I would proceed slowly, keeping my eyes peeled for signs of trouble—like decrepit Mexicans with treasure maps and drunken cowboys carrying racks of deer antlers.

For some time I deliberated on whether or not I should give up my practice of doing good deeds. It seemed the kindness I had done the old Mexican had led to all kinds of skulduggery. It became clear after an hour or so of meditation, however, that my curiosity and greed—not my thoughtfulness toward the old man—had led to the incident in the whorehouse. I decided to continue to pursue acts of helpfulness but to desist in any thoughts of buried treasure.

Buried treasure! Consider the lunacy of it. Of all the things I could conceive that would cause me to break into jail, buried treasure seemed the most outlandish. And yet five cowboys on some ranch were probably telling the story of it as I lay in the shade of my scrubby oak tree.

What *was* this supposed treasure the old Mexican's map had misrepresented to me, anyway? I put the canteen under my head and stared into the sky. *El tesoro.* The treasure. Such vagueness! What treasure? In Texas? The land of a thousand legends of buried treasure? From the shifting sand dunes of Galveston where Jean Lafitte buried his pirated booty to Castle Gap, west of the Pecos, where Emperor Maximilian's fortune waited to be unearthed? Treasure indeed! Trunks of it, mule loads, wagon loads, train loads—all for rubes and dreamers!

The clouds above took on the shapes of abandoned mine shafts and caches of gold nuggets; jewels and coins and gems; oaken chests trimmed in brass and bulging with loot.

I sprang up so suddenly that my mare jerked the slack out of her picket rope. I picked up a stone and hurled it into a little canyon and heard it clacking among boulders. I

shook my head, spit, pissed on a cedar bush. I had to work
all ridiculous thoughts of treasure out of my system and out
of my mind—a mind contorted with some nebulous form
of greed that was bound to bring me nothing but misery.

The map! The damned treasure map was at the core of
my greed. I rushed around under the oak trees and picked
up as many sticks as I could find. My mare stood and stared
at me, bewildered. I pulled dry grass for kindling and put
a match to it. Soon I had a fire going and I reached into my
saddlebag for the old Mexican's map.

I made one crucial mistake before tossing the sheepskin
into the flames. I unrolled it for a last look. Two points, a
line running between them. *El tesoro*—the treasure. One
hundred eighty-nine chains, seven varas. Forty-nine degrees northwest. *La piedra del cero*—the rock of the zero.

What and where in the hell was the rock of the zero?

I threw the map onto the fire and watched every grain
of it burn to ashes. It gave the smell of a branding iron
against a yearling's flank. The flames dwindled and the embers cooled and I scattered the ashes among the stones. I
sat and looked back at the sky. The map was gone and the
clouds were clouds again and my ambition was to work for
room and board, not to dig for buried treasure. The vin-
dictive old Mexican was dead, San Antonio behind me and
the treasure map a part of my past. I was, again, a man of
one ambition, one concern, one goal for life.

But the Spanish language is odd in its beauty and it rings
like music in one's memories. Like an old song, a phrase
heard often enough echoes endlessly in the subconscious,
weaves itself among one's thoughts, and trips from the
tongue in whispers when all else is silent. *La piedra del
cero . . . la piedra del cero . . . la piedra del cero . . .*

The first leg of my trip to Fredericksburg proved unevent-
ful. I rode at such a sluggish pace that my mare found it

possible to graze on tall stalks of grass as we went. The first day I made it only as far as Leon Springs. There was a fine stone stagecoach inn there where I took a meal. But I shunned drinks at the bar and slept in a field outside of town.

The second day I rode through Boerne, one of the German towns settled northwest of San Antonio. The town had neat stone houses, clean streets, and an overall look of prosperity. I was so pleased with the looks of the place that I stopped in the post office and asked if employment might be found in the area.

The postmaster, an immaculate man in suspenders and a bow tie, looked up and down my dusty assemblage, flared his nostrils, and said, "We have no work here for the likes of drifters and saddle tramps. This is a proper town."

I moved on, acutely aware of my slovenly appearance. I hadn't bathed since New Braunfels, before arriving at San Antonio. Bathing was a habit I had found difficult to keep up during my sentence in the state penitentiary. Convicts were expected to wash their faces and hands daily, but all from a common trough without a change of water.

I found the Guadalupe River running beside the town of Comfort. I decided to avail myself of the clear, cool waters rushing among the huge bald cypress trees. I rode downstream until I found a place where a fallen colossus had stretched its woody carcass clear across the shallow stream, forming a natural dam. I staked my horse, shed my clothes, and jumped in.

It was October but still hot enough to make a man lather nearly as much as his horse. The Guadalupe felt so good that I stayed in it until sundown. At twilight, a flock of wild turkeys wandered to within fifty yards of my bathing place and flew up to roost in a sycamore. I began to wish for a rifle and decided that when I found a place to settle, I would buy one. But I didn't want to carry one on the road. A weapon might attract trouble.

By dark, my clothes were dry—I had washed them, too—so I rode into Comfort and ate at the stagecoach station. Afterward, I found a couple of old boarders whittling by lantern light on the gallery.

"Good evening, gentlemen," I said.

"Vat's dat?" one said. The folks around Boerne and Comfort, I had found, spoke German as often as English. And some of them, when they did speak English, spoke with the thick tongues of the Old World.

"I said, good evening."

"Oh, yah. Goot evening."

"Sit down, stranger," the other whittler said. With him, no accent was noticeable.

"Don't mind if I do. Pretty hot."

"Yah, ist plenty hot."

"And dry, too," the other one said, "except for that rain we had while back." They continued to litter the floor of the gallery with cedar shavings. The smell of the freshly cut wood drifted to me on the evening breeze.

"I don't suppose there would be a place for a fellow to work for room and board around here?"

The knives became still and the two old whittlers looked at each other, then looked at me, then scratched their heads and stroked their beards and looked at each other again.

"*Nein.* Ain't no verk arount here like dat."

"Nope," the other said.

The knives went back to biting cedar, but after a few strokes the whittlers stopped and looked at each other again. They scratched their heads and stroked their beards some more.

"Nope, not around here, son. However . . ."

"Vat *vas* dat feller's name?" said the German whittler.

"Seems to me he had the first name of a woman."

"Yah! Dat's right! Marion. Marion! Hoh, boy, vat a name!"

"Marion Harkey," the second whittler said.

"Who is Marion Harkey?" I asked.

"He's a fellow that passed through here yesterday. He lost his help recently and was putting out the word that he wanted to hire a man."

"What kind of work does he want done?" I asked.

"Vants lots of fences built und den torn down. Lots of verk, ofer und ofer."

"Fences?" I asked, appealing to the other whittler for clarification.

"Yes. Marion Harkey is a traveling drummer selling bob wire. He goes around putting on demonstrations."

"Demonstrations?"

"Yah, but ve didn't git to see no demonstration here. Too many damned sheeps und not enough cows. Bob vire ist for der cows."

"No, we didn't see it, but we read about it in the San Antonio paper. Harkey built a pen of cedar posts strung with seven strands of his bob wire on Military Plaza and he throwed a rodeo. Beer, beef, bronco rides, and roping contests and cuttin' horses and all. Then, he turned a hundred longhorn mavericks from west Texas into the pen and had a Mexican try to spook them through the wire with torches. They got cut up the first time they tried it and wouldn't go at it again."

"Yah, dat vire helt dem vild cows in, alright. Und dat Marion Harkey, he sold plenty of vire."

"But it's a traveling show, son. Harkey needs a man to build his fences and then tear them down and roll the wire back up every place he throws his rodeo."

I tilted back on the rear legs of my chair and thought about the prospects of building fences so that I could tear them down again. "Where did he go from here?"

"Fredericksburg. He left this morning in his wagon."

"Yah. Dat Marion, he's got to go vest und find zum cows to sell lots of dat vire."

I didn't want to become a barbed-wire drifter on the frontier. Not everybody out there liked the thought of bristling strands stretched across what were once public ranges. Some parties made a habit of cutting fences and shooting fence stretchers. Marion Harkey could spend his wages on some other lackey. I wanted to settle.

"And that's the only work available around here?"

"Yah, dat's it."

"Sorry, son."

"Well, thank you, gentlemen. It's been a pleasure talking to you both."

"Yah, und you, too."

"Good luck, son."

I heard coyotes howling that night as I camped beside the Guadalupe. It was pretty country the Germans had settled a generation before. The hills and clear running streams appealed to a flatlander from the muddy end of the rivers. It was a little rocky, but good for sheep and goats on the hills and suitable for farming in the bottoms where the cedars and oaks were cleared. Cattle did well enough out on the flats. Rain could get scarce in the summer, but springs flowed between most of the hills and folks seemed to get by without getting rich. I asked for no more than that for myself.

The next morning I resumed my trek to Fredericksburg. I passed the stone houses and barns of little farms every few miles and envied the occupants. I had once lorded over two hundred laborers on the sprawling Huckaby plantations and never had to pitch a single fork of hay or throw a solitary calf. But now I wanted only to get intimately acquainted with a couple of thousand acres, work there, hunt, mind my own business. I wanted to live in a place where the name Huckaby caused no more of a stir than the name of a common peon.

Not long after crossing the divide from the Guadalupe Valley into the watershed of the Pedernales River, I caught sight of a two-mule wagon, stopped by the side of the road. I immediately reined my mare in to reconnoiter. A lone man was unloading something from the wagon and a wheel leaned against the sideboards. It looked like a good deed in the making, so I moved cautiously forward.

"How do," I said.

Marion Harkey turned with a heavy spool of barbed wire in his hands and regarded me with a suspicious eye. He wore the clothes of a ranch-man—from the bandanna around his neck to the boots on his feet—but the clothes hadn't come between Marion and much ranch work. He had the thick-waisted build of a prosperous drummer. Sweat streaked his shirt and he looked quite put out. "How would *you* do?" he asked. "Can't you see I've got a busted wagon wheel?"

"Yes, sir, I gathered that. Thought you might like a hand fixing it."

Harkey's tune improved almost immediately. "I would be grateful for some help. Yes, I would. Kind of you to offer, Mr. . . . ?"

"Royal S. Huckaby."

"Marion Harkey."

I got down from my mare and we shook hands.

"Royal. That's a fine name for a common man."

"Thank you," I said, rolling a spool of wire from the bed of the wagon. I judged it weighed in the neighborhood of a hundred pounds when I hefted it.

"Just throw that product down," Harkey said. "Manhandle it. It won't bust. The spool will, maybe, but the wire's indestructible. That's a double-steel strand twist with S-locked barbs. More points to the pound than any wire on the market and just one pound per rod—the lightest, strongest, and cheapest wire ever invented. Eight hundred pounds of bawlin' maverick can't bust that product."

I had four spools on the ground by now and Harkey was just rolling his second one out of the bed.

"I know. I've heard about your rodeo in San Antonio. They say you sold some wire there."

"If a man believes in his product, he ain't afraid to demonstrate it. This wire sells itself. I see the day coming when the whole prairie will glisten with these beautiful strands. We'll have better beef, improved breeds—fat, lazy cattle built for a dinner plate . . ."

While Harkey practiced his sales pitch, I lightened the wagon enough to prize the rear axle up so I could remove the broken wheel. Harkey sat on the cedar post we used for a lever while I put the new wheel on.

"I walked all the way to Fredericksburg for that wheel," he said. "I rode part of the way back in a wagon with a farmer, but rolled that wheel by hand the rest of the way. Whew! That's why I'm so give out. Lucky for me you came along."

He talked more about the future for barbed wire while I loaded the spools back into the wagon. "What do I owe you?" he asked when I had finished.

"Nothing. Just being neighborly."

"By Lucifer, that's decent of you, Royal! Where are you heading?"

"Fredericksburg."

"In that case, ride with me. Throw your saddle on those spools and give your old nag a rest."

Harkey drove a little fast for my taste, but I didn't complain. "Business in Fredericksburg?" he asked.

"I'm looking for work there."

"Work! Why didn't you say so? I need a fence builder for my rodeo. I had a couple of hands, but I lost them in San Antonio. They must have got drunk or jailed or something. I'll be damned if I'm going to wait on hired help. You can start—well, hell, you've already started, haven't you?

I'll have all the work you can stand between here and Wyoming."

"Actually, I was hoping to settle."

"Settle! I made you for a drifter, Royal. What use have fellows like us got for the sedentary life? The frontier is crying for barbed wire. Let's deliver! I'll start you right now and pay you a full day's wage for today. I've got the money in my pocket."

Harkey handed the reins to me and pulled out a roll of bills that he flashed in my face. He pitched a swell deal, but I had no ear for it.

"The frontier's not for me," I said. "I may look like a drifter, but I'm a civilized fellow." I handed the reins back to him.

The wire salesman had put on a hat with the kind of crease that was popular with ranchmen then. He pushed it back on his head and diverted his eyes from the road long enough to look me over with some surprise. "You've seen rough times, Royal. I can tell that by looking at you. The frontier's the place for you."

"I've seen enough of rough times. I'm just looking for someplace quiet to live."

Harkey persisted with his offers of employment for several miles. I turned him down flat, but he refused to accept defeat and started negotiating.

"So, you want to settle. Well, I'll tell you what I can do for you. Maybe I can find you some work. If I can sell some outfit around here a mess of wire, they'll want me to hire 'em somebody to string it. Cowboys won't have any part of that kind of work—they know a fence will just put them out of a job. Young Bob Wire can do the work of twenty-five old cowhands. And Bob Wire don't eat beef and he don't drink whiskey. Reckon you can build a fence?"

"I've seen it done."

"Can you build a windmill tower?"

"Windmill?"

"Yes, I sell windmills, too."

"Why windmills?"

"Why? You must come from a wet country, Royal, I can gather that about you right away. You must have plenty of water holes where you're from—down on the coast, I'll bet. Down there you can build a pasture just about anywhere and have water in it—a creek or a bayou or something. But in dry country, you need a windmill. You fence cows in a pasture and you better fence some water in there with them or you'll be out of the beef business and into the hide and tallow market. Out west you have to pump water up from the ground. I couldn't sell a single spool of wire out there if I didn't sell a few windmills to boot."

"I guess I could build a windmill tower if I had one to look at for a model."

"I won't sell many windmills around here. Them dang bubbling springs are running all over this hilly country. I probably won't sell much barbed wire, either. The Germans have built rock fences and got more sheep than cows. Awful tight with their money, too. But wait till I get into cow country out west. That's where I'll make my money, among those cattle speculators. I did pretty good south of San Antonio, too, but the high plains is where I stand to make a bundle. That country is made for fences. You ever been out there?"

"No."

"Nothing to get in the way of fences out there, now that the Indians and buffaloes are cleaned out. Ain't even any trees to clear. The only problem is, there ain't nothing to make fence posts out of. Say, now, there's some work for you! Can you chop a fence post?"

"Sure."

We came to the Pedernales River, shallow and running clear among rounded white rocks in its bed. We let the mules drink there and cooled our faces in the stream. Harkey began trying to convince me that my future lay with cedar fence posts.

"You aim to stay at Fredericksburg?"

"I hope to."

"Check the post office every now and then. Don't be surprised if you find me ordering fence posts. I'll pay the going rate if you can chop 'em and freight 'em west. There must be a million posts in all these cedar brakes around here. It's rough work, but if you round up a crew of men whose hands will fit an ax handle, you can turn a profit. Barbed wire is reaching west and they need posts out there on the plains, Royal!"

I took it all for mostly idle talk, so I told Harkey I'd consider throwing in with him as a post supplier. In truth, the thought of becoming a cedar chopper boss made me a little nervous. Too much responsibility. I wouldn't mind swinging an ax, but swinging business deals could lead to misunderstandings. I had seen it happen before. I had seen men get killed over minor disputes in ownership of property.

The mules were full of water and moving uphill from the Pedernales, so Harkey drove them easy. We made Fredericksburg in another hour. The town differed from the sticky, muddy, clapboard-and-brick coastal towns I had grown up around and that made it instantly appealing. They built with limestone and cypress lumber in Fredericksburg, and the Germans knew how to build things for the long haul. The town had sturdy stone houses, churches, public buildings. They weren't fancy, but they answered every aspect of practicality. Low hills surrounded the town and oak trees shaded the homes.

Main street was wide enough for freight wagons to turn around in. Harkey drove his mules past the White Elephant Saloon and the Nimitz Hotel. We proceeded to a wagon yard on the west side of town, Harkey tipping his hat at anyone on the street who looked like a cattleman.

"Let's have some dinner over at the hotel," he said as a towheaded boy unhitched his mules for him.

I didn't know Harkey's habits, but I thought it possible he would desire an after-dinner drink, so I declined to dine with him. "No, thank you. I'm going to ask around about employment."

"Where are you staying tonight?"

"I'm limited on funds. I'll find a field to camp in."

"That's no way to live. It's liable to start raining this time of year. Why don't you share a room with me at the hotel?"

"No, thanks. I'm comfortable outside."

Harkey shook his head. "You're an odd one, Royal. Look, at least do me the honor of sleeping in my wagon here in the yard so you don't get snake-bit. That way I can see you in the morning and tell you whether or not I hear of any work you might be interested in."

That sounded agreeable enough with me, so I accepted the invitation and left my saddle in the wagon and my horse at the yard.

I spent the rest of the day walking around town, looking for work. Every person I met gave me a sidewise glance. I figured the cheap suit from the state penitentiary was making me look like a low-rate confidence man or something so I decided to invest some of my dwindling cash reserves in a new suit of work clothes. I found a dry-goods store and bought a leather belt, a pair of heavy jean pants, a cotton shirt, and the first pair of underwear I had owned in three years. They were long-handles; winter was not too far off.

I took a good meal at the Nimitz Hotel in the afternoon and saw Harkey working the other side of the street, shaking hands, telling jokes, and making acquaintances. When dark came, the little town of Fredericksburg lapsed into silence. I used my old clothes for a pillow and settled comfortably in the bed of Harkey's wagon, surrounded by spools of barbed wire. Maybe the next day I would find a farm that needed a hand. I imagined making a little room for myself in one of the cool rock barns or outbuildings.

I dreamed that night that I was in a room of stone with chains on my wrists and ankles. But there was a hoe in the room and I used it to part the shackles as if by magic.

Then I floated out of the room, dreamlike, and started walking somewhere with the hoe over my shoulder, my legs and arms swinging free, unfettered. It was dawn, cool and foggy. I passed a stone cottage, and a pretty girl, a farmer's daughter, stepped out onto the porch and waved. In a moment there were three girls waving, sisters—like the three sisters I had grown up with, but prettier. I waved back at them, smiled, and strode to a field that appeared through the fog.

The soft dirt felt good under my feet and the magic hoe started cutting weeds between the rows. It went effortlessly up and down. I struck a rock in the dirt, dug it up, threw it to the side of the field. The hoe attacked the weeds again. I struck another rock, lifted it, and tossed it with great facility beyond the furrows, into the fog. The hoe went back to work, and I struck another object in the tilled ground. I stooped and felt for it with my hands. Lifting it, I hurled it high and hard into the mist. But the dirt fell away when it flew and it erupted into a hundred nuggets of gold, a thousand coins of silver, a million jewels of precious stone—all of which sailed away, hopelessly lost in the fog.

Then there was laughter, and when I turned, I saw the old Mexican standing between the furrows. He was doubled over with mirth. His hardened old hands slapped his knees and tears of joy glistened in the creases of his weathered face. His laughter sounded like the quick grating of a rasp against a coffin. He laughed as the fog swirled and thickened, then looked at me and said, *"La piedra del cero. La piedra del cero."* Then he spread his arms like the wings of a flying dove and laughed until he vanished in the fog.

SIX

It was the laughter of Marion Harkey that woke me up. A couple of spools of barbed wire had shifted and rolled in next to me in the night. I slept so soundly that I didn't feel them. On the other hand, maybe I felt them a bit too pointedly.

Harkey said, "Wake up, Royal, before somebody catches you humping that spool!" and "Say, you like them with bristles on, don't you?" and "I guess the rut comes this time of year for you Huckaby bucks," and he interspersed all his comments with spates of laughter.

It was dawn and Harkey was ready to hitch his mules and head west. "There ain't no wire or windmills to be sold in this town. These folks are too tight-fisted. They could pinch the scalp off an Indian-head penny. Here, I brought you some breakfast."

The Germans made a kind of sausage wrapped in dough and then baked. Harkey had brought me a couple of them along with a jar full of fresh milk. I barely had the capacity to finish it all. My stomach had shrunk after three years of near starvation as a convict and I didn't need a tremendous amount of sustenance to keep going.

"I want you to ride with me to a ranch west of here," Harkey said as I ate. "There's a big cow outfit out there, I'm told. If I can sell some wire there, they'll be looking for someone to string it. That ought to keep you busy until I start sending orders for fence posts. You don't know it yet,

Royal, but you're going to get rich with barbed wire and cedar posts."

I saddled Liberty and rode with the barbed-wire wagon as the sun rose behind us. Along the way, Harkey warned me about the dangers of fencing.

"Some of the cowboys will come behind you and cut every strand you stretch. These are mostly the lazier, no-account hands that know they'll be the first ones to get fired when the fences are in. Sometimes they'll throw in with rustlers, too. Barbed wire makes rustling more difficult, as you could figure.

"Mostly, it's the big outfits who start fencing because they've got the money for it. Lots of times the little men will throw in together and cut the fences of the big men. Especially when they fence in water holes and such. The fence cutters give theirselves names like the Blue Devils and the Hatchet Gang and the Nipper Brigade. One of those gangs caught a fellow building a fence down on the Nueces and they wrapped him in wire and drug him to death. I suggest you get yourself a pistol, Royal, if you aim to go into the fence-stretching business."

With that bit of intelligence, I resolved to part company with Marion Harkey at the first convenient opportunity. My future did not lie with young Bob Wire. "The wire cutters must be pretty popular if they can get away with all that," I said.

"Popular, hell. Sneakiness can make up for a great lack of popularity. Them fence cutters come out in the dark of night, cut some fence, maybe leave a message or something, then they're back in their beds before sunrise."

"How much damage could they do in that short amount of time?"

"Hell, it takes a while to build a fence, but it don't take no time at all to tear one down. There's all sorts of ways.

Some of them carry wire nippers with them and clip every strand between every post for a mile or more. Some of them rope the posts and pull them clean out of the ground, and others chop them down with hatchets. I've known them to pour oil on the posts and let them burn. Once they started a hell of a wildfire that way. Some brave fence busters down in Karnes County took the time to roll up two miles of wire and left it in front of the fellow's house who had stretched it. And down near Laredo . . ."

The longer Harkey talked, the more apprehensive I grew about riding beside a wagon loaded with barbed wire. I expected to meet a gang of anti-fence men at every bend in the road. "Maybe this country isn't ready to be fenced yet, if so many are that set against it," I said.

"Oh, don't think the big-pasture men are just putting up with it," Harkey said. "Down at San Patricio they lynched a fellow because he was carrying wire nippers in his saddlebags. And they patrol them new fences, too. They got a right to protect their property. Fencing is legal, you know. There ain't no laws against fencing your own land. The open-range days are over, Royal. Men are buying up those good pastures and those water holes and they have a right to fence them. You might just as well get used to that . . ."

We traveled on, past orchards of scrubby peach trees and rocky fields of crooked cornstalks. I was feeling grave, but Harkey kept talking. For a drummer, he was likable enough, but he was going to lead me into a fence war just as sure as Matt Cottle had led me into the whorehouse scrape.

I started thinking up excuses to turn back to Fredericksburg. Maybe I could say that I had left something there. But that sounded too lame. Maybe I could pretend to take sick and go back to see a doctor. But I wasn't sure I was enough of an actor to pull that one off. Finally, I came up with a possible solution.

"Harkey, where have you sold the most wire in this part of the state?" I asked.

"Oh, the folks in this rocky country don't care much for the idea of digging post holes. Business is slow around here. I haven't even bothered to put on my rodeo demonstration. I did sell a mess of wire back on the Colorado, though, just downstream of the Marble Falls. An old man there has decided to fence his whole spread."

That was my cue to turn back. The Marble Falls, I knew, was in Burnet County, right where the Flatt-Standard feud was going on. That was the next-to-last place I cared to go. But Harkey didn't know that.

"The Marble Falls! That's not but fifty miles from here. Why haven't you told me about it before? There's some work for me right there, building fences."

Harkey became serious. He twitched his whip nervously and shook his head. "It ain't a good idea to look for work there."

"Why not?"

"Because the old man I sold the wire to is named Eli Flatt and he's right in the middle of some trouble with his neighbors, the Standards."

I shuddered to know that I was in the presence of a man who had driven his barbed-wire wagon among feudists. But I continued to express my false desire to go to work for the Flatts, just for the excuse to travel a different path from Harkey's. "What difference does that make?" I asked. "I'm looking for work, not trouble. Besides, I've seen family fights before."

Harkey twitched his whip more expressively. "I don't know, Royal. Folks are mighty nervous in that country. You see, the Flatt-Standard thing is a *land* feud. Flatt wants to fence a piece of property on Double Horn Creek that both families are claiming. If you're the one doing the fencing, you'll be in the middle of the fight. I'd advise you against it."

"The thing of it is," I argued, "is that I need a job now. I'm low on money. If you sell some wire somewhere up the road here, I'll have to wait for weeks for the freight wagons to ship it all out before I can go to work. You can't let them have any of the wire in your wagon, here, because you'll need that for your rodeo. But since you sold your wire to Flatt some time ago, he's probably received it by now. I think there's a good wagon road from Burnet to the Marble Falls and Burnet is on the railroad." I felt peculiar pretending to argue my way into a feud.

Harkey shook his head and worried. It was gratifying in a way to see him fret like that on my account. "It's dangerous, Royal. Barbed wire is liable to be dangerous anywhere in Texas right now, but especially in between the Standards and the Flatts. I spent a night with the Flatts. You ought to see the eyes of those men—old Eli and the two sons he's got left. The other two are already dead. Seeing family die like that makes a man's conscience turn cold. The Flatt brothers murdered two of the Standard boys while I was stayin' with them."

"While you were there?"

"Well, I didn't see it happen, but I saw the Flatt boys come back to their house when it was over, looking wild-eyed and kind of pale. I didn't figure out what they had done until later that day when I went to the Marble Falls to put in the order for the old man's wire. There was talk about it all over the settlement there and the two dead Standard boys were laid out at the general store, filled with bullet holes. I got the hell out of town before somebody figured out that I had spent the night with the Flatts. I didn't want to be associated with them and I didn't want to answer no questions to no grand jury. The Standards are going to fight back, of course."

"I read that the Texas Rangers were coming to settle the question of who owned the land."

"The rangers are busy on the plains dealing with those fence wars I've been telling you about. They haven't had time to take care of the Flatt-Standard trouble yet. The way I heard it, the judge ruled that the rangers and an investigator from the General Land Office would come find the old boundary marker between the Flatt and Standard properties to decide who owned what. But right after court was over, they started shootin' at one another on the way home and the Standards killed two Flatts.

"Then, while I was there, like I already told you, the Flatts killed two Standards. That makes four dead. Now they'll keep fightin' one another till they're all dead, unless the rangers get there first. But the question of who owns the land hasn't been figured out yet because the investigator from the Land Office hasn't showed up. He and the rangers are supposed to come and find an old boundary marker."

"What kind of marker are they looking for?"

"I guess it's a stone one," Harkey said, "because they call it the zero stone."

For some reason I didn't grasp instantly, the term "zero stone" sounded familiar to me. Then, just after Harkey said it, a flock of doves flew up from a patch of dove weed beside the road and one of them flew right over me. By the way it beat its wings and by the cadence in its whistling voice, it seemed to be saying, *"La piedra del cero, la piedra del cero!"*

La piedra del cero? The rock of the zero! The zero stone! The point of reference on the old Mexican's treasure map! I flinched so hard that I jerked the reins and almost made my mare stumble. I lost a stirrup and fell halfway out of the saddle. When I pulled myself back into the seat, Harkey was looking at me as if he thought I was suffering convulsions. I belatedly slapped the back of my neck. "Damned horseflies," I said.

Harkey pulled his mules up and started laughing at me. "Horsefly? That son of a bitch almost knocked you off your mare! You sure it wasn't an eagle diving for those doves?"

"I'm not sure I heard you correctly about the Flatt-Standard thing," I said. "Did you say, 'the zero stone'?"

"Yeah, that's what they call that boundary marker."

"What and where in the hell *is* this zero stone?"

"Damned if I know. If they knew where it was, the Flatts and Standards would probably never have started exterminating one another in the first place. The zero stone marks the boundary that they're fighting over."

My mind all but imploded on itself and worked so fast that I lost control of it. "Harkey," I said, "I've made up my mind to go back and work for the Flatts. I've got an idea. First, I'll fence the part of their property that doesn't border the Standard land, then I'll just quit. By that time you'll be sending me orders for cedar posts and I can collect my pay from Flatt and go into business on my own." I did the smoothest lying I had ever done under the influence of the zero stone.

Harkey deliberated for a while. "Well, you're a grown man and I guess you'll do what you want to do. Just be careful. Keep your guard posted and don't trust neither Flatts nor Standards. I'll send for fence posts just as soon as I can and I'll see if I can get the buyer to pay for the first load up front. That way you can get started sooner and maybe get the hell out of Burnet County before the war gets you." He chuckled a little. "I had you figured, didn't I, Royal? I said you'd seen rough times and I can tell they don't scare you. You're liable to see more of them when you get to Burnet County."

His words were wasted on me. I was seeing the zero stone in my thoughts—a tall, polished monument standing above the trees, encircled by cavorting doves. "Good luck, Harkey," I said, moving my horse up next to his wagon seat. "Write me care of the post office at the Marble Falls."

"Count on it." He shook my hand.

I turned Liberty around and coaxed her into the first lope she had run since I had bought her at Huntsville. I heard Marion Harkey shouting behind me: "Trust your future to young Bob Wire!"

But I was seeing my fortune in old buried gold.

By pounding my heels against Liberty's flanks, I managed to goad her into a gallop. Spanish zeros rang in my ears and dashed to bits all my previous resolutions to abandon treasure hunting. I used my hat to fan the rump of my mare and grasped desperately for a mental image of the burned map. The line between *la piedra del cero* and *el tesoro* bore northwest. How many degrees? Forty-nine! The dust rose behind me as if in the wake of a whirlwind. How many chains? How many! One hundred . . . One hundred eighty . . . One hundred eighty-nine! Plus seven varas!

But, oh, my God, of what length was the chain? And of what length, exactly, was a vara? It didn't matter. I would find that treasure if I had to dig a trench ten feet deep and ten miles long from the zero stone, northwest, 49 degrees, to the buried treasure. I would use doubloons for skipping stones and ingots for trotline weights. God bless the soul of the old Mexican!

I rode so hard that I barely saw Fredericksburg when I passed it. I kept the gallop up, heading for the Marble Falls, Double Horn Creek, the zero stone, and the cache of long-forgotten treasure. Damn the Flatts and the Standards and their trifling feud!

The road forked ahead—one branch leading north and the other east—but the Marble Falls were due northeast and I had no intention of swerving. I held a beeline, taking neither fork, but making my own road between them. I plunged my mare into a gully and drove headlong into a tangle of mustang grapevines that yanked me from the saddle like a calf hitting the end of a lariat. It was probably the most fortunate accident that ever befell me, for it knocked a good deal of the treasure-hunting madness clear out of my brain.

Liberty ran halfway up the opposite slope and stopped, heaving. It took me several minutes to get my wind back and crawl to her. I loosened the saddle cinch and let her blow. I would have ridden her to death if not for the grapevine.

It was the zero stone. My knowledge of it thrilled me, but I had to learn control of it. What had happened to my plan? What of working for room and board? What of avoiding anything that smacked of my old vendetta in Matagorda County? I would have wished to God that I had never met the old Mexican, but I feared my wish might come true.

It was time to sit again against a slope and think things through. I dragged myself into the shade to ruminate.

SEVEN

If it was true that the old Mexican had given me the treasure map as his final hoax, then his laughter must have pealed somewhere as thunder when the grapevine unhorsed me. When I thought of that likelihood, I cursed his soul and damned the ashes of his sheepskin map.

If it was true that he had presented the map to me in a spirit of real benevolence, then his smile must have shone somewhere as sunshine when Marion Harkey told me where to find the zero stone. When considering that possibility, I worshiped his spirit and cherished my memories of his chart.

But even when I regarded the treasure map as a blessing, I had also to consider it a scourge. It tempted me with rumors of riches yet tortured me with threats of feud blood. Knowing what I knew about vendettas, how could I even consider approaching the haunts of the Flatts and the Standards? How could I?

Quite easily, really. I simply rationalized: My being in the vicinity of a feud did not necessitate my being drawn into it. True, it had happened to me in Matagorda County because one of the major combatants had been my friend and brother-in-law. But it would not happen with the Flatt-Standard affair because I had made no acquaintances on either side. My previous notion that jeopardy would increase with geographical proximity to a feud was a product of rampant paranoia. The real danger came from intimacy with the feudists.

With that matter settled, I decided I might just as well crawl out of the gully I had fallen in, tighten the cinch on my mare, and proceed to the Marble Falls. There was no longer any use in trying to avoid Burnet County. The lure of the treasure was so strong that even had I turned away, I would have walked back in my sleep. The spell of the zero stone owned me and I would not break it until I found my treasure—or my corpse—buried in the ground.

The trick was to master the spell. I would take no more mounted plunges into blind gullies. I would listen to no more twittering Spanish phrases from flying doves. I would rely on patience, discretion, practicality. And, most importantly, I would not approach the zero stone until I could do so without the slightest risk of injury or incrimination.

It occurred to me that if, as Harkey had said, an investigator from the General Land Office was coming with a company of Texas Rangers to find the zero stone, then I would have nothing to do but wait. Once the marker was found and the feud settled, I could snoop around 49 degrees northwest of the zero stone until I found the treasure— assuming the old Mexican's map was genuine. But it had to be genuine! The zero stone existed! At any rate, until it was located, I would have to find some kind of work around the Marble Falls to keep me busy.

That was my new formula and it made perfect sense. It required nothing but patience. I added to it a few elements from my former plan: be helpful, stay out of saloons, avoid prostitutes.

I backtracked to the fork in the road and took the east branch. It soon crossed the Pedernales and led downstream along the south bank. Questions I had not yet pondered began to arise: What type of boundary marker *was* this thing called the zero stone? Who erected it and when? How did it come to be considered lost? How did the old Mexican know about it? Who had located treasure in its vicinity and plotted the distance between the two by chain lengths? And what length of chain had been used in measuring?

Patience, Roy, patience.

I arrived at the settlement near Johnson Ranch well before dark. The Marble Falls were to the north on the Colorado, twenty-some-odd miles away. I decided to spend the night at the Johnson Ranch settlement, called Johnson City, and finish the final leg of my trip to the falls in the morning.

At Johnson City I realized another ill effect of my crazed attempt to ride cross-country to the zero stone. My charge into the gully had knocked one of my mare's shoes loose. This inconvenience was in addition to the bruises up and down my back that now had me feeling as stove-up as a grandfather.

I found a blacksmith in town. He was a bald-headed,

squint-eyed old codger named Samuel Jessom who looked more cantankerous than a roped bear. But I would soon learn that he was a deacon in the Methodist Church and a paragon of decorum.

"Passing through?" he asked me after fixing the shoe.

"Yes," I said, "I'm heading to the Marble Falls."

"You're not going to try to make it there tonight, are you?"

"No, sir," I said. "I'm going to camp by the river and start in the morning."

"In that case, I'll be honored to have you for a dinner guest," he said. "Come on. We better go kill a chicken." Deacon Sam walked abruptly out through the back door of his shop.

"Do you want me to help you lock your place up?"

"No doors," he said. "I leave it wide open. Somebody might need something. Come on."

"Don't you think somebody might run off with something?"

"Nothing in there I can't get along without. Besides, if they were to ask, I'd give them whatever it was they needed, anyway. Why make a person grovel? Let's go."

I had once seen a trained chimpanzee in a traveling menagerie and Deacon Sam Jessom so reminded me of that animal that I expected to see him flip over backward any second. His feet angled outward, his legs bowed rather remarkably, and he tottered from side to side, apelike, when he walked. His arms seemed to have been lengthened considerably from years of hefting anvils and wagon wheels. His fingers curled severely in toward his palms, permanently molded that way around the handles of hammers and billows and tongs. His shoulders dropped off at the angles of a church steeple, and if he possessed the ability to stand erect, I never saw him exercise it.

I led my mare and followed Deacon Sam down a

well-worn trail that skirted a native pecan orchard and came to a tiny cabin near the Pedernales. "How do you like them?" he asked. "Fried? Roasted? We could have some dumplin's or make up some stuffin'."

"Fried," I said.

"Good. That's what I had a taste for this evening myself. Corn crib's over there. Pick out some roasting ears while I kill a fryer."

It took me longer to shuck the corn than it took Deacon Sam to pluck the chicken, yet he seemed to move in the most unhurried way. He shucked the last ear himself. "Might as well fry some okra, too," he suggested. "I'll go pick some if you'll split some stove wood."

I was more than happy to handle the firewood chores, my bruised back notwithstanding, but Jessom had gathered a basket of okra and tomatoes before I could finish.

"Why don't you draw some water from the cistern?" he suggested, and finished splitting the stove wood himself as I picked up the bucket. He had fashioned tin gutters to the eaves of his cabin and outbuildings, all designed to carry rainwater through a system of filters into the cistern. By the time I carried the water into the cabin, Deacon Sam had already lit a fire, cut up the chicken, and started melting the lard.

"Mr. Jessom, I believe you represent the most fluid example of efficiency I have ever known."

"Call me what my friends do: Deacon Sam. And don't be intimidated by my ability to get things done. I'm like John Wesley—always in haste, but never in a hurry. You don't appear to be any stranger to hard work, either—a lean fellow like yourself."

Slices of battered okra dropped, sizzling, into the fat and soon a wonderful aroma filled the tiny cabin. Deacon Sam was stamping biscuits from dough on a chopping block with one hand and setting a coffee pot on the stove with his other.

"Actually, I'm looking for work," I said. "Do you know of anything in this area?"

"What do you do?" he asked, handing me plates to set out on the table. "Milk's in that pitcher," he added.

"Anything," I said. "As long as it doesn't require any particular skill."

Jessom paused to squint at me. "I don't know of anything for sure. But there is a rumor. There's a big granite hill just the other side of the Marble Falls—one huge solid dome of rock. A few years ago the fellows who own it said they'd give enough of it to the government to build a new capitol with. I hear they're getting ready to start quarrying the granite. They're going to build a narrow gauge track to haul the stuff to Burnet and put it on the Austin and Northwestern line there to ship to the capital. That's what I hear, anyway. Maybe they'll be hiring. There looks like enough granite in that hill to last two hundred years. It's hard work, but you might be interested."

I had not envisioned quarry work as my form of livelihood, but for temporary employment it might do. It would only have to last until the rangers came and ended the feud and allowed me to do my treasure hunting. Then a happy thought occurred to me: Something learned in quarrying might prove useful in making excavations for lucre!

"If you don't find work there, you're welcome to come back and work with me for meals and a roof over your head until you get settled," Jessom said.

"Thank you. I might have to accept that offer."

When we sat to eat, the deacon bowed his head and clasped his crooked fingers together. "Let us pray," he said. "Heavenly Father, bless this meal and look after young Roy as he finds his way in this world. Grant him only that which he needs to live in the Christian spirit. In Christ's name, amen."

I said, "Amen," too, habitually. But before I did, under my breath, I muttered a vague appeal for mammon.

Deacon Sam the blacksmith must have whet his appetite on a grindstone that day. He waded through his victuals with both hands, the same way he did his work, and he could lap every morsel of nourishment from a chicken bone or a corn cob. I was more contented in the humble home of Samuel Jessom than I had been in years. His cooking was adequate, his hospitality lacked nothing, and he had put me at ease with his offer of work for room and board. As I cut the lard from the roof of my mouth with a cup of hot coffee, I lapsed into a perfectly serene frame of mind.

I could hear Deacon Sam's beard stubble snagging against his napkin as he mopped his face vigorously. "If you're going up to the Marble Falls," he said, "there's one thing to look out for. There's a fight going on between two families, the Standards and the Flatts. They're crazy with hate for each other and a newcomer wouldn't do himself any service to associate with either clan right now. Don't ask questions about them when you get there. Just keep your mouth shut and your eyes open."

"I've heard about their feud. What do you know of them?"

"I don't know much about the Flatts. Oh, I've seen old Eli around a few times. He was one of the first white men in Burnet County. He was the settler farthest up the Colorado for a few years. But I don't know him and probably wouldn't even recognize his children. Two of them are killed now, anyway."

"What about the Standards?"

"Them I know. Lon Standard is a layman in the Methodist Church, and I see him every year at the camp meeting over at Hamilton's Pool. He's a fine man and it just makes my heart sick to see him in this kind of scrape. Two of his boys are dead, too. I've prayed that he would stop coveting that piece of land they're fighting over and put an end to all the killing."

"But what if the land is rightfully his?"

Jessom snorted. "The earth belongs to God. We may serve as stewards, but what right have we to claim a piece as our own? Land should be for everyone to use."

I grunted as if in approval, but had trouble concurring with old Sam on his ideas of ownership. As a Huckaby, I had grown up acquiring land. My father had lost thousands of acres during the War Between the States but rebuilt during the years I grew into manhood, passing to me the desire to bring the horizons under ownership of the Huckabys. It was a desire I no longer embraced, of course, but one of which I still approved.

After Jessom and I washed the dishes, he spread a pallet of blankets on the floor. Just as I prepared to lay myself down on it, he rolled in ahead of me, uttered a prayer, said good night, and fell asleep as quickly as if an anvil had dropped on his head. I slept in the deacon's bed—narrow but comfortable, the bed frame strung with rawhide and the mattress stuffed with corn shucks. It was the first home I had slept in for more than three years and I was ashamed to find myself covetous of my kind benefactor, the Deacon Sam Jessom.

I felt no compunction, however, over my avarice toward a certain trove rumored to lie under the soil somewhere along Double Horn Creek.

EIGHT

In the morning I took a dip in the Pedernales, washed my working togs, and put on my coarse freedom suit so my new clothes could dry. Jessom had some breakfast and some conversation waiting for me when I got back to his little cabin.

"You speak well," he suddenly said in the middle of our talk. "Are you educated?"

I nodded, my mouth full of bacon and eggs.

"I'm going to let you borrow my Bible, then. If you don't read it, at least read this page marker." He flipped the corner of a card sticking out of the Holy Book. "I have to go fire the forge now, but I hope to see you again. If you have no luck up at the Marble Falls, come back tomorrow and put up with me for a while. The latch string hangs on the outside of my door."

"Thank you," I said, gratified to hear him repeat his invitation of the night before.

"I packed you a lunch. It's in your saddlebag. Good luck." Jessom turned and waddled off toward his wide-open blacksmith shop, leaving me at his table in his cabin, eating his eggs and bacon, drinking his milk and coffee.

As I sopped up the last of the bacon grease with a biscuit, I slipped the book marker out of the Bible Deacon Sam had given me. It was a card printed with a heading that read, JOHN WESLEY'S RULE. Seven lines followed:

> Do all the good you can,
> By all the means you can,
> In all the ways you can,
> In all the places you can,
> At all the times you can,

> To all the people you can,
> As long as ever you can.

Yes, I thought. And you will never suffer a lack of character witnesses. I wondered if John Wesley would have allowed a treasure map to possess him after doing all the good he could by letting an aged Mexican ride his horse. If not, he was a better man than Royal S. Huckaby.

As I crossed the Pedernales and rode northward toward the Colorado, I began to imagine what might have caused the Spaniards to bury their riches in this region. If all I had learned about the conquistadors was true, they came to the hills of Texas not for the clear spring waters or the abundant game or the rolling, rocky vistas or the temperate climate. No, they came for riches.

Assuming that as their reason for going anywhere, they must have found some form of mineral wealth in the hills west of San Antonio and Austin. Evidence of their expeditions had certainly turned up. In Fredericksburg, for example, the earliest German settlers found a weathered wooden cross with Spanish inscriptions surmounting a hill. And I had heard of an Indian chief on the Llano Estacado known as Iron Shirt who wore the armored breastplate of a Spanish cavalryman, long since won on some unheralded battlefield.

Yes, the Spaniards had come here seeking riches, perhaps finding some, perhaps carrying much of it home to the king, and maybe even burying some as difficulties arose, hoping to return for it. The legends of those buried caches had haunted Texans for generations. I was not the first man to let a treasure map possess him. In fact, I had joined the ranks of some rather illustrious adventurers.

Jim Bowie—wielder of the world's most celebrated knife and hero of the fabled Alamo—had crossed the Pedernales River as I had, searching for lost treasure. He and his brother had led a party of treasure hunters in a quest for the legendary San Saba silver mine. They found only hostile Indians and survived a battle against odds similar to those that later killed Jim at the Alamo.

If Bowie and a hundred like him could believe in buried treasure, why shouldn't I? In fact, maybe the treasure waiting for me on the Double Horn had come from the lost San Saba mine—bars of smelted silver. Or maybe my treasure was gold diverted and buried by some corrupt Mexican paymaster who never returned for his ill-gotten wealth. Maybe it consisted of silver candlesticks and precious stones stolen from a cathedral by some fugitive who had hoped vainly to escape to Louisiana.

I had much to unravel. One particular question bothered me more than all the rest. Why hadn't the old Mexican used his own map? Then it struck me: Oh, my gracious, think of the volume of treasure there must be on the Double Horn if the old Mexican had been unable to carry it all away in his pockets! Either that, or there was no treasure to carry away at all and he was laughing at me in hell.

I knew only one thing for sure about the old Mexican. He had heard of a thing called the zero stone and passed the knowledge of it on to me. And until I found it, I would dream his ghost laughter and shrink from the twitter of doves.

A coyote loped, stiff-legged, across the road in front of me and I reached instinctively for a rifle stock under my left stirrup—a throwback to my hunting days on the Huckaby estates. Hunting had once been my all-absorbing avocation. I yearned to own a rifle again. I had enough money left to buy one and a little ammunition for it, and the area between Johnson City and the Marble Falls appeared to offer excellent possibilities for the nimrod. To hunt would be to indulge in the greatest freedom of the savage or the civilized man.

The deacon had familiarized me with the landmarks I would pass on my way to the Marble Falls, and I recognized them from his descriptions. For a long time the washboard wagon road led over successive wrinkles in the topography, slanting mostly upward to the divide between the Pedernales and the Colorado valleys. When I reached that divide, a rather low and inconspicuous one, I stopped in the shade of an old oak to eat lunch.

After a short nap, I saddled my mare and proceeded northward. Before me spread the wide valley of the Colorado River. In these hills the river coursed swift and shallow. Down in Matagorda County it ran slow and muddy through the great raft of driftwood and into the Gulf of Mexico.

To my right I passed a high hill that Jessom had mentioned—a flat-topped rise called Shovel Mountain. To my left, miles away, I saw the landmark known as Packsaddle Mountain where the last clash with Indians in the area had taken place several years before. It indeed struck the shape of a packsaddle against the horizon.

At last I came to a bluff and looked down on the Marble Falls. There was a little settlement across the river and beyond it I saw Granite Mountain—the mound of solid rock nearly two hundred feet high that would build the state capitol. I could tell the work had started there. A single boom was up and pivoting slowly over the virgin quarry.

I got off my horse and put on the clean suit of work clothes I had purchased in Fredericksburg and washed that morning. Thus outfitted, I prepared to procure employment.

Liberty carefully picked her way down the bluff and walked gingerly across the sand just under the falls. The ledge of black stone stood only four feet at the highest, but it stretched three hundred yards or more across the riverbed and split the current into a hundred spouts that gushed through timeworn channels in the rock. Three laughing, bare-chested boys were wearing out the seats of their britches sliding down some of the sluices. Their mothers would switch them through the holes in their pants whenever they got home, but I encouraged them with applause.

"'At a boy!" I said to one who went headfirst.

"Watch me, mister," another one said. "Watch me, watch me," they all chimed in.

There wasn't much of a town at the Marble Falls— perhaps a dozen buildings. When the quarry got going, the town would probably grow, I thought. There was undoubtedly a saloon or two on the main street so, to avoid them, I rode just west of there on a dirt road downhill from the main cluster of buildings. It looked as if the road would lead to the quarry and that's where I needed to go to find work anyway.

A couple of steep side streets led up to the buildings on the main street. As I passed the first one, I chanced a cautious glance that way, looking for trouble. All appeared calm.

I didn't look up the second side street because a gaggle of schoolchildren attracted my attention. Their little frame schoolhouse was at the bottom of the side street and the schoolmarm—that poor, haggard woman—had just turned them out. They swarmed like hornets. I knew the mothers of the boys at the falls would have to switch them twice now, for they were skipping their lessons.

I managed to guide my mare through the milling urchins and approached the schoolmarm. "Excuse me, ma'am."

"What is it?" she responded, speaking to me as if I were eleven years old.

"Does this road lead to the granite mountain?"

"Yes, yes," she said impatiently, pointing up the road. But she didn't get a chance to utter another word because at that moment we all—schoolmarm, children, Liberty, and

I—heard an unusual but distinct harbinger of impending disaster. Imagine listening to a two-horse surrey racing toward you across a long, wooden-planked bridge and you will have some idea of what the racket sounded like.

The schoolmarm screamed: "Children!" The students ran, seeming to get nowhere. My mare turned toward the noise, trembled with fear, and tried clumsily to back away.

A large barrel came rumbling down the hill, bouncing heavily, swerving, and building speed. It was big enough to smash three underclassmen or two advanced mathematicians and there was nothing between it and the children but a steep pitch and fifty yards of dirt street. Instantly I decided to sacrifice my poor mare by throwing her into the path of the calamity.

Children scrambled, screamed, and fell as I made my mare move in between them and the rolling barrel. Liberty pranced and snorted and jerked her head, but I held her in the street. The schoolmarm was virtually yodeling in distress.

The barrel came on like a boulder loosed by a mountain avalanche. It rolled faster and angled to one side. Just up the hill from me it came hard against the corner of a staircase that bashed in one of the staves. It bounced, whirling, and began spewing a spiral of pure, white, stone-milled flour into the air through the broken stave. My mare reared, kicked, and grunted at the spectacle, but I held her fast in the path of the keg as it hit the ground just in front of her and burst. A tremendous white cloud enveloped me and barrel staves flew like canister, one clobbering me on the ear.

No amount of horsemanship could have held my mare then. She whirled like an outlaw mustang and it was all I could do to hang on. Above the ringing in my ears, I heard the schoolmarm shrieking and the children, blast their ungrateful hides, laughing like a choir of hyenas.

Blinded and choked near to death by the flour, I had no idea where I would light when my mare flung me from her back. I simply covered my head and hoped for a safe landing. Instead, I crashed through a window and came to rest on something that felt like the cargo in Marion Harkey's barbed-wire wagon or the walls of Albert Friedrich's Buckhorn Saloon.

I must have been unconscious for a few seconds. When I came to, I caught myself murmuring, "'. . . In all the places you can,/At all the times you can,/To all the people you can . . .'" My vision cleared and I could see my legs sticking out of the schoolhouse window. I was on my back, the remains of a previously sound school desk splintered around me. I reached for something that I felt jabbing me in the rear end and found it to be an extremely sharp pencil. I heard scores of little bare feet stomping up the steps and knew the schoolchildren were rushing in to finish me off.

I started to lapse back into unconsciousness, but before I could slip away, I beheld the lines of a marvelously angelic face peering at me through the window between my boots. In my dazed state, she was all waving hair and batting eyes, glistening lips and heaving bosom. I smiled at her crookedly.

"Thank God, he's not killed," she said. Then she turned her angelic face to rail at someone outside and I knew immediately she was made of mortal flesh. "Damn you, Nat! I told you to put that barrel upright in the wagon! I told you the son of a bitch would roll out!"

"Annie Standard!" screamed the schoolmarm. "You watch your filthy mouth around these children!"

Standard? Two minutes in town and I had fallen through a window on account of a Standard.

"Oh, forgive *me,* Miss Teeter," Annie said testily. Then

she turned to look through the window again. "Don't just stand there, children. Get him up."

The students had gathered around me and began pulling in ten different directions, but eventually coordinated their efforts and put me on my feet. They bolstered me as I wobbled toward the door. There I saw the full length of Annie Standard, waiting to help me outside. She wore a faded print dress, tied in tight around her waist and rolled up at the sleeves. Everything about her reminded me of fine sand—her tawny hair, her dunelike curves. And her finely freckled skin looked like the smoothest brown beach of the most exotic island. I must have stared at her like a convict at an open door.

She slung my arm over her shoulder and helped me walk outside. Then she sat me down on the front steps of the schoolhouse. She began ineffectually dusting me off with a handkerchief. Through the white cloud she stirred up, I saw that Liberty had completely gotten over the keg scare and was standing patiently as some schoolboys climbed all over her.

Then I spied the two men. One of them, I supposed, was Nat, who had loaded the barrel in the wagon on its side. Both of them, I supposed, were Standards because they were holding rifles, keeping their eyes peeled for trouble, and looking down on me with distaste. Annie appeared to be the youngest of the three.

"Oh, fiddlesticks!" Miss Teeter said, looking in through the broken window. "Sir, you've shattered this glass and crushed an entire desk. What have you to say for yourself?"

I had nothing to say, but Annie did. "Is that all you can think of?" she demanded. "This man was trying to save those children from getting smashed. Why haven't you thanked him yet?"

Miss Teeter gasped.

"That barrel wouldn't have smashed anybody anyway," grumbled one of the brothers. "It busted open right there."

"Shut up, Lum," Annie snapped. "You're lucky it busted or it would have lamed this man's horse and you would have had to pay for it."

"Me?" Lum said. "I didn't put any barrel in the wagon sidewise. Nat did it."

"It was your idea!" Nat said.

"The heck it was," Lum countered.

Annie continued to flog me with her handkerchief while they argued. I took her by the wrist and stood up. "Thank you, miss. I'm alright now. No harm done."

"I was the one that told you not to leave the wagon so close to the hill where somethin' might roll off the tailgate," Nat said.

"You never opened your mouth to say any such thing," Lum said.

Annie followed me as I hobbled toward my horse. "What's your name?" she asked. Lum and Nat ended their argument to look out for their sister. She shooed the children off my mare as I went to put my foot in the stirrup.

"Roy."

"What brings you here?"

"I heard the quarry was hiring," I said, struggling up to the seat.

"If it's work you're looking for, come home with us and we'll put you to work on the ranch," Annie said.

"No, we don't need any hands on the ranch, Annie," Lum said. "You know better than that. Let that saddle tramp alone and get back in the wagon."

Annie's angel face turned fierce. She clinched her fists and took three menacing steps toward her brother, who backed away cautiously. "You go straight to hell, Columbus Standard."

Miss Teeter gasped again.

"Excuse Annie's language, Miss Teeter," Nat said. "She only talks that way when she gets het up. She's been cussin' up a storm here lately. Daddy gave up whippin' her."

"You go on up to the quarry, stranger," Lum said. "They're hiring, alright."

"And you can use your first week's wages to buy a new window and a new desk for my school," Miss Teeter said.

"Lum, pay Miss Teeter for the damages," Annie ordered. She had taken my horse by the bridle, as if she did not intend for me to ride away just yet.

"*Me* pay her?"

"Pay her!"

Lum heaved indignantly and went to negotiate with the schoolmarm.

"We've had some trouble lately," Annie said to me. "We don't have any work to hire out on the ranch right now, but soon we could have. I hope you'll stay around until then. It'll be better work than you'll get at that so-called quarry."

"Thank you," I said. I was still somewhat fuddled—as much by Annie as from my mode of entering the schoolhouse—but I knew enough to recognize a stroke of luck when one dropped into my hands. One of the Standards—undoubtedly the prettiest—had just invited me to work on the family ranch as soon as the trouble with the Flatts had passed. What better way to search for treasure? "That sounds fine," I said. "I'd rather work at a ranch than a quarry, but I have to take what's available for now."

"Come on, Annie," Nat said. "Daddy and Clay are waiting on us. You've slowed us down enough."

I tilted my hat and smiled at Annie. "Good-bye for now, miss," I said.

"Good-bye," she said, turning away. "Well, come on and get the wagon loaded," she said to her brothers. Then she turned and waved quickly to me.

The last I saw of Miss Teeter, she was counting her money.

"What about all that flour?" I heard Nat ask as I rode toward Granite Mountain.

"What about it?" Annie said.

"Well, shouldn't we scrape it up or something? We'll have to pay for it, you know."

"If you want to eat dirt in your hot cakes, Nat, by all means, scrape it up."

"Scrape it up," Lum said. "We'll make mush out of it and feed it to the hogs."

"Why don't *you* scrape it up?" Nat asked, and so the conversation went until I rode out of earshot.

NINE

My seal brown mare looked something like a roan after the sprinkling the flour barrel gave her and I looked like a veteran of the chalk mines. I dusted myself off as much as possible as I rode to the quarry. I was sore on the head and all over the back, but I plugged ahead, dauntless.

Granite Mountain loomed before me—a great bulge of beautiful reddish stone flecked with black and glistening with tiny crystals—overall about the color of a red brindle steer. As I got closer to it, I began to have a strange feeling. At first, I passed it off as an aftershock to the way I had met Annie, or to the fact that I had met her at all. I was thinking more about her than the quarry. She even seemed to make me forget, for the moment, about the zero stone and the buried treasure. But as I continued to approach Granite Mountain, I began to realize that the quarry was the thing making me feel peculiar.

When I rode close enough to see the workers scrambling about the rough face of the monolith, something about them made me uneasy. They had started the quarry work; several huge blocks of granite had been sheared from the flanks of the hill. I dipped down into a creek bed then and lost sight of the laborers. When I saw them again, I was much closer. A pitiful realization came to me and chilled every bit of warmth I was feeling for Annie Standard, the zero stone, and buried treasure.

The workers at the quarry came in two classes. One consisted of white men who sat in the shade and fondled shotguns. The other class wore dirty, striped uniforms. They were lean from a lack of food and an overabundance of hard labor. Most of them were black men. I reined in my mare, afraid to get any closer. I couldn't work at this quarry. The actual labor was being done by convicts. The only hiring going on was for guards.

As I sat on my horse and stared and pitied the men among the slabs of granite, I noticed that a couple of the guards were watching me. One of them got on a mule and rode out to me. He looked me over carefully, resting his scattergun across the withers of the mule. "What do you want?" he asked.

"Are you the sergeant?"

"Yeah, who the hell are you?"

I could judge a guard at a glance with almost invariable accuracy, and the subject on the mule struck me as the most reprehensible sort of bully.

"I heard y'all were hiring," I said, not attempting to hide the distaste in my voice.

"Maybe. What the hell is that white stuff all over your clothes?"

"That's the bone meal of the last fool I met who couldn't mind his own business."

The sergeant grew red in the face and hooked his thumb

over one of the hammers of his double-barrel. Then he settled down and chuckled. "Alright, you're a rough enough customer. Do you know anything about convicts?"

"Yes, I have had three years experience among them."

"Where at?"

"Huntsville."

The bully on the mule seemed impressed. "Come on over and talk to the captain, then."

I sat on my mare for a moment, sick with guilt, for some bizarre reason, that I was not among the quarry gang. If only the sergeant on the mule knew how many times those convicts would like to murder him today. "How much does it pay?"

"Forty dollars and grub twice a day."

I laughed with a mocking tone in my voice. "Mister, I wouldn't take ten times that much to work beside the likes of you."

I turned my mare back toward town and listened for the sound of the hammer latching back on the double-barrel. But the only shot the guard fired was, "Then why in hell did you ride out here, you crazy-assed lunatic?"

I had disobeyed John Wesley's rule. I hadn't done the sergeant at the Granite Mountain quarry one lick of good in any way and I was proud of it. In fact, I probably took more pride in what I had done than any man ever did for any such stupid stunt. "The bone meal of the last fool . . ." What wonderful, wicked inspiration had caused me to think up that reply on short notice?

By the time I got back to the town, however, I was regretting my venomous comments. That kind of talk fit nowhere into my plans to avoid trouble. What I needed was a good dose of Deacon Sam Jessom's virtuous influence. I resolved to start immediately back to Johnson City and stay with Jessom until the Flatt-Standard thing blew over. But I would not show up at his modest cabin empty-handed this time. I had just enough cash left to buy a rifle and some cartridges and I intended to do so and kill a fat deer for Deacon Sam and me to butcher.

I avoided the schoolhouse on my return route and rode up on the main street to the store that I knew to be just up the hill from the site of my late catastrophe. The Standards had scraped up their flour, finished loading their wagon, and gone home. I was still embarrassed about breaking the window out of the schoolhouse and for that reason I was glad Annie and her brothers had left. But for some opposing reason, I wished for another glimpse of her.

I entered an establishment with a hand-painted sign hanging over the boardwalk that read, "Lynn's Store," and below, in smaller letters, "United States Post Office." The proprietor was happily counting the large wad of money Lum Standard had left with him. He glanced up at me once, glanced again, and started laughing. "You must be the poor devil who got run over with the flour barrel!"

I spotted some weapons in a counter and looked them over. "Yes, sir. But I'd rather be addressed by name. Royal Huckaby."

"Glad to meet you. I'm J. L. Lynn. Be with you directly." He put his cash away in a drawer. Lynn stood about six feet and weighed in at over two hundred pounds, I guessed—a healthy-looking fellow who appeared to enjoy life and thrive on the mercantile business. "I guess you're wondering what those Standards needed with an entire barrel of flour."

"Forting up, I supposed."

"Oh, you've heard about their trouble, then."

"Yes, it was in the San Antonio newspapers."

"Lum told me they've been afraid to sleep in their own house for fear the Flatts would lay siege on them. But now they're stocked up with enough food and ammunition to supply a garrison for a month. The rangers ought to be here by then."

"What will they do for water?" I asked.

"They already have water in the house. Annie made them boys put a pitcher pump in the kitchen for Mrs. Standard. The boys didn't want to. They said it would rot the floor timbers out, but Annie usually gets her way. Them Flatts will have to catch them out of the house somewhere if they intend to fight. Of course, I hate to see them kill one another like they have been, but, my Lord, I never dreamed it would be so good for business. I never sold the likes of guns and bullets in my life and now there's a run on foodstuffs."

"I'm interested in buying a rifle myself. I need something in a caliber for hunting deer and turkeys and such."

"Oh, is that right? I figured you had your eye on a shotgun. Lum said you were going to hire on at the quarry."

"No, sir. That's no business for a gentleman. How about this Winchester?"

I haggled with Lynn for a while and we struck a deal that included the rifle, a scabbard, and a hundred rounds. I had only two dollars left after the trade, but I felt satisfied when I hefted the weapon and worked the lever a few times and smelled the grease in the action. It was a beautiful rifle with a checkered pistol grip, a shotgun butt, and an octagonal barrel over a full-length magazine. I picked a popular caliber: .45-60.

"I'm going back to Johnson City," I said. "Any chance of finding some good hunting on the way there?"

"Oh, sure," Lynn said. "If I was you, I'd go across the divide and turn west and hunt along the Sandy. There're turkeys and hogs there by the hundreds and enough deer, too. You might even find a bear, but they're getting scarce. Of course, the best hunting around here has always been on the Double Horn, but I would advise you against going there. That's a war zone with the Flatts and Standards."

"I understand. I don't want to get mixed up in any of that

trouble. In fact, I would consider it a favor if you would tell me just where the Double Horn runs, so I can be sure to avoid it."

"Do you know Shovel Mountain?" Lynn asked.

"Yes, I rode past there today."

"Well, Double Horn Creek starts at the foot of Shovel Mountain, runs north about six miles, and then empties into the river a few miles downstream from here. It's all on the east side of the road to Johnson City. That's why I told you to stay on the west side of the road and hunt the Sandy, that way you'll have no chance of making a mistake. Of course, you'd be okay hunting up on the head of the Double Horn, under Shovel Mountain, but being a stranger here you wouldn't know where the Flatt and Standard lands take up along toward the mouth of the creek."

"I guess I'll just go on to the Sandy, then."

"That's what I'd do. There's game enough there for a good hunt."

My eyes had been trained for rifles since entering the store and I didn't think until then to look around at the other kinds of goods Lynn had for sale. He had pretty fair supplies of coffee, salt, sugar, dried beans, bacon and tobacco, plus some dry goods and tools. Behind his counter I saw rows of pigeonholes stuffed with parcels and envelopes of different sizes and colors. Two or three piles of unsorted mail lay nearby.

There were three volatile barrels of flour standing innocently against the wall, looking like powder kegs set to roll and explode in bursts of white smoke. There had to be a mill nearby, I reasoned, to supply that much flour.

I must have regarded the barrels with a little too much caution, making Lynn chuckle. But I soon forgot them when my eyes found the willow basket. It didn't seem to belong in Lynn's Store. His goods stood haphazardly on dusty shelves or hung crookedly from the walls. But the

willow basket looked as if the hands of a woman had built
it and arranged its marvelous contents in a manner almost
artistic.

It was shallow, but all of four feet wide, woven of slender branches stripped of bark. In the center stood a collection of glass bottles filled with a fluid of the most remarkably
amber hue, the stoppers sealed in wax. A cornucopia of
vegetables surrounded the bottles—red tomatoes, green
okra, yellow squash. And the whole of it rested atop a bed
of the largest pecans I had ever seen.

"Annie brought that," Lynn said, following my stare.
"She and I trade often. Crack two of those pecans together.
You've never tasted any like them."

I had squeezed pecans together all of my life and knew
how much force to clamp on them to get them to crack. But
the shells of Annie's pecans crumpled like paper in my
hand. The nuts tasted smoother and sweeter than any
county-fair, blue-ribbon winners I had ever sampled.

"Ain't they somethin'?" Lynn said. "Annie's got her a
prize-winning pecan tree on their land and she takes limbs
off of it and splints them onto other trees and makes them
grow. You won't believe it, but that's honest. She calls it
the mother tree and its limbs put out these kind of pecans
even when they grow on a regular tree."

"You mean she grafts the limbs?"

"That's what she calls it! It sure is! And them are the best
pecans I ever et. But just wait till you wash it down with a
swallow of this."

Lynn peeled the wax from one of the bottle necks, pulled
the stopper, and poured some in a shot glass he kept behind his counter for just such occasions. I sniffed the liq-
uid before tasting it and inhaled an aroma so rich that I
thought myself in some parlor holding a crystal snifter. It
was the smoothest and most potent brandy I had ever swallowed, flavored of peaches.

"Got her a peach orchard alongside her pecan grove, and a vegetable garden alongside that. A big one, so I've heard, though I've never had the pleasure of seeing it. Nat told me there's a little spring that runs through all of them and Annie uses it to irrigate her plants. She brings me stuff in the spring of the year like dewberries and vegetables and peaches, and in the fall she brings more vegetables and pecans and brandy. She should have some wine ready soon. She makes some good spirits from them old mustang grapes."

"If it's as good as the brandy, you'll have no trouble selling it," I said.

"Hell, no, I'll have no trouble. You better buy a bottle of that brandy yourself if you want some. It'll all be sold in two days."

"No, thank you," I said. "I normally abstain from drink."

"Oh, I see. Well, that's wise if you have the weakness for it."

"Give my compliments to Miss Standard on the brandy," I said, tipping my hat and leaving with my new rifle.

"I will, sir. Good luck on the Sandy."

I made my way back over the same ground I had passed earlier in the day, before fending off the flour keg and before meeting Annie Standard and her brothers. It was getting late and the good hunting would soon commence. My hand kept reaching down to stroke the gun stock sticking out from under my left stirrup. The wood felt smooth and warm, like the taut skin of a living thing. I longed to level my sights on game, but it was clear that I would not get to the Sandy before nightfall.

As I trotted my mare past Shovel Mountain, I got an idea to ride up on top of the hill and look over Double Horn Creek to get a feel for the lay of the land and try to figure out where the zero stone might lie. I thought I might even camp there and start out for the Sandy before sunrise next morning. That way my scent or that of my campfire wouldn't spook the game out of the vicinity.

Shovel Mountain stood just a few miles to the east. It didn't prove much of a hill to climb, but it put my mare and me high enough above the rest of the territory that we could see for miles in every direction. I saw the colossal Pack-saddle lying on the ground out to the northwest. I could see way off toward the Sandy and Johnson City to the south. To the east I found the valley of the Colorado snaking down toward Austin. And to the north I saw an undulation of greenery marking the path of Double Horn Creek. Just as Lynn had said, it started on the north face of Shovel Mountain, right under me, and ran northward six miles to the Colorado. The moment I laid eyes on it, *The Feeling* struck me.

Now, The Feeling was something that gripped me from time to time in life. It was something I never talked about for fear I would be committed to the lunatic asylum. The Feeling smacked of sorcery and mysticism and other things people shunned in serious conversation. The Feeling had even spooked me the first several times I felt it and acted upon it, but later in life I began to welcome it.

I first felt The Feeling as a boy while hunting for deer along the cane brakes of the Colorado River in Matagorda County. I was following a deer trail one day, trying to find a place to take a stand and ambush a big buck, when I came to a fork in the trail. Naturally, I had to decide which fork to follow. They both led into the thick hardwood bottoms along a creek. Each fork looked as well used as the other. I looked down the one to the left and sensed nothing out of the ordinary. But when I observed the trail to the right, The Feeling struck me and I knew, somehow, that I would find success down that path. It was no mere hunch or trifling whim—it was an overwhelming certainty, a knowingness. It was The Feeling.

I snuck down the right fork and crouched behind a fallen tree and within a minute the biggest buck I had ever seen in my life strolled up about thirty yards away from me. I killed it with one shot and went to get a friend of mine, a black boy named Rafe.

Rafe and his family sharecropped some Huckaby land. He had a knack for training dogs and had the finest pack of bear hounds in the county, therefore we became friends and hunting partners. It was a rather lopsided partnership, however—he doing all the work and me having most of the fun.

Rafe gutted the buck I had killed, an old twelve-pointer, and tied him on a mule while I told him what had happened. "How do you think I knew he would be there?" I asked him.

"Don't know," Rafe said. "Let's go ask ol' Uncle Pie."

Uncle Pie was a savant to the black people who lived and worked on the Huckaby estates. He stayed in a broken-down shanty near the river where he sat on his porch all day and cracked pecans or whittled or sharpened knives or gave advice. He had spent sixty years of his life as a slave, but was supposedly as free as I was the day Rafe and I went to him to tell him how I had killed the buck. We had to talk loud, for Uncle Pie was hard of hearing.

When he finally got the story straight, he said, "Boy, you done got The Feelin'."

"The feeling?" I said. "What feeling?"

"The Feelin' that tells you where things is. The Feelin' that shows you where to go to see a turkey if you huntin' a turkey and bear if you huntin' a bear. Some of you white folks calls it a 'sixth sense' and some says you gots to have Indian blood to feel it. But it ain't everybody can have it, boy, so you thank Jesus you gots The Feelin' and you re-member ol' Uncle Pie told you about it."

For a long time I considered myself somehow gifted. The

Feeling continued to strike me from time to time when I was hunting and never failed me if I waited long enough where it told me I should hunt. I grew to trust it and even found it occurring in places other than the hunting field.

When I looked at a total stranger, for example, and felt a twinge of The Feeling, I knew I could trust that person with life or money. When I looked at a piece of farm land my father, Champ Huckaby, had asked my opinion of and shivered with The Feeling when I saw it, I invariably told him to buy and knew the crops would flourish.

It is a frightful thing to know something and not know why you know it. For this reason, The Feeling disturbed me and I contemplated it often. Finally, to convince myself that I wasn't a mental freak of some kind, I conjectured that everyone must have the power to possess The Feeling, but that few harnessed it. Most people passed it off as intestinal gas or nervous tension and generally drank some catnip tea and bitters or went to bed when they felt it.

I, on the other hand, would not deny it. As Uncle Pie had advised, I would be grateful for it and rely upon it. The Feeling, I thought, would set me on the correct course in life. I trusted it to point out every advantageous opportunity that crossed my path. The Feeling told me what to do and when to act.

Unfortunately, I had no opposing feeling that could tell me what *not* to do, where *not* to go, and whom *not* to trust. I possessed only the power to recognize the positive things, able to sense nothing of oncoming ill fortune. I had only begun, after three years in prison, to develop the ability to sense disaster. Some kind of feeling had warned me about the guard at the Granite Mountain quarry, for example. But it was not yet a sensation highly advanced enough to steer me away from things like whorehouse fights or runaway flour kegs.

But The Feeling *was* mine and it had become so powerful

that I never failed to follow it. Only now will I admit that The Feeling virtually seized me with my very first glimpse of the old Mexican as he tottered along with his walking stick in front of the Buckhorn Saloon. Is it any wonder, then, that I should keep coming back to the possibility that his sheepskin map bore the brand of veracity?

I should explain also that I detected a powerful surge of something in the settlement at the Marble Falls, when I first saw the angelic face of Annie Standard—framed by the broken pane of the schoolhouse window and clouded by the white swirl of drifting flour. But that was not *the* feeling. That was a sensation of a completely original order.

TEN

I had never before disobeyed The Feeling, but I had questioned it on occasion. I had questioned it many times in the past several days as it pertained to the old Mexican and now I questioned it concerning Double Horn Creek.

Yes, there was undoubtedly good hunting along the creek. The Feeling couldn't be wrong about that. There was plenty of cover for wildlife. Brushy draws led into the creek from both sides, like veins to the center of a leaf. Cedars, oaks, and pecans grew thick along the draws. Among the coppices were open meadows where game could browse. Even without The Feeling, I would have wanted to hunt there.

But if I hunted too far down the Double Horn, I might stumble into Flatt or Standard territory and get accidentally murdered. As Lynn had pointed out, I was a stranger to the area and didn't know where one man's land ended and another's took up.

As I stood on the crest of Shovel Mountain and struggled

to reason against The Feeling, I heard a rustling of leaves moving toward me up the north face of the hill. It came nearer and grew louder, like the wing beats of waterfowl flocking low overhead. Then I saw branches waving in the oncoming gust and when the blast finally whipped over the summit it knocked my hat off.

The season's first cool front had arrived—an annual cause for celebration in Texas. It was no blue norther and would probably do little more than drop the temperature ten or twelve degrees for the next few days. But when a Texan turns to the north in October and feels the breeze in his face, he knows blessed autumn will come to drive summer down to the tropics. It is a time of year that indulges the children of every generation. Even old men and women step outside to smell the crisp wind as if they had never before seen a summer lapse.

A fresh northern breeze could move a man from a hot climate with mysterious energies. The same energies that make the snow geese long to fly down from Canada. The energies that cause whitetail bucks to polish their antlers against oak saplings. Energies that tell predators of the world to stalk their prey. The wild energies of freedom that a captive creature must deny. I was uncaged for my first norther in three years. Did my will consist of the stuff that would enable me to ignore both The Feeling *and* the northerly draft? I should scarcely think so.

I had only enough sense left to notice that about halfway between Shovel Mountain and the Colorado River, Double Horn Creek ran between two pointed hills. The line between those hills, I decided, would serve as my boundary. I would assume the Flatt-Standard feud began on the far side of it, and beyond it I would not venture. Under the combined sway of the zero stone, The Feeling, and the sudden cool snap, that seemed like a substantial precaution.

Liberty eased down the slope of Shovel Mountain as I

sniffed the cool, dry aroma of the north and quivered with its energies. At the first clearing I came to along the rushing Double Horn, I staked the mare to graze. I filled my canteen and looped its strap over my shoulder. I also filled the magazine of my new rifle, levered a round into the chamber, and struck out through the thickets.

I stayed in the shadows to make myself less conspicuous to the wary eyes of my prey. I walked in close to the cedars but avoided the oaks as the ground under them was strewn with dried leaves and crunched loudly underfoot like eggshells. I stopped every fifty yards or so and hunkered down to look and listen. I saw no fresh sign the first mile. No moist deer droppings, no freshly shed turkey feathers, no distinct tracks in the mud or the dust. Ah, but the breeze blew in my favor and the prime hour had yet to arrive and The Feeling called me northward.

I blundered up to a place where one of the brushy draws came in from the east to meet the creek. I heard a whistling snort and turned just in time to see the white, waving tail of a doe disappear up the draw. I heard other sets of hooves escaping with hers. I was out of form as a deer hunter. I should have crept up to that draw and peered into it from behind a bush instead of stumbling into full view. I should have seen the deer before she saw me. It was as if I did not know what I was hunting for.

My failure at that draw did little to discourage me, however. To see a deer within rifle range, to hear her distinctive snort, that was no mean privilege to a recent inmate. I considered taking a stand at the mouth of that draw, thinking that other deer might use the trail before dark. But I looked down the creek bed and I could see one of the two pointed hills still a couple of miles off and The Feeling tugged me toward that place.

I moved more carefully now, pausing longer and walking slower. I found game trails and turkey feathers and tracks in more abundance. Here a squirrel chattered at me from a tree limb and there a cottontail rabbit paused before springing into the bushes. And, try though I did to ignore them, mourning doves burst from the trees in flocks around me as I passed. But I spared the small game. I was hunting for something else. Something bigger. Something farther down the Double Horn.

The best hour for hunting began. Sunlight no longer fell into the little valley of the Double Horn. Soon the deer would be moving to their feeding grounds and the turkey would be returning to their roosts.

I came to another draw, a well-wooded one, and this time approached with more stealth. Everything I knew about hunting told me to make my stand there. Game trails streamed in to the place where the draw slashed the creek bank. A huge live oak had dropped an early batch of acorns that would attract deer and turkeys. Fresh tracks lined the muddy places along the creek. Experience told me to hunt there. But The Feeling differed.

When I looked again at the one visible member of the twin hills flanking the Double Horn, not far from me now, The Feeling drew me there. I protested: Pass up a wooded bottom with still water and game food to hunt a half-bald hill? What did The Feeling expect to find up there? I leaned my rifle against a tree to debate. Should I press against the very boundary I had set for myself and risk crossing into Flatt or Standard territory? Or should I hunt the draw I had found and shun The Feeling for the first time since I had known it?

I tipped my canteen up to drink as I deliberated. I tipped it high into the air above my mouth and let the water pour in. But above the trickling noises from the canteen, I distinctly heard, in the direction of the hill downstream, a metallic click—the muffled but unmistakable ring of a lock tripping in its machinery. Though I knew exactly what instrument had caused that noise, I failed to react with proper haste.

The canteen flew from my hand, and the strap around my neck yanked me to the ground. The noise from the impact of the bullet rang in my ears as I staggered to my feet. I looked at my rifle against the tree, but knew not to reach for it. I had nothing to do but stand at the mercy of someone on the hill. The water from my canteen was spilling out of the bullet hole, down the front of my pants.

"Hands up!" a gruff voice yelled from the hill.

I raised my hands and heard a horse coming to me. Down into the draw galloped a gaunt old man with hollowed eyes and a long, white beard, yellowish at the tip. He jumped from his horse holding a carbine in hands as wide and hard as spades. His clothes had seen much service. The hat on his head was marked with the stains of sweat. He wore frayed suspenders over a patched-up shirt and had the legs of his frazzled pants tucked into the high tops of his boots.

He pointed the carbine at me. "I've got him, Topsy," he hollered over his shoulder, without taking his eyes off of me. Almost instantly I heard another horse coming down from the hill. "How many are you?" he asked.

"I'm alone."

"You better hope you're alone," he growled, "because if I hear somebody comin' besides Topsy, I'll kill you quick."

"I'm alone," I repeated. "Just doing some hunting. You don't mind a man doing a little hunting, do you?"

The old man squinted and moved around to pick up my rifle. "Depends on what you're huntin' for."

About that time, Topsy rode down into the draw, and looking at her, I almost forgot the danger I was in. She straddled a red roan horse about three shades lighter than her hair, which was the color of dried blood, but full and beautiful. She had the same thin face as the old man, with none of the creases worn in it. And where the old man's face wore an expression of grim certainty, hers appeared anxious. She rode lightly on top of the horse, moving with the animal like a part of it. She had fringed moccasins in her stirrups, and when she stopped the horse near me, her skirt billowed up over one knee and damned if she wasn't wearing buckskin britches underneath!

"Who is he, Pa?" she asked.

"Says he's a hunter."

"He looks like a hunter."

"Yes, I'm just a hunter," I agreed. "I'm almost out of money and thought I'd kill some meat on my way to Johnson City."

"Looks like you wet your britches," he said.

"Pa!" Topsy complained. "That's just the water from the canteen!"

"Where's your horse?"

"I staked her up the creek."

The old man gnawed on his lower lip and shot his eyes around in suspicious little glances. "You're a friend of them Standards, ain't you?" he said quietly.

I felt in immediate peril of my life, but Topsy came to my rescue. "I know most all the Standards' kin and I ain't never seen him before."

"Then what's he doin' here?" the old man asked.

I was asking the same question of myself about that time. It was that damned old Mexican's fault.

"He's just huntin', Pa," Topsy said, becoming more insistent. "I could tell by the way he was stalkin' down the creek that last half mile that he was huntin'. Tryin' to, anyhow."

"Who are you, boy?" The old man lowered his carbine a degree or two.

"Royal Strickland Huckaby of Matagorda County."

He stared at me for a moment, the northerly breeze

bending the yellow point of his whiskers to the south, as if mockingly indicating the place of safety whence I had strayed. "What would you give for me to let you go? How about this new rifle?"

"Oh, Pa!" Topsy bounded down from her horse. She yanked my rifle away from her father and levered the cartridges out onto the ground. She handed the rifle to me and picked up the rounds and put them in her father's pocket. "There," she said, "now he can't do us no harm even he had a mind to." She turned to me. "Sorry, Mr. Huckaby, but we've had some trouble with land grabbers and Pa's riled over it."

The old man's carbine swung up to cover me again and his eyes flared at Topsy's poor choice of words. "Trouble! Hell, the goddamn bastards are killin' us!"

I could tell he wanted to shoot me badly so I decided I would say something before I died. "I understand your pa's feelings," I said to Topsy. "I spent three years in prison on account of a feud in Matagorda County. Three years just because I did what I had to do there to do right by my family. I figure that's all your pa wants to do."

The old man relaxed a little. "What feud?"

"The fight between the Williamses and the Fitzhughs. Joe David Williams was my brother-in-law."

The old man lowered his rifle. "I remember hearin' about that. You're the one that killed the ranger, aren't you?"

I shrugged. "They said I did, but they couldn't prove it. They could only convict me as an accomplice. I only did what I had to do."

The old man finally let his guard down. "You'll understand why I treated you suspicious, then. I'm Eli Flatt. This is my baby daughter, Topsy. Maybe you've heard of our trouble with the Standards. They're trying to steal our land and they've murdered two of us."

"I read something in the papers."

Old Eli was watching me with less caution now and it looked as if he might tell me I could leave any second. Then we heard hoofbeats coming in a hurry. "Who's that?" he said, covering me again with his carbine.

I shrugged. "Let's take cover," I suggested, trying to look as if I was on Eli's side. I pointed to the brush up in the draw and Topsy helped out by leading her horse there in a sprint. The old man motioned with his gun barrel for me to follow her and he led his horse behind me.

It didn't take long for the riders to arrive along the opposite bank of the creek. The two men were strangers to me, but obviously cut from the Flatt mold—wild-eyed and hatchet-faced.

"Boone!" Eli hollered.

Topsy stepped out of the underbrush and waved. The two riders crossed the creek. I came out under the guard of Eli's carbine, feeling nervous about the new arrivals. Daylight was slipping away quickly.

"We heard a shot," Boone said. "What happened? Who's this?"

"This feller says he's Royal Huckaby of Matagorda County. Either of you seen him around?"

The brothers shook their heads.

"Pa, why don't you be more polite?" Topsy said. "Mr. Huckaby, these are my brothers Boone and Tobe."

I nodded. "Roy," I suggested.

Neither Boone nor Tobe returned any courtesies. "Looks like he peed in his pants," Tobe said.

"Tobe!" Topsy scolded.

"What are you doin' here?" Boone growled. He was obviously the oldest brother of the clan—a full-grown man, graying in the sideburns and probably twenty years older than Topsy.

"He just wanted to shoot a deer," Topsy said.

"That's not what I mean," Boone said. "What brings you to this part of the country?"

"I came looking for work. I heard they were hiring at the Granite Mountain quarry."

"They was," Tobe said. "How come you didn't hire on if that's what you were after?"

"They were only hiring guards for the prisoners. I don't have much use for prison guards."

"He says he was in prison himself for killin' a ranger in that fight between the Fitzhughs and the Williamses down in Matagorda County," Eli said.

"I ain't never heard of no fight down there," Tobe said.

"I have," Boone said. "Whose side were you on?"

"The side in the right. Joe David Williams was my brother-in-law." I was praying that Boone Flatt had no affinity for Fitzhughs.

Boone grinned. "The side in the right," he repeated. "Maybe you'd care to help us fight Standards, then."

"Oh, Boone!"

"Shut up, Topsy. What about it, Royal? You might as well throw in with us, you bein' experienced at feudin'. Unless maybe you think the Standard side is the one in the right."

"I have nothing against the Standards or the Flatts," I said. "I just got out of prison on account of a fight like yours and I don't care to go back right away. I'd just as soon go look for some less dangerous work somewhere else."

"We can't let him go," Tobe said. "He may be going to join Lum and them. I'll bet you a two-bit cigar they hired him like a professional gun to work with them."

"That's just stupid," Topsy said. "Does he look like a killer to you? He's a little rough, but he don't look mean. He don't even wear a pistol!"

"Tobe's right," Eli said. "We can't let him go now just

so maybe he can shoot us in the back of the head later. He's either got to be with us or he's again' us and if he's again' us, we'll have to shoot him."

"I just wanted to kill a deer to eat until I could find some work," I complained.

"Will you throw in with us or not?" Boone asked.

I tried to retrace my steps since my release from prison, attempting to figure out how in God's name I had ended up exactly where I swore I would never venture, but I could not think of a thing for the life of me. I could think of nothing to say and nothing to do.

Topsy saved me. "Look, if you want to keep an eye on him, just put him to work till we find out who he is. Pa, you said yourself we needed to start chopping fence posts since the bob wire got here. He says he's looking for work. There's no need to kill him if it turns out he's telling the truth. And if he hunts Standards as good as he hunts deer, you don't want him on our side, anyhow."

There were no immediate objections, but Tobe sighed heavily and frowned. He was about my age and size and looked tough as rawhide, but I didn't see any real meanness to him. I sensed that a simple fear of strangers was behind all his hard talk.

"Can you swing an ax?" the old man asked.

"Yes, sir."

"Twenty dollars a month and board," he offered.

I accepted by not refusing.

It turned out that I was not such a big liar after all in regard to what I had told Marion Harkey. It looked as though I really was going to join the ranks of cedar choppers and go to work for the Flatt family. And I was happy about it, too, inasmuch as it compared to being shot.

"Tobe," Eli ordered, "ride up the creek and get his horse for him."

Tobe frowned but followed the instructions immediately.

It was dark by the time we started riding to the Flatts' place. Eli questioned his sons about the movements of the Standards as we went along.

"It ain't good, Pa," Tobe said. "Lum and Nat went up to the Marble Falls and got their wagon loaded with supplies. They got enough stuff to hole up in their house now."

"What?" the old man shouted.

"He's right, Pa," Boone said. "They had their wagon loaded dang near full."

Eli cussed and pulled savagely at a branch he happened to pass by. "They sleep in their beds tonight and we still camp out like curs! Why in hell didn't you stop 'em, Boone?"

"Couldn't," he said.

"Yeah, they had Annie with 'em," Tobe said. "The cowards made her ride right between 'em so we wouldn't shoot."

"Not that they would have shot," Topsy said to me. "Us Flatts ain't no bushwhackers."

We stopped at the dark edge of a clearing.

"Go ahead and look around," Boone said to Tobe.

"What for? Lum and Nat couldn't have finished unloading those supplies yet."

"We haven't accounted for Clay and Lon," the old man said. "Just do what your brother tells you."

"Half brother," Tobe said before riding away. He was gone for about five minutes while the rest of us sat on our horses, perfectly silent. "No sign of anybody," he said when he came back. We started to ride again and soon arrived at the Flatt home, a weathered board-and-batten structure surrounded by the usual spate of outbuildings.

"You see what cautions we have to take?" Eli said. "We never know when they'll hit us again. They have us outnumbered now with Lon and his three boys. It's only me and Boone and Tobe left on our side—the three of us altogether. I don't count Topsy. She shoots better than her brothers, but it ain't a woman's work to have to kill men."

"It shouldn't be nobody's work." Topsy turned away and went into a little log kitchen next to the house. In the moonlight I saw the form of a burly little dog moving beside her.

The rest of us put our horses in the barn, merely loosening the cinches of our saddles. I knew we would not sleep in the house that night. Men who expected trouble from their neighbors could not be so predictable as to sleep in their own beds unless, like the Standards, they were prepared for a long siege.

Tobe and Boone disappeared somewhere in the night with their rifles while Eli and I went to sit in the dark under a tree. A light came on in the kitchen and I could hear Topsy rattling skillets. I saw the dog again, a mottled, bobtailed cow dog, standing just outside the doorway of the kitchen, licking his chops. About halfway between the dog and me, I saw a pile of objects I would never have recognized in the dark if I hadn't slept among them in the bed of Marion Harkey's wagon.

"You see those headstones right there?" Eli asked, pointing to a group of grave markers illuminated by the lantern light from the kitchen. "The one on the south belongs to Boone's ma, my first wife. The one next to it is my second wife. She died after Topsy was born. It was just their natural time to go, both of them.

"But those two new graves are for Reed and Bass, my next-to-oldest and my next-to-youngest. Standards killed 'em. Jumped 'em after the trial. They knew they would lose the land they were claiming and it riled their greedy souls. But it ain't their land to claim. Never was. It's mine, and they know it."

I thought I should acknowledge Eli's talk with some kind of response. "How did they ever come to claim it in the first place?" I was hoping to make use of my predicament by learning something about the zero stone, but I was prepared to take Eli's account with the proper measure of incredulity.

"I suspect old Lon had it on his mind to steal that land when he first set foot on his claim. Just took him several years to work up the nerve for it. Him and his family were ruined in the war back in Virginia. Lost all their land. So they scraped together everything they owned and sold it and used the money to buy their spread here, just upstream of mine. I had already been here twenty-seven years by that time. I was the first white man to live this far up the Colorado.

"Anyway, Lon and them didn't have a thing when they come here, so I taken 'em in, fed 'em, helped 'em build a house and all. It was Lon and Charlotte and all their offspring. The youngest one was just a sprout."

That would be Annie, I thought to myself, but I dared not mention any Standard names.

"They worked hard—I'll give 'em that. I was glad to have help in the neighborhood because the Indians had been pesterin' us like heel flies. Lon and me both was in on that last fight with 'em over to Packsaddle Mountain. He really had me blindfolded, thinkin' he was the finest kind of neighbor a man could get."

"When did he lay claim to the land?"

"The courthouse up at Burnet burned in '74," Eli said. "After that Lon started claiming Double Horn Creek was his, which was a damned lie. The creek's mine. Always has been. I settled here first and I have always owned that creek."

"What does the courthouse burning down have to do with it?"

"Can't you figure it out? Everybody thought for some time that the courthouse was burned by rustlers trying to destroy all the brand records. But I believe Lon done it. He done it to burn up our land patents, so it would be just my word again' his."

It had been my job in the Huckaby enterprises to evaluate land and oversee the development of it once purchased. My father had handled the details with the deeds and patents and courthouse records, so I was almost completely ignorant of them. When it occurred to me that records of cattle brands and rightful titles to land and such things could be completely lost by destroying a courthouse, I ceased to wonder why so many Texas counties had converted theirs to ashes.

"Why did it take so long to bring the case to court," I asked, "if the courthouse burned back in '74?"

"Because I'm a fool with generosity. I asked Lon one day why he would claim the Double Horn when he knew it was mine and he looked me dead in the eye and lied like a thief and said I should know damn good and well that it belonged to him. We might have fought right then if I hadn't been such a fair man. You see, boy, it didn't make any difference to me who owned the land because we both used the creek and our herds ran free on each other's land. There weren't no fences—and won't be till you get them posts chopped.

"So I compromised with Lon, bein' generous. I told him we would just keep sharing the creek and call it our boundary. I was giving up maybe a hundred acres along the other side of the creek by doin' that, but I figured that was a small price to pay to stay on good terms with my neighbors."

"And then?" I asked.

"Then Lon decides earlier this year that he wants the whole creek to hisself and starts talking about fencing it off. That's where he drew too hard on my generosity and I fought back. But I done it proper. Took him to court. That's the difference between us Flatts and them Standards. They done their fightin' like a mob. Jumped us after court. His boys murdered two of my sons."

"I was sorry to read about that in the papers," I said. "Land isn't worth the lives of good young men. That was a sore way for them to act just for losing the case."

"They haven't lost yet, but they will."

"You mean the trial isn't over?" I asked.

"No. The judge ruled that a company of rangers and a Land Office investigator would have to come and find the zero stone to locate the original boundary."

At last, the term I had waited to hear! "Zero stone? What in the hell is the zero stone?"

"It's a sack of shit, if you ask me. There's a sort of legend around here that a party of men who surveyed this place back in '38 left some kind of monument or somethin' chiseled in a rock. I've lived on this land forty-seven years and I ain't never run across it."

I let Eli's notion upset me for a moment—the notion that no zero stone existed. But then I remembered the old Mexican's map. Eli could waste his words on the stars. I knew better. But I played along. "You mean the survey party never was here?"

"No, that ain't what I mean, damn it. They were here, alright. I saw 'em. I talked to 'em the day before the Indians got 'em."

"Indians?"

"Yes. It was way back yonder in '38 when I was a pup about like you. I come up the day before it happened to see how them surveyors were coming along. They were platting my head rights for me. This was wild country then. Thirty miles from nowhere. They showed me about where the boundaries to my property would run and I can tell you the Gospel truth that my claim included Double Horn Creek as they showed it to me. But them surveyors never told me nothin' about no blasted zero stone."

"Why did those men come all the way out in the wilderness to survey a piece of land?" I asked.

"The Republic of Texas was trying to get settlers to take up the Indian lands, so they was givin' it away for almost nothin'. A man could get as much as forty-five hundred acres and not have to pay anything but the survey fees.

"The surveyors come all the way out here because they planned to make a great big survey of this whole valley, to open it up to settlers. When I heard about them getting up a survey party in Austin, I went to them and told them that I wanted the first plot myself. I wanted to be the first settler. So I asked them to pick out the finest piece of land along the river and start their big survey there and I would patent that first piece of land for myself. I offered them a bonus over and above the survey fees to do that for me.

"I rode up here several days after they got started to see what my land looked like. It included Double Horn Creek and a good portion of land along the Colorado and several little springs here and there. I asked them to send the field notes back to the General Land Office as soon as they got them written up so I could go ahead and get my patent. Then, the next day, I rode back down to Austin."

"And the Indians got them that day?"

"That's right. This piece of land was all they got surveyed before the Indians got 'em. The reds must have figured out what was up. They knew settlers would come after the first survey crew. Them surveyors must have let their guard down, because Indians killed and scalped 'em all except for one."

"One got away?"

"Yep."

"Who was he?"

"Hell if I know. But lucky for me he got away and took the field notes back down to Austin and turned them in, so I could use them to patent my land."

The old Mexican! The old Mexican had been a member of that survey party—maybe a cook or a guard or a horse wrangler. Being a young Mexican back then, he had managed to escape the Indian attack and had taken the field notes to Austin. He had probably found the treasure with the rest of the men in the survey party a day or so before the massacre and they had used their surveying equipment to plot the exact location of the treasure so they could come back for it later.

Yes, that explained the 49 degrees northwest, measured by the surveyors' compass! And the 189 chains! Didn't surveyors use chains to measure land? They all would have become rich if not for the Indians. And the old Mexican—the young Mexican, that is—was too badly scared to come back after the treasure himself, so he simply made a map of it. That dear, old vaquero had bequeathed to me a buried fortune!

My mind amazed me with the speed at which it could conjure up such possibilities. I wanted desperately to ask old man Flatt if he remembered any Mexicans being part of the survey crew or if the surveyors had seemed strangely excitable about something they wouldn't mention the day he talked to them. But what would Eli think of those kind of harebrained inquiries?

I heard the hinges creak as the door to the log kitchen opened wider. Topsy walked out carrying a big pot and a cake of cornbread. She paused to look for us, her dog watching for some morsel to fall from her hands.

"Over here, Topsy," Eli said.

She approached and put the food down in front of us.

The dog moved around downwind of the stew pot and started sniffing the air, inching nervously toward the steaming vessel.

"Git out of there, Speck," the old man growled.

Speck cowered and followed Topsy as she went back to the house for some plates and spoons. By the time she got back, Boone and Tobe had snuck in under the shadows with me and Eli. We all ate our stew and cornbread in silence, the Flatt men with their rifles across their laps, watching the dark, Speck sitting expectantly on his haunches.

I saw Topsy save a corner of her cornbread. She scraped a little stew onto it and gave it to the dog. I ate my fill and still had a little left on my plate, too. When I gave it back to Topsy, I gestured toward the dog and she understood I intended the leftovers for her pet.

We tightened our saddle cinches again, except for Topsy. She stayed home while Eli, Boone, Tobe, and I rode a mile or so into the oak thickets and made a dry camp with no fire. Topsy had loaned me a blanket from the house. The cool front made me grateful to have it. The Flatt men stretched out beside me, their guns in their hands.

My back was too sore from breaking school desks and the ground too rough with rocks to make sleep come easy for me. But the air was clear and the stars brilliant. I was still staring at them when the snoring started. If the Standards had come out to slaughter us that night, they could have located us from three miles away by the noise—provided they could have distinguished it from a chorus of sonorous bullfrogs. The grating lullaby eventually put me to sleep and, in my dreams, became the creaking and groaning of timbers as I wandered aimlessly through the shafts of an abandoned silver mine.

ELEVEN

A gun butt nudged me about an hour before sunup. I rolled out from under my borrowed blanket and saddled my mare. No one spoke as we rode back to the house. When we got there, Topsy already had eggs, bacon, biscuits, and coffee ready for us. We ate out behind the barn. Topsy was the only one who went in or out of the house.

By dawn Eli, Boone, and Tobe had mounted fresh horses. "We're gonna try to get some work done today," Eli said to Topsy, "after we account for them Standards. We'll look for some calves to brand back at Cypress Creek. You might want to take a rope and check them bogs along the river and pull out any cows you find."

"Alright," Topsy said.

Then Eli turned to me. "You'll find you an ax and a file in the barn. Topsy will show you." He took a canteen down from his saddle and tossed it to me. "Here, I believe I owe you a canteen."

"Where do you want me to start chopping?" I asked.

"Use your sense, boy. Find a big cedar brake where we can get a wagon in to load the posts. Cut them about as big as you are around the knee. Hundreds of 'em."

"Might as well chop some skinnier ones, too," Tobe said. "We can use 'em for pickets around the pens and staves on the bob-wire fence to keep the wires from saggin'."

"Alright," Eli said, "cut some smaller ones, too."

"And find you a few great big ones for corners and gate posts," Boone suggested. "Big as you are around the middle and ten feet tall."

"Ten feet," Eli repeated. "And don't take no ideas of pullin' stakes. We'll catch you wherever you run. You're with us now whether you like it or not until we find out just who the hell you are."

I nodded and the Flatt gang trotted to the south. When they called Speck, he kicked up a cloud of dust a whirlwind would have envied as he made his pursuit. Topsy watched them leave, then showed me where to find my tools.

In the dim light of the barn, her hair looked jet-black. But when she passed in front of the morning light streaming in through the open barn door, it shone with the color of rubies. Her moccasins moved silently across the dirt-and-straw floor. "Here's your ax." She handed the tool to me. "I'll get you a file. There's a vise by the door if you want to put an edge on it now."

I clamped the ax head in the vise and started smoothing the burrs from the blade with the file Topsy brought me. She went out with a bridle and brought a big gelding around to the barn door.

"He looks strong enough to pull those brutes out of the mud," I said.

"Yes, he's a strong one, alright." She went to the room the bridle had come from and came out carrying a saddle. She was only a switch of a person, but she didn't let the load slow her down. "Did everything stay quiet last night?"

"Yes," I said, "except for the snoring. I appreciate that blanket you loaned me. I slept well under it, but your pa and your brothers sure must be nervous to camp in the rocks like that."

"They're expecting trouble from the Standards."

"Do you think they'll give you any?"

Topsy was stroking the big gelding's back with a brush. She ducked under his belly to get to his other side. "I don't think they'll come after us. But if any Flatts and Standards happen to cross paths, they're sure to start shooting."

I turned the head of the ax around in the vise to work the other face. I was grateful that it was a double-bladed head so I could spend twice the time on it and work Topsy for more information. "Last night your pa told me how the trouble got started between y'all and the Standards. Too bad about your brothers, Reed and Bass."

Topsy grunted. "It's too bad about Virgil and Cal Standard, too. It's too bad about all of them. But I'm sure Pa didn't tell you how he's the cause of it all. I bet he forgot to mention that."

I stopped in midstroke with the file, shocked to hear Topsy speak out against her father. "What do you mean?"

"It's none of your concern," she said, "but I guess I better tell you so you'll know how much trouble you've stumbled into. It was Pa that caused us to go to war with the Standards."

"I thought the Standards grabbed some of y'all's land."

"They didn't exactly grab it. The boundary never has been marked that any of us know about, so we just sort of shared the creek as a boundary and that worked out fine for years."

"Until the courthouse burned down," I suggested.

"No, that had nothing to do with it. That's just Pa's story. He's told it so often that he's got Boone and Tobe believing it and I think he may even believe it hisself."

"Well, what was it that caused the land dispute, then?"

"You may not believe me but I'm going to tell you." She swung the saddle around in a half circle to get it on the gelding's back. "Pa was the first settler to come to this part of the country. He's always bragged about that and thought he should get more credit for fightin' Indians and all. When they formed the county, he wanted them to name it after him—Flatt County, Texas. Only problem is, this ain't no flat county. So they called it Burnet County, after that old politician, David Burnet. That burned Pa up double because he's an old Sam Houston man and Houston hated David Burnet."

"I don't understand what that has to do with . . ."

"Just hold your horses," Topsy said, "I'm gittin' to it. Since he couldn't get the county named Flatt, Pa's had it on his mind to get a town named for him around here. Well, a few years ago, we had a wet year and the river stayed up running deep all summer. There was a steamboat in the Colorado then—I've heard it sunk down at La Grange since then—but that little steamer came all the way up to the Marble Falls because the river was so high."

"Yes, but what has a steamboat to do with . . ."

"Dang it, Mr. Huckaby, just keep your shirt on. I'm going to make sense in the long run." Topsy was hanging by the cinch strap, using her weight to snug it through the saddle rings. "That steamboat gave Pa the idea that he should start a town on the river and name it Flatt, Texas, and let the steamers service the town. And he figured he'd put this town where that steamer tied up on its way to the Marble Falls. And guess where that was."

"The mouth of the Double Horn?" I asked, finally beginning to grasp the route Topsy had taken.

"Yes, and so Pa figured that's where he'd put his docks."

"But that was all several years ago, you said."

"Yes, and we didn't hear no more whistles from no more steamers this high up the river and Pa more or less forgot about that idea. Then, a few months ago, the papers had a story about the Colorado River Navigation Company. Pa read it and got all excited because this company was going to clear the raft out of the mouth of the Colorado and open up the river to steamboats that could come in and out of the Gulf of Mexico. Pa figured we'd get rich if we had our own steamboat town, so he up and told Lon Standard one day that he was going to fence off the Double Horn and start his town."

"Now, wait a minute," I said, working the last face of the

ax. "Your pa told me that Lon Standard was going to fence *him* out."

"That's not true," Topsy said. "It was Pa that said he would fence first. Well, the Standards have always believed that that land was theirs, so they took Pa to court to try and prove it and that made him madder than a hornet. He wanted that town bad. He wanted it so much that he couldn't think straight. And he still wants it. He keeps sayin' that we could be rich as kings if only that damned Lon Standard would stay away from what didn't belong to him."

I began to see what drove Eli Flatt. He was an old man who felt life had shortchanged him on his dreams. He wanted to leave his name on something and he was ready to grasp any idea that could turn his fortunes before he had to die poor. And that was a polite way of saying he was a greedy old bastard.

But of all the nonsensical schemes to pay for with the lives of one's own sons! Steamboats on the Colorado! What did Eli Flatt know of building towns? What did he know of the indestructible raft at the Colorado's mouth? What did he know of steamers? To think that he would go to war with his neighbors in hopes that a line of steam-powered vessels would ply the river this high up! This river—the Colorado—that jumped its banks every other year and all but dried up the years in between! The idiot who would follow his greed into that kind of ridiculous speculation had no more sense than the fool who would . . .

The fool who would risk his life and his freedom against the sorry chance of digging up some unknown treasure once mentioned on an old Mexican's map.

"Well, just who *is* it that rightfully owns the creek?" I asked. "The Flatts or the Standards?"

"I don't know. I always thought it was us, but now I'm not sure. The Standards always thought they owned it and said the land patents that burned in the courthouse would have proved them right. But now I just don't know who's right. For so many years it just didn't matter. We *shared* the creek."

"What about the zero stone?"

Topsy had coiled a hemp lariat and was fastening the end of it to her saddle horn. "Nobody knows where it is. Sometimes Pa says there ain't no such thing. Other times he says that if there ever was a boundary marker like that, the Standards would have already dug it up anyhow, so they could steal our land."

If I had to hone the ax head much longer, I would reduce it all to shavings. I paused to take a drink from the canteen Eli had given me. "How come you said your pa caused the killing to start between your brothers and the Standards? He told me last night that the Standard boys jumped your brothers after the trial."

"It was Pa that told all my brothers to take their guns to the courthouse the day of the trial," she said. "He had told them that if the judge couldn't settle the case that day, that us Flatts ought to settle it ourselves. That's what Reed and Bass tried to do and that's why the Standards shot them down."

"You mean to say that the Standards only shot in self-defense?"

"Yes, and the grand jury saw it the same way. Then Pa sent Boone and Tobe out to get even."

"What do you mean get even?" I said.

"You know what I mean. You must have heard how Virgil and Cal Standard got shot."

"You mean Boone and Tobe ambushed them?"

"I told you last night us Flatts ain't no bushwhackers. Boone and Tobe said they came across Virgil and Cal on the road to the Marble Falls. Virgil and Cal started shooting first and so my brothers had to shoot back."

"I read in the paper that the Standard boys were shot in the back," I said.

"It was a running fight. They turned their backs at the wrong time. The point is Pa shouldn't never have sent Boone and Tobe out looking for them in the first place. Now two more are dead and everybody thinks Tobe and Boone are murderers.

"There was a bob-wire salesman staying with us then and Pa wanted to kill him, too, so he wouldn't say anything about where Boone and Tobe had been that day. I talked Pa out of it, though, just like I talked him out of shooting you yesterday."

"I have neglected to thank you for that," I said.

"You can thank me by not letting Pa know what I've told you today."

"I won't say anything." I took the ax out of the vise and slipped the file into my hip pocket to take with me to the cedar brakes. "In fact, there's a secret or two I would like you to know, since you told me yours."

Topsy tossed her red hair over one shoulder as she turned to look at me. "What do you mean?"

"I didn't say anything to your pa because I was afraid he would misunderstand me. But I think I better tell you in case he finds out and takes it the wrong way."

"Finds what out?" she asked.

"I've met some of the Standard family."

"What?" she said. "Which ones?"

I told her about my altercation with the flour barrel. I told it as humorously as I knew how to, but Topsy only cracked a smile for a second or two.

"What about Clay?" she said. "Was he there, too?"

"No, just Lum and Nat and Annie. They did mention Clay, though. Said he and their pa would be waiting."

Topsy sighed and looked beyond me. It made sense now how she could go against her father when her own brothers were getting killed. She was in love with Clay Standard. If not for Clay, she would have hated Standards as much as old Eli, and she might have shot me herself the day before for getting too close to Flatt land.

"What are the Standards like?" I asked. We were standing in the doorway of the barn, ready to go to our jobs.

"They were good neighbors. But there was always something between Pa and Mr. Lon, even before the land argument."

"What was it?"

"Mr. Lon came from Virginia. He fought four years in the war. I think he was a major or something. When the Yankees won, he lost almost all his land and property. His house burned. He had to turn his Negroes out. He didn't have work for them all after the war. So he came here to start again."

"And your pa?"

"Like I said, Pa is an old Sam Houston man. He voted against Texas going with the Confederacy, just like old Sam did. In fact, most of the people in this county voted against quitting the Union. We ain't never had no slaves around here and we didn't want no war. Pa said we never should have gone to war."

"So your pa and Lon Standard differed about the war?"

"I never heard them argue out loud. But whenever they were together and Pa said something good about the Reconstruction Government I could see Mr. Lon getting sort of hot. And whenever Mr. Lon would talk about Jeff Davis or something, Pa would just get up and leave. Boone and Reed fought with the Confederacy, and Pa was proud of them for it, but he never thought Texas should have been in it in the first place."

"What about the rest of the Standards?" I asked.

"There was five brothers and two sisters before the feud started. Cal and Virgil are dead now. Susan got married to a fellow she knew in Virginia and went back there. Lum is the oldest and used to lead the militia before the Indians were run out. Some folks wanted him to run for sheriff here while back, but he didn't do it.

"Nat's about your age, I guess. It was Nat and Cal who shot my brothers after the trial. Nat's got him the fastest two racehorses around here.

"Then there's Clay," she said.

"What's he like?"

"He's a nice feller. Took me to a dance once last year."

"You like him?"

"Sure, I like him," she said, fiddling with the gelding's bridle. "He treated me nice. He liked to joke around a lot. Always told me I was the prettiest one of the Flatt family. I ain't got no sisters, you know."

I smiled and looped the canteen strap around my neck. "What about Annie?"

"Annie? She's a friend of mine now—or would be if it wasn't for the feud—but in school we used to fight every day."

"Fight?" I asked.

"You bet. Rasslin' and fistfights, too. We got so tough the boys wouldn't even pick on us."

A bizarre image came to mind. It *would* be a good fight, I was thinking. Topsy versus Annie in a hair-pulling, toe-to-toe bout of fisticuffs. I felt strangely disloyal when I thought I would have to put my money on Topsy in the long run.

"We've growed up since then," Topsy continued. "She's a better cook and keeps a better house than I can. Course, she's got her ma to help her. And she's got the biggest garden and orchards you ever seen. She used to send over lots of it for us."

"I guess she must be the prettiest one of the Standard family," I said, before I could stop myself.

Topsy caught me blushing. "Why, Mr. Huckaby! I do believe you took a shine to her yesterday at the Marble Falls! You better watch yourself. She's a hellcat. I have never heard the likes of cuss words in my life as when Annie gets riled!"

"I know," I said. "Well, I guess I better start chopping."

"Yes, you better before you turn any redder," she said. "I'll bring you some biscuits or something to eat this evening. As long as I don't have too many cows to look after." She hitched her skirt up over the knee of her buckskins, took a short hop to get her foot in the stirrup, and then sprang into the saddle. "There's a good cedar brake on that road to the Double Horn," she said, pointing. "You can't get in any trouble as long as you don't cross the creek."

I watched Topsy ride away, then I walked past the spools of barbed wire, past a post-and-rail corral where Liberty was standing with some of the Flatt horses, and on toward the creek. A cool, pleasant stroll of two miles or so brought me to the edge of a cedar brake just off the road. It was a good place to start chopping.

I got my muscles limbered up on two or three trees, then began lopping limbs off at such a clip that the whole out-of-doors smelled like the inside of a brand-new cedar chest. The smaller limbs I piled up in one stack, to be used as the pickets and staves Tobe had suggested. The larger limbs would become posts, big around as I was at the knee, as Eli had specified.

Most of the cedars branched right above the ground into multiple trunks of the fence-post size. It was a rare one that had a single trunk and then the trunk would be just a little bigger around than my leg—still too slender and short for corner or gate posts. I would have to find some old trees for the big posts Boone had ordered me to produce.

As I swung the ax, I began to take Lon Standard's side in the land dispute. His side was Annie's side. His side was the side that went against Eli Flatt and if Eli's own daughter could blame him for the dispute, I figured I could, too.

But, most prominent in my mind was the hope that Lon Standard was right because, if he was, it meant the lost zero stone stood somewhere east of the creek, where my ax was currently making fence posts of cedar trees. It was foolish to hope for such things, but I held to a fancy that I might actually stumble across the rock of the zero somewhere in the cedar brakes while chopping posts.

Why not? I had stumbled across the old Mexican and Marion Harkey and Annie Standard and Topsy Flatt. Why couldn't I stumble upon a lost boundary marker the same way the old Mexican had happened across a lost treasure in the years of his youth? I felt a gold coin or a faceted gem drop into my pocket with every limb I hacked from the brakes.

TWELVE

Topsy must have come across more bogged cows than she expected, for she didn't arrive with any edibles that afternoon. I subsisted on water from Eli's canteen and a couple of biscuits I had saved from breakfast.

It was almost dusk when I saw Tobe riding toward me, leading my mare, picking his way around the cedar stumps. He stared at the piles of posts and pickets around him as if he had never before seen a day's work thus accounted for. "My word, Royal," he said. "Did you have an ax for each hand?"

I had almost finished stacking the day's posts in their appropriate piles and Liberty was a welcome sight. "Thanks for bringing my mare," I said.

"If I didn't know better, I'd think Topsy spent the day

chopping with you," he said. "She can rough it with the best of 'em but she's got nothin' on you." He helped me carry the last couple of dozen posts to the stack I was building of them. "She's cooking us some game and some roasting ears," he said as we mounted. He took a last look over his shoulder at the wreckage I had made of the cedar brakes and shook his head in wonder and admiration.

We ate in the dark again, this time in a thicket out beyond the corral. The Flatt men ate three squirrels and two roasting ears apiece. Topsy and I split a rabbit.

"He don't burn much hay," Tobe said, "but he sure makes splinters fly."

Boone scoffed. "The man's bein' paid to work, ain't he?"

"How much you reckon he chopped in one day?" Tobe asked.

"How much *did* he chop?" Eli asked.

"I'll bet you a plug he cut four hundred pickets and two hundred posts and he's got 'em all ricked up like cordwood."

Boone risked a low laugh. "Tobe, you'd bet on spoilt milk."

"That would be almost a post every minute," Topsy said, having figured the question mathematically in her head.

"He couldn't have chopped that much," Boone said.

"Yes, he could have, couldn't he, Pa?" Tobe asked.

"I guess mite near anybody could cut sixty posts in one hour, but I don't know whether or not he could keep it up ten hours straight."

"We'll go count 'em in the mornin'," Tobe suggested.

"The hell we will," Boone said. "Got better things to do."

"Boone's right," Eli said.

After tossing my rabbit bones to Speck, I rode with the men to another campsite somewhere in the dark. I didn't know the trails the way they did, so I just had to follow along. We left our horses in a hollow and threw our bed-rolls down nearby. Tobe still hadn't stopped bragging on my prowess with the ax.

"Let me see your hands," he said, once we had seated ourselves among the rocks and tree trunks.

I held them out, palms upward. Tobe felt them.

"Good gracious, Pa, they feel hard as hooves. I thought *I* had thick skin."

Boone and Eli had to inspect my hands then. It was almost pitch-dark, the moon having not yet risen, but Eli was about to light his pipe, so he let his match illuminate my calluses after his tobacco had taken the flame. In the flickering light, I saw that his long white beard had snagged a few kernels of corn. Then it was dark again and the Flatts smoked silently.

"I don't know why in hell a man would want to work that hard afoot," Boone finally said.

"I didn't have much choice in the matter," I replied. "I built those calluses in the penitentiary."

"What did you do to get put in there, anyway?"

"Hush, Tobe," Eli said. "That's a dangerous question to ask of a man."

"That's alright, Mr. Flatt," I replied. "It might do you all some good to hear what I did because it was not much different from what y'all are doing right now. I was just trying to do what I thought was right by my friends and my family."

There was another stretch of silence. "How long you say you stayed in prison?" Tobe asked.

"Three years."

"How'd you like it?"

Boone started laughing. "Hell, it wasn't a damn holiday he went on. They put chains on him and made him earn his keep. What did you think?"

"That right?" Tobe asked me.

"More or less. Except it wasn't my keep I was earning. It was the contractor's."

"The contractor's? What's that mean?"

"The prison's been under the lease system since '71. They hire convicts out like mules at so much a head to various contractors who work them as hard as they want. When I was in there, sometimes they even subleased us to somebody else. They paid for us by the day, so, of course, to get their money's worth out of us, they worked us as long as we could stand up. Boone's right about the chains, though. We wore them often enough."

"What kind of work did you do?" Tobe asked.

"All kinds. I worked in hide yards and brick yards, built railroads, made charcoal, chopped cotton, dug ditches, pitched hay."

"They must not have fed you too good," Eli said. "Or have you always been that skinny?"

"No, sir, not always," I replied. "I cut a wider wake before I went to prison. The amount of food we got depended on the generosity of whoever it was that was leasing us at the time. Some of them fed us better than others, but none of them fed us enough."

Boone snorted as if he thought I was telling windies.

"What's the hardest you ever worked?" Tobe asked.

"The hardest I ever worked was the time I was given the choice to pump or die."

"What in hell's name is that supposed to mean?" Boone asked.

"I'll explain it to you. You see, I never did much work before I went to prison. Not the kind of work you men are used to, anyway. My daddy owned a lot of land and it was my responsibility to oversee it and make sure other folks were doing the work. My hands and my muscles were soft then."

"Nobody asked you to back up that far," Boone said.

"I'll get to the point quick enough," I said. "When they sent me off to prison I'll admit I was scared. I imagined it would be something like a big dog pit and I knew I wouldn't be the toughest dog to get thrown in. Like I say, I was soft then. But the real danger of the state penitentiary was something that never even crossed my mind until I found out about it firsthand."

"What was that?" Tobe asked.

"The danger that I would be worked or starved or beaten to death by the guards."

"I thought you were gonna tell something about pumpin' for your life," Boone reminded me.

"I'm leading up to that."

"Just let him tell it," Tobe said.

I continued: "I had been in prison just a couple of days when they sent me out with a chain gang to work in the hay fields of some farmer who was subleasing a bunch of prisoners. I spent all day in the sun, forking hay into a baling machine. I didn't have these calluses then, so by the end of the day my hands were bloody. They locked us up in a little shack that night and had a few men there to guard us. I started to tell one of the guards that I needed medical attention for my hands, but there was a black prisoner there by the name of Reuben who sat me down and told me I had better not mention any of my problems to the guards or things would go rough for me. I took his advice that night."

"What did you have to eat that night?" Tobe asked.

"What the hell difference does it make?" Boone said. "Don't start him to branchin' out or he'll really take the bridle off."

"Everything I've said is true, Boone. But if you don't believe it so far, I warn you that you'll never believe the parts I haven't told yet."

Boone snorted again.

"I don't remember what they had for us to eat that night, Tobe, because I was too cramped up from the work and the sun to keep anything down.

"Anyway, the next day they worked us just as hard and I figured about noon that I wasn't going to live if I had to keep working like that. Old Reuben knew what I had on my mind, though, and he whispered to me not to try getting out of any hay baling. He stuck with me all day and made it look like I was getting my share done, when really it was him doing his work and mine, too.

"My palms were two big blood blisters that night when they locked us back up in the shack. I managed to eat that night, some kind of gruel. At least they gave us all the water we wanted."

"Is that the water you had to pump to save your life?"

"Shut up, Boone, and let the boy tell his story," old Eli suggested.

Boone heaved a sigh of disgust and settled back against a small oak.

"It was the next day that I had to do the pumping. The black man, Reuben, tried to keep me from complaining to the guards, but the blood from my hands was running all the way down the handle of my pitchfork. I just knew I couldn't live if I had to work that way and I figured it was high time I said so.

"I went to the guard who looked the friendliest and said, 'Sir, I need another kind of job. This work is ruining my hands.' The guard looked at them and, with the most sincere expression of concern on his face, asked me what kind of work it was that I had in mind. I told him I didn't know, but that I was college educated and was not used to working out in the sun.

" 'Would you like a cooler place to work?' he asked.

" 'Yes, sir,' I said, 'I would be grateful to have a cooler

place to work,' and it didn't seem to me that the guards were going to be unreasonable at all.

"Then the guard said, 'Men, this prisoner is college educated and wants someplace cool to work. Let's oblige him.' Well, they left just one guard to watch the hay pitching and the rest of them came at me laughing and dragged me back to the shack and locked a ball and chain on my leg and told me they were about to put me to work in the coolest place they knew."

"Where did they put you?" Tobe said.

"They threw me down an old well."

"Oh, my foot," Boone said.

"I said you wouldn't believe it, Boone, but I'm telling you the truth. What was to stop them? Nobody was around who gave a damn about any convicts."

"How deep a well was it?" Tobe asked.

"Yes, and how long a yarn is this?" Boone wanted to know.

I ignored the second question. "It wasn't too deep. About twenty feet or thereabouts and there was only about three feet of water in the bottom. And it *was* cool. The leg iron cut my ankle a little falling in and I got scraped up some on the rocks lining the inside of the well. But I didn't break any bones, and overall, I was happy to be out of the sun and I figured I might get some rest. I thought it was a kind of solitary confinement they were putting me in. I figured they would throw me some food down that evening and then take me out the next morning."

"That what happened?" Tobe asked.

"Nope. About ten minutes after they threw me in the well they lowered a pump down to me. It had a pipe attached to it that ran all the way up and out of the well. And they had sawed the handle off shorter than usual."

"What was they about?" old Eli asked quietly.

"Well, sir, I soon found out. Before they threw me into the well, I had noticed that there was a windmill right nearby and a water tank up on stilts. And they began letting water gush out of the tank and into the old well I was in. It took me about thirty seconds to figure out that I was going to drown if I didn't start pumping."

"I'd have swum," Boone said.

"He had a ball and chain on his leg," Tobe reminded his half brother with a tone of superiority in his voice.

"Pay closer attention, Boone," the old man said.

"They had figured out every way possible to make it tough on me. The pump stood on a pedestal that put it about a foot too high to make pumping easy. And they had sawed that handle off to reduce the leverage."

"I'd have clumb that pipe sticking out of the well," Boone said, "and I'd have dragged that ball and chain right up with me."

"Maybe you could have made it," I said. "You might be strong enough. But I wasn't. Besides, I figured those guards would be on the top, waiting for me. No, I just had to pump and I mean I had to pump quick to keep the water going out as fast as it came in. Even then, I was losing ground. The water level climbed steadily up my chest."

"And with them sore hands, too," Tobe said.

"That was the worst of it, even after I used my shirt to wrap them up in, they still hurt something terrible. But I learned pretty quick not to think about that and I figured I would survive because I estimated about how much water was in that tank on stilts and I knew it would run out sooner or later and I could quit pumping. And I figured out ways to use different muscles. I would squat up and down for a while and use my legs to do the work . . ."

The moon had risen and there was enough light for the Flatt men to watch me as I demonstrated my method of squat-pumping. It was worth a laugh to Boone.

". . . and to give my hands a break, I could catch that pump handle in the crook of my elbow on the way down. Then I would go to using my back muscles, bending over and straightening up. But that well was narrow and I kept bumping my head against the other side. So then I would pump with my arms again and then start over with the squatting method."

"How long did it take for that water tank to empty out?" Tobe asked.

"It never did," I said.

"I knew it!" Boone shouted, laughing. "I knew it was a windy and ol' Royal hooked you good on it, Tobe!"

"No, it's the truth," I said quickly. "The tank didn't run out of water because I was pumping it right back in. I was pumping water in circles."

Two hoot owls called to each other during a brief silence.

"How'd you come out alive, then?" Boone asked skeptically.

"I almost didn't. I gave it all of what I had. I was pumping for my life. But a man has just so much and I was getting used up. I made it until after dark sometime, but the water was climbing higher up on me all the time. Then strange things began to happen to me."

"Explain that better," Eli ordered.

"Well, I don't know if I can. You see it got pitch-dark in that well and there was that constant noise of the water falling in on me. And I had gotten so cold from standing in the water that I had gone numb all over. I was completely worn out from the work and I couldn't feel or hear or see a thing and my head started to play tricks on me. I saw things I couldn't explain—things that didn't make sense."

"Haints?"

"Yeah, something like that, Tobe. Just strange lights and things. Visions. I guess I kept pumping, though. I guess my body worked longer than my mind."

"Well, did they shut the water off or what?" Boone asked. "How come you didn't drown?"

"The next thing I remember, I could feel something warm in the water with me."

"You mean you pissed yourself again?"

That one even made Tobe laugh, and he was right with me in the story.

"No, it was another man in there with me. That black man, Reuben, had taken all his clothes off and climbed down into the well."

"What do you mean to say, boy?" old Eli growled.

"He took his uniform off because he didn't want to be caught and the guards would figure out that he had come to help me if his clothes were wet the next morning. He had a handful of that gruel and he shoved some in my mouth and made me swallow it. He started doing the pumping for me, too. I told him to shut the water off, but he said he couldn't do that because the guards would wake up if they didn't keep hearing that noise of it flowing.

"The way Reuben pumped that water was something. He got it down below our knees, then told me he would have to climb up the pipe and go back to the shack. He told me to rest until the water got up to my waist and then to start pumping again. He said they would let me out at dawn."

"Did they?"

"Yes, they did. It was the sweetest silence I ever heard when that water quit falling in on me. They hauled the pump out, then lowered a rope for me to loop under my arms. I thought that ball was going to pull my leg off, but I stayed in one piece until they dragged me out."

"You sure that's all true?" Boone asked.

"I swear by everything holy that it's true."

We sat in the dim silence for a while, the embers in Eli's pipe pulsing orange.

"Was that the worst they ever done you in jail?" Tobe asked.

"Nope," I said. "The worst came right after they pulled me out of the well."

The Flatt men didn't have the heart to ask what more the guards could have done to me, so I had to tell them on my own initiative.

"They forced me to watch as they whipped the life out of poor old Reuben for climbing down in the well to help me out. They stripped all his clothes off him and made five convicts hold him facedown by the arms, legs, and head. Then they used the bat on him."

"What's the bat?" asked Tobe with a touch of dread in his voice.

"It's a handle attached to two straps of leather as thick as the soles of your boots, about four inches wide and up to six feet long. It can turn a man's flesh to jelly. They must have lashed him fifty times with it until he was limp as a rope. The screams he made will never let me be as long as I live. I wake up hearing them sometimes."

"They whipped him to death?" Eli asked.

"I suppose so. At least I never saw him again after that. They just dragged him off and I figured they buried him somewhere. I probably saw or heard a thousand others get beaten with the bat the next three years. It killed a good many of them."

I stretched out under my blanket and put my hat over my face to block the moonlight from my eyes. "But you men are tougher than I was," I said. "When those rangers show up here to break up this feud between y'all and the Standards, if they happen to want to send any of you to prison to make an example of you to the rest of the county, I suspect you'll fare better than I did that first few days."

I had worked hard enough that day to make my body crave rest, and mercifully I soon fell asleep.

THIRTEEN

The next day Eli, Boone, and Tobe made a sweep through the Standard spread, looking for cattle. They wanted to round up a small herd to drive to Austin. Topsy tried to talk them out of cow hunting on the Standards' property, but Eli was adamant. He said some crick in his shin bones told him a hard winter was coming and he needed to cut some cattle from the range. They passed through the cedar brakes on the way back that afternoon.

"We got us six head of cows, four of calves, and nine of yearlin' steers," Tobe reported.

"But not a single head of land grabbers," Boone added.

They moved a herd of about a hundred out that day, planning three days to get the beeves to Austin and one day for their return ride.

Eli and his sons had loosened their guard on me and given me their trust by now, although Boone didn't like to admit it. It's difficult to mistrust a hard worker. I moved my overnight headquarters to the barn. There were beds in the house, of course, but it wouldn't be proper for Topsy to sleep alone under the same roof with the hired man.

She seemed relieved to see her father and brothers ride away from Double Horn Creek for a few days. And I much preferred her company that evening on the gallery of the Flatt home to that of Eli, Boone, and Tobe out on the hard ground in the hills. We got to talking and I told her how the Colorado seemed an entirely different river where I came from, where it snaked through the level clay prairies.

"Do you ever miss your home?" she asked.

"Some things I miss."

"Like what?"

"I miss the colored folks."

Topsy glared at me with her wild green eyes. "Why? You don't mean the colored girls, do you?"

I laughed. "No, I mean the whole lot of them."

"How come?"

"Lots of reasons. I used to go down to their settlements for an evening with a black boy I grew up with named Rafe. Things were usually dull around the white folks' homes, but down there the colored folks always had something going. They had more fun."

"What do you mean?"

"Well, for example, some of my family were violinists but Rafe's people were fiddlers. Us white patties—that's what they called us—we may have passed as storytellers, but the colored folks were raconteurs."

"Raccoon what?"

"A raconteur is somebody who can just flat naturally *tell* a story. Old Uncle Pie was the best yarn spinner of the bunch."

"What kind of stories did he tell?"

"Oh, about any subject you could name. Huntin' stories, fishin' stories, tall tales. But he especially liked to talk about buried treasure."

"Oh."

"You know—those old legends about pirates or lost gold or abandoned mines. I guess y'all have those kind of stories around here, too."

"Yeah, some," Topsy said.

"Like what?"

"Oh, I ain't no raccoon-teer, but I've heard stories. Some folks say that old Gail Borden found gold on his place down along the Sandy before he invented that Eagle-Brand milk-in-a-can and got rich."

"Oh, really? What else?"

"Well, let me think. Some of the old-timers say that a fellow named Harp Perry buried twelve hundred pounds of silver somewhere on Packsaddle Mountain."

I was trying to find a level place on the warped porch to make my chair sit flush on all four legs. "Twelve hundred?" I asked.

"Yeah. They say he melted it and poured it inside pieces of cane. And then there's an old Indian cave between the Marble Falls and Burnett where they say Sam Bass hid some gold he stole from a bank, but nobody can find it because the cave branches out underground and you can get lost in it. Then there's all them stories about Dead Man's Hole."

"What's Dead Man's Hole?"

"It's a cave right across the river from the town at the Marble Falls. It goes about three hundred feet straight down."

"Why do they call it Dead Man's Hole?"

"Some fellers tried to climb down it a long time ago but they never came out. I've heard you can lower a chicken down on a rope and pull it up dead in a minute or so. The air's poison. Well, naturally, that would make a fine place to put your treasure if you didn't want nobody to get at it."

"Yes, it would," I replied. "That's how most of those old treasure stories end up. There's always something to keep you from getting at the gold."

"Back during the war," Topsy said, "there was a lot of trouble around here with bushwhackers. They killed a bunch of Union men, like Pa. Some of their bodies were never found and everybody says they were throwed down into Dead Man's Hole. There was some talk that Pa's carcass would be the next one down there, but he was too sneaky for the bushwhackers. He stayed hid out like he's been doing here lately and they never got him."

I didn't care about old bushwhackings. I was interested

in treasure. "I don't suppose you've ever heard of any treasure buried along the Double Horn," I said.

Topsy laughed. "If we had, Pa'd have dug for it to build his town."

I let the conversation branch into other subjects then, not wanting to seem unusually interested in buried loot. I was hoping for some talk about Annie Standard, but I was too bashful to initiate it. I knew Topsy would have been pleased to talk about certain members of the Standard clan herself, but she didn't have the nerve for it, either.

We did talk about the Standards in general, though, and speculated on when the rangers were likely to show up.

"I heard the rangers were scattered out dealing with the fence wars. I don't guess we'll see them until they get some of that mess under control."

"Is it true that you killed that ranger down in Matagorda County?" she asked abruptly, caressing a tin cup of coffee.

"No," I said, "I never killed him and I never killed anybody on purpose. I feel responsible for getting some other men killed." I turned to look her in the eye. I needed her to trust me. "But I don't think I could have done anything to prevent any of their deaths. I just didn't know enough to be able to see what was coming."

"What about now? What do you see comin' for us and the Standards?"

I tried to come up with some shred of optimism. "I hope to see the rangers coming one day soon. If they can't stop your feud, nobody can." That was the most hope I could hold out to her that evening.

I spent the next three days dealing death to cedar trees. By the end of the third day the cool front that had blown my hat off on Shovel Mountain wore out and the wind shifted back around to the south. The heat made the work tougher, but I managed to keep the production rate up to roughly that of my first day.

About midmorning on the fourth day I finally found a stand of cedar trees tall and straight enough to use as corner posts. I could see their dark green tops sticking up above the rest of the scrubby evergreens in the brakes. I was so anxious to tie into one that I passed through about fifty yards of smaller trees to reach the biggest of the big ones.

It stood every bit of thirty feet tall and rose in one perfectly straight trunk that would have served just as well for a rafter beam as a corner post. The trunk was probably too big for me to reach my arms all the way around, although I didn't intend to embrace it before killing it. The limbs that branched off from the main trunk would provide as many as thirty regular fence posts and an incalculable number of smaller pickets for hog pens, staves, and garden fences. I spit on my palms, wrapped them around the hickory handle of my double-bladed ax, and took my first swing at the granddaddy of all Double Horn Creek cedars.

There was a small bush of some kind at the base of the trunk where I aimed my first blow. The ax scattered its little branches and lodged firmly in the trunk of the big cedar. Instantly I heard a familiar sound that struck a tremor through the entire length of my spine and caused the hairs to stand on the back of my neck like the pikes of an ancient army.

A diamondback rattler of no less than five feet in length writhed wickedly from the bush at the base of the big cedar, its dozen or more rattles blurring in wild vibrations. It looked as big around as the fence posts I had been chopping. It coiled almost at my feet and prepared to strike. I jumped straight up, using the handle of my ax as a springboard and breaking it off in the process. Catching hold of the lower limbs, I pulled myself up into the tree and stuck the crown of my hat smack into the biggest nest of red hornets in the Texas hills.

In a second the buzz of wings accompanied that of snake rattles as the first of many wasps stung me on the right earlobe. I flinched so hard that I lost my toehold and my legs swung pendulum-like in front of the singing rattler, causing it to strike. Luckily the viper failed to lead my legs, as they swooped by quickly, and it completely missed its target. But I didn't care to test its aim again so I swung my feet back up into the tree, hooked one leg over a branch, hung there in a horizontal attitude, and thereby exposed my face to the nest of hornets.

Poisonous pinpricks peppered my neck, face, hands, and even my body through my thick shirt. The world was red with hornets. The only merit I could see to them was that the humming of their wings in my ears almost drowned out the chilling hiss of the rattler's tail. When one wasp stung me on the eyelid I quickly concluded that a giant hornet nest was no proper matter for point-blank scrutiny. I let my legs swing down again so I could expose the crown of my hat rather than my face to the hornet nest.

I must have forgotten that the rattler would strike at my flailing legs again. One look at its scaly shaft of a body lunging arrow-quick at my boots made me hook my legs back around the limb and turn my face to the hornet nest once more. Hanging on with one hand I pulled my hat down over my face to protect it from the marauding insects. The maneuver cost my hand three or four shots of hornet venom.

I had heard somewhere that a wasp would sting only once, then die. I decided to ride out the hornet attack until all the malicious little bugs had spent their single shots on me. I hung horizontal in the tree with my hat on my face, flinching like a worm in an ant bed until I simply could not take it any longer. Certainly two snake fangs could hold no more venom than a hundred wasp stings! I dropped from the tree and landed flat-footed in front of the coiled rattler.

The snake struck at my left shin. It was not a direct blow, so the fangs did not penetrate my jeans and boot tops. Instead they got snagged on my trouser cuffs. I don't know how long I danced the jig of a crazy man, trying to sling that reptile from my leg while swatting at the last two dozen red hornets who had yet to give their lives for their nest, but finally the fangs broke loose and the rattler sailed through the air as if someone had hurled the letter S into the cedar brakes.

I was dizzy either from doing the snake dance or from absorbing wasp poison, and once the danger had passed, the pain increased by degrees until I reached the Flatt home. Topsy was splitting wood when I staggered up to her. "What are you doin' back this time of day?" she asked.

I took off my hat. She gasped. I could feel the skin tightening around my neck and knew I must have swollen up like a poisoned pup. Topsy ordered me to sit on the front porch. She went to the kitchen and came back with a box of baking soda and a pan of water.

"Take off your shirt," she said.

"I will not," I replied.

"Oh, for Pete's sake, take off your shirt, Mr. Huckaby, before I have to take it off of you myself!"

I knew she would do it, too, and I couldn't stand the thought of someone else pulling my shirt off over all those wasp stings so I removed it myself. It didn't really matter. Blushing couldn't have made me any redder than the wasps already had. "I'll have you know that not one of them stung me below the belt," I insisted.

As I told Topsy what had happened, she made a cool paste from the baking soda and water and put a glob of it on each of the stung places, starting with my face. My eye had almost swollen shut where the hornet had stung me on the eyelid. When she worked around to the back of my neck, she stopped for a few seconds, then continued to smear the paste on.

"What caused them scars?" she asked.

"The prison guards whipped me for falling behind in my work one time when I was sick."

She continued to put the cool paste on the stung spots across my shoulders and down my back. Despite the pain, it was pleasant to feel the touch of her slender fingers. I knew then that if I hadn't already met Annie, I would have given Clay Standard some competition for the affections of Topsy Flatt.

"Who gives them guards the right to treat prisoners that way?" she asked.

"They do whatever they want. Some of them used to be convicts themselves. Hey, don't poke at those stings so hard. They're getting sore."

"I'm barely touching you."

I was almost drunk with pain, but the baking-soda paste felt like ice on burns.

"You landed in prison on account of a feud," she said. "What if that happens to Tobe or Boone. Or . . ."

"Or Clay Standard? Ouch! Son of a gun, that hurts!"

"Well, don't wiggle so much. You'd think a man who could take a whippin' on his back like that could stand to get stung some."

I squinted but that made my stung eye hurt, so I just gritted my teeth.

"Ain't you scared of going back to prison?" she asked.

"Not right now."

"Well, you ought to be. You're in the middle of another feud. How do you aim to get out of it?"

"Pray," I grunted.

"Pray for what?"

"Pray for rangers. They know how to stop a feud."

I looked like a spotted mule by the time Topsy finished daubing me with baking-soda paste. "Leave that paste on till it dries," she said. "It'll cool them bites and draw the poison out. Then you can rinse it off."

About the time I got my shirt back on, Speck came running up to the house panting. In the next minute or two, Eli and his boys had returned from Austin. "How come you ain't choppin'?" the old man asked.

I looked up at him through my one open eye and smirked. Boone and Tobe started laughing.

"Why you wearin' polky dots?" Tobe asked. "What'd you tangle with?"

Topsy told them the story.

"Treed by a rattlesnake!" Boone said. "That beats all the dumb-assed stunts I ever heard of."

"Here are the fangs," I said, remembering the snake teeth stuck in my trouser cuffs.

"Go bury 'em," Eli said. "Don't prick yourself on 'em or they'll kill you just as sure as a bite from a live snake. Bury 'em deep and put rocks on 'em."

I got up to get a shovel so I could satisfy Eli's superstitions. Topsy said I shouldn't be made to work in my condition, but I told her not to worry. I got a shovel from the barn and made a good show of burying the fangs, though I didn't bury them very deep and I didn't put very many rocks over them. When I got back to the front porch, there was an argument going on.

"Don't go," Topsy was saying. "You'll have to drive right through their land. It's too dangerous."

"Go where?" I asked.

"Pa wants to take the money from the herd he sold and stock the house with supplies," Topsy explained, rolling her green eyes.

"Damn right," Boone said. "I'm tired of beddin' on the ground."

"But it's too dangerous to cross the Standard spread," Topsy said.

"That's right," I agreed. "They might be laying for you over there."

"We ain't scared of them," Boone said. "We can fight 'em off any day. Me and Tobe had no trouble with Virgil and Cal in a fair fight."

"That's exactly why they won't fight fair anymore," I said. "They'll shoot you in the back from the bushes as you ride by. They think that's what y'all did to Virgil and Cal so they'll do the same to you."

"Yeah, but you ain't been sleepin' on the ground as long as we have, Royal," Tobe reminded me. "That's no way to live. We're ready to risk it."

"No need to," I said. "Let me go for you. They have no reason to kill me. I'll drive the wagon to town and get the supplies. Besides, I need to get a new ax handle to replace that one I broke."

"You ain't got but one eye to see with," Eli said. "And who will help you load all them supplies? You don't look up to heftin' much, swol' up like you are with them hornet stings."

"I'll go with him," Topsy said. "They won't shoot me neither."

"Oh, hell, Pa, we don't need girls and no-'count drifters to do our work for us," Boone said. "It's just a trip to town."

"Could be your last trip," I argued. "There's no way to defend yourself against an ambush. It's not a question of bravery, it's a question of strategy. Let Topsy and me get the supplies and you all can get some water barrels filled up in the house for a long siege if it comes to that."

"Makes sense," Tobe said.

Eli agreed. He ordered Tobe to help me hitch two mules to the wagon. Tobe had to laugh every time he looked up at me. Soon Topsy and I were pulling away from the Flatt home with a list of supplies and a wad of cash to buy them with. Boone scowled at me as we left.

"Come on, Speck," Topsy said in a singsong voice, and the dog bounced off a spool of barbed wire and jumped to the bed of the moving buckboard, wagging his stump of a tail for glory.

We passed through the Standard spread without seeing a single one of its clan. Of course, we didn't take the road that led by their house. We crossed the Colorado at a sandy ford on the Standard Ranch, and when we reached the other side of the river I got out to rinse the dried baking soda from my face and neck. It had helped some, but my skin was still taut and felt feverish, especially in the places where several hornets had conspired to make their attacks close together.

A good road led to the Marble Falls settlement along the north bank of the Colorado. Topsy and I stopped at a road ranch to have a dinner of roast beef served to us. She said Eli wouldn't miss the cost of one dinner and she wanted to eat something for once that she didn't have to cook herself. I didn't eat very much. I saved my scraps for Speck. The wasp stings seemed to have affected my appetite.

After Topsy ate some apple pie and drank some coffee, we went on toward Lynn's Store. As we approached, I saw three guards from the Granite Mountain quarry sitting on the boardwalk in front of the store, passing around a bottle of Annie Standard's peach brandy. I forgot all about being stung by hornets or treed by rattlesnakes. One of the guards was the sergeant I had spoken to the day I went to the quarry.

Topsy and I ignored them as we stopped the mules in front of Lynn's Store, but we had just put our feet on the ground when the sergeant recognized me and spoke up.

"Well, look who's here. It's ol' Royal." He passed the bottle to one of his cohorts and picked up the sawed-off shotgun resting across his lap. "I don't see no bone meal on your clothes today, Royal. In fact, it looks like something got the better of you."

I stopped and glared at the sergeant through my one open eye. "How do you know my name?"

"That storekeeper told me all about you and your fight with the flour barrel," he said. "We asked around about you after you come to the quarry smart-mouthing me that day. We thought maybe you were trouble. Turns out you're just a convict yourself."

"How would you know?"

"A couple of them prisoners recognized your name. Said they knowed you when you wore stripes at Huntsville."

Topsy was standing at the door of Lynn's Store, waiting for me to go in with her, wondering what kind of previous acquaintance I had forged with the guards. I handed her the wad of money Eli had given me and told her to go on in the store for the supplies.

"What the hell bloated your neck up so bad?" asked one of the other guards.

"Oh, leave it alone," the sergeant said. "You'll embarrass that little redheaded thing. Can't you see that Royal has been lifting her skirt and she's been biting him to keep him off."

I could ignore just so much in my attempts to avoid trouble. I did not intend to stand by and listen to a sergeant of prison guards dishonor feminine virtue. I had listened to such men slander my mother and sisters often enough when I was in chains and helpless to defend womanhood. Now I meant to make the sergeant with the scattergun pay for every foul word I had ever heard cross the lips of a prison guard.

"Don't pay them no mind," Topsy said, but I was already stalking toward the trio of guards. The one with the shotgun laughed as I approached, assuming I was bluffing. When he saw the angry glint in my eye it was too late.

I wrestled the shotgun from his hands and applied the butt of it to his stomach. Then I used it like a club to strike him over the shoulders. The other two guards grabbed me, took the gun away, and pinned me against Eli's wagon. My swollen neck smarted terribly when one of them hooked the crook of his elbow under my chin to hold me still. I heard Topsy yelling and Speck growling low from the far corner of the wagon bed.

The sergeant threw a couple of punches into my midsection, but they hurt me less than the blows I had given him with his own gun. Then he hit me hard in my good eye. When he backed off and prepared to kick me between the legs, Topsy rushed in to stop him, but he grabbed a handful of her blood-red hair and threw her down on the boardwalk.

Suddenly I felt fur leaping over my shoulder and knew Speck was lunging for the sergeant. The dog sank his fangs into the back of the sergeant's thigh and wrenched his head as if shaking a snake to pieces. Topsy scrambled for the nearest weapon—the brandy bottle—and had just reared it back to throw when a rifle shot went off.

Speck ran to hide behind Topsy's skirt. I saw Lynn standing at the door with a brand-new brass-bellied Winchester smoking from the muzzle. The two guards turned me loose immediately and when they did I kicked the sergeant where he had intended all along to kick me. Then Speck tore into the thigh again and Topsy had to call him off.

"That's enough, Roy," Lynn said. "Topsy, kick the shells out of that shotgun and give it back to them."

When Topsy had done so Lynn said, "You two pick him up and get on out of here. And don't you ever suppose to harm another one of my customers."

"What the hell are we?" asked one of the guards as they helped the sergeant onto his mule. "We buy our supplies for them prisoners here."

"You spend more on liquor than you do on food for them convicts. Now, git!"

Lynn never took his sights off the guards until they had ridden completely out of sight.

"Mr. Huckaby," he said, turning to me, "every time I see your face, you are fresh from some form of calamity. Your luck must run over some pretty rugged country."

"My soul craves trouble," I admitted. "I can't seem to avoid it."

"Have you been robbing bee hives?"

"No, I've been chopping cedar posts. I got into a big nest of hornets."

"I'd say you're in a nest of something worse than that. What have you joined up with the Flatt family for?"

I had to explain how I had been captured while hunting on the Double Horn.

"Oh, I see," Lynn said. "If only someone had warned you about hunting there, I suppose you'd be living elsewhere under much healthier circumstances right now."

I shrugged sheepishly.

Lynn helped us load rations of bacon, beans, coffee, salt, sugar, pepper, and flour. We also bought ammunition for the rifles of the Flatt men.

When I went to look at the ax handles I found a collection of tools nearby including a pickax. It looked like just the implement to use in excavating buried treasure from the rocks. I picked it up and tested its balance in my hand. I found myself longing to bury its point somewhere 49 degrees northwest of the zero stone.

Why wouldn't the rangers come to locate that marker for me? Where were they? I touched the steel point of the pick and imagined the sound it would make when it poked into the buried treasure chest. I was hearing that sound. I was digging for treasure. I was clawing back the dirt and throwing gold, silver, and jewels over my shoulders.

"What do you want with that pickax?" Topsy asked.

"What? Oh. I was thinking this might come in handy for digging post holes in the rocky places."

"We already got us a pickax," she said. "Don't forget to git you that ax handle, though."

When we settled our account, Lynn told us to be careful on the way home and he stepped out on the boardwalk with his slightly used, brass-bellied rifle to make sure no one was waiting for us with shotguns.

"Oh," he said as I took up the reins. "I almost forgot to mention it. Those guards aren't the only ones who have been asking questions about you around here."

My neck was so swollen and sore that I couldn't turn my head to look at Lynn. I had to shift sideways in the seat to face him.

"Another fellow came by a couple of days ago. Said he was an old acquaintance of yours. Called himself Little Jimmy Fitzhugh. I told him you had gone back to Johnson City."

The throbbing in my head doubled and my heart flopped over once or twice in my rib cage. I turned to the mules and stared over their backs. Someone at my bank in Matagorda County had let it slip that Royal Huckaby had wired for money to pay a fine in San Antonio. Little Jimmy Fitzhugh had trailed me from there to Burnet County and had come to resurrect the Williams-Fitzhugh feud, three years dead.

Where had it all gone wrong? At what moment had my plans for a trouble-free existence become unworkable? No matter which way I traced it, it all came down to the exact instant I saw the old Mexican. That wicked old mapmaker had caused me to stray from my formula. It was his fault and none of my own. He had started me on the trail to senseless greed and self-destruction.

If I could just find that zero stone without getting killed by Flatts or Standards or Fitzhughs or prison guards. If I could just satisfy my lust for the unnamed treasure. If only I could break the spell of singing doves, I swore I would never seek riches again as long as I drew breath.

If only the rangers would come. Where in hell were the Texas Rangers?

"Thanks, Lynn," I said, and whistled at the mules to get them moving. The eye that the sergeant had punched was beginning to get puffy.

FOURTEEN

W ho's Little Jimmy Fitzhugh?" Topsy asked on the way home.

"A fellow who's waited three years to kill me."

She didn't say anything for a half mile or so, but her curiosity finally got the better of her. "I guess he was part of that Williams-Fitzhugh feud you got mixed up in."

"Yep."

"What started all that trouble, anyway?"

"A calf."

"A calf?"

"Yeah, a couple of Williams brothers accidentally put their brand on a Fitzhugh calf."

"And they started a feud over one little bitty ol' calf?"

"Well," I said, turning painfully in the seat to make sure the load was riding alright in the wagon, "that was what touched it off. But it really started with my sister Chastity."

She shook her head. "You Huckabys have the funniest names."

"That's exactly what Chastity always said. My father's

name is Champion and he named my two older sisters Opal and Spirit. Then he named me Royal and then came Chastity."

"What's Opal mean?" Topsy asked.

"That's a kind of precious stone they use in jewelry."

"That's a pretty name," she said, scratching behind Speck's ear who was perched right behind the seat atop the highest barrel in the wagon bed. "What's Chastity mean?"

"What's Topsy mean?" I asked evasively.

"Short for topsy-turvy. I used to romp and roll around a lot when I was a sprout so they took to calling me Topsy-Turvy, then just Topsy. My real name's Jane, but I suspect most everybody has forgotten that by now."

"Well, nobody is likely to forget Topsy," I said. "That's a memorable name."

"You didn't say what Chastity means."

"Oh, yeah. Well, let me explain it the way Chastity herself always did. She said all of us Huckabys had horse names and hers apparently meant she was supposed to stay a filly all of her life."

Topsy thought for a moment. "What kind of a name is that to give a girl?"

"It was my father's idea. Chastity hated it. She always made me call her Chaz. She hated her name so much that she just set out to let everybody know it didn't fit her. She used to slip out at all hours with her beaus and she ran with some pretty wild young bucks."

"Oh, goodness, gracious. Pa would tan my hide if I acted like that."

"Old Champ did tan her hide on a regular schedule, but she kept at it. She finally settled down with one fellow, though. A fellow my mother used to call 'that reckless cowboy.' His name was Joe David Williams."

"Was that one of the Williamses from the Williams-Fitzhugh feud?"

"None other," I said. I was riding the brake against the wheel because we were dropping down to the river. Speck was clawing wildly on the barrel, trying to keep from falling in our laps. "You see, the day Chaz married Joe David, one of her old beaus, Sloan Fitzhugh, showed up at the wedding drunk and wanted to fight the groom. Well, some Williams men dragged him off and roughed him up a little and he never forgot it."

"But what about the branding of that calf you were talking about?"

"Well, back in Matagorda County," I said, "the cowboys of the neighboring ranches used to carry each other's branding irons and they'd brand one another's calves. It was just sort of a favor you could do for your neighbor and everybody did it for each other so it saved a lot of work. Well, for a wedding present old Champ gave Chaz and Joe David a spread of twenty thousand acres right next to the Fitzhugh League. And Joe David put two of his brothers to work on his new ranch."

"Get to the branding part," Topsy said. "And give me those reins. Your eye has swollen up so bad that you can barely see out of half your face."

I passed the leather to Topsy and sat back in the seat to enjoy the ride as much as I could, being covered with hornet stings and hunted by an enemy in an old feud. "I *am* getting to the branding part. See, one day these two Williams brothers, Tom and Milam, were branding calves—some of their own and some of the Fitzhughs—and they roped a Fitzhugh calf and just happened to pick up the wrong iron out of the fire and put a Williams brand on it."

"Uh-oh," Topsy said.

"Yeah. The worst of it was that they didn't even catch their mistake. And Sloan Fitzhugh just happened to see the smoke from the branding fire and rode over to see what was going on. Well, he noticed one of his cows nursing a calf with a Williams brand and right away he accused Milam and Tom of rustling. They called him a liar, so Sloan pulled out a gun and started shooting. There was already all that bad blood between the Williamses and the Fitzhughs because of what had happened at the wedding."

"Did he kill them?"

"He killed Milam but Tom got away. Those were the first shots fired in the Williams-Fitzhugh feud, but they wouldn't be the last."

"What happened then?"

"Well, Joe David and Tom Williams wanted to get even right away for Milam's murder and they were going to do it, too. But I heard what had happened from Chaz and caught the Williams brothers and talked them out of taking revenge. I told them they would get more pleasure and less trouble out of seeing Sloan hang. So we took Milam's body to the sheriff and did everything legally."

"And that Fitzhugh boy went to trial?"

"He certainly did," I said. We were nearing the ford that would cross us over onto the Standard Ranch. "But he got off."

"How? Didn't you say that the Williams boy named Tom saw the murder?"

"Yes, but here's what happened. They put Sloan on trial at the county seat in Matagorda. That's right down at the mouth of the Colorado River. The day he went on trial the town was packed with spectators who wanted to watch the proceedings. Then the storm hit us. Maybe you remember hearing about it. It was the big storm that swept about half of the town into the bay."

"Yes, I do remember that from a few years ago," Topsy said. She was just easing the wagon into the river for the crossing. The ford was a little sandy, but the mules were strong and could pull the wagon across easily. The river wasn't up enough to get the supplies wet in the bed.

"Well, when the storm really started blowing the judge had to adjourn court and everybody took refuge in the houses around town. Except for Sloan. They locked him up in the jail. Stop right here," I said, once we had reached the middle of the river.

"What for?" Topsy asked.

"I want to show you something."

She pulled the mules up and made them stand in the rushing current.

"You see how fast this water is flowing by us?"

"Of course I see it. I ain't the one whose eyes are swollen shut."

"Well, this is about how fast the water was flowing through the town of Matagorda the night of that hurricane. Except it was about three times as deep."

"My Lord!" she said, quickly urging the mules toward the south bank.

"Houses were swept clear into the bay. Dozens of people drowned. And Tom Williams, the only witness to the murder of his brother, was one of the ones who was never found. The courthouse was flooded and a lot of the evidence against Sloan was destroyed, including Tom's written statement and the shirt with the bullet holes that Milam had been wearing when Sloan shot him."

"What happened to the murderer?"

"Sloan? They let him out when the jail flooded. He survived the storm and went free. There wasn't enough evidence left to convict him. The charges were dropped."

"Were you there?"

"Oh, yes. I was in one of the houses that didn't get swept away, thank God. My brother-in-law, Joe David, was there with me. We both survived. But Joe David went crazy with hatred because both of his brothers had died on account of Sloan Fitzhugh and Sloan was free."

"And Sloan was your sister's old beau, too, right?"

"That's right. That was at the heart of it. Sloan Fitzhugh was probably the biggest mistake Chaz ever made, though she hadn't courted him very long."

"It don't take long to give a feller ideas. When did you git mixed up in it all?"

"I was already in it to a certain degree, just because Joe David was my sister's husband. But there was more to it than that. I had a hunting lodge down on the river and Joe David and I used to hunt together a lot. And that black boy I told you about, Rafe, the one that I grew up with, he used to serve as our guide and cook. He had the best pack of hunting dogs in the county."

At my mention of dogs, Topsy started scratching Speck behind the ear again.

"Joe David asked me one day after the hurricane if he could use the lodge. I told him of course he could. He didn't say what he wanted to use it for, but, naturally, I figured he wanted to go hunting. I got to thinking about it and decided I would meet him there and hunt some with him. So Rafe got his dogs together, and I brought some of my best jumping horses because I wanted to run a wolf or two. We went to the lodge to wait for Joe David to show up."

We were on Standard land now and it made me balk to be talking about how I had entered one feud knowing I was now stuck in the middle of another one.

"Well?" Topsy prodded. "What did your brother-in-law want to hunt for? Fitzhughs?"

"Exactly. Joe David showed up at the lodge after dark and told me he had just shot Sloan Fitzhugh dead. He said he had waited up under an old rose hedge fence by the cow pens where Sloan came every evening with a colored man to feed a big bremmer bull they had penned there."

"Did he shoot the colored man, too?"

"No. He had no reason to. Anyway, while Joe David was telling me what he had done, Rafe's dogs took to growling

at something in the pecan bottoms by the hunting lodge.
Rafe said it was probably coyotes prowling around out there
so Joe David grabbed his rifle. Just as soon as he reached
for that rifle, the shooting started."

"Shootin'? Who was shootin'?"

"The rangers. Poor Rafe got hit in the head and I dragged
him into the lodge, but he was already dead. Joe David was
hit in the leg, but he kept on fighting. I swear, though, it
didn't take those rangers any longer than a minute to kill
Joe David and bust the door down on the lodge. They
wanted to kill me, too, because Joe David had managed to
kill one of the rangers and they were thirsty for blood."

"Is that the ranger they said you killed?"

"Yeah, the other rangers said so, but I never picked up a
gun during the whole fight."

"How did they catch up to your brother-in-law so quick
after he killed that Fitzhugh feller?"

"That was just luck. That colored man who was with
Sloan when Joe David shot him went to tell the sheriff.
There just happened to be four rangers in town staying with
the sheriff that night. Sloan's hired colored man also happened to be coonhunting partners with my friend Rafe.
Rafe had told him many a time how Joe David hunted at
the lodge so he figured Joe David might be going there to
hide out and he was right."

"How come they sent you to jail if you never picked up
a gun?"

"I guess the county just wanted to make an example of
somebody so feuding wouldn't get too common. Everybody
figured Little Jimmy Fitzhugh would come after me next
because some people said I had helped my brother-in-law
murder Sloan. You know how gossip goes. My lawyer got
me off of all the murder charges, but they convicted me as
an accomplice to Sloan's murder. They said I had brought
fresh horses to the lodge to help Joe David escape."

We were easing the wagon over the rocks in the crossing at Double Horn Creek. We hadn't seen any sign of life on the Standards' ranch. It seemed they had forted up and were waiting for the rangers.

"Is that what you brought the horses for?"

"No, of course not. They were just hunting horses, but nobody believed that other than my family. Us Huckabys were not real well liked by everybody in Matagorda County because we had bought up so much farm and ranch land and run the old owners off."

"So they gave you three years for something you never did?"

"I don't know whether I deserved those three years or not. I'd like to think I served them for something. I guess Little Jimmy Fitzhugh might have killed me by now if I hadn't gone to prison. I thought I had spent those years learning my lesson to stay out of family fights, but here I am in the middle of all your troubles with the Standards. I guess maybe it's just my fate to get mixed up in these things."

"My foot," Topsy snapped. "I can't believe the Good Lord would make it anybody's fate to kill their neighbors."

"I wish you could explain that to Little Jimmy Fitzhugh. He's Sloan's brother, you know. He probably believes I had something to do with Joe David killing Sloan. He's the main reason I didn't go back to Matagorda County after I got out of prison. I figured he'd be gunning for me as soon as I got home. Now he's come after me anyway. I guess Lynn's right about the way my luck runs."

The mules were quickening their steps because they knew the barn was nearby and they wanted their oats. The drab Flatt home came into view around the next bend and I saw Eli and sons carrying buckets of water from the springhouse to the back door and knew they had moved their rain barrels into the house and were brimming them.

None of them seemed particularly pleased to have Topsy and me back, but they were glad to see the supplies, and Tobe condescended to pat Speck on the head once or twice.

"Git out of the wagon," Boone growled, and the dog bounded down.

Tobe came over to check on the progress of my face. "Let's see how them sores look. Oh, my word, his other eye has nearly bloated shut now."

Topsy explained what had happened at the store as we unloaded the supplies. Eli thanked me for taking up for his daughter and Tobe mentioned that I had some kind of gumption to take on a man with a shotgun.

"Sounds like the damn dog got the most licks in," Boone said.

Eli ordered us to carry the goods inside and stack most of the kegs and crates in front of the windows so the Standards couldn't shoot in. "We still can't rest easy," he said. "We'll have to take turns standing guard so they don't sneak up and set fire to the place. This old house would go up like fatwood."

I was informed that I could continue to sleep in the barn and wouldn't be expected to stand guard. Boone added that I wouldn't be trusted to stand guard as far as he was concerned.

"There's somebody you might want to keep an eye out for besides the Standards when you're standing guard," I mentioned.

"Who's that?" Boone asked.

I explained about Little Jimmy Fitzhugh coming to Burnet County for my hide.

"Hear that, Pa?" Boone said. "Now we've got the damned Fitzhughs comin' after us and we don't even know 'em. Let's get shed of this saddle bum. We can't trust nobody but our own till we win this fight and he ain't one of our own."

Tobe looked me over as if trying to make up his mind whether or not to agree with his half brother. Topsy held her breath. She would never say so, but she felt some comfort in having me around to help keep the old man from causing trouble. I was wondering just how Boone planned to get shed of me.

But Eli didn't give Boone's suggestion much consideration. The old man had the misconception in his mind that if it came to shooting I would fight with the Flatts. He said, "No, Royal's handy to have around the place with us spending so much time watching them Standards. He can help us keep this place runnin' and he don't eat much, anyway."

Boone grabbed a rifle and went to patrol the perimeters. Eli sat down on the gallery to smoke his pipe. Topsy went to the log kitchen to fix something for supper. I went to take care of the mules and Tobe came along to ask me how it felt to get treed, stung, and ganged up on all in one day.

FIFTEEN

Before I approached the tree the rattler had chased me into, I threw about two dozen rocks into the remains of the bush at its base to make sure no other snakes were hiding there. I got the ax head loose from the trunk, then knocked the hornet nest out with the new ax handle. There were still a good many hornets on it and they swarmed but I was too quick for them and got away without getting stung.

I started a small fire and burned the old handle out of the ax head and wedged the new one in while the wasps settled down. Then I made that tree pay with its life for all the pain and embarrassment it had caused me. I took pleasure in chopping off each and every one of its limbs.

I spent the next several days chopping and stacking cedar posts and still there was no word of the Texas Rangers. I was getting nervous. I had so many posts cut that I knew Eli would order me to start building fences any day. I had conflicting feelings about building fences. On the one hand I feared stretching wire would rile certain members of the Standard family and cause them to put a stop to the practice.

On the other hand, digging the post holes interested me considerably. It seemed like a perfect way to test a lot of ground for treasure. Maybe I would get lucky and find the trove without having to wait for the Land Office investigator to come and locate the zero stone.

Finally, Eli indeed told me to start building fences. To my relief, he decided to start by patching up the corrals and picket pens around the barn. "Tomorrow I want you to use the wagon," he said as we looked at the dilapidated enclosures, "and haul as many pickets and posts as you'll need to fix up these pens. You can stack 'em over there by the bob wire. And hitch the mules to some of them big corner posts you chopped and drag 'em up here. These old ones have plum rotted out."

The next morning I harnessed the mules and drove them to the cedar brakes. I intended to drag the big corner posts first while the mules were still fresh. The first one I hitched up to was all that remained of the old cedar the snake had chased me into. I had kept it singled out because I wanted to plant it deep on a prominent corner and let it stand as a memorial to the great hornet and rattler war.

I dragged it and a dozen more big cedar trunks to the house without interference from any of the Flatts. They had gone to find some wild hogs they had trapped and castrated in the spring and then turned loose again. It was time to kill some bacon to smoke for the winter. Topsy went along to keep the old man from wandering onto Standard land.

After dragging the corner posts, I hitched the mules to the wagon and drove back to the brakes to start loading pickets and posts and rails.

It was almost noon when I thought I heard a voice call my name. It came in a whisper. I stopped and glanced around, but saw no one, so decided I must have misinterpreted some natural sound. I had been working too hard.

Then it came again: "Royal."

I turned all the way around and still saw no one. I was alone.

"Royal," it said again. It was the ghost of the old Mexican, leading me to treasure!

I took a step in the direction I thought the voice had come from.

"Over here, Royal."

I looked into the shadows of the brush along Double Horn Creek and saw the vague shape of a man crouched behind the bushes.

"Who is that?" I asked. Maybe it was Little Jimmy Fitzhugh. Maybe it was one of the Standards. It could have been Tobe playing a trick on me. But I still hoped it was the ghost of the old Mexican, he having acquired English in the great beyond.

"Come here. I don't want to git out in the open."

I neared the dark place in the undergrowth and saw that the man hiding there was just as dark as the shadows—a black man in the soiled uniform of a convict. "Who are you?" I asked.

"You know me. You ain't forgot me, I know."

I walked cautiously into the shadows of the underbrush and the man stood part of the way up, looking nervously all around. "My God," I said. "I can't believe it's you."

"I knowed you'd remember me. I knowed you'd remember ol' Reuben."

I suddenly realized that Reuben was standing as straight

as he was going to stand. Years of forced labor had bent his body. His frame had wasted to bone and sinew and his hair had taken on a frosting of white. I wondered if he still had the strength to crawl down a dark well shaft and cheat death for a stranger.

"I don't believe it." I put my hand out and he shook it. "How did you get here?"

"I got away last night. Been walkin' in the river all night to find you."

"How did you know where?"

"I listen. I always listen. I heard them guards talkin' about you and that redheaded white girl they said lived down here. That bull-driver was plenty mad about you grabbin' his shotgun and hittin' him with it. He stayed mad a long time. He didn't go easy on us."

I looked at the ground between my feet. "I'm sorry. I should have known he would take it out on y'all."

"Don't worry no more about him. He won't never beat no more convicts. He got drunk last night, come around and told me to go with him outside. When I saw him pick up that bat, I choked him to death, Royal. I squeezed him so hard around the neck his eyeballs stuck out." Reuben wrapped his hands around an imaginary neck and choked the guard all over again in his thoughts.

I sank back against the trunk of a tree and drew in a breath of dread. "Did they come after you? How did you get away?"

"They was all drunk. They didn't know ol' Reuben was gone till this mornin'. I just need a little help. I need clothes to wear. I need a hoss."

"But, where do you expect to go? How long do you think you'll last before they catch you?"

He grinned, teeth missing. "Last time I was out three months. This time I won't never go back. Give me a hoss, Royal. I swear they'll never know you give it to me."

"You know better than that. You know they'll beat the truth out of you if they catch you."

Reuben grabbed me by the arm and squeezed with all the strength he had once used to save my life in the flooded well. "Ain't nobody ever gonna beat ol' Reuben again. They got to kill me. They won't never chain me again."

I pried his fingers from my arm as he glared at me. "Okay," I said. "Okay. Wait here." I couldn't get over the shame I felt for not wanting to help him. I knew I would help him, of course, because I owed my life to him. But I didn't really *want* to help him. I only agreed to aid him in his escape to repay a debt. Reuben hadn't owed me a thing the night he descended the well shaft for the sake of my wretched life.

I drove the wagon back to the Flatt house, took Liberty out of the corral, bridled her, and tied her to lead behind the wagon. Then I went into the barn to get my saddle and the suit of clothes I had worn the day I left the state penitentiary at Huntsville. I turned the wagon around and ran the mules back to the creek.

"Give me your clothes," I told Reuben when I got back to the brakes. "I'll burn them over here. I already had a fire going this morning so nobody will question the ashes."

"What about the hoss? What are you gonna tell 'em about the hoss?" he said, stripping down.

"I'll tell them she must have wandered off," I said. I tossed him the freedom suit.

The old convict turned his back for a moment to pull on the pants and I saw a horrible mass of scars stretching from his heels to his neck—great welts of deformed flesh. I heard the sickening screams and the wasted pleas for mercy.

He caught me gaping. "They give me the bat whenever I escape. But I won't take it again."

When Reuben got dressed, he came to stand by the

wagon as I stirred the ashes of his striped uniform to make sure it had all burned, just as I had stirred the ashes of the old Mexican's map. My coat hung awkwardly from his shoulders and we had to cut a piece of rope to keep the pants up. "It looks good on you," I said.

"Yeah, feels good, too," he said, keeping his eyes trained for pursuers.

"Where will you go?"

"Don't know."

"Here, take this." I pulled the page marker from Sam Jessom's Bible out of my shirt pocket. "Go south to Johnson City. There's a blacksmith there called Deacon Sam. Show him this card and tell him I gave it to you. He'll help you with some food and anything else you want."

Reuben took the card and looked at it. "What's it say?" he asked.

"Never mind. Just take it and give it to Deacon Sam."

He nodded and put the card in his pocket. "I don't want your saddle. Don't want your bridle neither," he said, picking up a length of rope from the wagon bed. "Take it off that mare. I'll make a hackamore."

I did as he said because it would make my story about Liberty wandering off sound better. She didn't usually put her bridle and saddle on before wandering.

"You like this job?" Reuben asked, glancing around at the cedar posts.

"I guess."

"Good," he said, tying another knot in the hackamore. "Stay with it. Don't worry about them rich men with all that money. You don't need that. Just work here and keep what you make. You'll be alright. Just be glad you're free, that's all. That's all you need."

"Good advice."

"You know why they put me in prison, Royal? I wanted

me a Christmas ham. I tried to sneak me a pig out of a white man's pen, but he caught me. I was a boy. Didn't know better."

"That's all you did to get all those years?"

"No, not all," he said, grinning at me under Liberty's neck as he slipped the hackamore on. "I escaped when I thought I learned my lesson not to steal no more pigs. Then I escaped again when I thought I learned my lesson not to escape no more. Five times I been out. This here's the last time. They got to kill me before they chain me this time." He flopped across Liberty's bare back and threw his leg over.

"Stay well on the west side of this creek," I said, "or you're liable to run into some of the Flatts. If they see you riding my horse, they'll shoot." I was praying that Topsy was holding Eli on his own side of the Double Horn. "And stay off the road on the way to Johnson City. They'll be looking everywhere for you."

He laughed down at me from the back of my mare. "Don't tell me nothin'. I know where they're gonna be. Who kept you alive in that well?"

I half smiled and nodded. "Good luck."

"We're even, now, you and me." He looked across the cedar stumps. "You best start loadin' them posts again. You got to earn your honest way." He nudged Liberty in the flanks and turned toward Johnson City, and I picked up another post and threw it in the wagon bed as if nothing peculiar had happened.

I was piling cedar posts by the spools of barbed wire when the Flatts came back. Boone and Tobe were dragging hog carcasses behind their horses. I was relieved to see that Reuben's carcass was not being dragged along with them. Topsy put her horse away and started gathering wood to build a fire under the big kettle in front of the kitchen.

It didn't take long for Eli to miss my mare and ask where

she had gone. I had already put my saddle and bridle away and had taken a couple of old cedar rails down from the corral. "I guess she jumped the corral where I took those rotten rails down," I said. "I wouldn't worry about her. She never wanders far. I'll go hunt her up in the morning."

"That fat old mare jumps?" Eli asked.

"I reckon she does," I said.

"I'll go find her," Tobe said.

"The hell you will," Boone said. "You ain't slippin' off while there's work to be done." Boone was preparing to slip off himself, though. It was his turn to patrol the perimeters for Standards.

"Get your ax and cut us some gambrels," Eli said to me.

I found a couple of stout green cedar pickets in the wagon and chopped sharp points on both ends of each one. Tobe and Eli dragged the hogs up under the big live oak behind the kitchen and poked holes through the skin at the hocks so we could shove the gambrels through to hold the back legs apart. Then we tied ropes to the gambrels and hoisted the hogs up to hang head-down from a tree limb. They weighed about three hundred pounds each, so we had to grunt some to get them hung.

"I'll go see how the water is coming along," I said as Eli and Tobe tied the ropes. I walked around to the front of the kitchen and asked Topsy if the water was hot enough yet.

She dipped her hand quickly into the big cauldron with the wood burning under it. "No, it will take a few more minutes."

"Where did y'all find the hogs?"

"I saw sign of them the other day over by Sandy Point when I was checking the bogs for cattle, so I got Pa to go there and look first. We hunted all morning and finally came on them. Just in time, too. Pa was wanting to go over across the Double Horn."

Reuben had been lucky to avoid the old man, I thought,

and he was probably almost to Johnson City by now. "Who shot them? Looks like both of them were hit clean in the head."

"I shot one and Pa shot the other."

"You're a good shot."

Topsy shrugged, but smiled a little. "He was only a hundred yards off." She leaned toward me and whispered. "Listen, you better watch out for Pa because . . ."

Eli came around the corner of the log kitchen and Topsy moved quickly away from me. "How hot is it?" the old man asked. "Don't make it boil or it'll set the hair. Make it just shy of boiling."

When the water got just hot enough, I carried a bucket of it around behind the kitchen and poured it slowly over the carcass of one of the hogs. Topsy carried a bucket for the other one. Eli and Tobe scraped the hogs with their knives as we poured the hot water on them.

"That's just right," Eli said. "The hair's slippin' good." As we applied pail after pail of hot water, Eli and Tobe scraped every hair off right down to the knuckles and the snouts until the carcasses looked as smooth and clean as porcelain. They seemed out of place in their rough surroundings. Eli cut their throats to let them bleed.

I gutted one hog and Tobe did the other. We let the entrails fall into tubs positioned under the carcasses.

"Take the hearts and lights and let the dog eat 'em," Eli told Topsy. She plunged her knife into the tubs of viscera and cut away the morsels for Speck. Tobe and I then carried the rest of the guts away to throw in the woods. By the time we got back, Topsy had rinsed the blood out of the body cavities and we were ready to take the carcasses down and butcher them on an old plank table built against the side of the kitchen.

We cut the heads off first and I carried one for Topsy and

we put them into the now boiling water in the cauldron. "I guess we're going to have headcheese for supper," I said.

"What?"

"Headcheese."

"Is that what you call it? We call it hog head souse. Have you et it before?"

"Only with the colored folks." I lowered my voice. "Say, what was that you tried to tell me a while ago about watching out for your pa?"

"Oh, that. He's got him an idea that he can get you . . ."

Topsy clammed up again when Tobe brought some pig feet around and threw them in with the heads. "Pa wants you to help with the butchering," he said to me.

I winked at Topsy and went back around the kitchen where Eli was chopping along the backbone of a hog carcass with a hatchet, separating the ribs from the spine. "What do you want me to do?" I asked.

"You can handle this backbone soon as I get it loose. You know how to do it, don't you?"

"Yes, sir. We did a hundred hogs a day sometimes on the prison farms."

Eli grunted and shoved a side of pork out of his way as I picked up my ax. "Somethin' I want to talk to you about," he said. "I've come to trust you, Royal. Me and the boys have been talkin' about it. It's plain to us you're on our side now. I guess Topsy's told you that we plan to build us a town on the river as soon as we get over this trouble with them Standards. We'd like you to have an equal share in it. It's sure to mean a fair profit for us all once the steamboats start running up the river."

So this was what Topsy had tried to warn me about. Eli had plans to draw me into his fight and make me one of his own. He needed another gun on his side. Lon Standard had one more son still among the living than Eli. Eli probably even had plans of making me a son-in-law. "What would you expect in return?" I asked.

He had chopped the backbone loose and tossed it in front of me on the table. "Expect? Nothin'. Oh, I'd expect you'd want to be up on a level with the rest of us, take your turn standin' guard and all, and we're willin' to allow that. But we don't expect nothin' particular out of you."

He was willing to let me get shot at by Standards for a share in a town that would never be built! I almost had to bite my lip to hold back the sardonic laughter. I was using my ax to chop the backbone into lengths of about six inches and I figured my proposed stock in Flatt, Texas, would be worth about as much as a couple of those chunks of backbone out of a wild pig. "That's a generous offer, Mr. Flatt. But I'm not the sort to bother with investments and such."

The yellow tips of Eli's beard had dragged through some pig blood. "I ain't after money. You're a hard worker. I could use your help. Think about it for a while. It'll grow on you. You could have streets and parks named after you. How would that sound?" he asked, elbowing me. "Royal Avenue and Huckaby Park."

"That sounds fine, but I'm not so sure about the government being able to clear the raft out of the Colorado to let the steamers in. I used to live alongside of that raft, you know, and they haven't been able to clear it yet."

"Uncle Sam's cherry picker cleared the one on the Red River, didn't it? I ain't goin' into nothin' half cocked, boy. I've studied it. That raft can be moved."

"I know they have the machinery to do it," I said. "But I'm not so sure they have the funds. The government tends to run out of money every time it just gets to work on removing that raft."

"They'll git the job done, boy. I have connections in the gov'ment, you know. They'll clear the damned raft this time."

The old man tossed the other backbone in front of me and I let my ax rive another section of spine.

"Even if they do clear it," I said, "I'm not so sure those steamboats will come this high up."

"What the hell do you mean? We already had one come plum up to the Marble Falls!"

"Yes, but that was a wet year, wasn't it? Do you think the river will be deep enough for steamers year to year?"

"When I was a boy, before I come to Texas," Eli said, "I took a ride on a steamer up the Missouri, clean up into the plains. Don't tell me a steamer can't come up this river. Them pilots don't need but two feet of water for them stern-wheelers."

"The Missouri's wider," I said. "More room to navigate."

Eli buried the blade of his butcher knife in the wooden table and glared at me. "We're gonna' have us a town here, boy. Now, I'm offerin' you a chance to be a part of it. You best think about it real serious. It's the smartest thing for all of us to throw in together. With that Fitzhugh feller after your scalp, you could stand to make some friends about now. You can take the first watch tomorrow evenin'."

I didn't answer. Tobe had come out of the house with a twenty-five-pound keg of salt to cure the knuckle joints, square shoulders, and hams. "What do you want me to do with these ribs?" he asked the old man.

"Put 'em in the springhouse to keep 'em cool. We'll have 'em for dinner tomorrow."

I helped Tobe salt the quarters and hang them in the smokehouse to cure for a couple of weeks before the actual smoking would start.

By the time we finished the butchering and salting Topsy had boiled all the meat off of the heads and feet and mashed it up and mixed in some peppers and salt and sage. When the souse cooled and jelled we ate it on the table against the side of the kitchen. Topsy took some out to Boone. I wondered what Boone had said that afternoon about taking me into the Flatt gang.

I also found myself wondering about other individuals—where they were and what they were doing. Where was Marion Harkey? Was he selling a lot of barbed wire? Where were the Standard men—Lon, Lum, Nat, and Clay? And what was Annie doing? Working in her garden? Where was the old Mexican? Heaven or hell? How far had Reuben gotten? Was he eating better fare at Deacon Sam's? Where was Liberty? Where was Little Jimmy Fitzhugh? And where were the cotton-pickin' Texas Rangers when you needed them the most?

SIXTEEN

The morning came on cool and wet. The mist fell so fine I couldn't feel the drops, but I still got soaked after staying out only a few minutes. Boone and I were tearing down the old corral and I looked forward to burning the pile of rotten posts and rails. It was a good day for burning. No chance of starting a wildfire in that mist.

We had been at work a few hours when Tobe came running to the house from his guard post. "Get Pa," he said to Topsy, then turned to watch the road that led toward the Double Horn and the Standard Ranch.

Boone and I trotted over to the house to see what had upset Tobe. He was breathing too hard to tell us. Eli came out with Topsy, pulling his suspenders up and rubbing his eyes. He had been catching up on sleep lost during his midnight watch. "What is it?"

"Two strangers coming," Tobe gasped. "A big feller on a big horse and a little one on a Spanish pony. And they're leading a pack mule and Royal's mare."

I felt the clammy grip of the wet day seize me like death and knew some ill fortune had befallen poor old Reuben.

"They armed?" Boone asked.

"The little one's got guns all over him. The big one has a rifle, but I think that's all."

Eli turned to me. "You think it's that Fitzhugh feller?"

I shrugged. "I can't tell until I see them."

Eli rubbed the sleep out of his face. "Get your rifle and hide behind that pile of old rails," he said to me. "If it's Fitzhugh, blast him out of the saddle and we'll get the other one."

"Hold on a minute," I said, but Eli was already giving other orders:

"Tobe, get up in the loft. Boone, you and me in the house. Topsy, you get a pistol and hide in the kitchen. If one of them comes in, shoot him."

The Flatts scattered to their posts.

"If it's not Little Jimmy, I'll talk to them," I said. But I couldn't be sure whether any of them had heard me except Topsy, who paused to look at me, wild-eyed, before she ducked into the kitchen.

I took my place behind the rotten timbers and waited. Speck came to stand beside me, looking alert, sensing my fear. I soon saw the horses appear through the mist, turning the bend in the road. I didn't recognize either of the riders. The little man on the mustang was leading Liberty and the big man on the big horse had the pack mule in tow. When they got almost within rifle range, the little one stopped and yelled in a high-pitched voice: "Eli Flatt!"

The dog ran out from behind the pile of rotten timbers and started barking. "Shut up, Speck," I said. The dog obeyed, but continued to growl and glower at the men on his road.

I stepped out from behind the pile of old corral rails, holding my rifle muzzle down. I waved for the men to approach. The little fellow waved for me to approach him instead. The big man shook his head and said something to the little one. I made Speck stay and started walking out to see what the men wanted. I hoped they were not prison guards. I hoped Reuben's body was not tied to the pack mule.

I got close enough to see rainwater dripping from their brims and beading up on their slickers. The big man tipped his hat at me and, with a graceful stroke of his hand, sculpted the handles of his salt-and-pepper mustache into an elegant curve. He straddled a beautiful smokey black horse fitted with a silver bridle. A couple of poles of some sort stuck out of the tarp-covered pack his mule was carrying. He appeared to fall in somewhere between the ages of Boone and Eli. He slouched casually in the saddle.

The little man on the silver buckskin mustang had a big Sharps repeater in his hands, cocked. His slicker was tucked inside the grips of his Colt revolvers. A shotgun hung from his saddle horn by a thong. I could see a shaggy bit of pale yellow hair sticking out from under his black hat and his eyes were glaring spots of lucid blue. He had the build of a jackrabbit: narrow across the shoulders, weak-chinned, and scrawny. He seemed to be about equal to Tobe or me in age. "Who are you?" he asked in a throaty little voice.

"Who are *you?*" I asked. "And what are you doing with my mare?"

"Shut your mouth, mister. I'll ask the questions."

"Oh, settle down, Cotton," the big man said. "We've been here thirty seconds and you've already made us an enemy." He smiled at me. "I'm Dub Coe of the General Land Office. And this little firebrand is Cotton Anderson of the Texas Rangers. We're here to talk with the Flatts."

"And serve them with subpoenas to appear at an inquest concerning . . ."

"When the time comes, Captain," Coe said, interrupting the little ranger. "Take your spurs off for once, will you?"

"Why do you have my mare?" I asked again.

"We'll explain everything if we could get out of the rain and have a cup of coffee," Coe said. "You must be Roy Huckaby if this is your mount."

"A convict and a ranger-killer," Anderson said with disgust. "You must like prison. You're liable to go back."

Coe sighed and rolled his eyes. "Don't mind him," he said, jerking his head at the ranger. "Cotton's mammy weaned him young on a sour pickle and he's been rankled over it ever since." He returned Anderson's scowl with a smirk, then looked at me again. "How about that coffee?"

"Stay here a minute," I suggested. "I'll go tell them who you are, then wave you in. You have to be careful with these Flatts. They're expecting to go to war with the Standard family."

Cotton Anderson didn't wait for me to wave. He trotted his mustang past the house and into the barn before I could tell anyone what was going on. "It's alright, Tobe," I yelled. "He's a ranger." Speck barked and growled like a rabid wolf.

Topsy came out of the kitchen to call the dog off. The old man and Boone stalked out of the house about the time the boundary investigator got down from the saddle.

"Howdy. I'm Dub Coe of the General Land Office. Would it be alright if I put my stock in your barn?"

Eli's eyes lit up like lanterns and he instantly put on a cheerful face I hadn't seen him wear. "Land Office! Why didn't you say so? Help him with his animals, Royal. Topsy, put some coffee on for the gentlemen. We've been waitin' on you, Mr. Coe."

Dub tipped his hat and turned to lead his horse and mule into the barn. The ranger had already availed himself of the facilities without asking. He had unsaddled his mustang and was using one of Eli's saddle blankets to dry the little horse off. When I entered the barn with Coe, Tobe began to come down from the loft. His rifle butt bumped against the ladder.

In a snap, Cotton Anderson had dropped to one knee, whirled, pulled both of his Colts from their holsters, cocked them, and aligned their sights on the loft ladder. Tobe's eyes bulged and he dropped his rifle onto the hay below.

"Who are you?" the ranger asked.

"Tobe Flatt."

"Where're the others?"

Eli and Boone walked into the barn behind Coe.

"They're all right here," Coe said. "Now, put those Peacemakers away. These men don't aim to bushwhack you."

Anderson jammed his pistols back into their holsters and pulled some folded papers out from under his slicker. "Tobe Flatt, Eli Flatt, Boone Flatt," he said, handing out the summonses, "you are ordered to be at an inquest the twenty-first of next month in the county courthouse to answer some questions about the way you murdered those two Standard brothers. Then you'll be put on trial and most likely hung."

Tobe felt insulted enough to pick up his rifle while Eli and Boone glowered and trembled with anger. Boone took a step toward the ranger.

"Mind your authority, Captain!" Coe shouted. "Just serve the papers and keep your mouth shut."

"Damn it, Coe, stop calling me that," Anderson said. "You know I ain't no captain."

"Maybe not yet. But you intend to make a captain, don't you?"

"I intend to see that you find that damned boundary marker and then I intend to bust up this feud."

"In the short run, yes," Coe said. "But on the long haul you intend to make a captain, don't you?"

"I don't reckon it's any of your damned business what I intend."

"None of my . . . !" Coe pulled the saddle from his smokey black stallion. "You are a servant of the public trust, Cotton, and I am a taxpayer and a representative of the popular vote. It concerns me a great deal what you intend."

Anderson swore and stalked into the mist.

Coe chuckled. "That boy wouldn't back down from a whole nation of armed outlaws, but he can't last two minutes in a good debate."

Eli watched the little ranger walk away and then told Boone and Tobe to help Coe with the pack mule.

"Now," Coe said to me, "I promised to explain how we came across your mare. I imagine you thought her lost."

"She got out yesterday," I said. "I didn't think she'd wander far, but she looks spent. Where did you find her?"

"Me and Cotton got to Johnson City yesterday about evening time. Just as we trotted into town, a bunch of men came galloping by, and of course Cotton just had to find out what they were up to. Turned out they were prison guards from the granite quarry over at the Marble Falls and had chased an escaped convict into town. It seems the convict was riding your mare."

"What?" I said.

"Don't act so dumb," said Anderson's grating tenor voice. He had snuck around and come in the other end of the barn and now stepped from the shadows to glare at me. "You brought horses to help your murderin' brother-in-law escape Matagorda County, didn't you? It's plain you gave that horse to that convict yesterday, too."

"How the hell would you know who I give horses to," I said.

"When somebody kills a ranger, I make it my business to know what they do."

"He didn't give no horse to no convict yesterday," Tobe said in my defense. "He was here all day haulin' fence rails in the wagon. He must have hauled five hundred or more. That don't leave no time to mess with convicts."

Anderson simply walked out of the barn again when Tobe started talking. I saw him prowling around the house, peeking into the kitchen where Topsy was, reading the tombstones in the family plot.

"How did y'all come to get my mare away from that escapee?" I asked Coe. Boone and Tobe were helping him unpack a strange cargo from his mule.

"Well," he said, "the fugitive jumped off your mare and holed up in the blacksmith shop and was yelling at the guards that he had a gun and would shoot the first man that came after him. Cotton had to be the first man, of course. When he charged the shop, the convict ran out with what looked like a pistol in his hand and pointed it at Cotton and Cotton shot him dead. Turned out it was just a piece of pipe that convict was holding."

"He must have wanted to get shot," I said. "Can't say that I blame him. I've seen what they do to escapees when they catch them."

Coe nodded. "It did appear that's what he wanted. The blacksmith recognized your horse and so did the prison guards. The guards said you were working out here with the Flatts, so I volunteered to return your mare for you. The blacksmith vouched for you. Said you were a fine individual. The guards didn't agree, but I tend to believe that blacksmith over those guards."

"Not me," Anderson said. He had appeared in the doorway again. "I think he's just a murderin' convict joined up with a gang of outlaws."

Eli, Boone, and Tobe turned their eyes together to stab the little ranger.

"Damn it, Cotton, quit poppin' up like a mud duck," Coe said. "Stand in here among us if you want to auger."

But Cotton was already gone again.

Coe reached into his pocket and pulled out a sealed envelope. "The blacksmith asked me to deliver this to you," he said.

I took the envelope and saw it addressed to me, from Deacon Sam Jessom. "Thanks," I said.

"My pleasure."

Topsy shouted to us, saying the coffee was ready.

"Royal, see that Mr. Coe's animals get some feed," Eli said. "Come on, Mr. Coe, have some coffee and get that slicker off."

After I fed the horses I stopped to look over the equipment Coe had taken from his mule's packsaddle. It included an old surveyor's compass almost as big around as a dinner plate, a staff for mounting the compass, and two poles with a chain running between them. I imagined it was the same type of chain the old Mexican had used to measure the distance between the zero stone and the treasure. In fact, every tool I would need to locate the wealth was lying on the barn floor in front of me. And Dub Coe was the man who would find the zero stone for me.

The tremor of greed I felt filled me with shame. I should have been mourning Reuben, but all I could think of was treasure. A strange truth came to me. I didn't want to buy anything. I didn't want to spend my treasure. I only wanted to find it. I owned a gentle horse and a good hunting rifle and I desired no other possessions. The treasure had come to possess *me*. It was hunting for *me*. It was getting closer and closer to claiming *me*!

I stood by Liberty and scratched her on the withers as

she ate her oats. She seemed destined to carry convicts to their fates. Reuben had found his. The fate he preferred to imprisonment. When would Liberty carry me to mine?

I remembered the letter Coe had given me and went to stand by the door to read it in the dull light that came through the drizzle.

Dear Roy,

The prison guards tell some bad stories about you, but they are a sorry lot and I don't trust what they say. Why are you mixed up in that business with the Flatts and the Standards? Leave immediately and come to work with me. An old acquaintance of yours who called himself Little Jimmy Fitzhugh stopped by here to find you. I sent him to the Marble Falls, but he came back having failed to locate you and went on to San Antonio yesterday. Now that I know where to find you, I shall send a messenger to catch Mr. Fitzhugh and tell him you have been located. He is quite anxious to see you.

Samuel Jessom

Quite anxious to see me, indeed, I said to myself. And more anxious to see me dead. But Deacon Sam had no way of knowing that. That was the trouble with John Wesley's rule. When you do all the good you can, to all the people you can, in all the ways you can, you sometimes commit well-intentioned debacles. It is better to let people do good for themselves.

I walked through the mist toward the house and found Topsy making more coffee in the kitchen. "That Land Office man wants to stay and talk to Pa today," she said. "Then he's going to talk to the Standards tomorrow, then he says he's going to find the zero stone."

"Good," I said. "Maybe he can end this trouble before it goes any further."

"I hope so," she said. "Where do you reckon the rest of the rangers are?"

"I was wondering the same thing. They must be coming. Surely they'll be here before Coe goes to hunt for the zero stone."

"I hope so," she repeated. "I have to cook something. Pa says to put out the best we got. Would you go get those spareribs out of the springhouse for me? I guess I'll cook them up with some fixin's."

I fetched the ribs for Topsy, then carried a fresh pot of coffee into the house. The men had pulled every chair in the house into the front room. The fireplace was burning for the first time since I had lived among the Flatts. Eli's clothes were dry, so he sat back from the fire. Boone and Tobe and Dub Coe were drying themselves right in front of the hearth. Cotton Anderson was as wet as any of them, but he sat apart from the rest, in the shadows of a corner.

"Oh, 'investigator' is a fancy handle," Coe was saying as I came in with the coffee. He had taken his hat off to reveal an unexpected bald spot in the middle of his graying head. "I'm just an old surveyor is all I am. My pappy was a surveyor, too, and he taught me the profession. He surveyed for the Republic of Texas and knew all the methods they used to locate lands back then. I learned about all that from him and so the Land Office likes to send me out to find the lost boundary markers because I know a thing or two about how they were probably located in the first place."

"You won't find ours," Eli said. "I'm sure you know your business, but you won't find no boundary markers between us and them Standards."

"Why do you say that?" Coe asked.

"Because if there ever was a zero stone, I'm sure old Lon Standard has taken and destroyed the thing."

"The Bible says something about that," Coe said.

" 'Cursed be he who removeth his neighbor's landmark.' That's in Deuteronomy, chapter twenty-seven, verse seventeen. That's about all the Gospel I can quote, however, so don't ask me to preach come Sunday." Coe laughed and thanked me for refilling his coffee cup. "But, you see, Mr. Flatt, even if your neighbor has removed your landmark, that don't mean I can't find where it was."

"How's that?" Eli asked, stroking his beard.

"Them old-time surveyors left more than just corner stones behind. They left all kinds of sign. You just have to know what to look for."

"Like what?" Eli asked.

"Oh, they built little stone mounds, drove stakes, blazed trees. That sort of thing."

Eli laughed. "This place was surveyed forty-seven years ago. The stones have been scattered, the stakes have rotted, and the blazes have growed over if the trees ain't burnt down altogether."

"You'd think so, wouldn't you?" Coe said. "But I think we'll find some sign of that old survey party. You'd be surprised how long some of those marks can last. I have even found that if you rub a stone with your hand you can sometimes find marks left by a chaining pin where the old surveyors ran their original lines. Even if it was fifty years ago."

Eli looked worried for several seconds, and Coe glanced at him and read the expression on his face. Then the old man put on his false laughter again. "Look if you want to, Coe, but I don't think you'll find anything. You'll have to go by my testimony on where the boundary was because I'm the only man alive who was here when the surveyors were. They showed me my land, and though I don't remember exactly where the boundary ran, I can swear the west line was on the other side of the Double Horn. That creek is mine. But you won't find no zero stone. No, Lon Standard has destroyed it."

"Won't hurt to look some," Coe said.

Cotton Anderson jumped up from his chair and walked out of the room and out of the house.

"That boy squirms more than a wormy pup," Coe said. "Can't stay put no longer than a cricket in a chicken yard."

I took the ranger's chair from the corner and pulled it up to the fire to warm myself. "How will you know where to start looking for the zero stone?" I asked.

"I'll have to start by going on Mr. Flatt's word. And, to be fair, I'll have to go by what Major Standard says, too. I have the field notes from the old survey, but they don't help much."

"Why not?"

"Oh, them old-timers, they did things sort of slipshod. Didn't have much choice in it, though. Not everybody wanted to go and survey among Comanches and Apaches. You know what the Indians called the surveyor's compass? They called it 'the thing that steals the land.' Them Indians knew what a survey party meant and generally didn't hold to it. So them old surveyors were mostly rough frontiersmen. Some of them didn't even learn how to figure magnetic variation of a compass needle. They just ran the lines the best they knew how and took field notes and put up markers. And when Indians were around, like they were when this place was surveyed, why them surveyors didn't mess around and run the whole boundary. They'd just locate a couple of corners and move on.

"The field notes didn't have much to say in a survey like that." Coe took a folded piece of paper from his pocket. "I've got a copy of the field notes for the old survey done in '38 on this place. You can see what I mean. These were written up the day before the survey party was massacred."

Coe unfolded the paper, held it to catch the light from the fireplace, and recited: " 'Beginning at inscribed rock.' That's the zero stone. 'Thence north 4,433 varas to Colorado River.' So the zero stone should be about 4,433 varas from the river, depending on how high the river was that day in '38 and assuming the river hasn't changed course too much since then. 'Thence 5,702 varas downstream.' I guess that means as the crow flies and not on the meander, but you can't be sure with these old field notes. 'Thence south 4,433 varas to stake about 45 varas southeast of a bunch of bushes. Thence west to the place of beginnings.' "

"That's it?" Eli asked.

"Yep."

Eli started chuckling and his laughter, of a genuine type this time, built until he was guffawing and slapping his knee. "It's been so long since I read them notes, I forgot what a worthless mess of writin' it was!" he finally said.

"I agree," Coe said. "It doesn't make any mention of any creeks, hills, canyons, trees, or any other landmark except for that clump of bushes, and God knows there must be enough clumps of bushes around here to shelter a million head of jackrabbits. The only information of any help these notes have is the reference to 4,433 varas from the river. That's between two and three miles."

"What is a vara?" I asked.

"A vara is thirty-three and a third inches. It's an old leftover from the Spanish and Mexican days. This is the only state in the Union that uses the vara for surveys. Texas never adopted the system of township, section, and range used everywhere else in the States. I've got my chains set for ten varas, just like they did during the Republic of Texas days when this place was surveyed. So the zero stone should be about 443 chains from the river."

Everything before my eyes suddenly turned golden in the firelight. In one breath Dub Coe had told me the last two mysteries surrounding the interpretation of the old Mexican's map: the length of the chain and the length of a vara. My mood took an instant swing toward improvement. It became suddenly clear that Reuben's death was not my fault. I had done everything expected of me to help him. The first of the rangers had arrived. The zero stone would be found within days. The feud would end and I would dig for buried treasure. Maybe, just maybe, it had all been worth the trouble. If only I could dig up my reward and scat before Little Jimmy Fitzhugh caught me.

"Those field notes," I said, thinking of the old Mexican. "How did they get to the Land Office if the surveyors were attacked by Indians?"

"Looks like somebody survived the massacre and brought the notes in," Coe said. "The Indians understood about field notes and generally tried to find them and burn them when they raided a surveyors' camp. That and bust up the compass. But somebody got away from the Indians here in '38 and brought the field notes in to the land commissioner. That's the only way Mr. Flatt here was able to patent his land. At least those field notes had some use to somebody. They're dang near worthless as horse apples to me.

"Yes, I'm afraid the only way we're going to settle this dispute is to find the zero stone itself. Or what's left of it if it's been destroyed. Even if somebody up and carried it away, we should find some chips of stone left over from the chiseling of the inscription on the thing. That and a blazed tree or a stone mound or two will be enough to settle the case. That much will stand up in court. I've seen it happen before."

"Shit," Eli said. "You won't find no zero stone. I guarantee that. That stone is long gone and the only thing that can settle this fight is my testimony. I'm telling you, Coe, I was here in '38, the day before the Indians wiped out that survey party. The surveyors showed me my land. Double Horn Creek was a part of it. That's what you'll have to go by to settle your case. You'll never find no zero stone."

Coe shrugged and changed the subject.

SEVENTEEN

When Topsy finished cooking, she called us into the dim dining room in the back of the house that faced the log kitchen outside.

She had done her best. She had fried the spareribs and cooked turnips and greens seasoned with one of the lengths of backbone I had chopped with my ax. She had also made biscuits and gravy and had put out all the milk, buttermilk, and butter she found in the springhouse.

Cotton Anderson came in as the rest of us pulled our chairs up to the table. "What's all these boxes and barrels in front of the windows for?" he asked in his accusing whine.

"Them is our supplies and that's where we like to put 'em," Boone said.

Cotton pulled a length of ribs loose and sat on one of the kegs against the wall to eat. "A Sharps rifle will shoot right through it," he mentioned, to Boone's chagrin.

"Miss Flatt," Coe said, taking a couple of biscuits and handing the platter to me, "this is the finest spread of feed I have witnessed in many a day. Pass the gravy, please."

As we ate, Dub declared how unfair it was for him and Cotton to put the Flatts out of all that grub.

"Don't mention it," Eli said.

"No, I want to make it up to you. Maybe I'll go huntin' if the weather breaks and bring in some game for supper."

"I'll go with you," I said.

Though I didn't look up from my plate, I could tell Eli

was glaring at me. The room became silent except for the chink of tarnished silver utensils against chipped bone china.

"Where are the rest of the rangers?" Topsy suddenly asked in a small voice. Everyone turned to look at her, surprised to hear her speak.

"Beg pardon, miss?" Dub Coe said.

"They said a whole company of rangers. I ain't seen but this single little one."

Boone chuckled with his mouth full.

Cotton Anderson flushed and scowled. "There won't be a company. Just me. The rest got to stay down on the border and fight rustlers and I had to come up here to clean up this damned feud."

The Flatt men glanced at one another quickly and almost gloated. But Topsy sank breathlessly back from her plate.

"Just one ranger to stand against two feuding families?" I asked, to the deep resentment of Cotton Anderson.

"You know what they say," Coe said. "If you ain't got but one riot, you don't need but one ranger. Same goes for feuds, I guess. And don't slight Cotton. He ain't much of a diplomat, but when it comes to war, he's got him a reputation."

Reputation or not, the puny ranger looked mighty insignificant perched on his keg against the wall when I thought about all the Flatts and all the Standards and all their guns coming together in one place.

To Topsy he looked worse than insignificant. He looked invisible. Dub Coe might just as well have come alone. She knew one ranger could never overcome the treachery of Eli Flatt.

After dinner the men sat on the front gallery to smoke while Topsy cleared the table—except for Cotton, who was prowling around somewhere. The mist had died down to almost nil and the clouds were getting thinner.

"Roy, I believe it will stop raining and turn out to be a good day for hunting," Coe said.

"I think so, too."

"I sure would like to leave the Flatt family with some game hanging to make up for all their hospitality. Let's load up and go kill something."

Eli followed us out to the barn where our weapons were.

"I'll just need to make a trip to the privy, first," Coe said, "then we'll go."

When he left for the outhouse, Eli pulled me aside. "What are you up to?" he asked.

"Just going hunting."

"Be careful of what you say. Don't give that surveyor no ideas."

"Ideas on what?"

"On where he ought to find that zero stone."

I scoffed. "What interest do I have in the zero stone?"

"An interest worth your share in our town."

"I never agreed to help you build that town. Besides, if the zero stone lies where you claim it does, your town site is secure."

"It don't matter what I claim. Only what Coe claims."

"Huh?" I grunted.

"Use your head, boy. That surveyor is fishin' for profit like everybody else. You heard what he said. He claims he can find marks of chainin' pins fifty years old on rocks where nobody else can see 'em. Says a few chips of rock'll stand up in court as evidence where the marker was chiseled. Hell, he can place that damned zero stone wherever he pleases. He'll favor whoever makes him the best offer."

"You mean, you think he's after bribes?"

"Works for the gov'ment, don't he? Just don't let on that I'm broke. When he asks, tell him far as you know Eli Flatt is flush with money and has got it to spare. Here he comes."

Coe came into the barn, picked up his rifle, and began

meticulously filling it with cartridges. "When it rains all day the game likes to crawl up under the brush and loaf," he said. "But when you get a break in the weather like this, they're liable to get up and move around. That's why I like to hunt this kind of weather."

We were just about to step out of the barn when Coe noticed an old set of deer antlers, covered with dust and cobwebs, tacked up in the barn above the door. The ten-point antlers were connected by a strip of skull that a hunter had sawed from the buck's head after killing it.

"Say, Mr. Flatt," the surveyor said, "would you object to my using those deer horns?"

Eli's eyes squinted. "Use 'em for what?"

"For me and Roy to rattle up some bucks. I'll have to break that piece of skull in two, but I could tie them back together whenever I get through with them and tack them back up on your wall."

"What do you mean rattle up some bucks?" Eli asked.

"Well, some vaqueros that ran my chains for me down in the chaparral showed me how to rattle up the big bucks and bring them runnin' right at you like you never saw."

"How do you do it?" I asked.

"Well, you just rear back and rattle a couple of old horns together to make it sound like two big ol' bucks fightin'. If there's any big bucks around, they'll come to join in on the fight."

Eli looked skeptical, then glanced at the antlers and grinned. "Oh! Rattle 'em up! I see, you want to show Royal how to rattle 'em up." He snickered and pulled at the antlers above the door.

"Yes," Coe said. "It only works two or three weeks out of the year, when the bucks are ruttin' and lookin' to fight each other for does. But I think the rut is on right now in these hills. Me and Cotton saw a buck running a doe in the rain this morning."

Eli put the piece of deer skull in the vise beside the door and broke the antlers apart by pulling on one of them. "Oh, sure. The time is right to rattle up some bucks," he said, winking at Coe.

Coe took the antlers from the old man and held one in each hand as if testing the weight of a new pair of revolvers. Suddenly he spread his arms like the wings of an eagle and banged the antlers together, twisting them, grinding them, gnashing the tines. He struck them together like a plowboy trying to knock cakes of dirt from a pair of boots. A cymbal player in a military marching band wouldn't have hit his instruments together as hard at the height of the "Star Spangled Banner."

"They've got a pretty good sound to them, don't you think?" he asked.

"Loud," I said.

Eli laughed. "Open the gates and we'll rattle 'em right into the stalls!"

We left the old man slapping his knees and walked eastward to look for game. Coe stopped at the water trough to rinse the dust and cobwebs from his rattling horns. "Old Flatt thinks I'm taking you on a snipe hunt," he said. "But this rattlin' business is genuine. I've seen it work many a time. On a day like this I'd say we have half a chance to rattle one up. Could be colder and clearer. But the bucks are runnin' the does and that's the main thing. You do believe me, don't you?"

"I'll believe you when I see the bucks running at us," I said.

The big surveyor who had lumbered through the Flatt house clopping his boots against the floorboards now became the epitome of stealth. Every step I took crunched or scraped something, but Coe's strides fell silently under him. Finally he turned to frown at me. "Walk quiet," he said.

I shrugged.

"Put your heel down soft and then roll onto the rest of your foot."

I tried it, with better success, but I stepped into a circle of dried bunch grass and the stalks collapsed and crackled under my soles.

"Step on the grass like this." Coe used the side of his boot to sweep the dry stalks of grass down flat against the ground and then put his weight on them. The maneuver was almost perfectly silent and he performed it with the grace of a waltzer.

I mimicked his moves, concentrating hard on walking in silence. To Coe the gait was natural and he poured his concentration into studying the sign around us. He pointed his rifle barrel at a shed snakeskin lying crooked over a low mesquite branch. He stooped to pluck a square-ended turkey feather from the ground and tucked it into a buttonhole on his shirt. He picked up a shiny pellet of deer dung and smashed it between his fingers. "Fresh," he said. "Not even cool yet."

I must have turned my nose up.

"What's the matter?" he asked, amused at me. "It washes off. They just eat leaves and stuff."

I spotted a few full tracks of deer and turkey feet pressed into the damp ground, but Coe found tiny pairs of dents made by the cloven toes of deer on hard ground. He recognized the depression of a single toe of a turkey in the gravel. "Fox," he said, pointing to a mound of dung perched on top of a rotten log. Then he showed me a small cedar tree whose branches had been mangled and whose skinny trunk had been stripped of bark by some force unknown to me.

"Buck rub," he said quietly. "Some big old boy has used this place to polish the velvet from his horns. This rub marks his territory and he'll fight to keep it. As soon as we find a clearing we'll try to rattle him out into it."

I had spent many days hunting and had swapped yarns

with many a hunter and never had I heard of things like buck rubs and horn rattling. But, not presuming to know everything under the sun about deer hunting, I went along with Coe's strategy.

We pressed on through the oak motts. Coe showed me places where deer had browsed on their favorite shrubs and he knew the names of all the plants. At last we came to a clearing about eighty yards wide on the side of a hill.

"You set against this tree," Coe suggested. "That will give you a full view of the place. I'll hunker down beside you behind these agarita bushes. I'll do the rattlin' and you do the shootin'." He squatted behind the agarita, put his rifle down, and took an antler in each hand.

"We're upwind," I said. "Shouldn't we hunt on the other side of this clearing?"

"Not when you're rattlin'. The bucks usually come in downwind to get the smell for what's going on, so you want a clear spot downwind where you can get a clean shot at 'em. Even if they wind us, I can bring 'em back with the horns."

I smirked and sat down against the tree. "Alright, if you say so. But I've never been on a hunt like this before."

"Just keep your eyes open. They might come galloping right out in the open or sneaking in cautious through the woods."

I drew my knees up and put my rifle across them. Coe took a firm grip on the old antlers and raked the tines together for about fifteen seconds, but not with the same ferocity he had used in the barn. He settled back against the tree with me to watch.

After five minutes we had seen nothing move so Coe took the antlers in hand and bashed them together again, louder than before. They clacked and scraped and rang with the dull timbre of a padded tuning fork. I frowned my disbelief.

"Just wait," he said. "It sometimes takes a while."

A while went by and still no bucks had charged, fighting mad, into the meadow. Coe started gathering sticks around him. "Here," he said with a perfectly straight face, "break these while I rattle this time. And rustle that agarita some with your foot."

I rolled my eyes as I took the sticks from him. "What in hell for?"

"It sounds like two fightin' bucks stamping down the bushes. If this don't bring 'em runnin', we'll move to another spot."

He crashed the antlers together. I sat idle. He looked at the sticks in my hands, urging me to break them. He gestured toward the agarita bush. I sighed and kicked half-heartedly at the bush and snapped some of the smaller twigs in my hands. I could already hear him telling the story to the Flatts: *I had ol' Roy hunting upwind of the clearing, breaking limbs across his knee and stomping hell out of an acre of agarita bushes!*

Two minutes after Coe allowed me to stop the foolishness with the sticks and bushes, he nudged me with his elbow. "See him?" he whispered.

I looked into the empty clearing. "I don't see anything."

"Keep watching. To the right. There's a pretty good buck coming in through the shadows." Coe kept his eyes fixed on a spot across the clearing.

I followed his stare and saw nothing. "Look here, Coe. You better not be pulling my leg."

"Watch, Roy. You'll see him directly."

I leered casually toward the phantom buck. There was absolutely nothing there. Then a movement came to me and the buck materialized as if suddenly carved from the trees around him. He came strolling toward the clearing, his head held low, the great curve of his antlers bobbing among the branches.

My heart rhythm doubled in one beat. I eased my shaking rifle into shooting position.

"Eight-pointer," Coe whispered. "A good one. Wait till he gets in the open."

The buck stopped two steps shy of the clearing and looked our way. His horns swept wildly through the air as he craned to glimpse the struggle he had heard.

The horn rattler touched his instruments together, locking the tines and grinding them. The eight-pointer quivered with excitement and sniffed the moist air. Still he avoided the clearing. He stayed among the trees and moved farther to our left, intending to use the wind to scent us.

"He's a smart one," Coe said in the lowest whisper. "Get ready to break some more sticks."

When the buck got just downwind of us, he whirled with his nose in the air, leapt, and vanished in the shadows. I dropped my rifle and wrenched a handful of sticks to flinders. Coe smashed the rattling horns together. He attacked the agarita bush, whipping it violently with the antlers as he rattled them. He thrashed his cover to shreds as he banged the old bones together. He produced the most astounding spectacle I had ever seen until the buck went him one better.

I dropped the sticks and groped for my rifle. The eight-pointer was galloping headlong at us across the clearing. He stopped so close I could see his nostrils quiver. A single shot through his neck reduced him to a carcass.

"Good shot!" Coe hollered, springing to his feet.

I rose and followed him to the dead deer. Coe put his hand around the base of the antler and hefted the lifeless head. "Damn, we did alright together!"

The smell of burnt powder was in my nostrils and the ring of the rifle shot was still in my ears. I stared dumbly at the dead buck. "He knew we were here," I said. "He smelled us. Why did he come back?"

Coe pulled a folding knife from his pocket and stropped the blade against his boot top. "They can't help theirselves. They get a craziness for the sound of rattlin' and they'll charge into sure danger to find it. They lose all their good sense, I guess."

I understood such insanity better than Dub Coe. He had seen it work on rutting bucks, but I had felt it in myself every time I heard mention of the zero stone. For an instant I saw myself in the eight-pointer's place, my eyes clouded in death, a bullet hole between them. The slain buck's death knell was the rattle of old horns; mine was the jingle of ancient specie.

We hung the buck by the antlers in the fork of a tree to gut him. The branches showered us with rainwater as we shook them with the dead weight of the deer. Dub told me more about horn rattling as we worked. Then he showed me another way to call animals, putting two fingers across his pursed lips, sucking air in and making the most pitiful squeaks and squeals imaginable.

"What does that attract?" I asked.

"That's the wounded rabbit call. It'll bring all sorts of carnivores down on you. Coyotes, foxes, bobcats. Even wolves and bears and mountain lions. You should learn how to call your game, Roy. It saves a world of footwork.

"I surveyed some in the caprock country in the fifties and I had some Delaware braves scouting for me who used a folded leaf or a blade of grass to call antelopes. Tried it once myself. Spotted some pronghorns away off and crawled up through the grass, I guess three hundred yards from them. Then I took a wide blade of grass and made it squeal like the Delawares had showed me. It sounds like a fawn bleating for his mammy, you see."

"Did you call one in for a shot?"

"No, I worked on that blade of grass for fifteen minutes or so, then I heard something rushing me off to the left. It was the biggest old panther you ever saw in your life coming to kill that fawn he had heard bawling. I whirled my old muzzle loader, pulled the trigger, and broke his neck with the ball. He was in the air on his last jump to get me and he fell across me and knocked me down."

We finished field-dressing the buck and headed for the Flatt house to get a mule. With the hunt over, Coe turned his eyes to things other than game sign. Picking up a stone he said, "Looks like there's some iron ore in some of this rock."

He found a trail of ants carrying tiny leaves to their underground den. He called them "umbrella ants" and was not satisfied until he had back-trailed them to find the bush they were cutting the leaves from. "Wonder why they picked this one?" he asked.

About a half mile from the house, he pointed out some little plants on the ground and asked if I knew what they were. "Bluebonnets," he said, laying his rifle down beside him. "It amazes me that just about nobody recognizes them when they ain't bloomin'." He knelt and picked up a handful of tiny pebbles that he poured into my palm.

"Thanks," I said. "What am I supposed to do with gravel?"

"Now, that's what leads men into trouble—jumping to conclusions. Those are bluebonnet seeds. They just look like gravel so the birds won't eat them all up. Give those to your gal and tell her to plant them shallow in a sunny spot and next spring she'll have bluebonnets blooming."

"I don't have a gal," I said.

"What about that redheaded one back there?"

"She's not interested in me," I said. "Just between us two, she's sweet on one of the Standard boys."

"Do tell? Maybe she can keep her old man from killin' off all the Standards if she's pining for one of them."

"Maybe," I said.

"It's not my habit to give advice, Roy, but I'd urge you to help her keep that clan of hers out of trouble if you can. And don't let them talk you into fighting on their side by any means. Cotton won't hesitate to shoot any one of them or you either. I know how little he frets over spilt blood."

"I don't plan to be anywhere near when the shooting starts," I said.

"Good. I'd hate to see you get into hot water." He raised his hat above his scalp. "See what happens when you can't stay out of hot water? Your hair starts slippin'!" He grinned and dropped the hat back over his bald spot. "Anyway, just hold on to those bluebonnet seeds and give them to your gal once you find her. No hurry. They'll keep a couple of years or more. You see, that's what happens to them in nature when a drought sets in, they have to keep until it starts to rain again and then . . ."

Coe continued the lesson in natural history as we approached the Flatt home to brag on our kill. We failed to convince Eli that bucks could truly be rattled up.

That night, after eating fresh venison, Coe got to rambling and started telling a story about a survey line he had run in the pines of east Texas: "The line ran right near a log cabin and I was sighting through the telescope on the transit when a woman came out of the cabin with a broom and beat me well nigh to death with it. Turns out she thought I was a Peeping Tom . . ."

As I listened and laughed, Topsy brought me a cup of coffee.

"I reckon Mr. Coe is what you'd call a raccoonteer," she said quietly.

"Yes," I answered. "He rivals old Uncle Pie."

EIGHTEEN

Cotton Anderson probably weighed little more than Topsy but he had more fight in him than a pit dog and he seemed always eager to engage it. When he and Coe got ready to leave for the Standard Ranch after breakfast, while the rest of us stood out in front of the house, he stepped up onto the gallery and began to lecture us from his makeshift lyceum.

"I got somethin' to say," he declared in his peculiar tone. We all looked as he started pacing the gallery, his thumbs hitched over the hammers of his revolvers. "And make sure you listen good because I ain't gonna say it but once. It's my duty to see that Coe finds the boundary between here and that other ranch and you can be damned sure of one thing. I don't need your help and I won't stand for your interference. While we're huntin' the marker, you all best stay clear. If I see a hair of any one of your murderin' heads, the whole lot of you will soon be joining your kin." With that, he pointed a bony finger at the fresh graves in the family plot.

"Why, you little runt," Boone said, cracking his knuckles and mounting the bottom step of the porch.

Coe stepped quickly in front of him, grabbed Anderson by the collar, and led him down from his platform. "Shut up and mount your mustang. Don't you know better than to threaten men from their own front porch? You'll have to pardon Cotton," he said to the Flatts, "he was raised by mad coyotes and still thinks frothin' at the mouth is good manners." Coe made sure Cotton got on his horse and then mounted his smokey black stallion. "We thank you for your hospitality, Mr. Flatt." He tipped his hat at Topsy. "And good day to you, miss."

Coe turned, driving the ranger in front of him like a stray jackass. But he had gone no farther than thirty yards when he stopped his stallion to look at the pile of cedar posts I had stacked near the corral. He leaned from the saddle to look closer. Then he got down and knelt beside the pile of big corner posts. He reached down to stroke one of them. It was the big one. The one I had climbed to escape the rattler.

Cotton turned to see what was holding Coe back while the Flatts and I approached the pile of posts. As usual, Eli, Boone, and Tobe picked up their rifles before wandering that far from the house.

"Now what's he lookin' at?" Tobe said.

"Who chopped these posts?" Coe asked when we came close.

"I did," I said.

Eli glared at me and nervously stroked his beard. "What difference does it make to you?"

The surveyor stood and faced me. "Can you tell me where you chopped this post? I mean the exact spot. For this big one right here." He kicked the cedar log.

"Yes," I said.

"Are you sure?"

"Positive."

"What difference does it make to you where we chop our posts?" Eli repeated.

Coe knelt beside the big corner post again. "Look right here." He ran his fingers over an indentation in the face of the cedar trunk. "This tree was blazed. It's been a long time. Decades. The bark has healed over. But I've seen old blazes and that's what this is, I'm sure. This is a witness tree from the boundary. If you remember where you chopped it, Roy, I'll have to ask you to come with us and show me. It will most likely lead us right to the zero stone."

"He won't go with you to show nothin'," Eli said. "He works for me."

"He'll come with us if I say so," Cotton said from the back of his silver buckskin.

"The hell," Boone said.

"Now, go easy, men," Coe said. He stood up and sighed. "Roy, we can't make you go with us without a court order of some kind. But you're a free man. If you think it's best that you come with us, I'd be obliged. If you don't want to, you can stay until we get the order. The choice is yours."

The ranger and the three Flatt men glared at me as if they would kill me no matter what I said. Topsy wrung her hands. Coe waited patiently for me to make up my mind. But there was no choice for me to make. I possessed information that would lead to the zero stone and it looked as though the old cedar, having come from the east side of the creek, would place the survey marker on that same side— the wrong side for Eli. I could imagine all kinds of fatal accidents happening to me if I chose to stay among the Flatts with that kind of knowledge in my head.

Besides, it was my destiny to locate the zero stone. That fact became suddenly clear. How else could I have stumbled across the old Mexican, Marion Harkey, Dub Coe, and the blazed cedar tree in one lifetime? I had no choice to make. "I'll get my mare," I said.

"Damn you, boy, I trusted you!" Eli shouted. He trembled with an animal ire so deep that his words came out in an unnatural quake. "If you help these bastards steal my land you'll get just what you deserve. You go with them now and I'll . . ."

"You'll what?" Cotton said, jumping down from the mustang. "You'll kill him? Do it now, then. Go on, point your rifle at him and kill him dead right here. But you better reckon on dealing with me next. I won't just stand by and watch a murder."

"Put a scabbard on it, Captain," Coe said.

The ranger ignored him. "Go ahead. One of you can shoot Huckaby and the others can try me. This is your best chance. There's three of you against just the one of me. I can't kill all of you. I'm not *that* fast. One of you will get me. You've got the odds. I'm a dead man if you'll just go ahead and kill me right here. Of course, I'll get one, maybe two of you, and you don't know which ones I'll shoot at first, do you? What's the matter? Why don't you shoot?"

Tobe licked his lips and glanced at his father. Boone and Eli stood silent, but rumbled with anger within.

"I know what it is," Cotton said. "You damned bush-whackers are used to shooting men in the back. You hide safe in the bushes and shoot when they ain't lookin'. But I'm standing right in front of you and lookin' you dead in the eyes. No, you don't have the guts for this kind of fight."

Eli shook as if he had taken the palsy and I knew he would raise his rifle to shoot any second. Suddenly Topsy was shoving her way through the men. She pushed her brothers aside and marched straight at Cotton Anderson, her red hair bouncing after her. She balled up her little fist and punched the ranger right on the chin, staggering him back a step or two.

Speck appeared at Topsy's ankles, growling and popping his teeth at the ranger.

"The Flatts ain't no bushwhackers," Topsy said. "And you. You come here to keep people from killin' one another and all you can think about is killin' us yourself. You call yourself a lawman but you ain't no better than a hired killer." She turned to me. "Well, go git your mare. You can't stay here now, that's for sure."

I saddled Liberty in short time, got my few belongings together, and joined Dub Coe. I didn't bother to ask for my wages. Anderson was still eyeing the Flatt gang, but he was on his mustang now and Topsy had taken a good deal of the fire out of him. As we rode away, I heard Boone say to Eli, "I knew we should have killed him the first day we seen him."

The relief I felt at riding beyond rifle range was something akin to the feeling I had experienced during my first hour out of prison. Cotton became even more surly than usual, but I was almost cheerful to be free of the Flatts and so was Dub Coe. Then a welcome thought came to me. We were going to the Standard Ranch. I was going to see Annie.

I asked Dub if he didn't think it would be a good idea to bathe in the Double Horn before arriving at the Standard place. He said the same thought had possessed him and that he had spotted a fine swimming hole from the road the day before. The weather had cleared somewhat and the sun was coming through the clouds.

We stopped by a pool of clear water with a canyon bluff against one side and a gentle slope against the other. It was ten feet deep or more and there were fishes swimming around in it. Coe and I began shucking our clothes, but Anderson had no intention of divesting himself of guns much less clothing.

"I've been wondering about something," I said to the surveyor. "Where does the name Dub come from?"

"He won't tell you," Cotton squeaked.

"I will so tell him. It's a short way of saying my real name."

"What is your real name?" I asked.

"William Westfall Coe."

"I told you he wouldn't tell you," the ranger said.

"I just have told him, Cotton. The difference between Roy and you is that Roy is smart enough to figure it out."

I'm afraid I disappointed Dub on the capacity of my intelligence. I couldn't think of any way Dub could be short for William Westfall.

"It'll come to you," he said, wading into the cold swimming hole, his big white body glowing like a full moon underwater.

Cotton climbed the bluff on the other side of the creek and stood guard. I kept my back turned away from both of them. I didn't want them inquiring about the scars.

My clothes were still a bit clammy when I put them back on, but they were clean and that made me feel more at ease about facing Annie.

"That was some shot that little redhead give Cotton, wasn't it?" Coe asked as we pulled our boots on.

I chuckled and looked up for the ranger only to find that he had vanished. Then I heard his sharp voice right behind us in the bushes.

"She packs a good punch for a gal," he said.

Coe turned around. "Why, Cotton, that's the first respectful thing I ever heard you say about a woman."

The ranger shrugged. "I still think there'd be a bounty on 'em if you couldn't breed 'em."

Coe frowned and shook his head. "I swear you must have never had a mammy."

Cotton rode in front as we took the fork leading to the Standard house. We were listening to Dub tell how a survey party of his had once gotten caught in a buffalo stampede when another voice interrupted.

"Stop," it said. "Put your hands up."

We obeyed.

A young man in buckskins stepped out of the bushes aiming a rifle at us. The skins he wore were not of the greasy, blackened variety seen on frontiersmen. His were still new and golden. He was clean shaven and had his hair cropped so short that barely any stuck out from under his hat. "Identify yourselves," he said.

"Identify your own damn self." Cotton refused to hold

his hands up any longer. "And point that gun at something else or I'll take it and jam it . . ."

Dub interrupted and made the necessary introductions and the young man in deer skins lowered his rifle. But he looked at me with particular enmity even though I hadn't smarted off the way Cotton had.

"Sorry about the gun," he said to the ranger. "We've been keeping a watch out for bushwhackers. I'm Clay Standard. The house is this way. I better walk in with you."

As we turned the next crook in the road, the plantation home of the Lon Standard family came into view. It stood in the middle of about ten acres that had been cleared of growth except for the largest oak and pecan trees. Blooded horses cavorted behind whitewashed fences on either side of the road that led to the front door of the house. Rows of pecan trees had been planted to flank the road, but were only half-grown.

The two-story limestone house stood in front of all the barns and outbuildings, rising high among the boughs of centuries-old live oaks. On both floors, galleries ran all the way around the house, lending space here and there to rocking chairs and porch swings. Trimmed shrubs grew in front and a flagstone walk led to the broad steps.

As we rode between the rows of young pecans the pastured horses followed along behind their fences. Coe's stallion was particularly excited about them and pranced sideways down the drive, making Coe beam with pride.

Clay had a hunting horn looped around his neck and he blew it to announce our arrival. Half a dozen hounds answered the call and came loping around the corner in a pack, baying and barking. They swarmed around Clay, wagging their tails, jumping and nipping at his elbows.

Major Lon Standard came around the house then, walking ramrod straight, suspenders bulging around the barrel of his chest, sleeves rolled up above his hairy forearms. He wore a wide-brimmed panama and striped trousers. He had the kind of legs that buckled inward a little at the knees, but otherwise looked as sound as an ox.

"They're here, Daddy," shouted Clay. "It's the man from the Land Office and the first of the rangers."

Lon walked out to meet us at the hitching rail and Dub made the introductions followed by the initial explanations. Up close, the old major looked more haggard than he had from afar. The mask of mourning was still on his face. There were gray hairs in his thick pork-chop sideburns and black circles under his eyes. But when he shook my hand, I knew he had plenty of life left to fight with.

"What did *you* come for?" he asked me.

"I think I can help find the boundary marker. I happened to stumble upon a blazed tree on the other side of the creek."

"And he's volunteered to help us at risk to his own skin," Coe said.

Cotton scoffed, hitched his mustang, and began prowling. Clay still looked at me with some distaste.

Mrs. Standard appeared at the front door about that time. She wore an apron around her waist and had her hair tied back in a bun that seemed to pull the rest of her features smooth and taut across her cheekbones. I could easily see the resemblance between her and Annie. She invited Coe and me into the house for some arrack punch.

"Arrack punch!" I exclaimed involuntarily. "That's a specialty of my mother's. I haven't tasted any in years."

"You should go see your mother more often," she said.

"Yes, ma'am," I admitted.

"Son, ride down to the pens and tell your brothers we've got company," the major said to Clay. "Then go by Annie's garden and ask her if it wouldn't inconvenience her too much to come, too. Your mother could use her help."

Clay trotted for the stables with his dogs as the rest of us went inside.

The Standard home could have served equally as well as palace or fortress. It didn't quite rate with the house I had grown up in on the Huckaby estates and it probably stood a notch or two below the Standard home the Yankees had burned in Virginia, but it was a house that would stand for generations and one to take pride in.

Charlotte Standard led us to the kitchen table where we would drink our punch. Dub downed an entire glass in two or three gulps and asked for more. Cotton glanced at us through the window from outside and then passed by.

"What is that ranger doing out there?" Charlotte asked.

"He's avoiding us," Coe said. "Cotton doesn't get on real good with people."

Lon slipped his hand around his wife's arm. "Mother, Mr. Huckaby here says he found the old boundary across the creek and is going to lead Mr. Coe there tomorrow."

Charlotte studied my face. "God bless you for that. The sooner we can end this trouble the better."

Charlotte's kitchen included a fireplace, a wood stove, an icebox, and an indoor pitcher pump with a basin that drained somewhere to the outside. She chipped some more ice for Dub's drink, and we made small talk until we saw Lum and Nat returning to the house. Lon suggested that we go out to meet them in the stables and he would show us around the place.

"You have a string of nice-looking horses," I mentioned as we walked to the stables.

"Thank you," the major said. "We used to breed racing horses in Virginia before the war. Now we deal mainly in cow ponies. Quarter horses, mostly, although we have kept a couple of Spanish ponies before."

Dub was surprised to learn that I had already made the acquaintance of the two newly arrived Standard brothers. They had a fine time telling him how the flour barrel had turned my mare from a seal brown to a roan.

Cotton Anderson interrupted the laughter. "Is this all the men of the family here?" he asked, appearing suddenly at the door to the stables.

"Except for Clay," Lon said. "He's gone to get Annie."

"Well, I have something to say so I'll just tell y'all now and talk to him later." He began his pacing motion in the broad doorway. "It's my duty to see that the boundary marker gets found between you all and that other ranch. Tomorrow morning Coe and Huckaby and me are going out to hunt it. We don't need no help and we won't stand for no . . ."

"What he means to say is this," Dub said. He gave the Standards their orders to stay clear of our party with more diplomacy than Cotton could have mustered on his happiest day.

"We'll keep out of your investigation," Lon promised.

"I appreciate that," Coe said, giving Cotton a smirk. "But I do want to hear your side of the story. If you can tell me where you think the marker is, I'll check for sign of it there."

"I can show you exactly where I always figured it to be," Lon said. "Come on around front."

We all followed Lon around to the hitching rails where our horses were tied. Lon stepped up on the porch and pointed to the hills. "The land patent I had before the courthouse burned seemed to indicate that the marker was on top of that hill. You can just see the crest of it up the creek valley."

"Which hill?" Cotton demanded. "I can't tell which one you're pointin' at."

Lon asked to borrow a rifle, so I pulled mine from the saddle scabbard and handed it to him. He pushed an armchair sideways against the rail on the porch. He knelt and rested the barrel of the rifle across the porch rail and the stock across the arm of the chair, looking down the sights from his kneeling position. He took a pair of leather gloves from his back pocket and put them under the barrel, doubling them over until they had become thick enough to prop the rifle barrel at the correct angle. Then he stepped away.

"That hill," he said. "Look down the sights and you'll see the peak of it."

We all took turns kneeling behind the rifle to sight down the barrel like astronomy students taking turns at a telescope. I recognized the hill in the gun sights as the one from which Eli Flatt had shot my canteen just before I made his acquaintance.

"The first time Eli claimed my land, I went up on that hill to find the corner," Lon said. "I didn't see a trace of it. Of course, I didn't really know what to look for, either. I don't know what kinds of marks those old surveyors used. But the patent I had when I bought this place indicated that the hill you're looking at is the one with the zero stone on it."

"We think old man Flatt dug it up and moved it," Nat said.

"Who thinks that?" Lum asked.

"Well, I do."

"Nobody asked you what you thought."

"Hush, boys," Lon said. He gave my rifle back to me and I returned it to the scabbard. Clay came trotting up on his horse then and I heard the rattle of a buggy coming from behind the house and knew Annie was returning from her garden. I asked Clay if I could put my mare in the stables, and he looked disgusted but said he guessed it would be alright.

As I led Liberty into the stables I saw Annie jump down from the spring seat of her buggy. Her eyes grew wide when she recognized me, and she quickly tossed her hair over her shoulders and straightened the fabric of her dress. "Roy!" she said. "Clay didn't say *you* were here."

"It's a pleasure to see you again," I said.

Instantly her bright eyes narrowed and she looked as though she would scold me for something. "How are you getting along with the Flatt family?"

"Not well. Not since I refused to cover up the location of the boundary for old Eli."

One of Annie's eyebrows peaked, but she continued to glower at me. Even her anger was beautiful.

"How's Topsy?" she asked with an accusatory tone in her voice.

I shrugged. "Fine," I said. Then I reached a wonderful understanding. Annie was jealous of Topsy for the days I had spent with her at the Flatts' house. I rejoiced and panicked all at once. "Except that she's worried sick over your brother Clay," I added, pleased with my own quick thinking.

Annie gasped. "Is she still sweet on him?"

"I should say so."

"Well, I swunny! I told Clay she wouldn't have him for a pet after everything that's happened. It was hard on us all when those Flatt boys murdered Virgil and Cal. But Clay took it harder than any of us because he figured he had lost his girl along with two brothers. I bet he hasn't done a lick of work since we buried them. He started wearing those buckskins and spending all his time spying on the road to the Flatts' house. Says he's watching in case they want to come shoot some more of us, but I think he wants to get a glimpse of Topsy. He saw you and her go to town in the wagon one day and it sure made him jealous."

"I'll have to set him at ease, then," I said. "She's got her mind on no other fellow but him."

Annie beamed again and I saw an opportunity.

"I brought you something," I said, reaching into my pocket. I pulled out a little bundle of cloth in which I had wrapped the bluebonnet seeds Coe had found for me. Annie knew exactly what they were.

"I've heard a lot about your garden and thought you might want to grow some wildflowers there."

"Thank you," she said. "That was nice of you to think of it."

She put the seeds away and asked if I would like to help unload the cargo in her buggy. She had several tow sacks filled with pecans that we put away in a feed room. One of the sacks contained nothing but the paper-shelled variety, she told me. We kept it separate from the others because it was worth more.

We stripped the gear from our horses and gave them some feed. I also helped her carry baskets of fall vegetables to the kitchen. But then I was chased out of the house so the women could cook.

I decided to hunt up Clay and tell him that he had occupied a lot of Topsy's thinking of late. When I convinced him of the fact, he started treating me like his oldest pal instead of his vilest enemy. I had to keep scratching dogs as I sat on the front steps and talked to him, for they followed him everywhere, and it seemed that any pal of Clay Standard's was good enough company to set their tails wagging.

NINETEEN

When Major Lon Standard said grace, I couldn't help peeking at Annie. I figured all the eyes around the dining-room table would be closed, and the heads bowed in prayer. They were, except for Annie's, who risked a glance at me, too, making us both blush.

I noticed something else unexpected as Lon blessed the food. Cotton Anderson had his hands clasped as tight as anyone. He even quivered with the Spirit of the Lord and when Lon finished, he said amen louder than anybody.

We had chicken-fried steaks, mashed potatoes, gravy, corn, and mustang wine from Annie's native vineyard. Coe asked where all the vegetables and wine had come from and Lon told him about Annie's garden.

"I love a garden," the surveyor said. "When we finish our job tomorrow, I'd like a chance to look at it."

"Me, too," I said. "I'd like to see how you graft the pecan limbs from the mother tree to the other ones."

The Standards stopped and stared at me.

"The storekeeper at the Marble Falls told me about it," I explained.

Cotton was sitting at the corner of the table, his arm wrapped around his plate as though he thought one of us would try to take it away from him.

As the conversation evolved over dinner, I learned that the feud with the Flatts had caused Lon to postpone his political aspirations. He had intended to run for a seat in the state house of representatives.

"What'll your platform be?" Coe asked.

"Oh, Lord," Charlotte said, "now you've done it."

"Don't get him started on politics," Lum said. "You'll hear nothing else all day long."

"Don't worry, I'll be brief," the major said. "I wouldn't want to bore the ladies."

Annie started to say something, but her mother elbowed her.

The major dabbed his chin with a napkin. "Transportation's my main objective. We need more railroads in Texas and we still have plenty of public land to trade for them. Not the school lands, of course. We need to protect them so we can educate our upcoming young men."

"And women," Annie said.

"Now, Annie, don't start," Charlotte said. "Not while we have company."

The major ignored Annie and went on with his stump speech. "And I think it's high time we stopped letting every saddle bum in the state carry a revolver on his hip. Side arms should be for lawmen only."

"Amen," Cotton said.

"I have nothing against a man carrying a rifle to hunt and shoot varmints, but a pistol is for combat. Now that the Indians are all on the reservations, there's no need for men to carry revolvers everywhere they go. We need legislation against them."

"You'd get my vote, Major," the ranger squeaked.

"Then there's the fencing controversy. I know the free-range days are drawing to a close, but, by golly, those big-pasture men don't have the right to fence everything under the sun. We need laws requiring gates at three-mile intervals on the fences so other cattlemen can drive their herds to market. And no one should be allowed to fence a public road. And there should be penalties for those who fence in public range before they acquire legal ownership."

"I agree," Coe said. "We can't jump from free range to private ownership overnight. We should ease into it."

"Exactly," the major said.

"What about that other idea of yours, Daddy?" Nat said, sidling his eyes toward me.

"Oh, yes. I've been observing the operations at the Granite Mountain quarry. I think it's an abomination the way those convicts are treated. I don't care if they are criminals. We need prison reform."

Before I could contain myself I snorted rather mockingly. Everyone at the table gawked at me.

"Do you find that amusing, Mr. Huckaby?" Lon asked.

"On the contrary, there's nothing funny at all about the need for reform in the prison system. It's just that I've heard it all before and know how the politicians are misled to think reforms are being enacted, when actually the abuses just continue or get even worse."

Lon tapped his knife against his plate. "Not to pry into your past, but I've heard you have some firsthand knowledge of the system. Perhaps you could tell us about some of the abuses you are talking about."

"I'll be glad to. But not now. The dinner table is not the place for it."

We had biscuits and butter and peach preserves for dessert and then retired to the parlor for a smoke. Cotton ordered Nat to show him around the grounds, expressing particular interest in seeing the family burial plot and the fresh graves of Cal and Virgil.

"I can't figure that ranger, Dub," I said after Cotton left. "He thinks more about killing than anybody I ever knew and yet I saw him praying like a parson over dinner."

"Cotton belongs to that religion where they think the Good Lord has everybody's time to cross over marked on his calendar and nothing nobody can do will change it."

"You mean he's a fatalist?" the major asked.

"Yes, that's what they call it. It's a convenient way of thinking for lawmen because then they don't have to fret about whether or not they'll get shot. They know all the frettin' in the world will do them no good."

"But he was praying at dinner," I said. "He said amen and everything. What's the use of praying if it won't change anything?"

"Cotton only prays to give thanks. He never asks the Lord for nothin'."

When we had exhausted the topic of fatalism, Lon asked me if I didn't think the time appropriate to tell him about the problems within the prison system. I said it was as good a time as any and started by decrying the use of the bat.

"But there must be discipline," the major said.

"The bat is seldom used for discipline. It's used as an instrument of torture and intimidation and nothing else. I'll wager that in all your years as a slave owner and a Confederate officer you never saw a human being or even a dog treated the way those convicts are by their guards."

"Wasn't there a chaplain installed in the prison system a few years ago? The chaplain should be the man the prisoners go to to report abuses."

"Any chaplain who reports an abuse soon finds himself looking for another congregation," I explained. "The system works him out right quick."

The major puffed broodingly on his pipe. "Did they ever use the bat on you?"

"Just once," I said. "I was lucky. Except for that once I managed to stay healthy enough to keep up with the work expected of me. And my skin was white. That helped some, too."

"How severe are the beatings?"

"In my case I was unable to sit or lie down on my back for eight days. One fellow I know of was paralyzed below the waist. Many men have been beaten to death."

"What?"

"Yes," I said. "Once I worked with another convict in a sawmill. He took sick and couldn't finish the day's work. The guards took him for a slacker and whipped him without mercy. The next day he was sicker. He knew he couldn't last for sixteen hours and that's what they expected of us. So he cut his own hand off with the saw blade so the guards would send him to the infirmary back at the walls. He knew he wouldn't be beaten there."

Major Lon sat stone quiet across the parlor, the smoke from his pipe swirling around him like a storm cloud. Wordlessly he rose from his chair and went to a writing table near me. He opened the ink well, took up the quill, and made a note or two on a sheet of stationery. "What else?" he asked.

I told him that the contract system should be abolished and that prisoners should no longer be hired out to work for private farmers and businesses.

"But I have read the reports of the commission," he argued. "I was led to believe that the prisoners enjoyed getting out of their cells for the exercise and work. And I know for a fact that the disease and death rates are lower on the farms."

"That's because the sick and injured men are sent back to the walls to recuperate or die. The healthy ones are sent out to the farms and kept there until they are too sick or worn down to work. And they beat the weakest ones as examples of what will happen to those who don't work hard enough. It would be easier for them to do the work expected of them if they were fed enough."

"How can they be fed too little?" the major asked. "The legislature appropriates a set amount for food. Where does it go?"

"The guards take it. They openly take the food from the commissary and use it to feed their families."

The major scribbled on his stationery. "Go on," he said.

As I preached the evils of the Texas penal system, the men in the parlor left one at a time until only Lon was there to listen to me. "I don't understand how it could happen," he said. He shook his head and scratched one of his bushy sideburns. "The commission inspects the prison units and the farms and has never reported any of these crimes to my knowledge."

"The guards know the commission's schedule," I explained. "Before the inspectors arrive at a farm, all the sick or injured convicts are sent somewhere else and the ones that remain are told to keep their mouths shut. We used to look forward to the inspections, actually, because the guards had to feed us properly when the inspectors were there."

"The solution, then," the major said, "would be to conduct unannounced inspections. Then the guards would have to treat the prisoners properly all the time or risk getting caught and charged for the abuses."

"And the contract system must be done away with."

"Yes, that, too."

"And standards should be set when hiring guards."

"Standards, yes. References required. Bonds put forward." The major stood and ran his fingers through his hair, paced the floor, rubbed his brow. He looked ready to sway the entire congressional delegation. "So much to be done," he said. "It won't be easy." Then he asked me what on earth a man of my temperament and training had done to get thrown into prison in the first place.

When I told him, he looked through the window at Nat who was trotting a colt in circles on a long lead rope. "It could just as well have happened to one of my boys," he said. "It could just as well have happened to me."

"It could just as well happen yet," I said.

Lon nodded. Then he clapped me on the shoulder. "We've been cooped up in here long enough. Come on, let's get some air."

Dub took a nap that afternoon, beneath the shade of a huge live oak in the Standards' yard. Cotton cleaned and oiled his armory. The Standard men worked with some horses, except for Clay. Mrs. Standard sent him and me to the watering tank to net some catfish Clay had caught and thrown in for safekeeping some time before.

The whisker fish, skinned and filleted, became supper, fried along with some of Annie's fresh okra and accompanied by sweet potatoes, green beans, and peach brandy.

After supper we all sat on the front gallery to watch the stars appear. It was a pleasant evening. A portent of something seemed to hang in the air. The conversation naturally turned to the subject on everyone's mind and Lon began telling Dub Coe his side of the dispute with Eli Flatt.

"When we moved here after the war," he said, "the fellow I bought this land from told me the patent was at the county courthouse. For some reason it was never sent in to the General Land Office."

"That's common," Dub said. "My pappy used to gripe about how unorganized the Land Office was in them days. Patents were scattered out all over the state."

"Well, this one had been drawn up in 1842," Lon continued, "after this plot was surveyed. At that time, the location of the zero stone was still known. The surveyors of '42 found it and connected their survey to Eli's land and drew up the patent."

"Where is the patent now?" Dub asked.

"Blown away to the four corners. It was still in the courthouse when it burned in '74. I regret that I never had it sent to the Land Office or made a copy of it. It had a plat drawn on it that seemed to place the zero stone on that hill I showed you this morning in the rifle sights. I have no proof, of course. Only my word."

"Old man Flatt was the one who burned the courthouse down," Nat said.

"No, he wasn't," Lum said. "It was rustlers trying to burn up all the brand records."

"Old man Flatt was probably a rustler on top of everything else," Nat argued.

"Now, Nat," the major said. "Let's stop speculating and just tell what we know as fact. The point is that the patent was the only document in existence to show the location of the zero stone. Now that it's gone, it's just my word against Eli's. He says the zero stone is on this side of the

Double Horn and that the creek belongs to him. I say otherwise."

"How come it took the two of your families so long to go to war over the land?" Cotton asked. "The courthouse burned in '74 and you've just now got around to killin' one another."

Coe grimaced at the ranger's phrasing.

"Eli's family and mine got along fine at first," Lon said. "He welcomed us here when we first arrived and he and his boys helped us build the log house we lived in before we got this place built."

"Yeah, the Indians were still bad when we came here," Lum added, "and we chased 'em with the Flatt brothers whenever they came around to steal stock or hunt scalps."

"That's right, we were good neighbors to one another," continued Lon. "We never even discussed exactly where the boundary ran at first. It wasn't necessary. Even though most of the land was privately owned around here, we used it like free range. Our cattle ran together and we rounded them up and branded them just like they do on the government ranges. Eli and I were the only landowners to actually live on our places. All the others were waiting for the Indians to get cleared out, I suppose. It wasn't until after the last fight at Packsaddle Mountain that the valley began to settle up.

"Even after the courthouse burned, Eli didn't try to claim my land right away. In fact, it wasn't until that stern-wheeler came up to the Marble Falls that year that he told me he was going to build a town at the mouth of the Double Horn."

"And that's when the shootin' started?" Cotton asked.

"No, not then. I simply told Eli the mouth of the Double Horn was on my land and I didn't see much future in building a town there and if he wanted to build one, he should put it farther downstream on his own land. He told me then that he had always considered the Double Horn his. We argued about it, but we weren't mad enough to shoot each other. After that argument I realized that I didn't have any proof to back up my claim since my patent had burned up. I hunted some for boundary markers, but didn't know what I was looking for. Anyway, Eli didn't mention the subject again for a while and I just forgot about the whole thing."

Lon sighed and reached for Charlotte's hand and squeezed it. "If I had known that damned strip of land would cost me two sons, I'd have given it to him in the first place. But, damn it, I swore when I left Virginia that I would never let another man take my land again. The carpetbaggers had taxed my plantation out from under me back there. I just wanted to leave my children something. The last thing I wanted was for them to die because of it."

We all sat silent on the gallery for a long moment. Cotton shoved his chair back and walked into the dark.

"You know why I never liked old Mr. Flatt?" Annie said.

"Why is that, miss?" Coe asked.

"He always looks in his handkerchief after he blows his nose."

"Oh, Annie!" Charlotte said.

"It's true, Mother. You can't a trust a man who does things like that."

Dub laughed, then asked the Standard men what had happened between them and the Flatts after the steamboat came upriver. Lon seemed unwilling to tell about it, so Lum did. "Well, nothing happened for a long time," he said. "Then, a few months ago, old Eli told us he was going to string a fence on this side of the Double Horn. The newspapers had run a story about clearing the raft at the mouth of the river so steamers could come in and old man Flatt figured he would make a fortune in the steamboat trade if he could just put his town at the mouth of the Double Horn. Daddy took him to court over it."

"Yeah," Nat said, eager to get in on the story, "and old

man Flatt tried to tell the judge that he was the only one who knew where the boundary was because he was here with the first survey party in '38 and that Daddy had torn the old marker down. The judge didn't believe him, of course. He sent out an order for you to come, Mr. Coe. That made old Eli mad and those Flatt brothers pulled guns on us on the way home."

"Dang sure did," Lum said. "Shot at us, too. Put a bullet through my hat. We just started shootin' back and killed Reed and Bass."

"We didn't have no choice," Nat said. "It was kill them or get killed ourselves. Then Virgil and Cal got bushwhacked on their way to town one day . . ."

Dub interrupted. "The shootin' part is for the courts to look into. All I need to know about is the zero stone."

The Standard brothers looked at the sky. Lon stared at the porch floor. I saw something move away in the dark and knew it was Cotton.

"I've always wondered," Annie said. She sat at the far end of the gallery from me. I could barely hear her voice and could not see enough of her face in the starlight. "Why do they call it the 'zero' stone?"

Dub threw a cheerful twang into his voice as if he had decided to single-handedly take the gloom out of the conversation. "It's called that because it stands on top of the first corner ever surveyed in this part of the territory," he explained. "It was supposed to be the starting point for all surveys to follow for years to come. And, as anybody knows, if you start somewhere, you start at zero. Of course, it didn't work out that way because the Indians killed the survey crew after they had platted just one square.

"A lot of old lines were lost in ways like that. Why, I remember the first lost boundary I ever had to find. It was up in the Cross Timbers between two families that was feuding over the land. Well, I was a young man back then, green as a red blackberry . . ."

Dub slipped into his story, but I had trouble keeping my mind on it. I strained to catch Annie's eyes at the other end of the gallery, but it had grown too dark. I turned my gaze to the sky. The stars began to twinkle and I let them play tricks with my eyes. I let them sparkle like jewels, like sunlight glinting on the face of a polished bar of silver. I invented my own constellations: the doubloon, the ingot, the chain of jewels, the pieces of eight.

In the morning I would find the zero stone, the place the old Mexican's map had told me to begin in my search for *el tesoro.* One hundred eighty-nine lengths of Dub Coe's survey chain, 49 degrees northwest—by that formula I would come to stand on the most valuable point of land in Texas. Stand? No, I would drop and kiss it!

And then? After I found the loot? Oh, why not? Why be greedy? Of course I would share it with the Standard clan. There would be enough for Annie and I to build our own limestone mansion, raise our children, send them to college.

Only one hitch could keep me from it. Eli would be watching tomorrow. So would Boone and Tobe. Little Jimmy Fitzhugh might even have joined them by now. Their guns would be loaded and leveled on the boundary hunters. But Topsy would try to stop them. And if she didn't, Cotton Anderson would take them all on by himself. And I had my rifle and Dub had one, too. The Flatt gang would not deny me my reward.

Think like a ranger, Roy. Your day is marked on God's circle of time. You have no cause to worry. Your fretting changes nothing. You are a fatalist, Roy. You fear no one. It is your destiny to follow this path to the zero stone and you have no control over it. It's above you, Roy, it's beyond your grasp or understanding. You must let the hand of One greater than you will you where He would.

" . . . and the other clan was a freckle-faced race of people and every one of them had the brains of a, oh, I guess a razorback hog or so—which is not all that ignorant, by the way. Both clans were so poor they left five-toed tracks on the way to Sunday school. They both wanted that land bad."

Dub's tale was coming through to me again.

"They had been feudin' for fifteen years. They had already fought over women, whiskey, horses, religion, politics, and then land. I had a dozen rangers with me the day I went out to find the boundary between them. It was a case just like yours because it was an Initial Monument—a zero stone—that determined the line. When I went out that morning to find it, those rangers had more guns on them than a battalion could carry . . ."

"What?"

"I say, more than a whole battalion, Roy, really."

"No, what did you say before that? You went to find what?"

"The zero stone."

"The zero stone?"

"Yes, that's what I said. I went to find the zero stone."

"But the zero stone is here," I said, pointing into the darkness.

"One of them is. 'Zero stone' is just an old-fashioned term for an Initial Monument. A starting point for one of the frontier surveys."

A paralysis seized my throat. "But . . . How many?" I wheezed. "How many zero stones are there?"

"How many? Heck, I don't know, Roy. Hundreds, I guess, all over the country. Anyway, those rangers had guns to beat an army that morning when I went to hunt the zero stone up there in the Cross Timbers . . ."

TWENTY

The stars died in the night sky. Blackness closed in on me and left me alone with my agony. The grip tightened around my windpipe. The blood pounded against my temples. The bile rose in my guts. I stood and walked but, blinded, knew not where I went.

I had known just one ambition the day the old Mexican gave me the treasure map. There was only one old Mexican. He gave me only one map. There was one Marion Harkey, one Eli Flatt. One Texas, one Burnet County, one Double Horn Creek. There was one Annie Standard and there was only one fool named Royal Strickland Huckaby. But there were hundreds of zero stones.

I staggered like a drunk. I reeled and swooned. Why had I failed to consider the possibilities of multiple zero stones? What had made me think I could see the term once written in Spanish on a worthless Mexican treasure map and then coincidentally hear it spoken from the lips of a complete stranger like Marion Harkey—unless the zero stone existed in a thousand manifestations across the entire country?

I had staked everything on a zero stone. My freedom, my future, my very life. In the morning I was expected to run a gauntlet of guns leveled by the sure hands of the Flatt gang to help Dub Coe find a zero stone. If I survived, what would be my reward? A one-in-one-thousand chance of digging up a buried treasure trove? I had never bet against those kinds of odds and I had no intention of starting now.

There was just one thing to do. Run. Turn my back on the Flatt-Standard feud and flee to some kinder destiny. When all the Standards had gone to bed, when Dub Coe and Cotton Anderson had kicked off their boots and pulled up their covers, I would sneak out to the stables, saddle Liberty, and ride like a lost soul in limbo.

"Roy," I heard the voice say.

I shook my head to clear it and found myself leaning against the doorway of the stables behind the house.

"Roy, what are you doing?"

It was Annie, her tawny hair collecting the sparse starlight.

"Oh, I just . . . I needed to check on my mare before turning in." Thank God it was dark. Perhaps she hadn't seen me weave and stagger. Or perhaps only my thoughts had tripped and my legs had swung true.

"Mother asked me to tell you that you'll be staying in the guest room tonight. At the top of the stairs. Mr. Coe and the ranger will get Virgil and Cal's old room. Mother hasn't opened it until tonight."

She moved closer to me. I heard the rustle of her clothing. "I'm glad that you came here, Roy. It helps to know this trouble may be ended soon. I think you're very brave to help us."

"Annie," I said.

"No, let me tell you. I know you're modest, but I want you to know how I feel. I knew when you put your horse between that flour barrel and those children that you were a thoughtful man, that you cared about people, and that you would help those unable to help themselves if you could. But I never dreamed you would risk your life to help us."

She came nearer still. I smelled the sweet aroma of her skin. I felt her warmth. She touched my hand. "It could be dangerous tomorrow and you haven't shown the least sign of fear all day. I want to give you something to bring you luck in the morning."

"Annie, there's no need," I began. But then I felt her body press against mine and I felt her breath on my chin. Her lips touched below my jaw and then found my mouth. The darkness overwhelmed me again and I reeled and swooned in a whole new way.

"Who is that?" Dub said.

Annie bit my lower lip and pulled away from me. "Damn it, mister! Don't you respect privacy?"

"Oh, I, uh, sorry, miss," the startled surveyor said. "I just came to look after, uh . . ." He started chuckling. "Well, how was I to know?"

Annie slid away from me. "Excuse my language, Roy, but . . . oh, never mind!" She stomped back to the house.

"Sorry, Roy, if I busted in on anything. The major was telling me how hard he had found it to raise a southern belle on the Texas frontier. Now I see what he means. He said he got his older daughter married off and sent back to Virginia. But that Annie, she's a hellion."

"Huh?" I said.

"Say, listen! Did you hear that?"

"What?"

"Listen."

I heard the faintest yelps somewhere in the sky. Scores of them.

"Geese," Dub said. "You know what that means?"

"Means?"

"Norther coming tonight. Those honkers are ridin' it down from Canada. It'll be cold in the morning. Mark my words."

We rose before dawn and it *was* cold. The windows were patterned with frost. I found occasion to wear my long handles for the first time since I had purchased them in Fredericksburg. The entire Standard family got up with us to eat breakfast and see us off on our quest for the troublesome zero stone—one of hundreds.

The peculiar thing was that I had dreamed of the old Mexican again overnight. He had implored me, pointing his gnarled fingers at the ground under his feet. *"El tesoro,"* he said again and again. But folly lingers in dreams.

Before we left the house, Annie caught my eye and ran her finger across her lower lip, wordlessly asking me what kind of damage she had done to me the night before. I smiled and winked to let her know the pain had been worth the pleasure. Major Standard caught us glancing at each other and narrowed his eyes at me.

We rode at first light, Dub trailing the mule loaded with his surveying equipment.

"I think I've figured it out, Dub," I said to the surveyor as we left the stables.

"What's that?" he asked.

"Your name. Did you ever go by your initials? W. W.?"

"Yes, in fact I did," he said, grinning.

"And when folks got tired of calling you W. W., I guess they just shortened it to 'Dub.' "

"See there," he said to the little ranger, "I told you he was smarter than you."

"If he's so damn smart, what's he doing here?" Cotton said.

The animals puffed white clouds of vapor. It mingled with the fog that rose from the river and drifted south on the breezes, clouding our movements.

"This fog'll help us," Cotton said. "They'll have to git in close to shoot us in this stuff."

The misty air gave me some comfort, too. I felt as if I could hide in it.

"Cold north air on that warm river water," Coe said. "That's where this fog's coming from."

We went back to the Double Horn, crossed it, and turned south off the road. Cotton rode with a hand on one revolver. "How come you remember where you chopped that particular tree with the blaze on it?" he asked as I led us through the cedar stumps.

"It was the biggest one. It made an impression on me."

Even in the fog, I had no trouble finding the place. I saw the furrows the big corner posts had dug when the mules dragged them to the Flatt house. Then I saw the circle of ashes where I had burned Reuben's convict uniform. I knew exactly where to find the stump from there.

"Here it is."

"Look's big enough," Dub said. "Are you sure this is the one?"

"There's no doubt."

Dub tried to count the number of growth rings in the rough ax marks on the cedar stump. "Must be almost a hundred," he said. "Look how much this tree grew during these three years right here, Roy. Must have rained a lot then. Looks like, oh, in the fifties sometime. That's funny. I don't remember the fifties being that wet."

"God Almighty," Cotton said. "Forget the weather and find the damned boundary marker."

"It'll wait on us, Cotton. It's been there well nigh fifty years already."

I helped Dub unload his surveying equipment. He mounted his big, dinner-plate compass on something he called a Jacob staff. It was a hardwood pole with a sharpened steel spike on the bottom. On the top, where the compass was clamped, it had a ball-and-socket joint that allowed for leveling the instrument. The compass had two bubble levels beside its face that enabled the surveyor to get it exactly horizontal.

"Why don't you use that telescope thing you were telling us about when the lady thought you were a Peeping Tom?" I asked.

"I'm using the same type of equipment they used when they surveyed this place in '38. That will give us the best chance of duplicating the original lines. This old peep-sight compass is an antique. Nobody uses them anymore."

Dub fastened a bracket to either side of the compass. The brackets had vertical slots that the surveyor looked through as if sighting along the irons of a rifle.

"I'll need you boys to move the chains for me while I line you up with the compass. The zero stone should lie 190 chains due south of this stump."

"How do you know that?" I asked.

"The blaze on that witness tree you chopped was a section mark. That means it was one mile from the zero stone. That's about 1,900 varas or 190 chains. Shouldn't take us but a couple of hours to run it."

"At this rate?" Cotton complained.

The ranger took one chaining pin and I grabbed the other. Like the Jacob staff on which the compass was mounted, the chaining pins had steel spikes on them that allowed them to be planted firmly in the ground. We stretched the chain and lined the pins up on a north-south course as indicated through the slots in Dub's compass brackets.

As we moved the pins south for the second chain length, Cotton refused to leave the horses behind. His Sharps rifle and scattergun were attached to his saddle and he would not stray from them. In fact, he kept the reins to his silver buckskin looped around his elbow, which slowed down the chaining process considerably.

By the time we had stretched several chain lengths to the south, a disturbing trend became evident to me. I noticed that I could see over a hundred yards through the fog. It seemed to be lifting and leaving us unprotected. But on the next ten varas, it thickened so much that I could barely see Cotton at the other end of the chain. It was coming across us in waves.

When the fog was thin, the little ranger ceaselessly swept his pale blue eyes across the cedar brakes and brush around us. But when a finger of mist shrouded us, he relied more on his ears, cocking his head at every sound like some hard-hunted game bird.

We rattled the links through the moist litter of cedar needles and hardwood leaves. We laboriously moved the horses southward with us, chain by chain. Dub lined up the pins, holding us dead on course, keeping a running tally of the number of chains we had stretched.

It was tedious work pulling the chain through the brush. We found many trees and bushes growing along the line we were running. If practical, Dub would chop them away with a hatchet he had packed on his mule. But some trees were too big and we just had to stretch our chain around them and estimate the number of inches taken off the length of chain due to the variation from the straight line.

"Runnin' around all these trees," Cotton said, "we ain't gonna come out like them surveyors did in '38. Hell, half these trees probably wasn't even here then. This ain't gonna come out right, Coe."

"No need to be that precise," Dub replied. "The men who left the zero stone didn't stretch their chains perfect, either, you can bet on that. Not with Indians breathin' down their collars. We'll git within spittin' distance and that'll be close enough."

After half an hour of work, we came to a rocky place on a steep grade. The surveyor began brushing away the leaves on either side of our line. He rubbed the rock with his palm in several places.

"What are you lookin' for?" asked the ranger.

"I'm trying to find a place where one of those old surveyors might have stuck their chaining pin."

Cotton scoffed. "Forty-seven years ago?"

Dub kept looking and rubbing the rocks and directly he called me over to look. "See those old scratch marks? Could be their trail."

"Damn cold trail if you ask me," Cotton said. A column of fog had just rolled onto us and he was listening carefully for unnatural noises.

"I *didn't* ask you," Coe said.

"How will we know for sure?" I asked.

"Let's measure due south from these scratches. If we find another set of them at exactly ten varas, we can pretty much bet we're on the old line."

We stretched the chains and found faint marks under the other pin as well. We stretched it again and found more old marks, almost illegible except to the practiced eyes of Dub Coe.

"We've strayed about a foot to the west of their line," he said. "But now we're back on center. There's no doubt in my mind now, Roy. That cedar you chopped was a witness tree. It will lead us dead straight to that zero stone."

"Don't yell it to the whole damned valley," hissed the ranger. The wave of fog had pulled away from us and there was nothing to muffle our voices or cover our movements.

We ran the line southward, moving the horses, chopping the brush, dragging the chain. Dub came to a large sycamore perched on the creek bank and paused for a long moment to study it. Neither Cotton nor I complained about the delay and sat to rest, holding our chaining pins upright in their places. I exhaled into my cupped hands to warm them.

"This looks like an old witness mark, too," Dub said, sighting along the side of the trunk with one eye. He pulled the hatchet from his belt and scraped some bark away. "Yeah, it's a hack. I'll just freshen it up a bit." He chopped a deep horizontal gash in the side of the tree.

"What's the difference between a hack and a blaze?" I asked.

"A hack goes crossways on the trunk. A blaze is like the blaze on a horse's face—up and down. Looks like these surveyors used the blaze for a section mark and the hack just to mark any tree standing on the boundary."

For another hour we worked in and out of fog until we had stretched the chain 180 times by Dub's tally. "Ten chains to go," he said.

We stood halfway up the hill that Major Standard had sighted in his rifle irons the day before. I had already become accustomed to judging distances in increments of ten varas. I could tell that our final stretch of the chain would leave us standing on top of that hill. If the Flatts were going to stop us from finding the zero stone, they would be waiting for us there.

"Makes sense that they would put the corner up there," said Dub. "The old-timers usually tried to pick a rise as a starting point when they could. That made the markers easier to find."

The norther had blown a million doves south. They burst from the trees in flocks as we dragged the chain and led the horses, their wings popping in the cold air and their little voices shrilling in spasms. The day before, I might have recognized one of them as the old Mexican. But today they were just annoying noise-makers.

A dense cloud seemed to have snagged on the ridge of the knoll and I was grateful for its presence. It covered our progress up the rocky slope. Despite the problem of moving the horses with us, we had fallen into a kind of rhythm over the last two hours and we made good time ascending the hill.

Cotton was braced for battle. Coe was eager for discovery. I was scared almost witless. The fight between my late brother-in-law and the Texas Rangers at my hunting lodge in Matagorda County—the only gun battle I had ever been in—had taken me by surprise and had spared me an incalculable amount of worry because of it. But my anticipations of the impending battle of the zero stone were almost too much for me to endure. I might have considered running, but I couldn't stand to think of how Annie would cuss the memory of me if I did. Besides, Cotton Anderson would probably shoot me in the back for deserting.

No, I had to charge up the hill with the surveyor and the ranger. I had to fulfill my wretched destiny. How would posterity remember me? I wondered. Roy Huckaby: bush-whacker, ranger-killer, convict, and whorehouse brawler. Could not stay away from blood feuds. Picked fights with strangers on street corners, broke hardened criminals out of prison, seduced the daughters of fine gentlemen. It was a great day for Texas when the hard-fighting Flatt men killed him at the shootout on Double Horn Creek.

But maybe Topsy would come through. Maybe she could hold off her father and brothers until we could find the marker and git. And the fog would help us, too. It was so thick on our hill that the Flatts would have to crawl closer than thirty varas to find us in their sights and we would hear them coming.

There is hope, Roy. There is always hope. Think like a fatalist.

We lacked only two chains to reach the summit of the hill when, through the fog, I saw a pile of rocks standing on the very crest. It had several scrubby bushes and a yucca plant growing out of it and seemed to be a natural part of the hill. I judged that two more chain lengths would bring the final pin down at the edge of the rock pile.

"We're here," I said, laying my pin down.

"Wait," Dub said, "run the last two chains. We'll have to run the whole line to satisfy the courts. Besides, we're looking for a chiseled stone and I don't see nothin' yet but a pile of rocks."

"Maybe it's buried under them rocks," Cotton said. His voice squeaked higher than ever with the excitement.

"Maybe," Coe said. "Run the last two chains and then we'll see."

The last stretch of the links brought my chaining pin down right on the edge of the five-foot-tall pile of stones. "This pile of rocks ain't natural," Dub said.

"How can you tell?" I asked.

"Did you ever know rocks to pile theirselves up on top of a hill?" he asked. "Rocks roll down, not up. You boys just relax. I'll look around before we move anything."

Cotton squatted down in front of his mustang and strained to listen through the fog. Dub took a little straw hand broom from his pack mule and started brushing away the dirt here and there around the pile of stones, especially in the low spots that carried rainwater downhill. He picked up several tiny objects as he worked.

"What are you looking for now?" I asked.

"These." He showed me a handful of small stone flakes of different colors.

"What are they?"

"I think they're chips left over from chiseling the zero stone. I don't see what else could break off so many little bitty pieces of rock up here. The marker must be under that pile of rocks, like Cotton said. Somebody's buried it, most likely." He poured the stone chips into a small paper envelope that he put in his vest pocket. "Come on, Cotton. Make some use of yourself and help us move these rocks."

We pulled at the bushes in the pile of rocks and they came loose without much effort. Then we started picking up the melon-sized boulders or rolling them aside. A couple of them got away from us and crashed down the hill. There was some dirt mixed in with the rocks and Dub used a small shovel from his packsaddle to scrape it away. With all the noise we were making, the Flatts would have no trouble knowing we were there in the fog, digging up the zero stone, disclaiming Eli's right to Double Horn Creek, smashing his dreams of becoming a town father.

Thank God the fog stayed with us. And the wind was just barely blowing from the north, letting the mist linger over us.

The rocks came away from the pile easily until we reached a point of stone jutting up from the middle of the pile. I pushed it, but it didn't budge. It was the same kind of red brindle stone that the convicts carved out of the Granite Mountain quarry. "This piece of granite won't move," I said to Dub.

"Of course it won't. It's part of the hill. It's what these flakes came from." He patted his vest pocket and grinned.

"It's the zero stone?"

"Most likely."

We dug more frantically, tossing stones into the fog all around us. My heart pounded—more from a strange, exhilarating sense of discovery than from the exertion or the fear. A layer of dirt covered the piece of pink granite. Dub scraped the soil off with his shovel.

I thought I could see a flat face on the stone but I couldn't be sure until Dub brushed more dirt away with his whisk broom. There were words carved into the granite outcropping, but the letters were still clogged with dirt and we couldn't read them.

"I'd have used this for a marker myself," the surveyor said. "It's perfect. Set high on a hilltop and permanent, too. You'd have to blast this away to move it."

I felt a strange pity for old Eli. His greed and treachery were exposed now. He was naked to the truth. He had buried the zero stone, never imagining anyone would have the skills to find and unearth it.

"Get your canteen," Dub said, "and we'll wash it off and read it. I hope they didn't deface it. I'd like to know what it says."

I poured the water down the flattened west face of the zero stone as Dub brushed it with his hand broom. The mud came away in streaks and the lettering became clearer. When we had the entire marker cleaned we stood back a foot or two to read it:

INITIAL MONUMENT
ORIGINAL SURVEY
1838
REPUBLIC OF TEXAS

Dub stood with his little whisk broom in his hand and his hatchet tucked under his belt. He breathed in a great sigh of satisfaction. "Don't let nobody ever tell you Dub Coe can't run a straight line."

As I smiled at the old surveyor, I realized the protective wall of fog was slipping away from us, bringing the surrounding trees on the hilltop into view. I heard a faint but familiar noise: the sound of a lock tripping in its machinery. Cotton was next to me. I tackled him, pulling him down behind the zero stone.

"Get down!" I yelled. But I was too late. A rifle crack sounded and a bloody hole tore open in Dub's back. The impact threw him and he slid down the hill.

Cotton jumped up cussing, both revolvers blazing, running to get his guns from the mustang. I huddled behind the zero stone, shards of it spraying all over the hilltop. A bullet hit the silver buckskin and the horse fell, almost on top of Cotton. Coe's stallion and Liberty spooked and ran down the hill. His horse kicking in agony, the ranger tried to pull his Sharps rifle out of the scabbard, but the buckskin had fallen on it. Another volley of bullets tore pieces of horse flesh away and the mustang stopped kicking.

I could hear footsteps running toward us from the other side of the zero stone. I had no weapon. I had been unable

to carry my rifle while running the survey chain and I had
never worn a pistol in my life.

Cotton got the scattergun loose from the saddle horn and
threw it to me. "They're trying to flank us," he said. "You
watch the south side and don't let them get around us over
there. I can't get you any more shells. They're in the saddle pocket and the horse died on them. Make both shots
tell."

The cold barrel of the sawed-off shotgun felt good in my
hand, but I longed to have a rifle with a full magazine.
Buckshot wouldn't carry far with any accuracy.

Cotton reloaded his pistols with cartridges from his belt
and tried one last time to get the saddlebags loose from the
dead mustang. Then the shots rang out and the ranger rose
to return them. He let both his double-action Colts fire as
fast as he could pull the triggers and ran to the survey
marker, falling in beside me.

"Are you hit?" I asked.

"Not bad." There was blood running down from his right
arm. Again, he replaced the spent cartridges.

The fog thickened for a moment and I lost sight of the
treeline I was guarding to the south. Then: shots and points
of fire and bullets hitting rocks in front of me. I aimed at
the gunfire and let one of the barrels loose. I heard a yell
and the fog swirled and I saw Boone scampering for cover.

"That's not buckshot!" I yelled at Cotton.

He shrugged. "It's a riot gun. Bird shot."

"How do you expect me . . ."

A twig snapped behind him and the ranger whirled to
shoot. His bullet struck Tobe in the knee, taking him down
behind a boulder. In a few seconds, he began to moan.

I heard Eli's voice. "Git up and fight," it said.

Tobe continued to moan, but put his pistol over the rock
and fired blindly. Then Boone came again from the south
side. I let my second load of bird shot fly ineffectually.

"Give me a pistol," I said.

"You can have my guns when I'm dead." Cotton rose above the protection of the zero stone and fired his pistols in two directions as the bullets shattered stone around us. I heard Boone coming behind me and Eli firing from the other side of our chiseled battlement. I saw Tobe rising above the rock he had fallen behind, his bloody hands leveling a rifle on the ranger.

Cotton's revolvers ran dry and clicked against dead cartridges. He started to empty the shells and reload.

"No!" Tobe yelled. His voice told the pain he was feeling. "Drop them pistols!"

"He said drop 'em." Boone's voice came from the other slope, below me.

Cotton let the pistols fall from his hands and stood at attention to face his death.

Boone came up the hill, parting the fog, pointing his rifle. He had a few points of blood on him where the bird shot had gotten under his skin. "Git up, Royal," he said.

I rose beside the ranger, dropped the empty shotgun, and stood in front of the inscribed face of the boundary marker.

"Kill 'em!" Eli's voice yelled from the trees across the zero stone. I saw him walk out into the open. "Land grabbers! Shoot 'em!" He was shoving cartridges into the loading port of his carbine.

But Boone didn't shoot. He came around the crest of the hill to look at Dub Coe's body. His eyes bulged out as if the sight of the dead man horrified him. He looked at Eli. "Pa, this ain't no hammer. It's a hatchet."

Tobe was using his rifle as a crutch, whimpering with every step he took on his shattered leg. He also gawked at the surveyor's body. He stumbled and fell beside the dead man and took the whisk broom out of his hand. "You said he had a chisel, Pa. This ain't nothin' but a broom. He wasn't gonna chisel no stone. Sweet Jesus, we killed him for nothin'."

"Kill them others, too," the old man said, still shoving cartridges into his saddle rifle with trembling hands.

"Sure, go ahead and kill us," Cotton said. "What are you waiting for?"

I backhanded the little ranger in the chest. "Shut up, Cotton. I'm not ready to die just yet." I stepped away from the zero stone. "Coe didn't have to chisel anything," I said to the Flatt brothers. "The chiseling was done forty-seven years ago. See for yourself, Boone. Here's the zero stone, where it's always been."

Boone gaped and lowered his rifle. "Pa," he said. "You were wrong. God in heaven, you were wrong."

"Shut up," Eli said. "This is my land. I was here first. Kill 'em. They're land grabbers."

Boone stared at the stone and Tobe moaned with his head against Dub's lifeless body.

"Kill 'em!" Eli shouted.

Boone set his jaw. "I ain't a murderer. I won't kill in cold blood."

"Now, son. You mind me and kill those land grabbers. We'll drag 'em across the creek and blame it on the Standards. We'll say Lon and them killed 'em to keep that surveyor from finding the boundary. Then we'll bury the marker again and nobody will ever know nothin'."

"I can't do it," Boone said. "You said the land was ours. You sent me and Tobe out to kill Virgil and Cal for nothin'." Boone threw his rifle down. "Goddamn you, Pa, you lied!"

I heard a single set of hoofbeats coming.

"I'll kill 'em myself, then," Eli said. He levered his rifle to work a shell into the chamber, but the action caught the end of his long white beard and he couldn't pull it loose. It was almost comical the way he struggled to get his whiskers free.

Suddenly Cotton rushed the old man, drawing a knife from his belt as he leapt over stones. The old man yanked half his beard out of his face to free the carbine and used it to club the ranger to the ground with one mighty sweep of the barrel.

The hoofbeats had grown louder and now I saw a horse coming through the fog up the east face of the hill.

Eli worked the action open and started pulling his whiskers out of the breech to make sure the gun would fire so he could shoot me. I glanced back to check Boone's position and found him standing stupidly, unable to act against his father. Before I knew it, I was running at Eli myself, my hands outstretched for his throat. He closed the breech, swung the carbine up, aimed it at my head. I closed my eyes and lunged and heard the shot and fell on top of the old man.

I heard Eli gasping. I was choking him. A powerful hand pulled me away. Boone threw me to the side and fell across his father, weeping. The old man was blinking at the foggy sky. Then I saw Topsy astride the big gray gelding, staring wildly at her father, the smoking rifle in her hands. Her skirt had blown up over the knees of her buckskin britches. Her red hair looked like a plume of blood against the gray mist.

Eli rolled his eyes and spoke: "My God, girl, you've shot me."

Topsy dismounted slowly and let the heaving gray gelding wander away. She dropped her rifle and stood over her father. She covered her face and began to cry.

I heard more hoofbeats coming and knew the Standard men were riding to join the fight. I ran to an open spot against the north face of the zero stone's hill and waved at the Standard gang. They saw me and came running, flailing their guns, but I held my hands high and told them not to shoot. I told them it was over.

They gathered on top of the hill to look at the dead and the wounded. They read the zero stone silently. Cotton Anderson moaned and pulled himself up on all fours. Boone was trying to stop the bleeding from Eli's chest. Topsy had shot him through both sets of ribs. Boone looked around at us all. "Help me," he pleaded. "Help me get him to a bed."

Eli's broad old hand grabbed Boone around the elbow and squeezed. He shook his head. "I'm killed, son."

Lon got down and knelt beside Eli. "You knew it was there all along. Why did you want this damned strip of dirt so bad?"

"My land," Eli said, wincing. "I come here first. I told them surveyors I wanted to patent this piece of land east of the creek. And I wanted the creek, too. Good runnin' water. I wanted to put up a mill. I told them to put the corner on that hill across the creek. But they had to put the son of a bitch here." He lifted his head to look at the stone. "Just because a good piece of rock stuck up on it for the marker. What kind of fool reason . . ."

Eli squinted and let his head fall back against the ground. "Somethin' you never knew about me, Lon. I was tradin' with the Indians for hides back then. I knew 'em good, chiefs and all. So I told 'em about the surveyors stealin' their land here. I knew they'd kill 'em, then I could hire me a new survey party. Put the damn boundary wherever I wanted it."

"You *let* the Indians massacre all those men?" Lon asked.

Eli nodded, grimacing. "Hell, I told 'em to, more or less. Then I come back to burn up the field notes. Couldn't find 'em. I found the chief surveyor, dead and scalped. The chain men, the flag men, the cook, the guards. All dead. The corner builder, too. Everybody dead and scalped but one. Mexican wrangler. Couldn't find him. Son of a bitch got away, I guess. Took the notes in."

As Eli paused, I collapsed and sat on a pile of rocks Dub Coe and I had thrown aside from the zero stone.

"So I had to bury the zero stone. Couldn't dig it up. Couldn't move it. Rooted too deep. Now you know how hard I worked to get ahold of this land," Eli said. "My land." His eyes stared blankly at the sky. "My land." He muttered about his land until he bled to death.

TWENTY-ONE

We carried the dead to the Marble Falls in the Standards' buckboard wagon. Cotton arrested Tobe and Boone for the murders of Cal Standard, Virgil Standard, and William Westfall Coe. He sat in the bed of the wagon with them and guarded them all the way to town, pouring water over his wounded head about every mile or so to keep himself alert. Neither of the prisoners offered any resistance. Clay drove the wagon and Topsy rode beside him.

Annie took her buggy and insisted that I drive it so I could tell her the story of the zero stone fight on the way. Everyone else rode saddle horses.

The sun had burned off the fog by the time we pulled up in front of Lynn's Store. We began attracting a crowd almost immediately. Miss Teeter somehow heard about our arrival and let her class out so the students could see the dead and wounded.

Tobe, Boone, and Topsy sat in the wagon like statues, refusing to acknowledge any of the conversation that went on around them. The shame they felt for their father's treachery seemed surpassed only by their will to sustain some measure of personal dignity. They lowered their eyes to no one, but looked through all comers. Even Tobe, who was pallid from loss of blood, sat upright and unwavering.

Lynn came out of his store when we stopped the wagons. Cotton climbed down, keeping his eyes on his prisoners. He raked the wet yellow hair back over his bleeding scalp and put his hat on. "I mean to hire a wagon to take these prisoners and these dead men to the county seat," he said to the store-keeper.

"Don't look at me," Lynn said. "I don't run no livery."

"Who does?"

"This town ain't got one yet."

Cotton turned to Lon. "Major, I hereby appropriate this wagon to take these prisoners to the county jail. I have the authority of the State of Texas behind me, so don't go refusing to . . ."

"Didn't any of Dub Coe rub off on you?" I said. "Just ask the gentleman and he'll no doubt lend you the damned wagon."

"Yes, go ahead and take the trifling wagon," the major said with a wave of his hand.

"I'm going, too," Clay said. "Somebody will have to bring Topsy and the buckboard back."

Lon nodded, tight-lipped.

"Then let's go," Cotton said. He sat between the dead men in the wagon bed to guard Tobe and Boone. "Don't go skippin' the county," he said to me as if I were a common fugitive. "You'll be wanted to testify sooner or later." He didn't bother to bid farewell to any of us as the wagon rolled out of town.

The crowd dispersed after the bodies and the prisoners left. I stood in front of the store with the Standards and J. L. Lynn and told what had happened half a dozen times until everyone was satisfied he had the story straight. Finally, Lon suggested taking a drink at the saloon catty-corner across the street from Lynn's Store.

"No, thank you," I said. "I made a vow to stay out of saloons and I intend to keep it."

Lum and Nat looked at each other and shrugged, but the major seemed impressed by my show of temperance. "Would you be so kind as to escort my daughter home, then?" he asked.

"I would consider it my pleasure," I said.

Annie put her hand around my arm as the Standard men walked across the street to the saloon. I started to help her into the buggy.

"Don't go just yet," Lynn said. "There's a letter for you here."

"A letter for me? Are you sure?"

"You know somebody else called Royal Huckaby?"

The merchant rummaged around in his pigeonholes for a couple of minutes and finally turned up the envelope. It had my name on it. I opened it to find a brief missive scrawled in an almost illegible hand:

Royal Huckaby, Esq.,
God help me if this letter doesn't find you alive and in good health. I have promised the XIT Ranch to supply 5,000 cedar fence posts before Christmas. Ten times that many after the first of the year. The ranch paid up front for the posts and I assured them the first shipment of cedar would get here on time. I opened an account in your name at my bank in Austin. Get the money, hire a crew, freight the posts. Hustle, man! More orders pending.

Marion Harkey

Annie read the letter after me and glowed with pride for my new venture. "You can clear the brakes from our place.

Daddy said he wanted to. There's wolves up in those cedars and they come out to get our foals and calves."

"I have a few thousand posts ready to ship on the Flatt place already. I guess I can claim them since I never got paid for chopping them."

"Sure you can," Annie said. "Topsy will let you have them."

I thanked Lynn for holding the letter and escorted Annie to the door.

The storekeeper held me back as Annie went to jump in the buggy. "It amazes me that you came out of it alive," he said. "And you got the prettiest gal in the valley on top of it all. I've changed my mind about your luck, Roy. You ought to get on alright in this country."

I shook Lynn's hand and walked around in front of the buggy horse to climb in beside Annie and enjoy her company on the ride back to the ranch. I got one foot on the step when I heard a voice that rang with a familiar timbre.

"There he is right now," it said. "Hey, Roy!" The voice belonged to Deacon Sam.

I turned to greet the blacksmith and saw five men in front of the saloon—the deacon, the three Standards, and a goliath that stood a full head taller than any of them and carried more bulk than half of them. He wore a hat the size of a butter churn and a sheepskin vest that had required the sacrifice of more than one sheep. Though I hadn't seen the face in three years, I immediately recognized it as that of Little Jimmy Fitzhugh.

I had grown up contesting the Fitzhugh boys at everything from wrestling to horse racing to target shooting and I knew how well Little Jimmy could use that iron holstered on his right hip. It seemed God had marked this day as my last on his calendar, and one way or the other, I was going to cross.

I stepped away from the buggy so Annie wouldn't get

shot, though I didn't think Little Jimmy would miss me by that much. I held my hands away from my body and turned my palms up to show that I had no weapon with which to defend myself, though I didn't expect that to stop him from killing me.

Little Jimmy, who had been grinning like a sunning alligator, began laughing wickedly, and to my horror, the Standards grinned and laughed with him. What lies had Little Jimmy told them? They obviously thought he had come in friendship. They knew nothing of the giant's intention to see my blood wash the streets. They wouldn't know to help me until it was too late. I couldn't even attempt to explain. I would be dead before I got a single syllable out of my mouth.

More than death, I feared that Annie would have to see another dead man, and she had witnessed enough of such for one day.

Little Jimmy took a thunderous step down from the boardwalk, laughing, shaking the ground below him as his strapping frame lumbered toward me. His eyes gleamed with wickedness, his hulking shoulders shook with the homicidal mirth rumbling from his lungs.

Then he mocked me! Oh, the insult of it! He held his hands away, palms upward, like mine, as if to suggest he had no weapon with which to shoot me dead. Then I understood. He wouldn't shoot me unarmed. He wouldn't have to. He would take me hand-to-hand. He wanted my blood under his finger-nails as well as my scalp on his belt. For three years he had waited, and now he would have his day. I saw a Bowie knife on his left hip. My God, it would run me clean through!

The human behemoth bore down on me, leering, rejoicing, savoring his moment of vengeance. His shadow engulfed me but still the knife stayed in its scabbard. When would he reach for it? Then the arms opened wider. Great

God in heaven! He was going to squeeze the life out of me
with his arms alone. I knew those arms—elephantine
limbs, keg-like in girth—arms that could crush an ox.

The huge hands pulled me in against the sheet-iron chest
and the arms enwrapped me. My feet left the ground, my
lungs collapsed, and my rib cage all but buckled and still
my murderer tightened his hold.

Laughing, he whirled me, my arms pinned against my
side, my heels flying out behind me. In terror, I heard the
Standard men laughing, too. And Deacon Sam. And Annie! They thought he was hugging me! They couldn't tell I
was being killed! They couldn't feel the heart fluttering in
my chest or the blood miring my veins.

There was only one chance. The pistol. I had to reach it.
I felt blindly with my left hand. I grasped the belt, felt the
cartridges. I used all my strength and pushed my shoulder
downward in Fitzhugh's hold. I touched the ivory handle,
but couldn't grip it. My fingers clawed like the talons of a
dying hawk until I had no strength left. I was limp, breath-
less, done for. The fog rolled back over me.

Then the ground came up under my feet and fresh, cool
air rushed down my windpipe. The murderous laughter was
still going, but Little Jimmy had stopped killing me. He
gripped me by the shoulders. I could barely see his face
through the tears in my eyes. His huge hand patted my
cheek like a bear toying with a carcass.

"Thank God I've found you," his baritone said. "Chaz
swore if I didn't bring you home, she'd bolt the bedroom
door and have me bunk alone on the floor rug." His laughter came like the winds of a cyclone. "A man wants his wife
beside him with the winter coming on!"

TWENTY-TWO

L ittle Jimmy was the only one of Sloan Fitzhugh's next
of kin to survive the hurricane that swept half of
Matagorda into the bay the day Sloan went on trial. He
was the only man who might have wanted to prolong the
Williams-Fitzhugh feud by killing me in return for the death
of his brother.

Chaz had realized this and made up her mind that she
would put an end to the feud herself before I came home.
She had spent three years mourning the death of her
husband and lamenting the imprisonment of her only
brother. She meant to make Matagorda County safe for my
return. A month before my release from the penitentiary,
she went to call on Little Jimmy.

As Little Jimmy Fitzhugh explained, "One meeting led
to another and, well, we wound up meeting all night and
decided to hitch up in double harness."

The Williams-Fitzhugh feud was dead. Little Jimmy said
he never believed that I had hidden under the rose hedge
fence with Joe David to shoot Sloan anyway, because
Sloan's black hired man had witnessed the whole thing and
named only Joe David Williams as the bushwhacker.

He said he had put some stock in the idea that I had acted
as an accomplice by bringing a fresh horse to the lodge to
aid in Joe David's escape, until he found out which horses
I had brought there.

"If you wanted to help Joe David get away," he said,
"you'd have brung that Spanish horse with the blaze on his
head. Now, that horse had good bottom. But those were
your jumping horses you had at the lodge that night. Good
on a wolf hunt, but not made for outridin' the law."

So there had never been any danger at all waiting for me

in Matagorda County. Chaz and Little Jimmy had meant to surprise me at the train depot the day I was to come home. When I didn't show, Chaz put her new husband on my trail. "I turned over dang near every rock in Texas trying to find you," he said.

I wouldn't let Little Jimmy take me back to the Gulf Coast, of course, because I had too many things to do in Burnet County. But when we got back to the Standard place, I wrote a long letter to my sister explaining why I could not come home right away and asking her to please let her husband back into the bedroom as a personal favor to me.

That seemed to satisfy my new brother-in-law's concerns and he left for home the very next day.

I spent the day after the battle of the zero stone counting cedar fence posts and making arrangements to fill the incoming orders from Marion Harkey. I would have to go to Austin the next day to hire a crew of cedar choppers and see about the bank account Harkey had established there in my name. That afternoon, after taking inventory of my cedar posts, I went back up to the zero stone to collect Dub Coe's surveying gear. I had decided to take it to the General Land Office while I was in Austin and give it to someone who would know what to do with it.

Wolves or coyotes had already torn the entrails out of Cotton's dead mustang and eaten off part of a hind quarter. I looked around at the bloodstains on the ground and the bullet holes in trees. I sat down and studied the old corner marker and thought about the men who had located it and the deaths they had suffered because of Eli's greed—except for that one who had escaped—the Mexican horse wrangler.

All the men in the survey crew were faceless personages to me except for that young horse wrangler who had escaped the massacre and returned the field notes. When I thought of him dodging through the brakes with the precious field notes clutched in his hand, I saw the face of the old Mexican.

Yes, the chances were slim. There were hundreds of zero stones mounting hundreds of hillocks all across the country. And hundreds of the old survey crews must have employed Mexican men as well as men of every other nationality and race. But something about the Mexican wrangler Eli had spoken of seemed incongruous to me. For a while I couldn't put my finger on just what.

I sat on the hill of the zero stone and pondered for half the afternoon until I figured out the thing that didn't make sense. Why would a horse wrangler bother to save the field notes with a band of murderous Indians grappling for his scalp? Why? Because he wanted to make sure the location of the zero stone remained known. Why? Because he wanted to return to it. Why? Because it would lead him back to the lost loot the survey party had found before the massacre!

Then I remembered something Dub Coe had said. Texas was the only state in the Union to measure land in varas. The treasure and the zero stone charted on the old Mexican's map had to be in Texas, for the distance between them was measured by chains and varas. How many zero stones were there in the state? How fair were my chances now?

I cradled my head in my hands and almost wept. When would my blood purge itself of the fever? After all that had happened, it still boiled in my veins. I didn't even want the damned treasure anymore. What would Annie think of me if she found out greed had fostered all my bravery? I scorned the tarnished treasure, but I could not turn away from the hunt for it. And despite every morsel of rationality I applied to my situation, I could not help being awed by it. I was, after all, alone beside the zero stone with a surveyor's chain and compass at my feet.

I decided to go ahead and do it. I decided to run that line to the northwest. Perhaps then I could get on with a more ordinary life and put the adventure of the zero stone behind me. It wouldn't be easy moving and aligning the chaining pins by myself, but I resolved to give it a try. One hundred and eighty-nine chains amounted to something less than a mile and I thought I could get through with the job by nightfall. Then I could lay to rest forevermore any oddball notions of digging up filthy lucre.

My first problem was getting the chaining pins to stand upright by themselves. I could stab them into the ground where I crossed deep soil, but in the rocky places I would need something to hold them up so I could align them. I solved the problem with Dub's hatchet that I found lying on the ground. With it, I chopped four cedar poles. With some strips of leather that I cut from my saddle, I tied two cedar poles to each chaining pin, turning them into crude tripods that would stand up on their own.

I planted the first pin at the base of the zero stone. I pulled the chain tight in a general northwesterly direction, then picked up the peep-sight compass mounted on the Jacob staff and sighted exactly 49 degrees northwest. The chain was off several degrees, so I had to move the second chaining pin. When I had it aligned perfectly, I moved ten varas to the northwest.

The line led me down the hill and into the valley of Double Horn Creek. I got my boots wet crossing the stream. I had to chop brush as I went, of course, and the going was slow. I maintained a very strict count of the chain lengths I had measured, repeating the tally under my breath as I worked.

Along the course I looked for old sign. I eyeballed the trunks of the largest trees for witness marks. I almost rubbed the calluses off my hands trying to turn up sign on the rocks. I saw nothing to encourage me and yet I had no doubts that I should continue.

I was working toward a terminus. There was perhaps only a chance in one hundred that I would find treasure, but the odds were much better that I would regain a certain serenity of spirit that had been absent from my life since I had met the old Mexican.

Once I fell into the rhythm of the job, the work entangled all my senses. I was so absorbed with the staffs and compass that, at forty-four chains, I was surprised to look up and find myself standing right in the middle of the wagon road that led from the Flatt and Standard ranches to the Marble Falls. I ran the line as quickly as I could across the road before somebody came along wanting an explanation.

One hundred chains found me ascending a slope, chopping brush, yanking the chain through snags. The novelty of the treasure hunt began to wear off and I still had eighty-nine chains left to run. It looked as though I might not finish before dark. My feet were sore and I was tired. I considered giving up for several chain lengths. Then I reached the crest of the ridge at one hundred and seven chains.

The moment I looked to the northwest from that summit, The Feeling seized me. The serpentine floodplain of the Colorado unfolded below. It stretched level, only partially wooded. There was good bottom land down there. The Feeling told me that. But there was something more than mere fertility of soil. There was a greater wealth awaiting me. Eighty-two chains would land me somewhere shy of the river—on Standard property.

With cheerfulness I hacked the brush from the downward slope and moved my chain ten varas more. I placed the pins precisely. I pulled the links snug against one another. I remained true to the line at 49 degrees northwest.

When I hit the floodplain, the chaining became easier.

The sun dipped behind the rim of the valley and took the glare out of the sky. I sank my faculties into surveying with more intensity than ever. I could not tell what kind of terrain or vegetation I passed. All that I saw grew on a thin line, 49 degrees northwest.

I whispered the tally as I worked: ". . . one-fifty, one-fifty, one-fifty; one-fifty-one, one-fifty-one . . ." I found fewer rocks and deeper soil. The Jacob staff and the chaining pins stabbed easily into the silt washed there by centuries of floodwaters. This was the kind of soil that facilitated the burial of things.

Daylight drained from the valley, funneling my senses ever more sharply to the line under my chain. ". . . one-seventy, one-seventy; one-seventy-one . . ." Yes, I would finish before nightfall, mark the final spot with a stake carved by Dub's hatchet, and return in the morning with a pick and shovel.

My heart pounded and mourning doves fluttered in my stomach. When I looked through the peep sight, I saw nothing beyond the farthest pin, lashed against the cedar posts that made it stand erect. My life at that moment measured no more than ten varas in scope.

I felt like a convict nearing the end of his sentence. I must not look ahead too far. I must take them one at a time. I must stay on the straight and narrow path until the end. Then and only then may I embrace my newfound liberty. Then and only then will I be free of chains.

". . . one-eighty, one-eighty, one-eighty; one-eighty-one, one-eighty-one, one-eighty-one . . ."

My only sound was the rattle of links—or was it the jingle of ancient coins? My eyes beheld only the wooden poles of the chaining pins—or were they tarnished silver? Five chains to go. Now four. Now three, now two. One chain. Precision! Don't look up! Don't lose the line. Move the pins, pull the chain, plant the staff. Line it up. There!

Don't look yet! Concentrate. Seven varas to go. How to measure them? Pace them off. Remember what Dub said. No need for pinpoint precision. The old Mexican and his party of surveyors would not have run a perfect line with Indians on them. You will come near enough by pacing off the last seven varas. Besides, the trove is huge. Too much treasure for the surveyors to have carried away with them.

I put my back against the chaining pin standing farthest to the northwest. I bent over and looked between my legs to align my course with the chain. I took a step of about one vara, then checked behind me again. Still on line. I took another step, lined myself up. I paced off the third vara. I tried the fourth, bumped my knee on something, felt thorns in my thigh. What was it? A rail covered with brambles. A rail to what? Never mind. Step over it. Five. Six. Seven.

My feet sank into soft soil. I stooped to grasp a handful of loam. What was that sound? A small stream trickled about twenty varas from me. I looked up the stream and saw it flanked by huge pecan trees draped with mustang grapevines. One marvelous specimen stood alone, cleared of vines, a ladder leaning against its trunk. Nearer to me I found smaller pecans, planted in rows. Some of their limbs wore bandaged splints.

Still nearer to me peach trees grew, also planted in orchard rows. Now I noticed trenches that branched out from the little spring-fed stream. They forked and carried water between the rows of trees.

I looked back toward the chain and compass. I had stepped over a rail fence covered with thorny dewberry vines. I could see beyond the chaining pins now, and on the southeastern horizon, at the other end of the line I had run, I saw the very peak of the hill of the zero stone. No wonder the surveyors had refused to move the zero stone for Eli. They chiseled it on that hill because they could sight its peak from the point of the buried treasure and plot a line to it!

And this tilled soil under my boots? I looked down the stream and saw a row of peas, killed brown by the recent frost. Then one of dead tomato vines tied to stakes and sagging as if still under the weight of the ripening fruits. Then a row of withered okra stalks. Then . . .

I staggered back from the point of the seventh vara, startled by the sight. It was Annie. Standing, staring, her hands on her hips, a bundle of dead plant stalks at her feet. She laughed. "Roy, what on earth are you doing? I've been watching you for the past ten minutes and for the life of me I can't figure it out!"

The facts were unspeakable. I couldn't admit that my greed for the treasure and not my concern for the well-being of the Standard family had been behind my quest for the zero stone all along. I resolved to utter the last lie she would ever hear spoken from my lips. I just didn't know what it was going to be yet. I stammered for a moment, but I did some pretty smooth lying under the influence of Annie Standard and I came up with a good one in no time.

"I was running a line. Dub got me to thinking. I figured I might like to take up the surveyor's trade. I just wanted to see how much I liked it before I had to take his equipment back to Austin."

"You might have asked for some help. You looked pretty silly moving those things by yourself."

I shrugged. "Didn't know anybody would be watching."

"Well, you were sure serious about it." She walked around the row of okra to approach me. "So, are you planning to make a surveyor of yourself?"

"No, I don't think so. I have an obligation to supply cedar posts for that barbed-wire salesman. Besides, surveyors have to wander too much. I'm looking to settle."

Annie wrung her hands in the apron she had tied around

her slender waist and walked closer to me. "Where are you thinking of settling? Going back home to see your family?"

"Maybe to visit. But I won't live there. Too flat. I like these hills around here."

"Good," she said. "I was hoping you'd decide to stay here with us." She swayed gracefully toward me, smiling, her eyes fixed on mine. She walked in close to me and then stopped over the point I had stepped back from. She stood exactly 189 chains and 7 varas, 49 degrees northwest from the zero stone.

God bless the old Mexican for now and for eternity! That wise and aged vaquero had known my own fate better than I. I would never doubt him again. *El tesoro* stood where his map had said I would find it. The only mystery to me was whether he somehow knew I would find Annie there or whether the treasure marked on his map was of the pecuniary variety.

Treasure is a thing whose qualities lie open to interpretations. To Marion Harkey, treasure came in the form of cash money. To Dub Coe, it had taken the shape of everything from deer droppings to wildflower seeds. To Eli Flatt, treasure had been an elusive vision of streets, parks, and buildings. Paper-shell pecans were treasure to Annie Standard, and Annie was treasure to me.

I kissed her in the garden as a flock of wintering doves vaulted from the mother tree and swooped low over our heads. From that moment forward I have cast aside any thoughts of excavating buried treasure.

Make no mistake, the spell of the old Mexican's map will burn within me the rest of my life. I will never quench it. I will always wonder about that spot in Annie's garden. I go there often to stand over it. I have witched for the riches with forked sticks. I have probed for it with steel rods. But I will not dig. I will never make excavations for the buried gold, the bars of smelted silver, the jewels, the loot pilfered from the Mexican cathedrals. If it is truly there, that treasure will remain for someone else to unearth. I have mastered the lust. I have found something better to hold.

I would like for my sons and daughters to own the loot if it is there, however. Annie, too, if she suspected treasure might lie under her garden, would want our children to own it. So I will, after a fashion, *order* the digging done someday. Then I will descend the shaft dug for me, slip the mortal bonds of rapacity, and let my soul find its lost peace in the cool river bottom soil under Annie's garden.

If a trove exists there, I will lie down in its place. For there is an odd clause in my will stipulating that when I die, my grave must be dug by my own children. They will bury me deep, on a line coursing 49 degrees northwest, exactly 1,897 varas from the zero stone.